THE

M000232674

THE MAN WITH
MUNNARI
EYES

NOVEL ONE

ML BELLANTE

The Man with Munnari Eyes
Novel One

The Munnari Chronicles:

ML Bellante

Copyright 2019 ML Bellante

Bookwise Publishing, Riverton, Utah
www.bookwisepublishing.com

Editor & Producer: K Christoffersen
Illustrator: Brian Hailes (cover, raster, metren, multipede, thrice, spear)
Illustrator: Juan Diego Dianderas (gorga)

Library of Congress Control Number: 2019940217

ISBN 978-1-60645-240-0 Trade Paperback
ISBN 978-1-60645-238-7 Ebook

10 9 8 7 6 5 4 3 2 1

Order online at Amazon.com
MunnariChronicles.com
MLBellanteBooks.com

12/18/2019 version

THE MAN WITH
MUNNARI EYES

NOVEL ONE

DEDICATION

To my wonderful wife, Denise,
who stands by my side through all things;
and to my marvelous children . . .
Kimberly, Aaron, Brian, Michelle,
Colleen, Keith, and Nicole
who challenge and inspired me.

TABLE OF CONTENTS

CHAPTER 1

AN UNEXPECTED PLACE

He opened his eyes and found himself in an unexpected place. Not the sterile grays of the rip chamber he was expecting, but a wilderness of lush greens, dense brush, and towering trees whose canopy blocked the sky. He was flat on his back, and as he peered through the visor of his environmental suit, he could see a triple layer of vegetation above. Obviously, this was not Tranquility's He-3 Base. His nausea began to subside, but a headache raged. As it slowly began to abate, he gathered his wits and made his first attempt to communicate.

"Houston, this is Coleman, do you copy? Over." He waited a few moments, but all he heard was dead air and the faint call of a bird's chatter. "Houston, this is Coleman, do you copy? Over."

He lay on his back looking upward through his helmet visor. Unexpectedly, he felt a tugging at his left boot. He raised his head high enough to see a huge creature pulling at it. The creature's body was over a foot across. It had eight legs, each covered in what appeared to be a hard shell encrusted with thorns or small spikes. The body had a thorny shell to match and was segmented in two places. Its coloring matched the greens and browns of the surrounding vegetation.

In a convulsive reaction, he kicked at the creature. It reared back on its six hind legs and motioned threateningly with its two pincer-tipped front legs. Suddenly, its body turned dark red as it started to wave back and forth threateningly. Coleman instinctively sat upright and scooted back a few feet. The creature continued its threat pose for a few more seconds, forelegs still waving from side to side, daring Coleman to approach. When he didn't, the creature lowered itself and scuttled away, disappearing into the thick, verdant cover.

In a slightly panicked voice, Coleman repeated, "Houston, this is Coleman. Do you copy? Over." He noticed a few ants or termites, each more than two inches long, crawling over the legs of his suit. He jumped up and brushed them off, stamping his feet and doing a wild dance in the process. "Giant spiders and big bugs are not what I signed up for! Houston, this is Coleman! Do you copy? Over." All he heard was white noise coming from his helmet's speaker.

He breathed deeply and took account of himself for a moment. His headache and nausea were gone. He had been warned by the med-team to expect these effects, and they were right. He was grateful they didn't last long.

"Houston, this is Coleman. Do you copy? Over." Nothing. "If anyone can hear me, please respond. Over." He touched the control panel on his belt and activated the beacon. "Houston, I've activated the beacon. I'll continue transmitting in case you can hear me, but I still can't hear you. I'm in a kind of jungle or rainforest. I've seen two-inch long ants and a spiny spider with a body over a foot long. I don't know where things like this come from, but I hope you do. Over."

Coleman started looking around the area. Not much to see except heavy vegetation. As he moved, a creature would occasionally dart deeper into the undergrowth, disturbing the bushes and leaves. He was never able to get a good look at what was moving. All he saw were flashes of movement on the periphery of his vision.

Surprisingly, he felt something hit his helmet and he watched as orange goo slowly slid down his visor. He turned, looked upward, and saw a monkey peering at him from around the trunk of a tree about twenty feet up in the branches. Again, he felt something hit him, this time in the back.

"Oh, that's just great. Now, I've got monkeys throwing rotten fruit at me. Houston, this is Coleman. I don't think I'm in the Everglades. There are monkeys here. They are about three feet tall, have light brown hair, and black skin. Oh, and they have tails about three feet long. Over."

Now, that should really make it easy for them to locate me, he thought sarcastically. *That pretty much describes half of all the monkey species.* He knew he needed to find something unique about the area to help mission control find his location. *Maybe I should try to find one of those spider things.* The thought of hunting spiders the size of basketballs didn't please him at all. He'd hated all arachnids since he'd been bitten by a black widow when he was a child. He still had a tiny scar on his left wrist from the bite.

He began moving around the small clearing where he had landed. He brushed aside the leafy fern under which the spider had disappeared. Nothing there and nothing moved. Whatever it was, it had left the area. He breathed a sigh of relief and continued his search, disturbing more creatures in the process. They scuttled away as quickly as they could, ensuring that he was never able to get a good look at them. He did, however, transmit detailed descriptions of all the plants he saw.

Coleman searched for an hour while his environmental suit continued to keep him cool and comfortable, but he knew it had only about twenty-four hours of battery life. Conserving his suit's batteries was going to be a priority. It was his only way of communicating with mission control. The beacon had its own power source and would continue transmitting for seventy-two hours. He hoped to be home by then. He flipped another switch on his belt and the suit turned off, releasing the stays of his helmet. He grabbed it between his two gloved hands, gave it a quick turn, and lifted it over his head. A blast of warm, dense air cascaded over him. In his first breath, he tasted an eternity of rotting debris.

"Man, this place stinks," he said aloud. He found a fallen branch, stuck it into the soft earth and put his helmet on it. It looked like a head on a pike. Thirst nagged at him. "I'm going to need water before long. I wonder if there's a fast running stream around here?" He listened intently for a few seconds, but all he could hear was the constant chatter of birds and the occasional hoot of a monkey.

"Runny stream," came a voice from the branches above. Coleman jerked his head in the direction of the sound. Staring back at him was a large parrot-like bird with green and black feathers. "Runny stream," it called again.

"Now, that's impressive, my friend," said Coleman.

The bird responded with, "My fend," and cocked its head sideways. Coleman laughed, and the bird spread its wings and flew away repeating, "My fend . . . my fend . . . my fend," until Coleman could hear it no longer.

All at once, a bright flash bathed the jungle floor in white light, accenting the black shadows. A few seconds later came the rolling thunder. "Nuts!" was Coleman's reply as he reached for his helmet. He had just enough time to secure it on his head before a torrential downpour began. Lightning and thunder flashed and boomed for what seemed to Coleman to be hours. During this time, he found meager shelter under a large leaf. His environmental suit kept him dry, but he continued to worry about its power supply and what he would do when the batteries were exhausted.

Slowly, the curtain of rain lifted and Coleman saw a horde of insects disgorge from the undergrowth. Quickly, they took flight and he became engulfed in a fog of flying creatures. They appeared to be winged termites with bodies over two inches in length. An even larger dragonfly-like creature darted in quick bursts through the horde of termites. It hovered using its twelve-inch wingspan in front of his face, examining him for several seconds before flitting into the horde of flying insects once more.

Coleman stood spellbound by what he was watching. As the termites hit one another, they seemed to embrace, their wings falling off, and the creatures dropping to the ground. As this phenomenon continued, he found his visor becoming covered with the discarded wings. Several times he had to wipe them away when his vision became obstructed. Eventually, the swarm subsided. He flipped the power switch on his belt again and the suit shut down. He removed his helmet and tucked it under his left arm. His throat was dry.

Lots of water around here, he thought. He found a small pool that had formed in the hollow of a large leaf. He gently held the leaf as he took a tentative sip.

"That's terrible!" he growled and spat out the bitter water. He tried a few other pools he found on other types of leaves but they weren't any better. He wasn't sure if it was safe to drink or not and he didn't want to find out the hard way. It was time to find some fresh water that didn't taste as if it came from a sewer.

He saw movement under one of the leaves from which he had tested the water. It looked like a snake. He watched intently and, as it moved, he could see it had legs, many legs.

It must be over eight feet long, he thought. The movement stopped. With a shudder, Coleman glanced up to see the head of a multi-legged creature slowly waving back and forth nearly four feet above the jungle floor. Its antennae were twirling in the air and its large mandibles were snapping a warning.

"What the heck is that?" he yelled and jumped back, moving away from the creature's head as fast as he could. "I think it's time to move on. I'm drawing too much attention here."

He moved forward in a straight line. He couldn't be sure of his direction because the triple canopy blocked the sun. He passed many mounds that stood ten to twelve feet high. Taking a closer look, he found large termites crawling in and out of holes in the hills. "I bet these beggars have a nasty bite," he mumbled to himself.

Onward he trudged. Several times he found his way blocked by dense foliage and had to backtrack. After about an hour, he thought he heard running water. He carefully moved toward the sound. Eventually, it began to grow louder and soon he came upon a huge, flowing spring. Water gushed more than five feet upward. *An artesian well?* He cupped his gloved hands, dipped them in it and took a taste. "Not bad," he said and began gulping down the refreshing liquid. He stepped back and wiped his mouth. *I didn't realize I was so thirsty.*

By this time, he could tell the sun was low in the sky. Dark shadows engulfed the jungle floor. It would be night soon and Coleman knew the most dangerous predators would be out to feed.

He began to feel hunger pangs himself. He had been required to fast for twenty-four hours before being ripped. The med-team told him fasting would reduce his nausea. Fortunately, his nausea hadn't lasted long and had removed any desire for food until now. Unfortunately, darkness was approaching and the most important thing for him to do was to find shelter and a safe place for the night.

He began moving around the spring looking for a place to bed down. As he did, he noticed a lone monkey scrambling down from the branches high above. It jumped to the ground and took a few tentative steps toward the water. It was very observant and kept swiveling its head back and forth. Warily, it dipped its head into the pool of fresh water and drank its fill. After that, several other monkeys gained enough courage to do the same. Down they came in what seemed to be a tide. It wasn't long before the entire area was covered in brown fur. Coleman remained still as he watched.

A new, deafening crack echoed from high above. The area again became bathed in white light and a deluge of rain gushed forth. The monkeys started shouting and chattering in surprise as they scurried into the trees. Coleman placed his helmet over his head and activated his suit's power supply. The rain poured down his visor, distorting his view.

"I hope this doesn't last long," he muttered.

Darkness slowly engulfed his surroundings, squeezing away what little light that reached the jungle floor. For the first time today he felt alone, isolated, and vulnerable. He still needed to find shelter, but the gathering darkness and the unrelenting torrent of rain weren't helping. Every few minutes, another round of lightning and thunder testified to him that the heavens were at war with the earth. He had never felt such uneasiness in his life.

Coleman had spent nearly ten years in the Army, most of that time serving as a Ranger, and he'd spent many a night like this one during training and while on combat missions in South and Central America. Nevertheless, he felt the darkness pressing in on him. The unseen threats and terrors of the night began to cause him to worry because he was unarmed and unprepared to protect himself if he needed to. He sensed danger. He slowly backed up until he gently bumped into a tree trunk. A large fern leaf covered him and provided scant protection from the rain. He remained upright but leaned against the tree for support. He checked his equipment. The beacon was transmitting and he still had several hours of reserve on the main suit.

First thing in the morning, I'm going to have to build a shelter. I'm not going to be able to rely on the suit much after that.

He thought he saw something moving ahead of him, so he turned on his helmet's LEDs and knelt to take a closer look at the biggest slug he had ever seen. Coleman's head was about a foot off the jungle floor when a feeling of foreboding swelled in his gut. He heard the snap of a twig or branch but before he could turn his head to look, he felt something heavy land on his back, forcing his head into the body of the slug and mashing it all over his visor. Instantly, he knew a powerful creature was attacking him.

He was lifted by his utility belt and savagely shaken from side to side. Horror filled his heart as snarls and growls filled his ears. Whatever had ahold of him dropped him to the ground and jumped on him again, ripping and tearing at his backpack. He felt a crushing bite to his right arm above the elbow. The pressure was excruciating but the bite failed to penetrate his environmental suit. The creature released his arm and attempted to crush his neck. He could hear the beast's teeth sliding off his helmet, causing his attacker to become even more enraged. He could feel claws raking his back and sides but, fortunately, none of the strikes reached his flesh. In the air, he could hear panicked screams and shouts, which he realized with a start, were coming from his own mouth.

The creature continued biting and clawing at him. Every time he attempted to rise to his knees or feet, he was knocked to the ground and suffered another pummeling by tooth and claw. He kept his back to the beast with his arms pulled tight against his sides, hoping this defensive maneuver would provide the most protection from the assault. In the light of the LEDs, he could see bits of fabric from his suit scattered around the area.

The attack began to subside and he thought for a moment the creature was about to give up. That thought fled his mind as another even more violent attack ensued. His com system sounded an alarm as the stays of his helmet released, and the LEDs turned off.

"I won't die like this!" he yelled.

He grabbed his helmet with both hands and gave it a twist and a pull. At the same time, he rolled to his left and grasped the helmet's neck rim with his right hand. As he did this, the beast leapt at him and began clawing at his chest with its forelegs. Again, the area was bathed in white light as another lightning bolt flashed above. For the first time, he got a glimpse of his assailant. Terror gripped his soul as his eyes stared into a foot-long jaw of razor-sharp teeth, accentuated by six-inch-long fangs. The monster's face resembled that of a long-snouted dog, yet its skin looked scaly, like that of a reptile or crocodile. It had a long scar chiseled across its snout. Coleman's body convulsed in a reaction of fear and anger. As the beast lunged for his exposed neck, he slammed his helmet into the side of its head, knocking the creature off him and dazing it. He jumped to his feet and turned to face the monster's next attack.

He could hardly see in the darkness and continuing downpour, but the creature's heavy breathing made it easy to guess where it was. A snarl announced the monster's next attack was on the way. Coleman swung his helmet at a flash of movement just as the creature hit him in the chest and drove him to the ground again. The beast didn't go for his neck this time but bit into his right thigh. The pressure was overwhelming and Coleman howled in agony, but the monster's teeth were unable to penetrate the suit's tough fabric. Screaming in pain, he sat up and nailed the creature hard on its left side with his helmet. It gave a yelp and retreated.

Coleman quickly scrambled up and awaited the next assault. Just as he regained his feet, the sky split with a streak of lightning and he could see his antagonist again. It was about six feet long with no tail. Coleman guessed it to be several hundred pounds. Just as quickly, darkness engulfed him, and he heard the creature snarling and circling to his left. In an instant, he was hit again, this time at the knees. He flew into the air and landed in a heap. In a flash, the beast was on him once more, tearing to get at his vitals. Coleman rolled onto his stomach as it began clawing and biting his backpack. A loud, hissing screech filled Coleman's ears as one of the rebreather tanks was punctured. The creature jumped back and scrutinized this unexpected cacophony. Coleman scrambled to his feet. His left knee ached from the last assault; his right arm and right thigh throbbed from the crushing bites they had suffered. He couldn't hear the creature this time, so he moved in a tight circle, expecting another attack. He didn't have to wait long. This time, he was hit from the rear and his face slammed into the ground. The monster picked him up by the belt again and shook him. The shaking lasted for more than ten seconds, and Coleman felt himself losing consciousness as a dark green fog invaded his mind.

"No!" he shouted as he pulled himself from the brink.

The creature continued shaking him, and just as the fog began to enter his mind again, he was tossed ten feet, slamming into something solid. Coleman lay crumpled against the trunk of a tree. He feared he might have a cracked rib, but he didn't have time to worry about it now. He had to endure the pain for his life was on the line.

He still held his helmet and prepared to use it in his final, desperate defense. He knew he was getting the worst of this fight and, unless he ended it now, he'd be slaughtered. "Okay, you ugly sucker! It's you or me this time. Bring your ugly face to me!"

He saw a flash of movement from his right so he swung the helmet as hard as he could. He felt it find its mark and the beast shrieked in agony. Coleman dodged to his side and the creature missed with its attack. Coleman jumped forward reaching out with his left hand, groping for the monstrous animal. His gloved hand made contact and he began pounding the beast repeatedly with his helmet. As he did, he began shrieking obscenities with each blow.

Coleman grabbed the creature's leg and pulled hard, forcing the monster to the ground, and then he started beating it again, striking it several times. He laughed with maniacal glee as he pounded the beast over and over. He grabbed the rim of his helmet with both hands and, with the strongest hammer blow he could muster, slammed it into the beast, splintering the helmet. He heard a crack and the creature howled in pain, regained its feet, and ran away whimpering. Quickly, Coleman staggered to his feet. A flash of lightning revealed an empty battleground.

"Did that thing leave?" Coleman wondered aloud.

He ached all over and was soaking wet. His environmental suit was destroyed and his helmet shattered. He wasn't breathing that hard, but each breath gave him a stabbing pain in his left side. The ache in his right arm began to grow more painful and was easily matched by the pain in his right thigh. He took a step, his left knee revolting in agony.

Coleman could tell that the rain was abating. Patches of a cloudless sky were filled by a few stars shining through the canopy. The glow from the sky increased until he began to see his surroundings.

"Well, it looks like a bright moon tonight."

As his battlefield brightened, he began scanning the trees for low hanging branches. When he found one, he dropped his shattered helmet and started climbing the tree as far as his aching body would allow. At about twenty-five feet, he nestled into a wide 'V' in the trunk and, for the first time since his battle with the beast, he began to relax. Exhausted by the day's ordeals, he leaned back into the tree trunk and attempted to make sense of his predicament.

"What was that thing, anyway?" he muttered aloud. He rested and thought, his mind reeling.

It was like a crocodile, but it wasn't. It was more like a big lizard, he thought.

"Where do you find giant lizards?" He realized he was talking to himself, but he didn't care. "The only giant lizards I've heard of are Komodo dragons. Are they really that big and that aggressive? Am I on some Indonesian island?" he blurted, his anger and frustration growing. "I should have listened to Megan. She warned me this could happen, but stubborn me wouldn't listen. Now, look at the mess I'm in," he grumbled.

He tried to calm himself and think things through. *I'm in a fine fix now. I'm supposed to be the first human to ride the ripple. Dimensional harmonic transference, the techs call it. Yeah, Megan said misses still happen. She reminded me that three monkeys were ripped and lost before the first success with a living primate; the first three were gone and never located. The techs said the odds of a miss were low. Well, lucky me. Here I sit in some jungle; target missed by only 240,000 miles. When I get back to Houston, the lead tech better not cross my path for a month or he'll need surgery to get my foot out of his . . .*

The thought was interrupted by a loud call. He quickly realized it was only a monkey. "Okay, okay, calm down! First, you gotta get out of this jungle and find civilization," he said, talking to himself again.

He slowly became drowsy and his mind began to drift. He cautiously fell asleep. Several times during the night, he awoke with a start when he thought he heard an aggressive sound. His battle with the beast had completely unnerved him. He had faced death before in combat, but, this was different. Struggling with a massive beast set on tearing him limb from limb was nothing he ever expected to face. Each time he awoke, a flood of questions entered his mind. *What else lurks in the darkness? What will I face after the sun rises? Can I survive until I'm rescued? Where am I?* Eventually, exhaustion overtook him and he got a few hours of sleep while propped up in the crook of the tree.

CHAPTER 2

MUNNARI EYES

Just as dawn began to break, a clap of thunder announced yet another deluge. He opened his eyes as he felt large drops of moisture begin hitting his face. This time he had little protection from the rain. His suit was in tatters and his helmet lay shattered on the ground. He felt water entering his suit through great gaps in its fabric. His boots began to fill with rainwater. Slowly and painfully he began to remove his mangled suit and waterlogged boots. His right arm and right thigh throbbed. His left knee ached and his left side rebelled with every breath. As the rain beat down, he started to snicker and then he began to laugh. He grabbed his side, searing pain burning there, and started laughing again.

I must be losing my mind. What an absurd situation I'm in. Is this someone's idea of a joke? I'm supposed to be the first human dimensional traveler, so what the heck am I doing in this awful place?

He calmed for an instant but soon began laughing hysterically again, at first with a low chuckle and then with maniacal chatter. After some time, he pulled himself together and realized that as pathetic as his situation was, self-pity wasn't going to help him. He had to survive if for no other reason than to get even with the senior tech who got him into this fix. He leaned back against the tree trunk and slowly slid down into the tree's crook in a depressed stupor.

After about an hour, the rain stopped. The sun was fully up now, and light filtered through the canopy of green. Coleman carefully examined his environmental suit. The backpack was gone; the belt had been torn away; the suit's fabric was shredded in many places, and there were gaping holes all over it. He considered moving to the ground but a stab of fear shook him.

What if that monster is still down there, waiting for me? he wondered to himself.

He took a deep breath, felt a twinge of pain in his side, though not as bad as before. *Maybe I don't have a cracked rib after all.* He began carefully and painfully climbing down from his perch. When he reached the ground, he stopped and listened. He could hear nothing threatening. He walked over to the spring and drank. He then walked around the area retrieving the scattered bits of his environmental suit. He found the homing beacon in the stream flowing from the artesian well. It was bent and crushed. The indicator light was off; the beacon had failed.

Now, what do I do? They'll never find me in this place. Fear gripped his soul again as the thought of another night in this hostile place left him empty and hollow. He walked over to his shattered helmet. Staring down at it, he thought of how it had saved his life. "If it weren't for you, my friend, I'd be history." He reached down, picked it up, and slowly turned it in his two bare hands. It crumpled and parts began to fall to the ground. He dropped it and watched it roll under a large leaf. "I guess I'm on my own now for sure. It's up to me to get myself out of this mess. When I get back to the Houston Plant, I'm going to strangle somebody!"

The more he thought about his situation, the angrier he became. But a hunger pang reminded him that something was more important than his anger. Food had been the last thing on his mind, but now he realized he needed to get some nourishment to keep up his strength. It looked like he was going to be stuck in this jungle for a long time.

"So, what's there to eat around here, if anything?" He heard the hoot of a monkey high overhead and looked up. "I wonder what they're eating." For the next ten minutes or so he observed the monkeys moving in the branches. He noticed they would reach out with their long arms and grab a fruit pod hanging from the branches high above. He also saw an inquisitive monkey move into the crook where he had spent the night. The creature tentatively examined his environmental suit and poked at it.

"Leave it alone; that's mine!" Coleman yelled. The monkey quickly ran up the trunk, stopped at a higher branch, and began hooting its discontent. Almost in slow motion, it reached out to a fruit pod, ripped it from its branch, and tossed it at Coleman while screeching in anger. The creature threw the pod with such accuracy and force, it caught Coleman unprepared and hit him squarely on the forehead.

"You hairy freak!" he yelled. He picked up the pod and threw it back as hard as he could. It bounced off the tree trunk and fell into the crook where his suit's remains had been stored.

Now, that was stupid, he thought. *That hairy ape offers you breakfast and you just toss it back.*

Coleman began waving his arms and yelling. "Hey, you

dumb ape. See if you can hit me again!" He felt something hit him in the back and he turned to look. A fruit pod hit the ground next to him and soon he was pummeled by fruit thrown from the hands of at least a dozen monkeys. Coleman picked up a fruit pod and tore it open as he had seen the monkeys do. He took a taste.

This one might be a little green. It's bitter. I'll try another. He found one that was redder in color, tore it open and took a bite. It tasted like a mix of strawberry and banana.

He lifted the pod above his head, waved it in thanks and continued feasting. He felt full after about six pods. "I hope these things don't give me a bellyache. They don't seem to bother the monkeys, though."

Coleman collected the remaining pieces of his environmental suit and moved them to his less than secure hideout in the tree. He didn't know if doing this was important, but he didn't want to regret inaction later. As he rested in the notch of the tree, he noticed the monkeys moving toward the ground again.

It looks like they're heading for their morning drink, he guessed.

They moved warily, the alpha male leading the way. Coleman remained in his perch for a couple of hours, watching the surrounding area. Several other types of odd-looking creatures moved to the spring and drank.

This seems to be a safe time.

Coleman knew he would have to depart this refuge soon. Since the beacon had been destroyed, he realized no one was going to come to his rescue. He would have to find his own way back to civilization.

Before he could leave, an unwelcome flash of lightning announced another downpour and for the next two hours, Coleman sat on his perch feeling miserable and alone, soaked to the bone. When the rain stopped, he decided to begin his trek, although he had no idea which direction he should go.

I'll head east and hope for the best, he mused, aiming toward where he thought the sun had risen. *First, I'll need to collect a few of those fruit pods.*

Slowly and painfully, Coleman descended the tree again. He found a downed branch that made an excellent walking staff and maybe even a decent weapon. Then he grabbed a shorter stick and heaved it into the branches above. The monkeys howled and hooted in protest and began pelting him with fruit again.

"Lunch is served. Thank you, my furry friends!" he yelled to the monkeys. They responded with angry shrieks and howls. He worked his way around the tiny clearing, picking up the fruit pods and stuffing them into his orange jumpsuit. He saw a nice ripe one peeking out from under a fern leaf and bent down to collect it. As he reached for it, he noticed something move into his view near the fruit pod. He focused on it and, with a start, realized it was a person's bare foot. He snapped straight up and found himself staring down into the brown eyes of a small man.

For an instant, their eyes locked, both widening in shock. Both men gave audible gasps as they jumped back in amazement. Coleman saw that the little man was holding a spear and was prepared to use it. His Ranger training kicked in immediately. He slapped the spear aside and charged the man, hitting him in the mid-section with a shoulder and driving him to the ground. Coleman's right hand was at his throat. The man began making gurgling sounds as Coleman kept pressure on the intruder's throat.

Kill him! a voice in Coleman's head screamed. *Kill him! There may be others. He'll warn them. Kill him, now!*

Coleman looked into the terrified man's eyes. He had once killed a man with a bayonet and had watched as the man's life drained away. He still suffered visions of that horror. The man he had killed was a known enemy. This one was not. In a split second, Coleman chose to let the man live. He released his stranglehold and the man sprang to his feet and darted off.

The intruder began shouting in words that Coleman didn't understand—words punctuated with clicks and pops. He heard other shouts from all around him.

Coleman looked for an escape route and then he charged in a direction that seemed to be free of calls. He tore through the ferns, trees, and bushes. He scrambled over fallen branches and logs. Several times he tripped, but immediately jumped to his feet and continued his headlong rush. He could hear shouts from behind and the crashing sounds of pursuit. Birds and monkeys screeched and hooted their discontent with the chaos below them. Occasionally, fruit pods flew toward Coleman, but he paid them no mind. He didn't know if the natives were friendly and he wasn't going to risk of finding out, especially after nearly choking one of them to death.

He ran for what he guessed was at least thirty minutes. The shouts slowly subsided and then stopped altogether. Even the overhead creatures quieted down. Coleman relaxed a bit and reduced his speed to a fast walk. His heart was pounding in his ears, probably an adrenalin rush, but he was not out of breath. As part of his personal physical training program, he jogged five miles a day and knew how far he could go without feeling winded. He was surprised to find his physical reserves little depleted. He didn't have any idea where he was going other than putting distance between himself and the natives.

As he walked, he began thinking about the person he had seen. The native was shorter than he was with tan skin and a wiry build. He was muscular and wore a loincloth of animal skin and a sheathed knife hung from his waist belt. His eyes were dark-brown, almost black in color and his long, dark-brown or black hair was held away from his face by a dark colored band around his forehead. His face sported no facial hair and there was a tattoo running horizontally down his cheek under his left eye: several simple, parallel lines that went halfway down the man's cheek.

He recalled the unusual words he'd heard. They were in a language that was completely foreign to him; it included pops and clicks. *Were there still wilderness tribes in Indonesia?* He didn't know. *If there were, could they be dangerous?* A chill ran down his spine as he recalled the battle for his life the night before, and he began to worry again about his ability to survive in this hostile land. His spirit dampened even further as he wondered if the natives would pursue him. He decided his best strategy would be to avoid getting captured.

He thought about his battle with the beast. He hadn't gotten a good look at it, but he was sure it was something he had never seen before. He was an avid reader and had read a few books about the animal kingdom, but he couldn't recall learning anything about the creature that had attacked him. It seemed almost prehistoric.

He quickly realized that he was letting his mind drift. *That's a good way to get yourself killed*, he thought.

"Better focus on the here and now," he said out loud. A flash of lightning announced the next downpour. In a few seconds, a crash of thunder reverberated across the land. "Oh great, another soaking," he grumbled to himself.

The rain began falling in torrents. In no time, Coleman was soaked to the bone, again. The orange USE (undergarment suit environmental) clothing worn under the environmental suit was like wearing a sopping wet pair of footsie pajamas with non-skid soles. The foot covers had already been ripped off his feet by the rough terrain. He wanted to stop and find shelter somewhere, but he didn't dare. The dread in the pit of his stomach forbade him from even slowing down. Onward he trudged, hoping the rain would obliterate his tracks. Thirst began to gnaw at his throat. He opened his mouth and tasted bitter water.

Why is the water so bitter? he wondered silently. He looked up and could see no opening in the green cover. *There must be something on the leaves that makes it bitter,* he guessed. *I wonder if the stream and river waters are potable. Will I be able to find a spring like the other one?*

He slogged along for another hour, slipping and sliding as he pressed on, his feet aching from the abuse. Fatigue began to erode his fear and he slowed his pace. An hour later, he stopped altogether. He found a hollow in the trunk of a large tree that provided relief from the drenching rain. He slumped to the ground and pulled his knees to his chest. For the first time since his arrival in the jungle, he felt cold. He began to shiver and could see his breath. He longed for his environmental suit, his comfortable flat in Houston near the He-3 power plant, and his close friends.

As he huddled in the tree's hollow, he thought about his girlfriend, Megan Klosky. She was a junior tech on the rip team who had warned him about misses. Megan was adamantly opposed to him volunteering. When he offered his services to be the first dimensional traveler, she was so distraught, she left him.

"Should have listened to her," he mumbled to himself. He shook his head as if forcing himself awake. "I will not succumb to self-pity," he said aloud. "Pull yourself together. You've got a long way to go." Soon, he fell asleep and thought no more of his plight.

He awoke with his head on his knees. The aches and pains from the night before throbbed with each heartbeat. He slowly opened his eyes and almost jumped when he saw a native standing only ten feet in front of his shelter; the native's head was tilted back as he sniffed the air. Coleman knew a person could smell his enemy; he'd done it himself more than once.

He had anguished over stopping when he did, for now he was in a fine mess. *These natives must be skilled trackers, able to follow me during a downpour,* he thought. He slowly drew his knees tighter to his chest, trying to disappear into a ball of orange shadow. Slowly, the native turned and faced him, but with eyes not meeting Coleman's. *He doesn't see me,* Coleman thought. He felt vulnerable, trapped in this hollow of a tree with only one exit. The native moved from Coleman's line of vision and gave a quiet shout. *That's it; he spotted me!* Coleman realized.

Kill him! the voice in his head shouted. *You let the other one go. Now, look where that's left you. Kill him before he warns the others!*

Coleman shook the thought from his head, jumped up in a flash, and darted from his hideout, scrambling through the ferns and undergrowth. The monkeys in the trees howled insults at the ruckus below and began pelting Coleman and the native alike with fruit pods. Unexpectedly, he felt his legs entwined, and he fell face first into the soggy muck. He quickly regained his feet, tried to take a step and fell again. He looked down and found his ankles wrapped in what looked like a bolo.

"No! I'm a dead man!" he shouted.

A fruit pod hit him in the face and pink goo slid down his cheek as three natives slowly and cautiously approached. One held a war club and two others had six-foot-long spears. Coleman fumbled with the bolo, but it was too late. A spear tip touched his chest, his gaze slowly climbed its shaft until he was staring into a very stern-looking face. Arms reached down, pulled him to his feet, and held him tightly. He chose not to resist unless directly threatened. One of the natives removed the bolo from his ankles, while another pulled both of his arms straight out in front of him. Deftly, the one with the bolo swung one of the balls with its leather cord binding his arms. He felt another strap tighten around his neck as he stood motionless. The native in front of him began speaking, his words falling foreign on Coleman's ears. He pointed to Coleman's face and then upward. One by one the natives stood in front of him, staring into his eyes in wonderment.

"What's the matter, haven't you guys seen baby-blues before?" Coleman questioned nervously. With those words, the natives drew back as if shocked. "Haven't you ever seen a white man?" The natives began talking among themselves, seemingly puzzled over Coleman's words. "I'm a dimensional traveler from the United States. Will you help me?"

The natives continued to speak one to another in what Coleman guessed to be increasing consternation and confusion. One of the more agitated natives raised a war club high above his head and then pointed it at Coleman. He recognized the man as the one he nearly strangled to death earlier. Another native stepped between them, grabbed the war club, and lowered it to the holder's side.

It appears I have an advocate, Coleman thought to himself.

A brawny young man tightly held the strap around his neck, almost choking him. As the natives continued to talk, occasionally one would drift over to Coleman and look into his eyes. This was done repeatedly as the discussion continued. *Apparently*, he guessed, *they are trying to decide what to do with me.*

He noticed that each man had the same tattoos as the first native—parallel lines running down their cheeks, some as far down as the man's neck. The younger natives had fewer lines than the older ones. The native whom Coleman guessed was the leader had a second string of tattooed lines part way down the other side of his face. He speculated that they granted status or denoted the age of the individual or both. As he continued his observation, he determined the lines couldn't indicate age because the younger natives had only half a dozen or so lines. He also noticed that the leader was the only one who had a large tooth or tusk hanging around his neck by a leather cord.

Soon, the leader walked over to Coleman and looked him in the eyes again. He gave a huff, spoke the word *Munnari* and glanced heavenward, then back to Coleman. He turned around and gave a clear command. All the natives fell into a predetermined formation surrounding Coleman. The group began to move, and with a shove, Coleman started walking, struggling to keep pace with the others.

The men continued their trek. Coleman had no sense of time. The perpetual gloom of the jungle made it impossible for him to tell what hour of the day it was. The natives moved almost silently in the undergrowth while Coleman stumbled and slogged his way forward, his bare and tender feet suffering with every step he took. Several times, he caught the annoyed gaze of a native as his heavy footfalls contrasted so noisily with theirs.

One of the lead natives held up his arm, and the party stopped. The point man tilted his head back and sniffed the air. Quietly he said, "Bataro." All the natives grinned in delight and one even licked his lips, but no one made a sound. The strap around Coleman's neck was drawn tighter and his guard whispered something in his ear, most likely a warning to keep quiet. The party fanned out with the spearmen taking the lead. Coleman noticed the spearmen had placed their spears in a lever device held in their hands. He recognized the spear and lever as an atlatl—a device which could propel a spear with great power and accuracy.

Coleman held his breath as one of the men took careful aim and loosed his spear. He heard the wail of a wounded animal that sounded like a swine. All the men, except the one restraining Coleman, rushed to the sound. He could hear war clubs crashing down on the wounded beast as it continued its death shrieks. Quickly, all was quiet again. The hoot of a startled monkey overhead was the only sound. Coleman's guard slapped a firm hand on his shoulder and said something that had the ring of kindness and gratitude to it. Coleman turned and looked at his guard whose broad smile and glimmering white teeth made Coleman smile widely, as well.

Shortly, the party returned with four of the men supporting a long pole with an enormous boar suspended from it by its feet. It was as ugly a boar as Coleman had ever seen. Even though the animal had already been gutted, the four men struggled with the massive beast. The leader was carrying a green woven basket in both arms. As he approached Coleman, he tipped it so Coleman could see that it contained some of the innards of the boar, most likely the heart, liver, and other delicacies the men probably favored. Laying atop the gore was a tusk like the one the leader wore. He patted Coleman's head with a bloody hand and said *Munnari* and some other words that Coleman couldn't begin to decipher.

"I hope this is a good omen," Coleman muttered. All the men turned their heads and stared at him. "What's with you guys and what's this *Munnari* I keep hearing?"

Many of the natives repeated *Munnari* and then one man, the target of his assault, began a tirade of hostile and angry words. The leader confronted the agitator and pushed the basket of entrails into his grasp. The angry young man stopped his diatribe and fell silent.

Soon, the party was on the move again. They trudged onward until Coleman heard running water. They walked into a small clearing and Coleman recognized it as the gushing spring that had given him both comfort and terror the previous night. He instinctively scanned the area, worried that the horrid beast was hiding in the shadows. The men stopped and dropped their loads. Two by two they partook of the fresh water while the others alertly scanned the periphery of the clearing. Coleman's guard motioned him toward the water and they both took their turns. After everyone drank, they rested.

Coleman was beginning to feel hungry again, so he reached into his undergarment with his tethered hands and pulled out a fruit pod. He broke it open and took a bite. His guard eyed him suspiciously at first and then grinned. Coleman offered him a bit of the fruit and his guard gratefully accepted. The other men looked at them and began to mimic monkey sounds as they pointed fingers of derision at the two. Coleman rolled his eyes and pulled out a second fruit pod and offered it to his deriders. A couple of men came forward and took the pod and began sharing it with each other while the rest of the party mocked and howled in laughter.

"Sorry guys, but that's all I've got. It seems I lost a few in the scuffle."

The laughter suddenly stopped and the men gawked at him. Comments were passed from one to another as the men stared in Coleman's direction.

"Quit looking at me like I've got two heads," he grumbled.

That came off a little too stern, he thought. His angry victim began another diatribe, but Coleman calmly turned and sat on a nearby log, his gaze fixed on the angry man until his grumbling subsided.

A flash of lightning foretold the coming of another drencher. Thunder rolled across the sky and the men stood up in unison.

Now, I'll see how these guys cope with this rain, Coleman thought.

Soaked to the skin, men collected their things and began moving quickly through the jungle with Coleman in tow. His captors seemed to give the storm no mind. Water washed over their almost naked bodies while Coleman's clothes soaked it up and stuck to his skin, but the pace of the march kept him warm. After another hour or so, as the rain began to subside, they came to a large clearing. In its center, Coleman could see a village surrounded by a wall of logs reminiscent of an old-time western fort. In front of the wall was a deep ditch filled with upturned spikes.

As the men stepped from the jungle, a cry of greeting came from the village. The leader replied, waving his spear above his head. He shouted, "Bataro!" and the village began to empty as a throng of joyous natives poured forth. The men with the pig, which Coleman assumed was a bataro, led the way while he and his guard brought up the rear. Men, women, and children gathered around the slain beast and began chanting and dancing in celebration. The party continued their grand march toward the village. One-by-one, the onlookers passed their gaze from the bataro to Coleman and a stunned silence slowly crept over the throng. All eyes were on the tall stranger in the orange garments.

When all was quiet, Coleman stopped and spoke, "My name is Coleman. I'm a dimensional traveler from the United States. Does anyone speak English?"

An audible gasp came from the gathered assembly. Every individual stared in silence at him. Soon, he could hear the murmur of their strange language. The only discernible word he could make out was *Munnari*. It seemed to be repeated over and over in whispers. A young female draped in skins tied tightly about her waist stepped forward and looked deeply into Coleman's eyes. She touched his cheek with her fingers and then touched her cheek and slid them down her tattooed lines. She uttered something loud enough for all to hear, something with the word *Munnari* in it.

"What does *Munnari* mean?" Coleman asked her. She cocked her head to one side and a strained look came over her countenance as if she were trying to understand the unfathomable. She slowly backed away, and Coleman's guard gave him a gentle nudge forward.

The party moved through the opening in the wall followed by a subdued crowd murmuring to themselves. Once inside, Coleman could see many lodges and huts. They were covered with fronds to protect the dwellings from the rain. He could see no window openings and the doorways were covered with animal hides. Smoke rose from the center of many of the roofs. He passed one that was different from the others. Hanging on poles near the doorway were feathers, bulbous tubers, several bones, and various animal skulls. Coleman couldn't help but stare at the grisly and unnerving sight.

The leader of the hunting party came to Coleman and he and the guard guided him to a lodge near the center of the village. Holding the door covering, the native stepped backward, then motioned for Coleman to go through.

When Coleman entered, he could see that the dwelling was illuminated by a central fire. The upper walls were exposed while the lower ones were covered in skins with many woven mats covering the dirt. The lodge was about twenty feet in diameter, and the hole in the center of the roof was about twenty feet above the floor. Coleman could see that these dwellings were well built and probably permanent. The hut was warm and offered comfort and refuge from the rain.

The leader removed Coleman's bindings, handed a skin filled with liquid to him, and pantomimed taking a drink. Coleman examined the skin, removed what looked like a cork, sniffed the spout, and took a tentative sip. It was water. He took a deep quaff and handed it back to the leader. The leader took a drink and passed it on to the guard to whom he said a few words, and then he left the lodge.

Coleman followed him with his eyes, then turned and looked at the guard. "Okay, now what do we do? You wouldn't have a chess set around here would you?" The guard looked at him in puzzlement. "Of course not." He thought for a moment, "My name is Coleman. What's yours?" The guard just shook his head. This required a different strategy. "Coleman," he said, and patted his chest. "Cole-man," he said his name slowly hoping the guard would begin to understand.

A light seemed to turn on in the guard's eyes as he grasped what Coleman was referring to. The guard attempted to repeat Coleman but failed miserably. His C was too harsh and guttural, and the letter L was more like an R. His attempt sounded like q-owr-mon.

"That's good," Coleman said in an encouraging tone. "What's your name?" as he touched the guard's chest with his open hand.

The guard's eyes brightened and he said something that sounded like a series of consonants rammed together.

Coleman attempted to repeat the sounds he'd heard, and it evoked a chuckle from the guard. "This is going to be harder than I thought," he mumbled. He plugged on. "What does *Munnari* mean? *Munnari*. Do you understand?"

The guard looked into Coleman's eyes and repeated, "*Munnari*," and pointed upward.

"I guess *Munnari* means the blue sky, right?"

His guard's expression turned to deeper puzzlement; then he repeated, "*Munnari*," followed by more words accentuated with unfamiliar sounds.

A feeling of weariness came over Coleman as he grappled with his exhaustion from the day's adventures and his fitful sleep the previous night. He continued the faltering conversation with his guard. Both he and the guard quickly became fatigued and impatient with their lack of success, so Coleman stepped away and sat down on a floor mat.

The guard sat down, too. Outside, the steady beat of drums followed by chanting entertained them. The guard smiled and uttered a sentence with the word *bataro* in it. Then he smiled and mimicked eating.

"Ah, *bataro* means pig. *Bataro*, pig," Coleman leaned his head forward, indicating it was his guard's turn to say the words.

The guard repeated, "*Bataro*, peeg."

"Yes, yes. *Bataro*, pig. That's it, you've got it," Coleman affirmed with a smile.

The guard rattled off a string of harsh consonants, ending with, "Peeg, peeg, peeg!"

Coleman just shrugged his shoulders and merely said, "*Bataro*, pig." They both fell silent and intently listened to the drumming and chanting.

Coleman could tell that night was approaching. From time-to-time, the guard would put another small log on the fire. The chanting eventually rose to a crescendo, then abruptly stopped. The guard smiled and gave an extended commentary on something concerning the bataro. He ended it by pretending to eat. Shortly after that, the skins covering the doorway were pulled aside and two female natives entered holding folded leaf packages. The smell of cooked meat wafted over the men. The women handed each of them a leafy package and quickly retreated, but not before they both took a brief look into Coleman's eyes.

Unfolding his package, the guard grabbed the seared meat with his hands and began to eat while Coleman watched. The guard stopped, looked down at Coleman's folded package and said, "Bataro," and bit into his own portion.

Coleman, carefully unfolding the leaf, stared at the meat and felt his hunger. He picked it up and took a bite. The taste of the meat was surprising. "That's odd. Bataro tastes like beef." The guard just smiled and continued to devour his portion.

After they had finished their meal, both men leaned back and relaxed. A few minutes later, the guard rose, moved to a collection of animal furs and rummaged through them. After a few seconds, he found what he was looking for: a large, supple hide with thick fur. The guard returned to Coleman and handed him the fur and motioned with his hands that it was intended to be used as a blanket. Coleman draped the fur over his shoulders and sat staring into the fire.

A female entered the lodge and Coleman recognized her as one of the two who had brought them their meal of bataro meat. The guard wrapped his arm around her shoulders indicating that they had a special relationship; probably husband and wife. Coleman returned a smile at the revelation. The two built a comfortable bed made of furs in front of the doorway and then retired for the night. Coleman laid back and after a few minutes was fast asleep.

CHAPTER 3

HANGING IN THE BALANCE

Coleman had a restful night's sleep for the most part. He awoke a couple of times when he heard the crash of thunder near the village. Rain fell most of the evening, but the lodge was a dry and comfortable shelter. The fire slowly died, but the coals kept the room warm. Before dawn, he awoke and lay staring at the hole in the center of the roof and the brightening sky above it. When he went to move, he immediately felt the pain from the injuries he had sustained the night before. He heard the guard or his wife rustle under their blanket of furs. After a couple of comments, they arose, collected their bedding, and stowed it away in tightly woven wicker-like baskets.

The guard moved to Coleman's side and said something, motioning for Coleman to rise and follow him out of the lodge. Once outside, Coleman looked around and noticed that many villagers were up and busily engaged in their daily duties. Although the rain had stopped, a blanket of clouds filled the sky. Inside the lodge behind him, Coleman's bedding was stowed away and the fire stoked. When they returned, the guard's wife was no longer there.

Coleman took some time to look at his clothes. They were ripped and torn, exposing his bare skin through its many holes.

It was obvious they would not last much longer. He slipped out of his shirt and set it aside. There was an enormous and ugly bruise on his upper arm. He found another nasty looking bruise just above his left kidney. The guard turned from what he was doing and noticed the bruises. He immediately walked over to Coleman, poking at them, causing Coleman to recoil in pain. The guard started talking, seemingly asking what had happened. Through pantomime and hand gestures, Coleman explained how he had been attacked the night before. He indicated the size of the attacking beast and its jaws of razor-sharp teeth.

The guard's eyes widened in amazement and he exclaimed, "Gorga!" grabbing Coleman by the shoulders.

"Gorgon? That seems an appropriate name for that monster."

The guard made a few more comments which Coleman didn't understand, but he felt the guard was surprised he had survived the encounter. When the guard had finished speaking, Coleman lowered his pants and looked at another huge bruise on his right thigh. He also noticed his left knee was swollen and purple.

The skins covering the doorway were pulled aside and the guard's wife returned. Coleman felt embarrassed as he stood there in his jockey shorts. He quickly pulled his orange pants up and turned beet red. The guard touched Coleman's reddened skin and said something in a questioning manner. After a quick glance in his direction, the woman went about her business as though nothing unusual had happened. The guard spoke with her for a few minutes, apparently relating to her what Coleman had communicated. She also had a look of amazement by the time the guard's description was finished.

For the next few hours, Coleman and his guard remained in the lodge. The guard's wife left earlier and hadn't returned. Coleman attempted to learn a few more words of the village language, but he made little progress. He couldn't get the clicks and pops right nor in the right places in the words. At first, it was humorous, but after an hour or so, he was becoming frustrated. He attempted to teach the guard a few simple words in English, like shirt and pants, and he thought he was making some progress; however, it appeared that the guard was having similar trouble pronouncing the English sounds and inserted extra consonants into the words.

It started to rain again. Thunder rumbled, lightning flashed across the sky. Coleman was hungry and pantomimed to the guard with his fingers to his mouth. The guard looked puzzled and said something that Coleman didn't understand. A few minutes later, a call was heard from outside. After his guard said something in response, the doorway skins were pulled aside and in walked the leader of yesterday's hunting party. He said a few words to the guard and the group left the lodge, Coleman in tow.

The trio walked across the village and after a few minutes, came to a structure that looked a bit different than the others Coleman had seen. On both sides of the doorway stood wooden totem poles with carved images on them. The men did not enter the dwelling but stood in the pouring rain. The leader announced their presence, and when a response came from inside the lodge, the men entered.

Coleman saw two men standing inside; one was elderly, the oldest villager he had seen so far. The man wore a brightly ornamented band around his head, and he had many lines tattooed down both sides of his face and neck. The other individual was a very peculiar sight to Coleman. He was adorned with feathers and furs of various kinds. He carried a large pouch and a staff of over six feet in length. Topping the staff was the skull of some unfortunate animal. It made Coleman's blood run cold.

The leader began to speak to the men while the guard stared at the floor of the lodge, his eyes never looking up. It was evident to Coleman that the elderly man was the village leader or chief and he guessed the other man was a witch doctor or shaman.

After the leader of the hunting team had finished speaking, the chief and the shaman moved closer to Coleman and stared into his eyes. The shaman uttered, "*Munnari.*"

Coleman offered a nervous smile and said, "Hello. My name is Coleman."

He got the expected response; both men stepped back and looked at him, astonished at what they had just heard. The guard made a few comments while still looking down. Coleman recognized the word *gorga*. The guard then indicated for Coleman to remove his shirt and Coleman did so, revealing his nasty wounds. The chief and shaman exchanged words. Then the village leader stepped forward again and stared up into Coleman's eyes. A look of concern filled his countenance as he began to speak. Coleman couldn't tell if he was talking to him or the other men. He got the impression that the chief had to make a decision about him and didn't know what to do. After a few more comments by the chief, Coleman, his guard, and the hunt leader were dismissed and returned to the guard's lodge. By the time they got back, Coleman was soaking wet and chilled.

He had given some thought to an escape attempt but had dismissed the idea as premature. So far, he had been treated well by the natives, although the sight of the fierce-looking shaman unnerved him. Coleman crossed his legs and sat by the fire. He began to doze as he basked in the fire's warmth. He awoke sometime later not knowing how long he'd been asleep. The wood in the fire was now reduced to only glowing coals, so he knew it had been at least a couple of hours. He could still hear the falling rain. He felt stiff and sore all over. He wasn't accustomed to sitting as the natives did. He slowly unfolded his legs, stood up, and stretched.

Looking around the lodge, he found his guard near the doorway. The villager had pulled back the skins and tied them open. He had a leather apron over his legs and was working with a slab of obsidian. Coleman watched for a few minutes as the guard continued chipping away at a long piece. It looked like the man was making a spear tip or a knife. Coleman reached for the waterskin and took a long drink, not allowing the spout to touch his lips. When he'd finished, he motioned to the guard if he would like a drink. The guard grunted something and continued staring out the doorway. Coleman capped the skin and returned it to its place. He thought it was mid afternoon, but that was only a guess. The overcast was so thick it was impossible to tell where the sun was in the sky.

He walked over to the doorway and squatted next to the

guard. He pointed out the doorway and said, "Rain," wiggling his fingers and motioning with his hands.

The guard understood and said, "Apour."

Coleman repeated, "'Apour,' rain," and both men smiled at their accomplishment. Coleman's stomach grumbled. "Food," he said and rubbed his abdomen.

The guard looked at him, pointed out the doorway and motioned with his hand what Coleman interpreted as the motion of the sun. When the guard's hand had dropped to the level of the horizon, he said, "Measha."

"Ah, so measha means food? Does that mean no measha until sundown?" The guard looked at him in puzzlement.

"Measha, food," and motioned with his hand indicating the setting sun.

The guard responded, "Ha," and went back to his obsidian.

He guessed that the people must eat only around sundown, meaning once a day. Coleman didn't feel much like struggling through more communication, so he just sat there, staring out at the rain, feeling more miserable in his predicament by the hour.

After a while, the rain began to ease and then it stopped. The sky glow was diminishing and Coleman knew dusk was approaching. A cry was heard from somewhere in the village and the guard's eyes brightened. He stepped through the doorway and indicated Coleman should follow. The two men moved at a quick pace to the village entrance where a throng of villagers had gathered. Walking across the clearing outside the village wall was a returning hunting party; however, it appeared they had returned empty-handed. There was no bataro slung from a pole like the day before. There were only ten men with sad expressions. They quickly and silently entered the village, each man going his separate way, disappearing into his lodge. The rest of the villagers moved to their homes with only quiet murmurs being shared. Coleman could tell that this was a big disappointment to everyone. He guessed, there would be no measha tonight.

Since it appeared the people ate only one meal a day, he feared it would be another day before they would be fed again; however, when the two men returned to the lodge, they found the guard's wife waiting for them with a basket of fruit pods. There was no bataro, but the fruit looked fresh and inviting. Coleman waited for the guard to start, and when he motioned for Coleman to indulge, he began to eat. He had never seen such fruit nor tasted such delicacies. What he ate was sweet and flavorful, but it wasn't meat. Coleman didn't care, though. He was really hungry after waiting all day for a meal.

After he'd indicated he was finished, the guard's wife ate her fill, and when she began to remove the basket, Coleman said, "That wasn't bataro, but it was good. Thank you, my friends."

She gave him a bewildered smile and took the basket out of the lodge. The guard said something about bataro and words that Coleman assumed meant other types of food. Then the guard took Coleman by the wrist and began speaking to him in a manner that was unnerving. He seemed to be quite earnest for the expression on his face indicated something serious was about to happen. Coleman thought about his meeting with the chief earlier, and how the village leader appeared to have a decision to make about his welfare.

Could this be what the guard was referring to? Could he be preparing me for some bad news? Coleman's thoughts turned to the scary shaman and the hostile hunter brandishing his war club threateningly. A shiver ran down his spine. He considered escape, but the thought of another encounter with the gorga was enough to change his mind.

Shortly after night had fallen, Coleman heard drums, and then the leader of yesterday's hunting party returned and talked with the guard. The two men looked tense as they conversed. After a few minutes, they indicated Coleman should go with them. He took a deep breath and stepped out of the lodge.

Coleman couldn't help but talk as the men walked. "So, I guess this is it. What will the chief do with me? This makes me a little nervous. Actually, I'm scared. I hope you two can offer a few words on my behalf."

The two natives said nothing as the group trudged through the darkness. Soon, they were standing in front of a huge frond-covered building. It was unlike the smaller lodges in which the villagers dwelt. It was obviously the central meeting place for the entire tribe. It looked to be fifty feet in diameter. No skins covered the large doorway. As they entered, Coleman guessed the inhabitants of the entire village were in attendance. A fire pit with unlit, stacked wood was in the center of the room, and the dirt floor was covered with large woven mats. Coleman could hear a low murmur of voices. On one side of the room sat the chief with the shaman at his right side. Both men were sitting on stools made of logs; a group of ten men squatted on floor mats in front of the two leaders. Every one of these men had a large tusk suspended from a leather strap around his neck. On the opposite side of the fire pit, sitting in a half-circle in front of this group and facing them were the rest of the adult men. None of these men wore a tusk. In another and larger half-circle near the walls of the grand lodge sat the women and young children. Coleman was directed to an opening in the center of the half-circle of men. There, he and his guard sat. The hunting party leader, who wore a tusk, moved to the tusk-men group and sat. The witch doctor stood and pointed his skull-topped staff at the stacked firewood. The wood burst into flame.

"How did he do that?" Coleman exclaimed. His guard silenced him by covering his lips with two fingers.

The chief stood, and a hush fell over the assembly. He began to speak to the assemblage in slow and moderate tones. Coleman recognized the words *Munnari*, *bataro*, and *gorga*. He didn't understand any of the meaning, but he could tell by the chief's demeanor he was remarking about a somber matter. The chief spoke for several minutes and then sat. The leader of the hunting party rose and began speaking. Coleman could tell that the hunt leader was explaining how he had been found, chased, and captured. He nervously shuffled in his position, thanking his lucky stars he hadn't acted upon the pressing urge he'd had to kill a hunter. When the hunt leader finished and sat, another of yesterday's hunters stood up from the group where Coleman was seated. He recognized him as the angry young man who would have split his skull open with a club if not prevented by the leader. The man went on another tirade. It was evident he didn't like Coleman and considered him a threat to the village. As he continued, others in the group shouted comments, some in support and some against his remarks. As the man finished his rant, he looked at Coleman, pulled his knife from its sheath, made a threatening gesture with it, and then sat down.

Coleman quickly realized his life was hanging in the balance. The fact that he could do nothing to defend himself both angered and alarmed him. It wasn't in his nature to remain a docile victim. He stood up, pointed his finger at his detractor and began to rage, "I don't know what your problem is, but maybe I should have killed you when I had the chance!"

The force of his words caught the assembly by surprise. Almost immediately, his guard yanked him down and motioned for him to be quiet by placing two fingers over Coleman's mouth again. The guard then stood and started speaking in Coleman's defense. He also mentioned something about *bataro, Munnari,* and *gorga,* finally raising both arms above his head as if in supplication to a higher power. He then sat and one of the tusk-men stood and began to speak. Coleman couldn't tell what his position was so he watched the angry man for signs of agreement. The angry man's expression soured. Coleman perceived that to be a good sign.

One-by-one, each adult male in the room took his turn and presented his view. Coleman studied the angry man to try to interpret whether the other villagers were in support of him or against him. His guard started to pat Coleman's leg when a speaker seemed to be for him. As the discussion continued, it appeared the men were evenly divided. After all the men had their say, the shaman stood and began to speak. As he spoke, Coleman heard the word *Munnari* mentioned several times, but he also began to recognize another oft-repeated word, *Munnevo*.

He leaned over to his guard and whispered, "What does *Munnevo* mean? *Mun-nevo?*" The guard didn't respond but covered Coleman's mouth with two fingers, once more.

After the shaman had finished, he sat; then the chief stood and said a few more words. Coleman stared at the angry young man, attempting to read every feature of his face, which revealed neither satisfaction nor disappointment as the chief spoke.

The village leader ended his comments and sat again. He then loudly spoke a word. One of the tusk-men grunted in recognition. He raised his tusk with the point down. A wicked smile crossed the angry man's face. Coleman quickly realized this was a vote for his life, and he had just lost one point. The chief called out another name and another tusk-man responded with his tusk pointing down. Coleman noticed his guard's head droop and his worry swelled. A third name was called, and again the tusk pointed down. Sweat began to form on Coleman's face. Fear gripped him as the chief called the fourth name.

They're going to kill you. Run! a voice in Coleman's head warned. He began contemplating escape and noted where he could make a fast exit.

Just as he was about to bolt, the leader of the hunting party that had captured him responded to the chief's call and turned his tusk point up. Coleman gave an audible sigh of relief and relaxed a bit. The chief called the fifth name. Everyone saw the tusk point was up. Coleman relaxed a little more. Other names were called and soon there was only one tusk-man left: he was the spearman from yesterday's hunt.

By his count, Coleman could tell the vote was evenly split, five-to-five. The young tusk-man gave a broad smile and turned his tusk point up. Coleman's angry detractor clenched his fists as his body stiffened. A subdued buzz of female voices came from the outer half-circle.

The chief stood, and instantly all became silent. He uttered the word, *Tondo,* and waited. Coleman's guard touched his leg and indicated that he must stand. Coleman obliged and waited for the chief to continue. The chief spoke for several minutes, often repeating the words *Tondo* and *Munnari.* Coleman could only guess that he was now referred to as Tondo. Other than that, he had no idea what the chief was saying. The chief stopped speaking for a few seconds and then called another name, Atura. A young woman from the rear stood up and approached the chief, her eyes downcast in submission. The chief spoke to her and pointed to Coleman. The woman did not look up but shook her head. Coleman recognized her as the woman who had examined him upon his entry into the village. He could tell she was being commanded to do something she didn't want to do.

The village leader spoke to her with a stern voice and Coleman could see the woman cringe in fear. The chief's words continued to flow even when tears began to streak down her cheeks. Finally, she broke down and covered her face with both hands. Coleman was sorry for her, but he didn't say a word. He felt he'd just passed through the valley of the shadow of death and he didn't want to do anything to jeopardize his narrow victory. He just stood in place, waiting in bewildered silence.

Finally, the woman nodded her head in forced agreement to what the chief was commanding her to do. Her body was stiff and her movements quick and jerky. She wiped tears from her eyes and looked at Coleman. He could see fear and anger etched across her face.

What is the chief doing? he wondered. *Is he giving this woman to me?* The idea hit him like an avalanche.

The chief then called out the name of Coleman's guard. Although Coleman couldn't pronounce the name, he recognized it. The guard stood up, took Coleman by the arm, and led him out of the great lodge with the woman, Atura, following closely behind. They returned to the guard's home and shortly after they entered, the guard's wife arrived. The women began preparing the beds, speaking in quiet voices. Atura did little to hide the fact that she was upset. Coleman watched carefully, fearing what he might see. His fear subsided when he noticed that three beds were made; one in front of the doorway where the guard and his wife slept, one near the fire where he had slept the night before, and one as far away from his bed as could be placed in the relatively small room.

"Thank you, ladies," he said. The guard and his wife smiled. Atura just scowled at him and said something that made the others chuckle as they all got into their beds.

Coleman lay under his furry blanket reviewing the trial or whatever it was he had just experienced. As the adrenaline finally drained from him and the weariness from the day set in, he wondered what his new status in the tribe was and if he would even be here long enough to experience it. As he pondered, he puzzled over how the witch doctor had magically ignited the fire.

Coleman was now accepted into the tribe and given free rein to walk about the village. Even so, he felt very conspicuous as he ambled around in his tattered orange USE garments. His throat began to feel scratchy and he figured he was coming down with a cold. Some villagers welcomed him, while others avoided him. For the next couple of days, he simply explored the village and greeted as many people as were willing to meet with their tall and unusual visitor. At first, his guard accompanied him, but it became obvious he considered it a bore and, after half a day, returned to his lodge to weave more wicker baskets.

On one of his sojourns about the place, he noticed a young woman and a boy returning to the village. They both had their arms full of wood branches for their dwelling's fire.

"Here, let me help you with that," Coleman said in his native tongue. The woman looked startled and resisted his help. Coleman insisted, "It's alright, I don't mind." He pulled the load of firewood from her and watched as the boy, most likely her son, dashed off, dropping his load outside a lodge and then disappearing through the doorway skins. The woman, appearing to be quite upset and constantly chattering in her indecipherable jargon, followed him as he walked toward the dwelling the boy had entered. About the time Coleman and the woman reached the hut, a male villager exited and grumbled a few terse words at Coleman. He seemed quite upset. He grabbed the woman by the upper arm and pushed her into the lodge. He then turned and faced Coleman. He knocked the bundle of wood from Coleman's arms, reached down, picked up a sturdy log, and raised it high above his head in a threatening manner.

Coleman thought he was about to be attacked and prepared himself to ward off the coming blow. *He wants to kill you. Stop him! Strangle him before it's too late!* Coleman's inner voice commanded.

Coleman prepared to attack, but just before he did, his guard intervened, placing his body between the two men. He faced Coleman's assailant and said a few calming words. The man responded in obvious anger, pointing at the tall visitor. Coleman quickly realized he must have violated some tribal custom by helping the man's woman. He felt foolish but nevertheless aggravated.

Why did my offer of help result in such a violent reaction? Coleman wondered.

He began to relax as the angry man tossed his makeshift club onto the firewood stack. He mumbled a few gruff words to the guard, glared at Coleman, and then disappeared into his hut. Coleman heard the man's angry voice and the woman's pleading response. He heard a slap and then sobs coming from the woman.

Coleman's anger was kindled, but his guard took him by the forearm and pulled him away from the lodge. After they had gone a fair distance, Coleman's guard began to lecture him. He stood, shifting his weight from one foot to the other. He knew from his guard's tone that he had done something wrong, but he didn't understand why.

"I only tried to help her; that's all. Was that so bad?" he protested. His guard continued his long, heated harangue until Coleman lowered his eyes and dropped his chin to his chest. "Alright, alright, I'll never help anyone in this village ever again. Now, get off my case!" Coleman grouched, his tone clearly reflecting his frustration. The guard marched him back to his lodge and pointed at the doorway. "Really, you're giving me a timeout? Good grief!" Coleman grumbled as he entered the dwelling and plopped himself down in front of the fire.

He sat in thought, reviewing the confrontation. *How could his simple act of kindness result in such a potential disaster?* he silently wondered. *Why did I have such a strong urge to strangle the man threatening me? That seemed out of character.* His assailant was at least a head shorter than he was. The man looked fit, but Coleman knew he was bigger, stronger, and better trained. The villager would not have been a threat. *So, why did I have such a strong urge to attack the man?*

As he thought, he recalled the other strong promptings he'd felt when he first encountered the hunters: a nearly overpowering desire to kill. *Was it simply fear and near panic that had driven me to such a state? I've been through worse, so why the desire to react with such haste and deadly violence?* It all seemed so foreign to him. He continued pondering for the remainder of the day, all the time noticing the symptoms of a worsening cold.

Coleman remained in timeout for the rest of the day. He enjoyed a meal of unfamiliar but tasty meat and fruit pods.

He listened to his three lodge mates as they carried on in their cryptic jargon, occasionally uttering one of the few words he recognized: *Tondo, Munnari, gorga.* Eventually, the beds were prepared, and everyone retired for the night. But, by this point, his cold had progressed to include a low-grade fever.

Several times during the night, Coleman awoke. His throat burned and felt parched. The waterskin was out of his reach, and he couldn't work up enough energy to rise and retrieve it. He saw the flash of lightning through the opening in the roof and, soon following the burst of light, he heard the distant rumble of thunder. Rain began to pelt the roof of the lodge. Coleman drifted back into a troubled sleep.

A thunderclap woke him just as a creature burst through the structure's doorway, scattering the door skins and sending splinters of fronds throughout the room. "Help, it's the gorga!" Coleman yelled, but it was too late.

The creature bit into the fur covers of the guard and his wife, slashing and tearing with its massive jaws and razor-sharp teeth. Neither one made a sound; their deaths were instantaneous! Atura rose from her bed and gave a stifled cry. The creature charged her, hitting her squarely in the chest and driving her into the wall of the lodge. She crumpled to the floor and didn't rise. The gorga turned and faced Coleman. He could see a chiseled scar across its snout.

"You're the same monster that attacked me before. How did you find me here?" Coleman was weak and could only prop himself up on his elbows.

The monster bit into his right leg, this time severing it at the thigh. The beast pulled back with Coleman's detached leg in its mouth, tossing it aside with a jerk of its head. It then lurched forward and bit into his right arm, severing it just above the elbow. He closed his eyes and wondered why he felt no pain. Something was tugging at him. When he opened his eyes, he saw a flinger monkey pulling at his shoulder. He felt paralyzed by his weakness and just stared in wonder at the monkey. In an instant, the gorga made another lunge and bit into his bowels.

"Gorga!" he yelled, wrenching his eyes wide open.

This time, he was staring into the face of his guard kneeling at his shoulder. The two women hovered above him with worried expressions. Light filled the room and Coleman realized it was dawn. He had just awakened from a horrible nightmare. He lifted his right arm, still attached but his skin was covered in red spots. He looked at his left arm and found it covered with spots, too. For an instant, his mind cleared enough to recognize that he had come down with some kind of local illness.

He pointed to the waterskin. The guard's wife took it down and handed it to him. He took several gulps directly from the spout and then poured water over his face. His clothes and bedding dripped with sweat, and he felt a burning fever ravishing his body. He grabbed the guard by the arm, his head swimming and the room spinning. Delirium overcame him and he uttered the word, "Gorga!" Then he collapsed into unconsciousness.

As he slipped into another hallucination, he felt hunted. He crashed through the jungle while the shouts of his pursuers filled his ears. Creatures scurried away from the noise and into the shadowy darkness of the thick undergrowth. The dank of the rainforest mingled with its darkness. All Coleman could see were shadows: shadow trees, shadow creatures, shadow pursuers. The jungle clawed at him as he stumbled forward, afraid to stop, afraid to listen. A crushing terror weighed upon his mind as he ran; the dread of being caught, again. He glanced over his shoulder and quickly glimpsed a staff raised above the ground shrubs. It had a skull attached to its top end. The shaman was after him, and he feared his skull would soon replace the one on the shaman's staff. He quickened his pace as he charged through the bushes and ferns, dodging trees and boulders that seemed to reach out and frustrate his advance.

The shouts became more distant as he ran. He thought he was outdistancing the huntsmen chasing him. This gave him some solace but he refused to slow his pace even a little. The jungle soon began to close in around him. His progress became impeded by the dense underbrush. As he struggled forward, branches and thorns ripped at his clothes and his bare skin. He had forgotten his pains but they now ached with a ferocity that could no longer be ignored. He had run so long and so far, that thirst also gnawed at him. It was overpowering, causing him to cry out for water, but to no avail. He didn't even know where he could find fresh water. He had no idea where the spring that had been his refuge and his torment was.

"I must have water!" he yelled.

Unexpectedly, an opening appeared in the jungle ahead. It was like a shaft through the wilderness. He plunged forward, his struggle eased by the opening he had found. Far in the distance, he could see a small light as if he were peering into a tunnel. His pace slackened and he began to walk. He felt his body being lifted, and he began to glide forward with no effort. The light grew larger and brighter. He reached out to it. It seemed to proclaim security and peace. His thirst and his pains were forgotten. His mind was spinning as he continued his headlong slide into the beckoning light. The feeling of peace, safety, and warmth embraced him. More than ever, he desired to reach it. It would be the end of his struggles, the end of his pain, the end of his fear. The light began to embrace him and he felt a loving warmth cascade over him.

A voice came from behind. He did not understand the mutterings, but he knew it was an urgent call. He looked over his shoulder and saw only darkness. He turned and looked again into the light. It was so inviting, so welcoming, but the voice continued its urgings, and he felt compelled to seek it out. He began to drift backward, away from the light. Sadness filled his soul and he watched the light shrink from view. Why had he followed the voice? The light offered so much more, yet the voice was compelling, demanding his return. Darkness filled his vision and he realized his eyes were closed. He struggled to open them but couldn't. He didn't have the strength. With a second great effort, he forced his eyelids back just enough to catch the light coming through the hole in the lodge roof. A ghostly image hovered over him. He heard chanting and the shake of a rattle. He thought he glimpsed a fan of feathers passing over his upturned face, blocking for an instant the light coming from the hole in the roof. Within moments, the struggle with his eyelids was lost, his eyes closed, and he drifted into an inky wasteland.

"Why did I leave the light? I must be crazy," he said to no one in particular. "The light offered such hope, such peace. I must find it again."

His mind drifted in a dark haze. He found it hard to focus on any of the visions that invaded his thoughts. He felt crazed by thirst and his aches and pains returned. He felt wracked by a fever that burned throughout his body.

"If I could only get a drink of water," he cried. "Water! Water!"

His calls went unheeded. He felt his arm groping for the waterskin, and then wonderful, soothing water trickled down his burning throat. "Oh, thank goodness! Where is the light? Where is the light? Peace is there. Safety is there. Let me return to it."

Again, he was overcome by his dark thoughts. Images of shadowy men on shadowy creatures flashed through his mind. "This makes no sense. Who are they? What are they? Where did they come from?"

He began to walk into the village clearing. He could see a gathering of the village inhabitants and he needed to know what was happening. He approached the chief, who looked at him with eyes full of sadness. He held up his arms and they were manacled at the wrists and attached to a long chain. The chain touched every villager and Coleman could now see they were all manacled and connected to the chain.

"What's the meaning of this? Who did this to you?"

Dark creatures patrolled the tree line—shadowy men riding on shadowy, spiral-horned mounts, the likes of which Coleman had never seen before. The villagers began to follow the gloomy forms, weeping and wailing with such ferocity that it tore at his heart. He followed them.

The shadows ignored him; it was as though he wasn't there. He passed burned villages and dead bodies of men, women, and children.

"What is all this? What has happened here?"

There were no answers, only more questions. He stopped and let the villagers disappear into the jungle, herded by the shadows. A young girl approached. He couldn't tell where she came from but she stopped in front of him and tugged at his leg. "Tondo; Munnari; Munnevo," she said. He dropped to his knees and looked the girl in the eyes. "Tondo," she called and she touched his chest with an open palm. "Munnari," she cried and raised both arms skyward, looking to the heavens. "Munnevo," she whispered as she lowered her arms and he could see they had become manacled.

"What are you trying to tell me, little one? I don't understand."

A tear ran down her cheek and her head bowed until her chin touched her chest. Her body began to shake, and she started to sob. As she wept, she spoke. "Tondo, Munnari, Munnevo," taking in great gulps of air as she cried.

Coleman wrapped his arms around the child and held her close. "Be at peace, little one. I will protect you."

She looked into his face and smiled as if she understood. Her arms were no longer manacled and she embraced him around the neck. He stood, took her by the hand, and they both followed the villagers. He heard a crack of thunder and looked into the cloud-filled sky. He looked down at the girl but she was gone.

He continued to follow the path the villagers took, although he could no longer see them. There was a clear trail winding its way through the jungle, making his progress easy. He picked up his pace, hoping to catch the others, but he saw no one. Unexpectedly, he heard a horn coming from the distance behind him. He looked back and saw shadow creatures moving his way. He felt hunted again and drove himself forward. The trail disappeared and he clamored through the bush and stumbled over rock and log. The horn sounded loudly, followed by beastly roars, growls, and the shouts of angry men. He distinctly heard the clanging of metal against metal.

Coleman scrambled forward with renewed vigor. He looked over his shoulder and glimpsed a shadowy man carrying a banner. The flag was black and had a large reddish-orange circle in its center. Coleman faced forward again and quickened his pace to a full run. But try as he might, he couldn't outdistance this horde. If anything, he was losing ground. He felt the wind of a missile pass near his ear, and then he heard a thud as a spear crashed into a tree trunk just as he passed it. He ran frantically through the jungle. He had to lose his pursuers or fall to their weapons.

Once again, he found the tunnel of light from whence he was pulled earlier. He stopped and turned for a quick look. The shadowy figures were still after him, led by the black flag with the reddish-orange symbol emblazoned on it. He turned back and began gliding into the light he could see at the end of the tunnel. It grew larger and brighter, and soon began to embrace him in its warmth and peace. All his troubles faded and he focused on the wondrous light that emanated such peace, love, and security.

He was about to abandon himself to the exhilaration of the light's glow when he felt a tap on his leg. He looked down and the little girl he had seen earlier looked up at him, her eyes pleading. Coleman wanted to push her aside and step further into the refuge of the light but his compassion wouldn't allow him to abandon the girl. He scooped her into his arms and stood transfixed as the light embraced them both. As he watched, the child faded from view.

Coleman slowly became aware of a faint voice deep within the recesses of his mind. It was not so much a voice as an impression upon his consciousness. He concentrated on it and soon began to hear words, some of them understandable. A white light filled his sight and his thoughts and he saw the face of the child as if he were in a dream.

"It is for this purpose you are here," the voice decreed without language.

"I don't understand! What purpose?" Coleman lamented.

The child began to speak in a voice that echoed and reverberated in his ears, "Tondo. Munnari. Munnevo."

"What does this mean? I don't understand." The girl's face faded from his view. He was alone.

The light began to fade and he felt himself being pulled from the tunnel. He heard chanting and felt a slight breeze across his face. His mind was spinning as he opened his eyes and saw a star shining through the hole in the lodge roof. A dark figure was hunched over him and he was startled at this realization. As his mind focused, he could see it was the shaman and he was chanting a song while waving his feathered fan over Coleman's face.

As he focused on the witch doctor, his mind began to clear, and he took stock of his situation. The first thing he noticed was a burning thirst. He groped for the waterskin and Atura helped him as he gulped the water down, nearly emptying the skin.

"Oh, thanks, that was good!"

Atura and the shaman looked at each other, then turned and smiled at him. Atura's smile was pleasant and serene. The witch doctor's smile was grotesque, almost gruesome due to his face paint and matted hair.

Coleman mustered a smile and dropped the waterskin to his side. He raised his right arm and examined the red spots marking his skin. "All this from the measles?" he muttered.

The shaman said something to Atura and she left the lodge. Soon, she returned with the chief, Coleman's guard, and the guard's wife. Coleman attempted to prop himself up on his elbows but he couldn't muster the strength. The shaman placed his painted hand on Coleman's shoulder and gently pushed him down, saying something that Coleman guessed meant to relax. The chief examined Coleman's face and said a few words to the small assemblage staring down at their stricken visitor. A discussion followed and, as they spoke, Coleman drifted into a peaceful languor.

He awoke sometime later. A bright star was shining through the hole in the lodge roof. The fire was down to coals with only a small whiff of smoke. Light from the moon shone, casting dark shadows throughout the interior of the lodge. He could hear the heavy breathing of his guard. Atura stirred in her sleep but did not wake. He felt the waterskin resting under his left arm. He took it and drank. The effort exhausted him and he recapped it, dropping the skin at his side; it made a loud plop as it hit the floor mat. The guard's wife awoke and came to him. She looked into his face, felt his forehead, and smiled. She whispered a few words and squatted beside him. Coleman raised both of his arms and examined the red spots. They hadn't diminished since the first time he'd noticed them. He tried to speak but couldn't get the words out. He had used up all his reserves of strength lifting the waterskin. Now, all he wanted to do was rest and recover. He drifted off into a dreamless torpor.

CHAPTER 4

THE MUNNA RISES

Coleman heard the chitchat of village voices passing by the lodge; that and the chatter of the jungle creatures in the distance seemed exceptionally loud to him. He noticed pressure in his ears and he yawned, attempting to clear them. He heard a pop, and his hearing returned to normal. When he opened his eyes, he saw his guard sitting next to him weaving a basket with intricate designs made from different colored reeds. The guard said a few words and laid the basket aside. He picked up the waterskin lying next to his stricken guest and offered him a drink. Coleman drank gratefully for several seconds and then raised his hand. The guard lowered the skin and recapped it.

Coleman attempted to rise on his elbows but couldn't muster the strength. "Whatever this thing is I've got, it's sure kicking my butt."

He felt his forehead and noticed he still had a fever. He examined the spots on his arms and could see they were still as red as the first day. The guard lifted a bowl of fruit and offered it to him, but he only shook his head. He had no appetite and no energy to eat. He pulled the blanket down to his waist and examined the red spots all over his chest.

"Where's my shirt?" he cried in shock. But it wasn't just his shirt that was missing; he was buck naked. "Where are my pants?" He motioned to the guard, miming putting on his shirt, and the guard pointed to the fire. "Now, ain't that just great? What am I supposed to wear? I can't go walking around the village in my birthday suit."

The guard just stared at him with a blank look. Atura entered the lodge with a gourd of water. She knelt beside Coleman and dipped a fur skin into the water and began daubing it on his face. The cool water felt wonderful on his fevered skin. After a minute or so of this, she touched his forehead with her bare hand and smiled. She then slid her palm down his face and quickly pulled her hand back. She moved closer for a look at his skin. Coleman thought she was examining the red spots he knew he must have on his face, but she started stroking his growth of beard. Her eyes widened in amazement as she felt the whiskers. She said a few words to the guard and both drew closer to examine him. Each rubbed their face and then touched his. He stared at his guard and noticed he didn't appear to have whiskers. Coleman managed to chuckle as he realized the men of this village didn't grow facial hair.

"I bet you guys save a lot on razor blades," he said out loud.

Atura and the guard just looked at each other with puzzled expressions. He then pointed to Atura and said, "Atura. Atura." She nodded in acknowledgment. He pointed to the guard and attempted to say his name, but he scrambled the pronunciation so badly, both villagers laughed at his feeble attempt.

Atura began to patiently pronounce the word, using

exaggerated mouth gestures to try and demonstrate how to pronounce the strange sounds.

Coleman made another attempt at the guard's name; "Zee-zo" was the result.

Both Atura and the guard nodded their heads in recognition of a decent job. All three smiled broadly.

"I'm Coleman. *Coleman.* Now, you try it." The guard just shook his head and didn't even try.

Atura stared at Coleman with the look of defiance in her eyes and then spouted, "Todo!"

The guard laughed. Coleman was confused but too tired to question. He laughed lightly and then rested. The effort had exhausted him. He closed his eyes and suddenly remembered his dreams of the light, the child, and the shadows of the reddish-orange symbol. He wanted to know why he had seen these things in his dreams. Were they just meaningless hallucinations or were they a warning? So far, they meant nothing he could understand, yet the impressions they left on his soul were disturbing, and he ached to know what their meaning was. He began to drift into slumber again.

The shaman pulled back the door skins and entered the lodge. Coleman and Atura were in a heated argument with him speaking in English and Atura speaking in the village tongue.

"My mouth doesn't make those sounds!" he yelled.

Atura responded angrily, neither understanding the words the other was saying, but the intent was clear.

"Oh yeah, well the student is only as good as the teacher," Coleman growled.

Atura gave as good as she got and ended her diatribe by calling him *todo* instead of Tondo. The shaman began chuckling quietly; that caught the attention of the two combatants.

Several days had passed since Coleman's near-death experience. The red spots were fading, but he was still very weak. Every time he attempted to stand, he had to be supported by the guard. Standing made him dizzy and walking was out of the question. Between his naps, Atura had begun grilling him with the village language. It had become clear to Coleman that teaching him their language was the assignment the chief had given her, and she wanted to get it over with as soon as possible. Coleman quickly discovered that she had a low frustration level and was easily annoyed by his failing attempts at the intricate sounds she was teaching him.

She began talking to the shaman in an angry tone, gesturing to Coleman with apparent disdain. The shaman said a few gruff words and Atura fell silent, bowing her head in submission. He then moved near Coleman and began examining him as a physician would. After a few minutes of this, the shaman took Coleman by the arms and pulled him to a standing position. Coleman attempted to grab the fur blanket, but couldn't since the shaman held both of his arms. He stood naked and embarrassed, but neither the shaman nor Atura seemed to care. The shaman pulled lightly on Coleman's arms forcing him to take a step. With dizziness overwhelming him, he fell forward toward the shaman, who supported him and gently lowered him onto his bed mat. He quickly covered himself with his blanket. Atura and the shaman had a short discussion and, when it ended, Atura left the lodge. The shaman squatted next to Coleman and began chanting. He pulled some dust from the pouch he always carried with him and tossed it on Coleman's face, causing him to sneeze. Then the shaman started waving a fan of feathers over Coleman's head while his chanting increased in volume. Coleman was exhausted by his effort to stand, and the shaman's chanting began to lull him to sleep.

When he awoke, the shaman was gone. Coleman sat up and rested on his elbows. The red spots on his arms and chest were nearly gone; he felt stronger, too. He stood, wrapped the blanket around himself, and walked to the lodge entrance. He pushed the door skins aside and peered into the dark and overcast sky. He turned and stepped back into the hut. He felt a little chilly, so he tossed a log onto the fire. The guard soon entered, walked over to him, grabbed him by the shoulders, and looked him over from head to toe.

"Ha!" he said excitedly.

Coleman examined his bruises and found them to be fading. His aches and pains had diminished quite a bit, although he could still feel them. Coleman put a hand on the guard's shoulder and said his name, "Tzeechoe." The word was pronounced perfectly and Tzeechoe nodded and smiled broadly. "Why do I feel so well, and how can I suddenly pronounce your name? I've been struggling with it ever since we met."

Atura and Tzeechoe's wife entered the lodge, each carrying a small basket of fruit. Tzeechoe spoke to Atura. Looking at Coleman, he said, "Tzeechoe." Then he gestured for Coleman to repeat it.

"Tzeechoe," Coleman said and smiled. Tzeechoe's wife laughed and clapped her hands. Atura uttered an audible huff and rolled her eyes as if to say, 'It's about time.'

Tzeechoe sat and motioned for Coleman to do the same. The women sat, offered the men the fruit, and the two men began to eat. The women waited patiently while they partook. Coleman motioned for the women to eat but neither would. They waited until both men were finished and then took their turns. Coleman was famished and the fresh, sweet fruit was a delight.

He said, "Thank you," and gave a curt bow to the women. For some reason, that set Atura off and she began berating him. He guessed it was because he wasn't speaking in the village language, so he just stared at her and smiled while she railed on. Finally, she calmed down but not before calling him todo. Tzeechoe and his wife both smiled wryly and turned their heads to hide their expressions. Coleman surmised that todo was an unflattering play on his village name, Tondo, and he took offense. He angrily chastised Atura in English and told her to call him Tondo. She grabbed the basket, rose to her feet, and stormed out of the lodge yelling *todo* repeatedly as she left.

"I'm not todo, you're todo," he shouted at the skins covering the doorway. He then looked at the bemused faces of his hosts. They sheepishly smiled back. Slapping his bare chest, he said, "Tondo." He then pointed to his guard and said "Tzeechoe," perfectly. He then pointed to Tzeechoe's wife and waited for her to respond.

She paused for a couple of seconds and then realized what he wanted, and said, "Tzeecha."

Coleman repeated, "Tzeecha."

Both Tzeechoe and Tzeecha responded in unison, "Ha!"

"That's interesting; your names sound almost alike." Then an idea crossed his mind. "Could Tzeecha be the feminine form of Tzeechoe? Do female villagers assume the name of their husbands?" he mumbled aloud. Tzeechoe and Tzeecha both looked at him with puzzled expressions. He picked up the waterskin and asked in the village tongue, "What this?"

Tzeecha responded in the village language, "Water."

Coleman then pointed to the fire, "What this?"

Tzeechoe said also in the village language, "Fire."

After asking about more of the trappings of their lodge, he said, "I think I'm getting it." The effort and excitement had used up a substantial amount of his recovering energy, so he stopped his comments and took a deep breath. Tzeechoe and Tzeecha rose and exited the dwelling. Coleman laid down, pulled the blanket up to his neck and started thinking about his dream again.

When he opened his eyes, he found the shaman looking down at him. "You are looking better," the shaman said.

"Yes, I feel a lot better now." He understood every word the shaman had said, and he was speaking in the village tongue!

The realization startled him. But as his head cleared of his drowsiness, the understanding fled. The shaman continued talking, but it had become gibberish once again to Coleman. "At first, I could understand every word you said, but now that I'm fully awake, I can't understand a thing you say. What gives?"

The shaman said a few calming words that Coleman couldn't understand and then began an examination of Coleman's body. After he had completed his scan, the shaman started chanting and waving his feathered fan over Coleman's head. Coleman closed his eyes and felt the dust gently cascade over his face. The chanting seemed to bring inner peace and Coleman just bathed in this gentle feeling. He felt invigorated and stronger as the shaman's chant continued.

As the days passed, Coleman became stronger; the dizziness began to fade and he felt surer of himself as he moved about the lodge, although this small effort still tired him quickly. During these days of recovery, Atura grilled him in the village language until he begged her to stop. This morning, with the help of Tzeechoe, he managed to make it to the village latrine. He felt like a furry beast as he moved through the village, wrapped in his fur blanket. A light drizzle fell and the earth was soft and mushy under his tender, bare feet; however, occasionally a foot would find a sharp rock or twig and he would jump in pain, stumbling, avoiding a fall only by Tzeechoe's steadying support. A few of the villagers stopped and stared as the duo passed. Coleman couldn't tell whether they were gawking at his furry wrap, his several days' growth of beard, or his blue eyes.

A couple of young teenage boys approached and one of them said, "Tondo, how are you feeling?"

Coleman smiled and, in the village tongue, said, "Better, thank you." The boys giggled and ran away. He had noticed, since the shaman's last visit, he'd found it much easier to learn the language. Although he still felt uncomfortable with some of the unusual sounds, he was beginning to learn how to form them and the more difficult words were getting easier to pronounce.

When the two returned to the lodge, Coleman collapsed on the floor, exhausted. They found Tzeecha and Atura waiting for them. "He needs something to wear," Tzeechoe said to the two women. Then he left the hut. Tzeecha rummaged through a pile of supple leather skins stored near the structure's wall and pulled out a large piece. The two women began cutting and shaping it with sharp obsidian tools. Coleman sat mesmerized by what they were doing. He couldn't figure out what it would be, but he was looking forward to trading his hairy blanket for something less cumbersome and awkward. In about an hour's time, the women had fashioned for him a smooth and pliant loincloth like the ones worn by all the male villagers.

Tzeecha handed it to him and he said, "Thank you." His words startled her and she looked at Atura and then back at Coleman, giving him a weak smile. Then she left the lodge.

Atura approached Coleman and said in a bitter tone, "Todo!" and she also left the hut.

"What did I say?" he asked in English, as he watched the door skins bounce back into place. He spent the next few minutes trying to figure out how to put on his new loincloth.

After he had dressed, in a manner of speaking, he exited the dwelling and gazed up into the continuously overcast sky. He found three boys standing near the door. He recognized two of them as the boys he'd seen earlier. "What want you?" he stammered.

The boys looked at each other and one of them meekly handed him a basket of fresh fruit. "Good boy. Thank you." The boys began to laugh and then they ran away. "Hey, what's so funny?" he yelled at them in English.

He found Tzeechoe sitting on a log working on a new reed basket. "Hello, Tondo. How do you like your new clothes?" Tzeechoe asked.

"Not used to wear this," was his reply. "Do it always rain here?"

"This is the rainy season. It is always like this, but it will end in its time," Tzeechoe instructed.

"Tzeechoe, Atura do not teach me what I want learn. She only teach me what she want. I ask her question, but she never tell me."

"Tondo, what is your question?"

"What do Tondo mean? It is my name in village, but I not know what it mean."

"No one can say your other name. It's impossible for us, so the chief calls you Tondo. Tondo means *the visitor*. Why don't you speak the language? Why must you be taught like a little child?"

"I not from here. I live in America, a long, long way from

here. Have you heard of United States? That my home. I am where? Is this Indonesia, Africa, South America?"

"Oonited t´atze? In-do-zia? What is that? This is the land of the Batru, the People of the Forest. We are the People."

"I need cell link, telephone, radio. I want talk to my people. I thankful you help me, but I need go home."

"I don't understand your strange words; I don't know what you're talking about."

"Where is nearest village?"

"You're in it."

"No, I mean big village, one with cars and buses and airplanes?"

"What are ar-p´an-ez?"

"They are machines that fly in the air, like birds, and people ride in them."

Tzeechoe stopped his work and stared at Coleman in disbelief. "Big bird with people inside?" He began laughing. "Tondo, you're funny. You tell Tzeechoe a very funny story."

Coleman noticed four boys meekly approaching him. Two held small baskets of fruit. The older boys pushed the smallest one forward who then handed Coleman his basket. He looked at it and then back to the boys. The other boy presented him with his basket and waited for a response. "Okay, thank you, boys." All four youngsters began to snicker. Then they turned and ran. As the two taller boys turned, they crashed into the approaching shaman, nearly knocking him over.

"Stop!" the shaman shouted. "What are you up to, you bad boys?" He waved his skull-topped staff in front of their faces, evoking expressions of dread from each one of them, and it made Coleman shudder, as well. "Are you followers of Munnevo? Need I punish you?" the shaman growled.

All four boys began to wail and begged his forgiveness. The oldest boy spoke for the others and pleaded, "Taahso, please forgive us!"

The shaman stared menacingly at the boys and finally said, "You must go now and be good. I will take you next time." The kids scrambled away as quickly as their feet could carry them.

Tzeechoe began chuckling to himself. Then he broke into a full belly laugh. "Tondo, you are very funny."

"What's going on here?" the shaman asked Tzeechoe.

"The boys gave Tondo some fruit and he said, 'I want to kiss your behind.' I think he meant to say, thank you, but he didn't say it right. Can you help him anymore?"

"I have done all I can. The rest is up to him," the shaman said.

Coleman became lost in thought. *Is that why those little urchins have been bringing me gifts all day?* he said to himself. He then thought of Tzeecha's shocked expression when he thanked her for his new clothes. He then hung his head in shame. *No wonder Atura called me todo,* he thought. "Tzeechoe, what do *todo* mean?"

The shaman answered instead, "Todo was a boy who lived in this village a long time ago. He wouldn't listen to his elders' advice. He'd always do things his way, no matter what. He never listened and he never learned."

"Is he still here?" Coleman asked.

"One day, he wandered out of the village alone and was eaten by a pack of betzoes."

"That bad! Did not anyone watch him?" Coleman wondered.

"Why? It's not anyone's duty to watch him. He should have watched himself."

"That bad," Coleman grumbled again in his limited vocabulary.

The shaman just looked at him and shook his head. "Now, the People say *todo* about anyone who won't listen and learn. Why do you ask about Todo?"

"Atura call me *todo*. Now, I know why. She think I stupid."

"Stoo-peed? Hmm, so she still calls you *todo*?" the shaman asked. Coleman nodded. "Then you must beat her."

"Beat her? You say, I hit her?" he asked as he pounded a fist into an open palm?

"She is your woman and you can do with her as you wish. The chief decreed it and so it is."

"What! The chief gave me Atura. What that mean?"

"Her father crossed-over recently. The chief waited to see if a man would take her into his family. No man wanted Atura, so there was no man to care for her. Now, you care for her. The chief is very wise."

"I cannot care for myself. How can I care for Atura?"

The shaman turned to Tzeechoe. "Tzeechoe, teach Tondo how to care for himself and Atura. If he doesn't learn, he will be sent away to die in the trees, and Atura will die, too."

Coleman rolled his eyes and hung his head in disbelief as his mind raced. *What am I going to do now? These people want me to stay, and the chief has trapped me with Atura's life,* he thought. "You say Atura die? Why she die?" he asked.

"A woman must be protected and cared for by a man; a father, a brother, a mate, a man of her family. If she has no man, she will be banished from the village and die in the trees. The chief thinks Batru sent you here to save Atura," the shaman explained.

"Batru?" Coleman wondered.

"The great god," the shaman told him.

Coleman groaned under this revelation. "Do she know this?" Coleman wondered.

"Yes, of course, she knows."

"Why she hate me if I save her from dead?"

"Atura is very difficult. That is why she doesn't have a man. Now, she is yours. The chief is very wise," the shaman said with a toothy and repulsive smile.

"Oh, no! How do I get out of this mess?" Coleman lamented. The shaman and Tzeechoe watched as Coleman slumped to the log and then jumped to his feet as a sliver poked a bare spot on his butt. He rubbed his wound and held up an inch-long splinter for the other two men to see. "Now, that says it all," he uttered in English. The two villagers looked at each other with confused but mirthful expressions.

The shaman turned and walked away and Tzeechoe resumed working on his basket. After checking the log for other sharp objects, Coleman gingerly sat, feeling as though a heavy weight was descending upon him. After a few minutes of brooding, Coleman asked, "Tzeechoe, anyone see white man like me before?"

"No, not like you. I have heard legends that the Anterrans are white. Are you Anterran?"

"No. Who Anterrans? Do they have big village?"

"The legend says Anterrans are very powerful. No one really knows if the legend is true."

"Do they have big village?" Coleman asked in a pleading voice.

"I don't know," was Tzeechoe's reply.

"I need to visit the Anterrans. Can you take me there?"

"Tondo, you are crazy. The legend says Anterrans live a long, long way away. It would be a very dangerous journey."

"I need to go there so I can talk to my people. I have to tell them I live. I want go home."

"What will you do with Atura? Will you take her with you?"

"That very big problem for me. My home very different and Atura will not be happy there."

Tzeechoe laughed and said, "Atura is not happy here. Maybe she'll like your home better."

"I do not think Atura wants to live in the same lodge with me."

"How did you get lost? Why are you here?"

"My mission took wrong turn and I got here, not the Moon."

"Mish-on? Munna?"

"Oh man, how can I explain this to you? I go to Moon and got here."

"Munna?"

"Yeah, big ball in night sky." Tzeechoe looked at Coleman, smiled, and shook his head. "Yes, I know. Tondo very funny," Coleman said, reading Tzeechoe's thoughts. "Tzeechoe, I heard one of the boys call the witch doctor Taahso. Is that his name?" Tzeechoe looked at Coleman as he tried to figure out the meaning of his question.

After a short pause, he said, "All men like him are taahso and have the name Taahso."

"Are there any other taahso?"

"He is the only one in our village. I've been told there are men like him in other villages. They are very powerful."

"How they powerful?"

"I don't know about the others, but our taahso can heal the sick, make it easier for us to learn, help us when we hunt, and he can control fire."

"Control fire? How he do that?"

"He uses taah."

"What taah?"

"It is the power he has in here," Tzeechoe said as he tapped Coleman's chest.

Coleman was skeptical of this tribal superstition, but his thoughts turned to the worst days of his illness. Each time he was on the brink of death, the taahso seemed to pull him back. The others also thought that this taahso appeared to have something to do with his ability to learn the language. And he recalled how the shaman had seemingly lit a fire by magic. Coleman sat contemplating what he had been told and his recent experiences.

The two men sat silently as dusk slowly crept over the village. The clouds began to part and for the first time since his arrival, Coleman could see large patches of blue sky. His gloomy mood began to lift. He saw the reddish disk of the sun.

"What that?" Coleman asked, pointing at the setting sun.

"P´atezas, the mother of life," Tzeechoe told him.

"P´atezas?"

Tzeechoe nodded and looked up from his work and scanned the sky. "Clouds go away. We will see many stars tonight and maybe munnas."

Just then, a shout was heard near the entrance of the village as the day's hunting party stepped into the clearing. A throng of villagers gathered to greet the hunters and to examine their efforts. Tzeechoe and Coleman were hungry and hoped for a good evening meal. From a distance, it looked like the hunters had something hanging from the poles they were carrying. As they approached, it became apparent that they had taken several monkeys.

Tzeechoe frowned, "Not good meat; monkey tastes bad."

Coleman didn't care; he was ready to eat anything. Now that the worst of his illness had passed, he was famished and he craved meat.

Coleman watched as the women gathered in the center of the village. The central fire was stoked; the meat was prepared and roasted over open coals. In about an hour, the taahso stepped forth, cut off a large piece of meat, and held it to the heavens. He uttered a few words that Coleman couldn't clearly decipher other than Batru and Munnari. He then laid the meat on the fire as a sacrifice. The women took turns getting their fair share of the remaining cooked meat. Soon, Tzeecha and Atura took their turns and brought the meat to their men. Tzeechoe frowned, grabbed a large piece, and started eating. Coleman took another large piece, making certain there was enough remaining for the two women. The smell of the cooked meat made Coleman's mouth water, and he took a bite. After a few chews, he could tell it was tough, stringy, and greasy. He chewed and chewed as if he were chewing on gristle. He finally swallowed and felt it slowly slide down his throat.

"This not best meat I eat, but it better than snail I eat for survival training," he said using English terms.

Tzeechoe continued chewing on his portion. The women looked at Coleman with befuddled expressions. "When I was a boy, there were no monkeys. Now, they are everywhere. No one knows where they came from," Tzeechoe explained. He grunted and pointed to the remaining morsels. That was the women's cue to take their turns. The four of them sat near the door of the lodge eating as the clouds separated and patches of stars could be seen.

Coleman scoured the heavens but couldn't get a clear view of the constellations. *Maybe later tonight I'll get a good look at the night sky and find out if I'm in the northern or southern hemisphere.*

When all four had finished eating, the women began preparing the bedding for the night. Coleman soon discovered that the meat did not agree with him and he had to make a quick dash to the latrine. Tzeechoe followed him and waited. As the men returned to the lodge, Coleman said, "Monkey meat not like me."

"Tondo, you were very sick. Your insides may not like meat for a while."

When the men entered the home, they found the women singing. Coleman found the tune uplifting and joyful. He didn't understand most of the words, but he thought it was a story of young love. The men sat and listened for a few minutes, then Tzeechoe joined in the singing. After a while, Coleman picked up the chorus line and sang, as well. When the song ended, Coleman leaned back on his elbows. "My good friends, thank you for helping me." Tzeechoe and Tzeecha began chuckling quietly.

Atura scowled and said, "Todo!"

"I guess I did it again. I sorry. Is there another way to say 'thank you'?" Tzeechoe's and Tzeecha's chuckles turned into roars of laughter. Even Atura cracked a smile and began laughing, as well.

A conversation soon began between Tzeecha and Tzeechoe. She was asking about the upcoming hunt. From what Coleman could understand, it appeared Tzeechoe's hunting team would soon have their turn and the responsibility of bringing food to the village. Tzeechoe told her that Tondo would be going with them by order of the taahso. He had two days to prepare Tondo for the hunt. That was not enough time to teach him how to use the spear—the atlatl—nor the bolo, but he could teach Tondo how to make and use a club and a knife.

"That is good. I want go," Coleman told the group excitedly.

"It is very dangerous to leave the village. Some men have died on the hunt," Tzeecha warned.

Coleman thought back to his encounter with the gorga. A shudder ran down his spine as he visualized the slashing teeth and claws of the beast. The nasty scar the monster carried across its snout was seared into Coleman's memory. He absentmindedly rubbed his thigh. He meekly uttered, "Gorga."

Tzeecha nodded and said, "Yes, the gorga has taken many hunters. You are the only one who has ever survived its attack. The gods favor you, Tondo. I think you will keep Tzeechoe safe." Tzeechoe bowed his head, either in agreement or shame, Coleman couldn't tell.

"Do all your people grow hair on their faces?" Atura asked.

"Most men do. There are a few who do not."

"Do the women grow hair on their faces, too?"

Coleman smiled, "No, most do not. There are a few who do."

Atura looked at Tzeecha and Tzeechoe, "Are all the people white like you?"

"No, some are black, some are brown."

"Will the hair on your face grow more?" Atura asked.

"Oh, yes. If I not shave, I mean cut it, my beard get very long," as he drew his hand across his waist.

Atura frowned, "You already look like a wild beast."

"Okay, I cut face hair tomorrow, if that make you happy. I need something sharp." Tzeechoe rummaged around the lodge and found an obsidian stone. It looked like the tool the women had used in the fashioning of his loincloth earlier in the day. Coleman took the stone and drew a finger across its blade. "Very sharp; I use in morning." Coleman then asked, "Atura, do not anyone have blue eyes like me?"

"No, no one has ever seen blue eyes before. They are the color of Munnari."

"So, Munnari the blue sky?" Coleman questioned.

"No, Munnari is the blue munna; the good munna."

"I do not understand. Do munna mean moon?"

"Come here; I'll show you," Atura said in a commanding voice. She then stepped through the doorway with Coleman following.

He scanned the night sky. It was a beautiful, clear night, with a multitude of stars shining in the heavens; so many were there, he had difficulty getting his bearings. As he scanned the sky from horizon to horizon, he was amazed at the vast number of stars. It was as though the Milky Way covered the entire night sky. He was searching for Polaris, the North Star, or at least the Big Dipper, but he couldn't locate either. He glanced over at the first quarter moon hanging just above the trees, near where the sun had set in the west. As he stared at the silvery moon, he noticed something odd about its appearance. The whiff of a cloud faintly obscured the view, but the moon's markings didn't seem quite right. As he watched the cloud pass, he heard Atura's call.

"Over here; Munnari is over here," she called.

"What? The munna is right here, just above the trees."

"Come here!" she ordered gruffly.

Coleman reluctantly moved to the other side of the lodge and found, to his utter surprise and amazement, a huge first quarter blue moon hanging just above the trees in the east. Coleman stopped in his tracks in stunned silence. He retraced his steps and looked up at the silvery white moon he had been watching and then back to the blue moon. He couldn't believe what he was seeing. His mind raced. *Could this be another hallucination? Was he dreaming?* He pinched himself and felt the pain. He stared into the night sky and noticed a first quarter reddish-orange disk rising above the trees near the blue moon.

He looked back at the silver moon and realized it was rising above the tree line, not dropping behind it. It was moving in retrograde, west to east.

"Wait! This isn't Earth? I'm on a different planet? Where have they sent me?" he cried in English as he dropped to his knees, his mind vacant with shock. He felt Atura's hands on his shoulders and he opened his eyes. He found himself staring into her face.

"What's the matter? Why are you so upset? I don't understand," she asked in a concerned voice.

Coleman could only shake his head slowly back and forth. Something had gone dreadfully wrong when he was ripped. He was expecting to ride the ripple to Tranquility's He-3 Base on Earth's moon, but instead, he had been sent by a dimensional shift to another world. He didn't know if he was in the same galaxy or even the same universe anymore. For all he knew, he was in an entirely different dimension of time and space. The ramifications of this thought crashed over him like a wave.

"What's the matter?" he heard Atura plead.

He looked into her worried face and mumbled in his native tongue, "Toto, we're not in Kansas anymore!"

Atura glared back at him as her expression changed from worry to anger, "No, you're todo! What's the matter with you? You're crazy!" she scolded as she arose and stomped back into the lodge. Soon, Tzeechoe came out and found Coleman still on his knees, scanning the night sky, looking from one moon to another.

Tzeechoe grabbed him by the arm and pulled him to his feet. "What's the matter with you? Atura said you went crazy."

"Tzeechoe, in my world there is only one munna, but there are three here. Do you know what this means? It means I can never go home. I am stuck here until I die."

"Oh, is that all? Go to bed. Things are always better in the morning."

"Not this time," Coleman sadly grumbled.

He returned to the lodge, plopped down on his bedding, and stared at the hole in the roof, his mind reviewing all he had seen and done since the time he entered the rip chamber at the Houston plant.

After a while, his thoughts changed from the mechanics of the rip to his home. He had thought little of his mother and father, his ex-girlfriend, Megan Klosky, and his other friends since he'd arrived here. He felt it would just be a matter of time before he returned to them. Now, with this new revelation, he began to miss them all. It was probable he would never see any of them again. He was sure the rip team would attempt to figure out what happened to him, but it was doubtful they would be able to do anything about it. Inanimate objects had disappeared during rips in the past and so had some monkeys. The rip team tried to figure out what went wrong in an effort to correct the problem, but never did they ever locate the lost objects, let alone recover one.

He felt a tear escape the corner of his eye and slide down the side of his face, but he quickly wiped it away. He couldn't think about this right now. Maybe he would be clearer in the morning. "Tomorrow is a new day and a new life," he voiced aloud in English.

From the darkness of the lodge, he heard Atura spout, "Todo!"

CHAPTER 5

THE OUTSIDER

In a hamlet a world apart from the Batru's wilderness, the hustle and bustle of daily life went on as usual. The settlement's residents plied their wares and services in the town's market. A boy made his way through the tables and barrows, his head turning from side to side and his eyes glancing in all directions. Without warning, a merchant holding a long, stiff switch swatted the boy on the shoulder.

"Begone Creeper! Every time you come around, I end up missing things. Begone and don't come back!"

The boy angrily turned over the merchant's table, snatched something shiny, and dashed away. The entire market was in an uproar as the boy zigzagged through the other displays as merchants either tried to snag him or hit him with whatever was at hand. But, the agile boy soon escaped, leaving behind a ruckus, and many furious men and women.

He dashed out of the hamlet and into the forest. He examined the shiny hairpin he had snatched and stuffed it into his tattered shirt while on the move. He eventually slowed to a walk, preparing to cross a stream. He had to be careful as he hopped from boulder to boulder, for he knew if he slipped and fell into the water, the creatures hiding under the surface would attack and they had sharp teeth. Two-thirds of the way across, he stopped and gazed into the stream. Sure enough, there was a big underwater creature as long as his arm staring back at him, just waiting for him to make a mistake. The boy took a deep breath and deftly hopped to the next boulder and then the next, quickly reaching the other side of the stream.

After he had reached it, he charged up the bank. "Ah, there you are," he said aloud to a wild berry bush. A few of the round berries had turned red, so he plucked them off the bush and gobbled them down. After he had picked and eaten all the ripe berries he could find, he moved deeper into the forest. Checking the ground, he began following a faint trail cut through the fallen leaves by small animals. He quickened his pace and came upon a small, furry, four-legged creature caught in a snare he had laid the day before. He extracted it, gutted, skinned it with his small knife, and started a fire in a cleared area. "I'll reset the trap after I eat," he said to himself as he roasted his catch on a spit.

He patiently waited as his meal turned a golden brown. As his meat cooked, he napped. He awoke with a start when he heard something crashing through the brush. A man-like creature stumbled into the clearing and dropped to its knees less than a stone's throw in front of the boy staring back at him. The creature's dark-brown eyes filled with desperation. The beast was wearing odd-looking yellow clothes with patches and strange symbols sewn onto its tatters. The man-thing wasn't wearing sandals. Instead, its feet were entirely covered in black leather coverings that went halfway up his shins. The most terrifying thing about this man-beast was the hair covering its face.

The beast dropped its stare from the boy to the roasting spit above the fire. It then charged toward the cooking meat, causing the child to panic and dash away. It grabbed the boy's meal and began devouring it as if it were famished. The boy stopped his flight only long enough to witness what the beast was doing. Then he continued to flee toward the village.

The boy rushed into the town shouting at the top of his lungs. When he reached the village center, he stopped as several stern-looking adults surrounded him. The boy pointed in the direction he had come from, shouting, "Monster! Beast! There's something out there I've never seen before!"

"Creeper, I'm going to give you the beating of your life for what you did this morning," an angry merchant threatened as he grabbed the boy by the arm and dragged him over to his barrow. The dealer picked up a stout wooden rod and was about to lay into the boy when a woman's scream was heard coming from the edge of the hamlet near where the boy had entered. Men grabbed clubs, quarterstaffs, wooden pitchforks, and anything else that might serve as a makeshift weapon, and rushed to the screams. The merchant dragged the boy along with him. When they arrived, they saw the same man-beast the boy had seen; the hairy face, the odd coverings, the strange footwear. The creature stood staring back at the people. It raised both hands, showing everyone it had no weapon.

"It doesn't have claws," someone noted.

"Be careful, it might have sharp teeth," another warned.

The man-beast made no threatening moves and began making sounds as if it were trying to communicate in some strange fashion. The leader of the hamlet, armed with a short sword, approached the creature and began speaking to it.

"Do you understand me?" he asked. The man-beast cocked its head to the side as if it were trying to comprehend. "What are you, beast or god?" the leader asked. The creature replied with a string of odd sounds that made no sense to anyone, some sounding threatening.

Everyone stood dumbfounded by the creature's appearance and strange noises. The boy being held by the merchant managed to shake free from his grip, and he dashed to the other side of the crowd. The leader attempted again to speak with the brute. "Have you been sent by the gods?" he asked.

The creature didn't answer and looked confused. By this time, it was surrounded and one of the other hamlet men holding a quarterstaff crept behind it. The leader nodded his head and the man standing behind the creature swung his staff, hitting it in the head, knocking it unconscious.

The boy sat on the ground near the cage where the hamlet men had stuffed the thing that had come out of the woods. The man-beast's outer garments had been stripped away. The cage was sturdy, made of stout wooden poles lashed together with strong leather cords. The last time the pen had been used was to capture a marauding wild beast that was raiding village flocks. That creature had sharp teeth, claws on all four paws, and its roar was terrifying.

This creature was nothing like that. *This beast is like a man with a hairy face and body,* the boy thought. *Could it be a lesser god?* After examining the unconscious creature for a while, the boy surmised it would look just like any other grown man if it didn't have hair on its face.

The beast began to stir, causing the boy to jump in fright, but his curiosity kept him in place. He was sure the well-built cage would securely hold the creature. The man-beast groaned and rubbed the back of its head. It then looked at its hand and saw blood. It looked around, examining its situation. It slowly stood but had to hunch over because it was taller than the cage was high. The creature's focus changed. It noticed the boy sitting on the ground, looking up into the cage. After a few moments, the beast started making sounds. The boy thought it was trying to talk to him, but the noises made no sense. Suddenly, the creature's focus changed again, causing the boy to look over his shoulder quickly, but too late. The merchant whose table he'd overturned earlier, was upon him, grabbing him by the upper arm with his left hand and jerking the boy to his feet.

"Now I have you, Creeper!" the merchant exploded.

"Let me go!" the boy shouted as he struggled to escape the merchant's clutches.

"I'm going to give you a beating you'll never forget!" the merchant growled. He raised the wooden rod he was holding in his right hand, preparing to swing it down hard on the boy's back. The lad dug his bare feet into the soft ground and pushed with all his might, crashing his tormentor into the cage's poles. The man-beast within grabbed the merchant, pulling him tightly against the cage and holding him there. The monster growled and grunted, the sounds terrifying the merchant, and he began screaming in panic. Several village men dashed to the merchant's aid. Two grabbed him by the arms and attempted to pull him free of the creature's grasp. Several other townsmen began jabbing the beast with the blunt ends of their staffs. The monster roared in pain and released his captive. It grabbed one of the staffs and jerked it from its abuser's grasp. The other men's attacks became more desperate and more vicious, pounding the beast until it was lying on the floor of the cage, nearly unconscious, bleeding from its nose and mouth.

The hamlet leader arrived and surveyed the situation. "Enough of this," he declared. "Secure the beast with ropes. I'm convinced it is a violent and dangerous monster. It will be driven into the mist. Let the gods deal with it."

The boy watched as the leather straps securing the cage's gate were cut. Two burly men grabbed the injured beast by its hairy legs and dragged it out of the cage. Its arms and hands were secured by ropes, and a rope was placed around its neck. The creature was then pulled and shoved out of the village as women and children pelted it with stones.

Every man in the hamlet followed the nearly naked beast as it was pushed, stumbling along on its uncovered feet. The trail wound westward through the trees and bushes. Woodland creatures scattered as the raucous horde approached. The boy followed, not wanting to get too close for he feared the men's wrath. Yet, there was something else he feared even more— the gods of the mist. If anyone got too close, the gods might seize them, and they would never be seen again. The boy hung back waiting to see what would happen.

By midafternoon, the mob drew near the mist-plains. All life seemed to have fled from this colorless place. No tree, no bush, nor flower grew here. No creature sounds could be heard. It was a desolate realm of gray that froze one's soul.

The men stopped a safe distance away from the dead place, removed the rope from around the creature's neck, and shoved the beast in the direction of the mist, its wrists still bound. Several men threatened the creature with sharpened poles and the hamlet leader waved his short sword, the only one in the village, in a threatening manner. The beast slowly and reluctantly trudged forward and disappeared into the fog.

The men waited until dusk and then began their trek back to the hamlet. The boy hid in the bushes as the village men marched past. He waited until their sounds were no longer heard; then he waited a little more. When he finally thought it was safe, he cleared an area of leaves and tinder and started a small campfire. Hunger gnawed at him. He knew he'd be cold by morning, but it wasn't the first time he'd been cold and hungry. He felt it his duty to remain and help the beast if he could because the beast had helped him, saving him from a sound beating. However, he doubted the creature would survive because no one ever returned once they went into the mist. He'd wait until midmorning; he owed the creature that much, at least.

He moved into the bushes, searching for small animal trails. Although it was difficult in the diminishing daylight, he found a path and set up a snare. He would return to it in the morning and hope for the best. He went back to his fire, leaned over it, and warmed himself. He placed a sturdy dry branch in the fire to use as a torch to fend off night predators, something he had learned was sometimes necessary. From time-to-time, he turned around, warming his opposite side. He did this throughout the night, catching naps in between. He looked above him and watched the three moons as they moved across the sky. Munnoga, the silvery moon, moved west to east. Munnari, the blue moon, and Munnevo, the red moon, moved east to west as they slowly revolved around each other.

The boy closed his eyes and managed to sleep a bit before his cold back woke him again. He turned around and fell asleep once more. When the eastern sky began to glow with the coming of day, he arose and went to his snare. When he arrived, a broad smile filled his face; first-meal was snared. He gutted and cleaned it; then he began roasting it over the fire.

As the glow of day increased, it chased away night's shadows. The boy noticed something laying on the ground near the border of the mist. He decided to risk getting a little closer to the dangerous fog and, as he did, he could see it was the body of the man-beast the others had forced into the mist the day before. The boy cautiously approached. When he was close enough, he pushed the creature's bare shoulder with a stick. It stirred. The boy recoiled but did not run away. The creature groaned and rolled onto its back. The boy waited, preparing to dart for safety. It sat up and looked around. When it saw the boy, a smile could be detected on its hairy face. The boy smiled back and motioned for the creature to follow; it did.

The monster was led back to the boy's fire and the meal roasting there. The boy pointed to it and then pantomimed eating. The creature grabbed the roasting animal and was about to begin devouring it; however, it stopped, tore the critter apart, and handed the boy a piece.

For the next several moments, the two ate and only the sounds of tearing meat and chewing could be heard. At last the boy asked, "What are you? You look and act like a man, but you've got hair in the wrong places."

The creature looked at him and began making odd sounds. The boy could tell it was trying to communicate, but the sounds it was making made no sense.

"Stop," the boy said. "I don't understand. What's your name?" The creature just stared at him. The boy touched the beast's shoulder and repeated loudly, "What . . . is . . . your . . . name?" At first, the creature looked at him with a confused expression, then its face lit up and it uttered an odd sound that the boy assumed was the beast's name. "I can't say that, but you understand. I'll call you outsider in old-speak; Tangundo. Your name is Tangundo."

The creature smiled and nodded. "Tan-gun-do," it repeated with a terrible accent. The boy nodded and smiled. The creature placed its hand on the boy's shoulder and made some odd sounds.

"Oh, you want to know what my name is. My name is Nevesant. Nev-e-sant," the boy repeated.

"Nev-e-sant," the creature said with a smile. It was then that the boy first noticed Tangundo's eyes were now the color of the red moon, Munnevo.

CHAPTER 6

HUNTER AND HUNTED

Early the next morning, Coleman, having learned the night before he wasn't on Earth after all, arose quietly and gingerly walked to the latrine with Tzeechoe close behind. As the men returned to the lodge, Tzeechoe told Coleman they would make a club for him to use on the hunt the next day.

"I hope I not todo on hunt. We hunt bataro?"

"We always search for bataro. It is a sacred beast. Its meat brings great strength and blessings to the villagers. We will always search for one, but we must bring food back to the village. We cannot waste our time. The longer we hunt, the more likely it is to draw the gorga's attention. That would be very bad," Tzeechoe explained as he pulled aside the door covering and entered the dwelling.

The men saw that the bedding had been collected and stowed away. Coleman found an obsidian blade, wet his face with water, and began scraping the sharp obsidian down his cheek.

"Ouch! This isn't going to be easy."

Coleman didn't have a heavy beard, but it still took him about twenty minutes to finish the task. The obsidian was razor sharp but jagged and he suffered many small cuts during the ordeal; however, a clean shave made him feel a lot better when he had finished.

"I not like hair on face," he told Tzeechoe, who had been watching him the entire time. Tzeechoe examined Coleman's face, used a finger to wipe some blood from one of the cuts, and examined it.

"Does this always happen when you cut the hair on your face?" he asked.

"Only with this," Coleman said as he held up the jagged obsidian tool.

"Now, we will make a hunting club. We need a strong branch and a round rock," Tzeechoe instructed as he grabbed his new spear and left the lodge with Coleman right behind.

The two men left the safety of the village and entered the trees nearby. Tzeechoe found a straight and sturdy branch and hacked at it with his waist knife. He then stripped the bark off it and handed it to Coleman.

"Okay," Coleman said reluctantly, "now what I do?"

Tzeechoe smiled, "That's mine. Go find your own."

Coleman looked around, found a similar branch, and using Tzeechoe's obsidian knife, hacked it loose, and stripped it clean. Tzeechoe then walked deeper into the forest with Coleman in tow. They soon approached a small brook with many round rocks. Tzeechoe selected one and showed it to Coleman. Following Tzeechoe's lead, Coleman found another and the two headed back to the village. When they got back to the lodge, they found several long strips of rawhide soaking in a gourd filled with water near the hut's doorway.

"Tzeecha and Atura made some bindings for us," Tzeechoe said.

Tzeechoe began cutting grooves around the pole at two-inch intervals. He then used his obsidian knife to shape one end of the pole so the rock would fit snugly against it. When he was satisfied with the pole's shape, he placed the rock in its perch and began laying wet leather strips over it. He then wrapped the entire handle with more strips as tightly as he could. Tzeechoe added a loop of rawhide at the heel end of the club, allowing the holder to slip his wrist through it to secure the club if he wanted to. He then laid the finished product in the sun and let the leather dry and shrink. *But it really isn't the sun,* Coleman thought sadly. *The villagers call it p'atezas, the mother-of-life.*

When Tzeechoe finished, the two men began working on Coleman's club. Tzeechoe corrected him many times during the process but after a couple of hours, Coleman had finished his club, as well. He wasn't confident it would hold up under extreme use, but Tzeechoe seemed to think it was done well enough, so Coleman accepted his praise cordially.

Tzeechoe then lifted a large obsidian stone that had been stowed near the hut's doorway and said, "You will now make a knife from this."

"Uh, okay," Coleman uttered sheepishly in English.

Tzeechoe collected a few stone tools and a leather lap skin. He began teaching Coleman how to make an obsidian knife. With Tzeechoe's gentle promptings, Coleman chiseled out a rough knife. Then Tzeechoe took over and showed him the finer points as he finished the job. It was late in the afternoon when the knife was fully formed and the handle wrapped in wet rawhide. Coleman examined his new knife and club, feeling proud of his accomplishments.

Just a short time ago, he was on the cutting edge of technology and today he was making stone tools. Yet, he looked at the tools with satisfaction. What he'd done today had a direct purpose to his life. In the morning, he would join a group of men and assist them in finding food for the village. If they failed, the village would suffer. If they succeeded, they would be lauded by the villagers. There would be risk and adventure, things which Coleman relished.

"I ready to hunt bataro," he said as he raised his new knife and club above his head. Tzeechoe nodded in agreement with a proud smile.

Coleman was awakened in the darkness by Tzeechoe shaking his shoulder. The men gathered their gear and left the lodge. Tzeecha quietly said something as they left. Coleman couldn't tell what she said, but there was loving concern in her tone.

As he walked, he scanned the sky. The blue and red moons had dropped behind the tree line in the west, but he could still see them through the branches. The other moon had already dipped below the tree line in the east. He shook his head, still hoping to awaken from a dream.

He could see a small gathering of men assembled in the center of the village. The chief and the taahso were with them. Ten hunters, including Coleman, formed a single line, much like a military formation, with the hunt leader at the left end of the line and Coleman at the far right. The leader left his position and moved down the line, examining each hunter. He stopped in front of Coleman, examined his new club and waist knife, gave him a smile, and returned to his position at the head of the line.

The chief looked up and down the line and then spoke, "Chashutzo, are your hunters ready?"

The hunt leader responded, "Yes, we are ready."

"Are your men prepared to sacrifice for the village?"

"Yes, they are!" Chashutzo yelled. All the men except Coleman shouted as they raised their weapons.

"Very good," said the chief. "Taahso, bless our hunters this day with the power and protection of Batru."

The taahso raised his arms high above his head and began chanting. The words didn't make any sense to Coleman's ears. He still had much to learn. The men began to hum and the taahso moved forward and faced Chashutzo. With his left arm raised above his head, the taahso lowered his right arm and placed an open palm on Chashutzo's chest. Chashutzo took a deep breath and continued humming. The taahso moved down the line and performed the same ritual with each man. After the third man, Coleman thought it best to begin humming, as well. When the taahso reached him, both men looked into the other's eyes and gave each other a bemused smile. Coleman couldn't believe he was taking part in this superstitious foolishness, but he thought it best to go along with it; however, when the taahso's palm touched his bare chest, he felt a tingling warmth radiate from the shaman's hand. The radiance slowly spread until it engulfed Coleman from head to toe. Coleman's bemused smile quickly changed to an expression of shock. This was not what he expected. Then they both felt a surge of energy course from Taahso's body into Coleman's. Coleman lost his balance and was steadied by the taahso. The shaman's eyes bolted wide open by this unexpected event. He quickly regained his composure, then asked, "Tondo, are you ready to make your first hunt?"

"Yes, Taahso, I am ready," Coleman responded as he raised his club, still dizzy from what had just happened. The taahso smiled his grotesque smile and returned to the chief's side.

"Chashutzo, may your hunt be successful and may your efforts bless the village." All the men but Coleman raised their weapons, turned, and filed out of the village, leaving Coleman standing alone, dizzy, and somewhat embarrassed by his ignorance of protocol. He gave a sheepish grin and staggered after the other hunters, stepping on a sharp stone and hopping on one foot for several yards.

Not the most graceful exit, he thought. As he hopped along, he was certain he heard muffled laughter coming from behind.

After the hunters left the village, Chashutzo stopped and the men gathered around him. "Today, we will start our hunt at the Sweet Waters." The men nodded in acknowledgment and started walking to the tree line. Coleman quickened his pace until he was walking next to Tzeechoe.

"What be *Sweet Waters?*" he asked.

"That's where the water gushes up out of the ground. Many animals go there to drink."

"The artesian well!" Coleman said confidently in English.

It took less than an hour for the hunting party to reach the gushing spring. During the trek, Coleman questioned

Tzeechoe and learned that each hunting party consisted of a tusk-man as the leader, a tracker, a scent-man capable of smelling prey from a great distance, and at least one excellent spearman. The remaining members of the party assisted the others and were considered students of the primary members. Tzeechoe wanted to become a lead spearman, although his best skill was with a bolo-like device that he and a couple of others carried. Coleman was told that the club bearers were the junior members responsible for finishing off the prey once it was speared or disabled. He felt it was an appropriate assignment considering his lack of any hunting skills in this venue. He was hoping his inexperience wouldn't cause a problem with the party's success this day. Several of the men were not happy with his presence, although no one said anything to him. His adversary, the villager named Ayascho, seemed most annoyed.

When the party reached the Sweet Waters, Ayascho gave Coleman a shoulder shove as he passed by. Coleman glowered at him. An inner voice growled, *Hit him! Take him down! Show the others you're not to be dissed!* Coleman's anger grew, but he reluctantly let the matter pass. He thought the young man to be either exceptionally brazen or foolish. Ayascho was a much smaller man than himself. *Before the day is through, that little punk and I better have this matter worked out one way or the other,* he grumbled silently to himself.

Namad, the tracker, began looking around the stream

flowing from the spring and, after a few seconds, stopped and stood bolt upright. "The gorga has been here. We must be careful," he whispered. A shudder ran down Coleman's spine at the thought of another encounter with one of those monsters.

"Tzeechoe, will gorga attack hunting party like ours?" he asked.

"The gorga does whatever it wants. If it is hungry, he will take one of us and drive the others away."

"How many gorgas around here?" Coleman asked.

"Only one, thank the gods," Tzeechoe replied.

Only one seemed odd to Coleman. *How do they breed?* he wondered to himself. He rubbed his upper arm, remembering the crushing pressure of the creature's bite. If attacked again, he wouldn't have the protection of his environmental suit. Suddenly, every sound in the forest caused him to start and peer into the underbrush.

"Get a grip, you're starting to jump at shadows," he mumbled in English.

After Namad had sounded the alert, he got back to business and found some interesting tracks. As he was homing in on them, Coleman scanned the trees and found the one where he sought refuge that first night. He noticed a monkey sitting in the crook, watching the hunters below. Coleman walked over to the tree and began climbing, wondering if there was anything left of the equipment he had stored there. The monkey departed as soon as Coleman started climbing. When he reached the nest, he found nothing there except for one piece of fabric from his suit. All the metal objects were gone, undoubtedly carried away by forest creatures. He collected the fabric piece and climbed down. The other hunters watched and wondered what he was doing. When he reached the ground, he showed them the material he'd retrieved. He was surprised and amused by their reactions. Although the piece was only about a foot square, the men collected together and took turns touching and pulling at the strange material. It had become such a distraction to their primary purpose that, in short order, Chashutzo grabbed it, scolded the other hunters, and handed the piece back to Coleman, giving him a stare worthy of an angry drill sergeant.

Coleman tucked it into his waist belt and meekly said, "I sorry."

The men refocused, then waited attentively, their eyes following Namad as he wandered around the creek flowing from the spring. He then headed off into the undergrowth at a slow jog, eyes fixed on the ground. The other men followed and scanned the surrounding area, watching for danger. Coleman stayed at Tzeechoe's side and asked awkwardly, "What he find?"

"It's a ghee; a large bird animal that runs and has fur. It tastes very good."

"How large?" Coleman questioned.

"As tall as a man," was his reply.

"They dangerous?"

"They can be. Ghees have powerful beaks and they kick with feet that have claws."

"So, how we kill it?"

"A spearman will spear it first, or someone will bolo its legs. Then the club men will kill it."

"That my job, right?"

Tzeechoe smiled broadly and shook his head up and down, "Yes, maybe today you will become a p´oez."

"What p´oez?" Coleman asked.

"A p´oez is the one who makes the killing blow and is honored. All the hunters want this honor." Coleman's competitive juices began to flow, and he gave Tzeechoe a broad smile. Then he assumed his game face, one which startled Tzeechoe, and slackened his pace.

After about a half-hour, Namad slowed his stride, then stopped and raised his arm. All the other hunters stopped in unison. Everything became quiet except for the creatures in the trees. A slight breeze rustled the leaves and branches, which helped to cover the men's heavy breathing. Coleman felt invigorated and was a little surprised. He was not a bit out of breath. But the men who lived like this were tired. Namad then held his spear in both hands and raised it high above his head.

"Danger," Tzeechoe quietly warned.

"Why?" Coleman wondered.

"Quiet!" Tzeechoe whispered sternly.

The men scanned the surrounding area while Namad stared intently forward. Chashutzo slowly moved to Namad's side and the two men exchanged a few whispered words. Chashutzo began moving warily forward as Namad placed his spear in its lever and brought it into a cocked position over his right shoulder. The remaining men slowly and cautiously moved forward, weapons at the ready. Coleman wanted to rush ahead so he would have a better chance of becoming the p´oez, but he restrained himself. He didn't want to be the one who caused the prey to escape. His feet gently felt the ground as he attempted to take each step as quietly as possible. His feet were still tender and sore from the abuse they had already taken, but he just gritted his teeth and endured the pain. Chashutzo continued moving forward for another fifty yards or so. Then he stopped. He looked down and scanned the area all around. Namad quickly moved to his side as the other men drew closer. When Coleman reached the gathered hunters, he found a large carcass laying in the center of the group. It resembled an eviscerated, furry ostrich.

Namad stooped over it and carefully examined the ground. "Gorga," he finally said, evoking a noticeable shudder from the other hunters.

Shadi, the scent-man, began sniffing the air. He then looked at Chashutzo and said, "He is very close. He may be stalking us." All of the hunters turned and faced outward, their weapons at the ready.

Tzeechoe whispered to Coleman, "Tondo, this is very bad. Be careful. If you have any influence with Munnari, call upon it to protect us this day."

Coleman swallowed deeply and asked, "Chashutzo, do we wait, or do we hunt it?" The men looked at him as if he were crazy. With a touch of bravado to bolster the hunters' flagging spirits, Coleman told them, "I have fought gorga, and it not kill me. I think we kill it." He could see a positive effect on some of the men, yet others stood motionless, paralyzed by the rising fear in their hearts.

Chashutzo finally said, "Follow me. Tzeechoe and Tondo protect our backs." The men filed past Coleman and Tzeechoe, two-by-two, and when all the others had left, they took up the rear and scanned the area behind the party.

A slight breeze brushed the men's faces, and Shadi sounded a warning, "He is near. He comes for us, now!" As the words left his mouth, they heard a loud noise to the right front of the line of men. Brush and tall grass parted as muffled grunts were heard. Chashutzo suddenly flew into the air as if in slow motion and collapsed several yards away. One after the other, men in the line were tossed in the same manner until the beast reached Coleman and Tzeechoe. Coleman managed to dodge the onrushing bulk, but Tzeechoe was too slow and was knocked into a tree, slumping to the ground, unmoving.

Coleman looked at the prone Ayascho and yelled, "Help Tzeechoe! I fight gorga." Ayascho's eyes widened and Coleman could see he was contemplating his next action. Would he run or help? In an instant, his mind was made up, and the young man jumped to his feet and darted into the forest, climbing the nearest tree. Coleman shook his head in frustration.

He could tell by the monster's grunts that it was circling to the head of the party. Coleman dashed in that direction and found Chashutzo lying on the ground with the bone of his left thigh protruding through the skin. Coleman slipped his hand through his club's wrist loop and grabbed Chashutzo spear, holding it at the ready as his club dangled from his wrist.

The gorga came into view, stopped, and pawed the ground like an angry bull. For the first time, Coleman got a clear view of the beast. It was nearly as big as a bull, but it looked more like an enraged and deformed dark-gray dog with scaly hide. Its body was muscular and powerful-looking, with threatening limbs tipped with deadly claws. Coleman shuddered in horror at the sight of its two huge, tusk-like incisors. He noticed, again, the

long scar chiseled across its snout. The monster snorted in anger and charged straight toward Coleman. He could feel the ground quake. For a split second, he felt his vulnerability, and panic chilled him. He wanted to run for his life, but just as quickly, his mental discipline, honed by years of military training and deadly combat, turned his fear into rage, and he charged forward growling like a wild beast, his spear at the level. Just before the two collided, Coleman dropped to one knee, planted the spear's heel in the ground, and held it at an angle. The spear caught the gorga in the chest, lifting the animal's front quarter off the ground, its death-dealing claws slashing at Coleman's face. Before he could pull back, a claw gouged him above the hairline.

The spear shaft suddenly snapped. Coleman rolled to his side just as the beast crashed to the ground where he had been kneeling. He gripped his club and struck the gorga as hard as he could in the head. The monster howled and stood up, shaking the pain from its head, quickly turning to face its antagonist. Coleman looked the beast in the eye and noticed the scar etched across its snout.

"You're just as ugly as the last time!" he yelled in English. His club crashed down upon the gorga's nose, causing the creature to yelp, step back, and attempt to shake away the pain. About two feet of the spear shaft was protruding from its chest. Coleman could somehow feel the resolve building in the beast's mind, and he knew what it was about to do. The beast rushed forward again. Coleman deftly stepped aside as if he were a bullfighter, and watched the monster pass.

The gorga stopped its charge about twenty feet away and turned to face Coleman again. As it prepared to charge once more, Coleman saw the futility of his situation and took off running in the opposite direction, a plan forming in his thoughts. The creature bolted after him, blood oozing from its wound. Just as it was about to catch him, Coleman stepped aside and darted in the opposite direction. The creature made a full turn and continued chasing him.

This time, the gorga did not charge but settled into a steady gallop. Coleman kept running, leading the beast away from the others. After a mile or so, he entered a large open meadow with the gorga about twenty yards behind him. He could sense the creature's weariness, so he slowed, taunting the monster by his proximity. The gorga picked up its pace, thinking it was about to overtake him. Ten to fifteen minutes later, the beast was completely winded and stopped, its chest heaving as blood continued to spill from its wound.

"Now, I've got you!" Coleman yelled as he wheeled about and approached the gorga from the flank. He could tell the monster was completely spent, so he approached with his club held high. He jumped up and crashed it down upon the beast's skull with all the force he could muster. When his club hit the monster's head, the rock dislodged from the club's handle and bounced off, disappearing into the grass. The blow knocked the creature to its front knees, and in a flash, Coleman was on it, driving his obsidian knife into the side of the beast's neck and shoving it downward, ripping open its neck. Blood gushed from the wound as the creature fell onto its side and began kicking in the throes of death. Coleman looked to the heavens, raised his bloody arm and knife above his head, and gave a yell of victory so loud that creatures in the nearby forest fell silent and birds took flight.

Three of the hunters led by Namad raced through the jungle and found Coleman and his kill. They greeted him like a conquering hero and patted his back. They called him the Sutro P'oez—the greatest slayer of beasts—for no one had ever taken down a gorga before. A rivulet of dried blood ran down the left side of Coleman's face.

"You're hurt," Namad noted.

"I okay, only scratch."

The men began preparing the carcass.

"How is Tzeechoe?" Coleman worriedly asked.

"He was only knocked out. He will be better soon."

"Chashutzo?"

"His wound is great. He will soon die," Namad told him with sadness.

"Take me to him. I need to see his wound."

The two men headed back to the forest while the other two continued working on the gorga carcass. Two more hunters approached Coleman and Namad when they reached the tree line. Namad told them to help the other two, then he and Coleman were on their way again. When they reached

Chashutzo, Ayascho was squatting beside him crying.

"Tondo, when they told me the gorga was chasing you, I feared you were a dead man," Chashutzo said in a strained voice. It was obvious he was in great pain.

"The gorga is dead," Coleman replied, "and village have measha like never before. Food brought to People by great hunt leader Chashutzo."

Chashutzo smiled and said, "I fear my time is short. My wound is great, and I will die. Then, my family will follow."

"What are you talking about?" Coleman asked.

Tzeechoe walked up to Coleman. A trickle of blood had run down the side of his face and dried. "Chashutzo is the keeper of his family," Tzeechoe said. "His sons are young and cannot hunt. They will have to leave the village after he dies."

"That be todo!" Coleman growled. "We not let Chashutzo die. He hunt after he heal. We fix leg."

"Even Taahso can't fix this," Tzeechoe said pointing to the bone protruding from Chashutzo's thigh.

"Tondo, can you heal Chashutzo?" asked Ayascho. Coleman felt like backhanding the young man for running when he needed his help, but he took pity on him and just nodded.

Coleman kneeled over Chashutzo and carefully examined the wound. The bleeding had stopped, indicating that no damage was done to an artery or vein.

Coleman instructed the men standing around him, "Get two long, straight poles; much longer than Chashutzo tall." The men dashed off and returned in less than five minutes with the poles. Coleman placed them on the ground and indicated he wanted the men to weave cords of leather or vines between them. Although they had no idea what they were doing this for, the men followed Coleman's instructions, and soon they had finished a sturdy stretcher. "Okay, I need four straight poles longer than Chashutzo's leg."

The men disappeared into the forest and returned in short order with the poles.

"I need something to tie poles to leg."

Again, the men disappeared into the undergrowth, returning in a few minutes, each held up long strands of vegetation that looked like horse hair. They began braiding it into strong cords.

When they had finished, Coleman had several six-foot-long cords for the bindings. He then looked at Chashutzo and said, "I set bone. My friend, it hurt." Coleman quickly set the bone, hoping there weren't any blood vessels damaged in the process. Chashutzo gave a scream that frightened the other men, but the deed was quickly done, and the bone was in place. Coleman carefully put the poles around the leg and tied them securely in several places. The pain had caused Chashutzo to pass out, but he quickly regained consciousness. Coleman examined his eyes and saw they had dilated, "He go into shock," he told the others, although they had no idea what he meant. "Okay, put him on stretcher . . . um, that," he finally said, pointing to the contraption they had built.

With Coleman and Tzeechoe securing his injured leg, the other men carefully lifted Chashutzo while Ayascho positioned the stretcher under him. Coleman could see, several of the men now understood what all their efforts were for as they smiled at each other and talked about how they could carry

Chashutzo back to the village. The men heard a rustling in the brush nearby, and they turned to face the perceived threat. The four other hunters struggled into view carrying the two halves of the gorga suspended from carrying poles. They had left the choice entrails behind because they could only bring the two halves. Chashutzo weakly ordered two of the hunters to return and quickly retrieve them. Coleman took a head count to make sure no one was missing. Everyone was accounted for.

It wasn't long before the others returned with two large, leafy baskets full of gorga innards. Coleman examined the baskets and could see they were filled with heart, kidneys, lungs, and a few other things he was afraid to identify. He also noticed one of the beast's huge fangs resting atop the gore in one of the baskets. He then organized the men, assigning two to each pole with half a gorga carcass suspended from it, four to the stretcher, and Tzeechoe leading the party back to the village, carrying a basket of entrails. The thoroughly lost Coleman brought up the rear, also carrying a bloody basket of entrails.

It was now mid afternoon and Coleman guessed it would take them a couple of hours to get back. Tzeechoe led them to the Sweet Waters. They each took turns refreshing themselves in the pure liquid. Chashutzo was in shock and this worried Coleman. They couldn't stay here long, so Coleman got the party moving after only a short rest. As they started, a light drizzle began to fall, cooling the men in their labors.

After another hour had passed, the men reached the village. The rain had stopped, and the clouds were scattered, exposing large blue patches of sky. The shout of welcome was sounded from the village as the inhabitants began to gather. At first, there was jubilation, but it quickly changed to worry as they saw the men carrying Chashutzo on the stretcher.

The taahso and the chief were waiting for the men as they entered the village. "What has happened? Why are you carrying Chashutzo?" the chief asked.

"His leg is broken and the bone came through his skin. Tondo has fixed it," Tzeechoe answered. The taahso examined Chashutzo and shook his head.

Coleman walked over to him and grabbed his upper arm. "Taahso, I do all I can do. He in shock and must have your magic."

"I cannot fix his broken bone."

"Do not fix broken bone. Use your dust and feathers. He very sick."

Taahso guided the stretcher bearers to Chashutzo's home. His wife and children were beside themselves with grief. Coleman had to restrain them from falling upon his wounded and broken body. "Stop! You make him feel bad! Go away!" he finally yelled in frustration, terrorizing Chashutza and the children. They retreated and sat near the wall of the lodge, bellowing their grief and fear. Coleman turned and faced the shaman. "I not know what power you have, but I have felt it. Chashutzo needs it now, so use it!" he bellowed.

The taahso was not accustomed to being talked to in such a rude and threatening manner, but he knew the truth when he heard it. He began chanting, pulling his feathered fan from his bag. Chashutzo closed his eyes and basked in the power that radiated from the taahso.

Coleman quietly moved over to the family and held out his arms to the youngest son, probably no more than three years old. The child jumped into his grasp and wrapped his arms around Coleman's neck. The other boy, around eight years old, quickly rose and embraced Coleman and his brother in a hug. Coleman reached out to their mother, and they locked hands on each other's forearm.

After a few minutes, the older boy drew away and stared into Coleman's eyes. "Munnari," was all he uttered, and then he crawled over to his mother's embrace.

The taahso chanted for nearly an hour and then abruptly stopped. He turned to the family and said, "Pray to the gods of Munnari for this man's life. I have done all I can," and then he left.

Coleman gave each family member a hug and began to follow the taahso. Before he exited the hut, he turned and warned, "Do not move him. His leg must not be moved at all until it heal." As he left the lodge and stood up, he found himself facing the chief.

"Tondo, the other men have told me what you did today. The power of Batru is in you. No one has ever killed a gorga before, yet now you have—and alone. The hunters told me what you did for Chashutzo. Will he live?"

"I not know. It up to Chashutzo and your gods. He strong and I think he heal in time."

"The village has been blessed by your presence, Tondo."

Coleman nodded his head in acknowledgment and then he felt exhaustion overcome his body. He had been through a lot this day and hadn't taken a moment to think about himself. The chief seemed to read his thoughts and dismissed him to return to Tzeechoe's home. When he arrived, Atura handed him the waterskin. Coleman drank and handed it back to her. "Thank you, Atura."

"Todo!" she growled. Coleman laughed but didn't feel like correcting himself. He slumped to the floor and rested.

It wasn't long before Tzeechoe and Tzeecha entered the lodge excitedly. "Tondo, the chief has called a special celebration tonight, after we eat. He wants to honor you," Tzeechoe announced in a delighted voice.

"What that mean?" Coleman asked.

"I don't know for sure, but I think he will give you the gorga's tooth, an award like no other ever given."

"Okay, I guess that good," Coleman muttered tiredly. "I rest now."

"Yes, yes, rest. You've earned it," Tzeecha chimed in.

Coleman began rubbing his sore feet. They were torn, bloody, and aching. "This stone age life is tough on the body," he grumbled in his native tongue. The three villagers looked at him and then at each other, no one having a clue as to what he had just said. Atura kneeled and began wiping his feet with dampened fur, removing the mud, dirt, and dried blood. For the first time since he'd known her, she looked at him with respect. "Except for Chashutzo broken leg, today be good day," he finally said to the assembled group. All nodded in agreement.

For the next couple of hours, the group rested in the lodge.

The women hummed a gentle tune while Coleman dozed. Tzeechoe, who was unconscious during most of the struggle with the gorga, squatted, waiting for Coleman to awake. He had many questions but did not want to disturb the Sutro P'oez. This morning Tondo was only a visitor; this evening he was the hero of the village.

Coleman's body shuddered and then his eyes opened. The women and Tzeechoe greeted him with smiles as he raised his arms above his head and stretched. "How long I sleep?"

"Not long. You are very tired," Tzeechoe said.

"I very hungry. When we eat?" Coleman asked. Just then, a shout was heard and the women left the lodge. Tzeechoe smiled and pantomimed eating. "I wonder what gorga tastes like?" Coleman asked as he rubbed the stubble on his chin.

"The Sutro P'oez will be given the heart of the kill. You will gain the strength of the gorga," Tzeechoe declared.

"What?" Coleman stammered.

"The heart of the kill is given to the p'oez and he can share it with his family or eat all of it himself. The heart holds the power of the beast and that power is passed on to the ones who eat it."

"I want sutro juicy steak," Coleman mused.

Tzeechoe cocked his head and laughed, "Tondo, you are very funny."

Just then, the women entered the lodge and the smell of roasted meat wafted over the men. "Hmm, that smell good," Coleman said licking his lips. Atura placed two leaf bundles in front of him and pointed to the one on his right. He unfolded the leaf and gawked at a large, raw gorga heart laying in front of him.

He looked at the villagers and said, "It not cooked. What I do?"

"You eat it," Tzeechoe said in a surprised tone. Coleman dropped his gaze from Tzeechoe to the raw heart and just stared. He had forced himself to eat strange offerings from friendly villagers on some of his Ranger missions, but he never liked that part of the job.

"Eat it," Atura commanded. "It will make you even more powerful."

Coleman's eyes brightened as a thought came to him. "I share with friends." He drew his waist knife and cut the heart in half and handed Tzeechoe the largest piece. He then cut the remaining half in two and pointed to the women to help themselves.

Atura grabbed the knife from Coleman's hand, cut one of the pieces in half again. She picked up the largest piece and held it in front of Coleman's face. "Eat!" she scolded. Coleman reluctantly took the raw piece and bit into it. The villagers smiled as a look of disgust and revulsion crossed his face. Tzeechoe gulped down his large piece and looked invigorated and proud, pushing out his chest. The women ate their share, and all closely watched Coleman as he forced down every bit of the piece Atura had pushed upon him. He then unfolded the other leaf, picked up the roasted meat, and took a bite.

He looked at Atura and said, "It tastes like chicken."

Atura's expression turned hard as she barked, "Todo!"

Coleman, Tzeechoe, and Tzeecha began to chuckle, and soon their chuckles turned into roaring laughter. Coleman rolled on the floor, laughing uncontrollably, releasing all the stress from his day. Try as she may, Atura could no longer contain herself and she, too, began laughing uproariously. When all had exhausted themselves, they relaxed. Atura gave Coleman a smile and said, "You are the Sutro P´oez, yes, but you are still todo." They all began laughing wildly again.

The big celebration was set to begin not long after. The women had learned that the chief had asked the taahso to tell the story of how the Batru came to be. After asking the three villagers what this was all about, Coleman learned that the taahso was not just the village shaman but also the oral historian for the tribe. Since the Batru had no written language, births, deaths, and major events were passed down from generation to generation via oral history.

As they continued to teach Coleman some of the more intricate details of Batru life, a drum sounded. Soon, several more drums joined in. They rose to their feet and exited the lodge. Coleman scanned the partly cloudy sky and found the silver moon's waxing quarter directly above the village. "What that one's name?" he asked, pointing to the silvery moon.

Atura answered, "That is Munnoga, the middle moon. It keeps balance." Coleman continued scanning the sky, but the other two moons had not risen.

"The blue moon name Munnari, and the red moon name Munnevo, right?"

"Yes," Tzeechoe said, "Munnari is the good munna and Munnevo is the evil munna."

"Why?" Coleman asked.

"You will learn that tonight. Taahso will tell us the story of how the Batru came to be."

CHAPTER 7

A STARTLING DISCOVERY

The villagers slowly moved to the great lodge. Teenage drummer boys stood in front of the doorway facing each other, beating their drums with a club-like drumstick. The villagers passed between them and entered. The chief stood facing the assembly with the tusk-men sitting cross-legged in front of him. The adult males squatted or sat across the fire ring facing them, and the women and children gathered near the structure's walls, forming a large half-circle. Wood was stacked in the fire pit but was unlit. Coleman noticed Chashutzo lying on his stretcher in front of the tusk-men and quickly moved to his side and knelt.

"They should not move you. Bad for leg."

Chashutzo grabbed Coleman's forearm and said, "This has been a special day and will be a wonderful celebration. I will not stay in my lodge. When I die, I can tell the gods I hunted with the Sutro P'oez."

"You not die if you do as I say. You die if you move too much," Coleman warned. He then took his place with the adult men, Tzeechoe at his side.

When all the villagers had arrived and positioned themselves, the drummers entered the huge edifice and seated themselves near the doorway. They continued pounding their drums with a slow, monotonous beat. When the last drummer was seated, the chief called for a blessing from the gods of Munnari, crossed his arms in front of his chest, and sat on his stool. The drummers resumed their beat and it quickened. Suddenly, the taahso burst into the room. He was dressed in full shaman regalia. He wore a headdress of antlers and a cloak of feathers, which ran the full length of his arms, and down his back to below his waist. His loins were girded in black fur like the ghee Coleman had seen earlier in the day. Gourds were strapped from his knees to his ankles and they rattled with every step he took. In his left hand, he held the feathered fan Coleman had seen so many times before. In his right hand he clutched the staff adorned with the animal's skull. Taahso's painted face and chest made him appear even more macabre than usual.

As he began moving around the outer perimeter of women and children, the men began chanting. Coleman did not understand the words or even if they were words at all. Suddenly, the men stopped chanting and the women started a different chant. After a minute or so, the women became silent and the men began chanting again. This went on, back and forth, for several minutes. It was as if they were calling to each other. While the chanting continued to rise in volume, Taahso danced. He whirled and jumped, dipped and spun. From time-to-time, he would stop and wave his staff in front of the faces of the villagers. When he did this, Coleman could see fear grip those near the staff, only to be replaced with relief when Taahso moved on. Coleman watched in puzzled awe as the spectacle continued. When Taahso strode past

Atura, Coleman noticed her expression. It was one that he had never seen on her face before. It wasn't the fear he had seen on others. It was a look of admiration; no, it was a look of adoration. A wry smile crossed Coleman's face as a plan was hatched in his mind.

Taahso's dance lasted for a while as the male villagers chanted their tune with the female villagers answering. With each round, the tempo grew quicker, the chants became louder, and Taahso whirled faster. Just as they reached a frenzied peak, he stopped and raised his staff high above his head. Taahso pointed his staff at the fire pit, and the wood stack exploded in flame. The effect was so violent and unexpected that Coleman fell backward. The men jumped to their feet and began slapping their chests with open palms while the women let out their long, wavering, high-pitched shrieks.

Coleman found himself seated on the floor mat, surrounded by a forest of hairless legs. Tzeechoe reached down and yanked him upright as the men continued slapping their chests and the women shrieked louder and louder. Taahso proudly strutted around the lodge, his sweaty chest puffed out and his steps deliberate.

Coleman watched Atura out of the corner of his eye. She was completely enthralled by Taahso's performance and demeanor. Nevertheless, Coleman's analytical mind scrambled to figure out how the shaman could pull off such a spectacular stunt.

Surprisingly, he felt Tzeechoe's elbow in his ribs as he motioned for Coleman to slap his chest like the other men.

He gave Tzeechoe a sheepish grin, and he began slapping his chest like the others, allowing himself to be caught up in the moment. Taahso strutted to the chief's right side and proudly sat on a stool made of logs.

The chief stood and raised his arms. The drumming stopped, the villagers became silent, and the men reseated themselves on the mats. The chief lowered his arms and slowly looked over everyone as he began speaking.

"My brothers and sisters, may the gods of Munnari bless you and keep you safe. They have certainly been kind to us this day. Never in the life story of the Batru has a hunting party returned to the village claiming victory over the gorga. Never have the Batru tasted of the most dreadful beast of the forest. Never have the Batru feasted upon that which would feast on us all. But today, my brothers and sisters, you have feasted, you have partaken of gorga strength. Chashutzo, our great hunt leader, has been severely injured by the gorga's attack, yet he lives. Taahso strengthened him, and Tondo has given us hope that Chashutzo will live." With those words, the men gave a guttural shout, which caught Coleman by surprise.

"Tondo, Chashutzo's family thanks you; the village thanks you; and I thank you." The chief then gave a curt bow in Coleman's direction, and all eyes fell upon the visitor. He gave a quick glance to his right and then to his left, unsure of what he should do. He then looked at the chief and returned the bow. The men gave another guttural shout and turned their faces back to the chief. Coleman noticed Taahso's proud demeanor had slackened.

"I have counseled with the taahso and he informs me that there is no history of a hunting party ever taking a gorga. He tells me, many villagers have died by gorga attacks. Yet, today gorga flesh strengthened the village. Who do we thank for this blessing? It is Tondo!"

The villagers began chanting, "Tondo! Tondo! Tondo!" over and over. The chief and Taahso joined in the chanting, and this continued for nearly five minutes. Coleman sat in his place feeling very uncomfortable with all this attention.

They adore you. Use this power to make them better. Guide them, strengthen them. Then you can use them for your own purposes, Coleman's inner voice chimed proudly.

The chief raised his arms again and the chanting ceased. "Tondo, tell us about the hunt!"

Coleman looked at Tzeechoe and whispered, "What I say?"

"You must tell us how you killed the gorga. You must *show* us how you killed the beast."

Coleman grabbed his head with both hands. *Oh good grief, this must be the villagers' version of instant replay,* he thought. Reluctantly, he stood and walked to the chief's left side. "I follow Chashutzo and other men and we got attacked by gorga," he uttered in a quiet voice. The chief shook his head and sat. Coleman immediately saw the disappointment in the eyes of the men in the front rank. Then Tzeechoe's words came back to him: 'You must show us how you killed the beast.'

Coleman took a deep breath and started over. This time he acted out every phrase and emphasized every threat. When he came to the part where he told Ayascho to help Tzeechoe, he watched as Ayascho lowered his head and stared at the floor mat, waiting for his shame and cowardice to be exposed to the entire village; however, Coleman only mentioned that he told Ayascho to help Tzeechoe and never said a word about the young man's cowardly retreat. Ayascho raised his head and, for an instant, their eyes locked.

Coleman continued, pantomiming his movements, grasping his imaginary club and Chashutzo's imaginary spear. His description of the charging gorga caused the men to shudder and the children to clutch their mothers.

The villagers sat transfixed by Coleman's exhibition. Audible gasps came from the women and guttural grunts came from the men during his thrilling presentation. As he pantomimed his run with the gorga hot on his heels, he would look over his shoulder, give an exaggerated expression of terror, and run in place faster. The villagers laughed wildly.

Finally, with the gorga exhausted, Coleman raised his imaginary club high. "The club crashed down on gorga's head, rock came loose and bounce into grass," he uttered through clenched teeth. The men leaned back and shook their heads while many of the women covered their eyes with their hands. "I pull out knife and kill gorga!" he yelled as he pulled out his waist knife and drove it into the imaginary gorga's neck. He raised the knife high above his head and gave a victory yell. All the men jumped to their feet, gave guttural shouts, and began slapping their chests. The women joined in with trills of joy. The chief and Taahso remained seated and moved their heads up and down in an approving manner. Coleman stood silently with sweat dripping from every pore.

The celebration continued for several minutes until finally, the chief stood and grasped Coleman by the upper arms. The men seated themselves again and all became quiet. "Tondo, you are the Sutro P′oez! Never has a story of the hunt been so thrilling. You have indeed earned the great tooth of the gorga." The chief lifted high for all to see a gorga fang suspended by a braided leather cord. He walked around the great lodge, showing it to all the villagers, causing many to marvel at its size. When he returned to Coleman, he said, "Tondo, this is your reward. Let this be a sign to all who see it that you are the greatest p′oez the Batru have ever seen!" With those words, he placed the cord around Coleman's neck and gave him a curt bow. Coleman returned the bow, and the assembly erupted once again. Coleman held the fang forward for all to see as he smiled from ear to ear. After another minute or so of celebration, the chief raised his arms for silence. The villagers quieted down and returned to their places. The chief motioned for Coleman to return to his place and sit.

"Now, my children, I've had a night vision; guidance was given to me by the Great Batru. That is why I have asked Taahso to tell us the story of how the Batru came to be. It is important for our little ones to learn this story. It is important for you to remember it and, most importantly, it is essential for Tondo to understand it." The chief then sat and looked at Taahso.

The shaman stood, his face as rigid as granite. So significant was the change that overtook him, Coleman thought he was going into a trance. After a few seconds, he began to speak, pausing after each phrase as he recalled each line from memory.

"In the beginning, Great Father searched the land for space for his wonderful work.

"Then, when Great Father found the place, filled with enough dust for all his creation, the spirits came to him.

"In their many voices, they said, 'We are weak and blown by the wind. Give us shells that we might learn to stand strong. Help us learn and grow wise.'

"The Great Father swept out his left hand and turned the dust into The-Land-We-Live-On. Then he swept out his right, and from the land grew all that lives.

"Then, the Great Father told the spirits to find the shell that would best please them and each went as they saw best. Some flew and became birds. Others wished to swim and became the fish. The fierce became the beasts of prey. But we became men.

"In those days, all living souls could speak with one another: the animals, the trees, the creepers.

"The living souls called upon Great Father for direction and guidance in their quest for knowledge.

"Great Father gave them instruction in all things. He taught the birds to fly and make nests. He taught the creepers to chirp in the night. And he taught the beasts of prey to hunt. Then Great Father granted them choice.

"He would see if they obeyed his counsel willingly, for in this way they would learn to freely choose between the good seeds and the evil seeds found within all living things.

"All living souls were thankful to the Great Father. They willingly obeyed the guidance of Great Father and fulfilled their purposes as they filled all of The-Land-We-Live-On.

"Harmony abounded and joy filled the hearts of all living things. They soon grew to fill all The-Land-We-Live-On. And as Great Father walked, he smiled always.

"And so it was for so many days that their number exceeded the leaves on every tree.

"However, after many days, there arose a corrupter. He claimed to teach Great Father's counsel, but he changed its meaning to support his own desires.

"He influenced others to stop following Great Father's guidance and live according to their own selfish desires.

"He sought to bend all living to his own will so he could become grand and supplant Great Father. Many followed him to gain power and dominion over others. The corrupter encouraged them to exceed Great Father's wise counsel, calling it foolish.

"Some trees doubled their size. Animals changed their natural forms. Plants began to eat their neighbors.

"The corrupter called himself Uragah, and his followers called his corrupted law the Uragah Code. Soon, the Uragah Code swept throughout The-Land-We-Live-On and, for the first time, suffering was seen as Great Father walked.

"But then, a powerful follower of Great Father arose. His name was Batru. When he saw the sadness in The-Land-We-Live-On, he wept and began to teach the true principles anew. His teachings are called the Batru Code.

"The living souls chose sides by the way they lived their lives and soon the contending codes brought strife to The-Land-We-Live-On. Great Father wept as he witnessed the discord in which his beloved creations had fallen, but he knew it had to be this way, for such is the consequence of choice.

"The struggle raged for many days and so fierce was the contention that it threatened to destroy all living. Batru saw that this destruction was bad for Great Father's creations. Uragah realized that this destruction would leave nothing for him to control. Great Father intervened and strove to bring peace to The-Land-We-Live-On.

"Batru told Great Father he would stop his fighting if Uragah would also stop.

"Uragah said he would stop fighting as long as Great Father did not take back the gift of choice.

"Thus, Great Father allowed Uragah to form the Tempter, the spirit of dissension; and allowed Batru to form the Whisperer, the spirit of harmony. In this way, balance would be maintained and all living souls would have choice.

"Both Batru and Uragah agreed. Great Father decreed that now both Batru and Uragah would have to leave The-Land-We-Live-On.

"Batru chose to dwell on the blue moon, Munnari, and the living souls who chose to live by the Batru Code would join him when their time of mortality had passed. By the Whisperer, the Batru Code is taught throughout all The-Land-We-Live-On and by the influence of the good moon, Munnari.

"Uragah chose to dwell on the red moon, Munnevo, and the living souls who chose to live by the Uragah Code would join him when their time of mortality had passed. By the Tempter, the Uragah Code is taught throughout The-Land-We-Live-On and by the influence of the evil moon, Munnevo.

"Today, Batru has greater power over The-Land-We-Live-On when Munnari covers Munnevo. But, Uragah has greater power over The-Land-We-Live-On when Munnevo covers Munnari.

"Planted in the heart of Great Father's creations are good seeds and evil seeds, placed there for all his children to choose for themselves which seeds they will nurture in this life. Balance is maintained and all the Great Father's creations are granted the power of choice."

Taahso stopped his narration and cast a stern gaze over the entire assemblage, scanning from left to right. He raised his staff and warned, "The followers of Batru, guided by the influence of Munnari, nurture the good seeds. Those who follow Munnevo nurture the evil seeds and must be cast out before their wickedness poisons the followers of Batru."

Coleman noticed the impact of these words upon the gathering. An air of reverence seemed to fall upon the villagers. Most of the adults and many of the children placed an open palm on their chest and began rocking to and fro. As though by a silent command, the conclave broke into song. As Coleman listened, a spirit of peace and contentment seemed to descend upon the great lodge. Joy filled his heart and he felt uplifted and secure. He closed his eyes and drifted into a dreamy haze.

The image of the young girl returned to him, her arms outstretched as if she were pleading for help. Coleman stretched forth his arms and embraced the little girl, comforting her as she quietly wept. Subjugated and weeping Batru villagers filed past him. In the distance, he noticed other enslaved people, and not just Batru. They, too, marched into the murky distance. He noticed a woman with dark hair, holding an infant, turn and look in his direction. After a

short delay, she continued her march into the distance, slowly
fading from view.

The singing continued in the great lodge and, as it did, he
could hear a faint voice giving him instructions. He focused
on the voice, but he could not understand what he heard.
The words were little more than whispers to his dreaming
ears, but he felt within his soul an urge to protect the girl
and, by extension, all she represented. *But what was that?* He
didn't know who the girl was and he had never seen her in
the village before. She didn't even appear to be Batru. Yet he
knew she was linked to this village and possibly all the good
people of this world. He was left with the strong impression
to help these people, both the Batru and the others he
had seen. Not only was it his duty, but it had become his
calling.

Coleman remained in this dreamy absorption, calling to
mind many more overlooked details of his previous visions.
He felt someone shaking his shoulder. He opened his eyes
and found himself looking into Tzeechoe's face. He shook his
head as reality slowly embraced him again.

Tzeechoe smiled and asked, "Were you sleeping?"

"No, I had dream like the one when I sick. I not understand
what it mean."

Tzeechoe nodded, "Tondo, the gods favor you and work
through you. I think you have a great duty to perform here. I
am honored to call you my friend."

Coleman placed both hands on Tzeechoe's shoulders and smiled. "I wish I understand what dreams mean."

"I am sure you will come to a full understanding of their meaning in time," Tzeechoe said in an encouraging voice.

Coleman looked around and noticed the meeting had ended and the villagers were departing. He and Tzeechoe stood and departed, as well. Tzeecha and Atura were waiting for them as they exited the great lodge. The women's smiles were infectious and Coleman couldn't help himself as a broad smile covered his face. "What?" was all he could say.

"You are the Sutro P'oez," Tzeecha finally said. "I wish I were a man and could do such great things."

"You think different when big, ugly gorga chase you," Coleman mused. The small group laughed and began walking to their home.

Unexpectedly, Ayascho approached Coleman from the darkness and stepped into his path. Coleman snapped to a stop and stared down into Ayascho's dark-brown eyes. He detected anger and frustration on his face, yet there was something more.

"Tondo, I will speak with you," he finally said. "I must talk to you alone," as he looked at the others accompanying Coleman.

"The rest of you go. I go to lodge later," Coleman said as he watched them disappear into the shadows. He noticed Tzeechoe was reluctant to leave and kept glancing back to see what Ayascho might do.

"What you want, Ayascho?" The young man stared at the gorga fang hanging from the leather cord around Coleman's neck. He seemed to be working up the courage to do or say something, so Coleman stiffened himself, preparing for the worst.

Finally, Ayascho spoke again. "I hate you! I have hated you since the time you attacked me. You don't belong here. You are not Batru. You know nothing of the Batru ways, and yet you have found favor with the gods and the People. I wish you had never come here."

"That too bad, Ayascho. I not harm you," Coleman responded awkwardly, wishing he had a better grasp of the villagers' language.

"Yes, you have! You have taken my honor and made me ashamed of myself."

"Why you say that?"

"You saved my life on the hunt and you didn't mention my dishonor to the village. I am in your debt and you are not even Batru!"

"Do not worry, Ayascho. It in past. You do better next time."

"You should have let the gorga take me. You shame me. Why have you come here?"

"Ayascho, I not shame you. You shame self when you run."

"Tondo, kill me here, where I stand and release me from this debt."

"No! I not do that. It todo!"

"I must repay this debt. I will not rest until it is done."

"Do what you must. Can we be friends?" Coleman asked as he extended his arm in peace. Ayascho seemed confused by Coleman's gesture. After a few awkward moments, Ayascho turned and left, leaving Coleman standing with his arm hanging in the air.

"That boy has some issues to work out," Coleman said aloud in English as he headed back to Tzeechoe's lodge.

As he walked, he scanned the night sky. It was another clear night with only a handful of clouds slowly drifting by. Both Munnari and Munnevo were at first quarter. Their location in the sky drifted slowly from night to night, whereas Munnoga's position changed quite a bit, like Earth's moon, he noted. He wondered if anyone in the village kept track of such things. He would ask that of Taahso in the morning, along with a few other things he'd been wondering.

When he entered the lodge, he found the others waiting in anticipation. "What did Ayascho want?" Tzeechoe asked immediately.

"He say he in my debt for saving his life and killing gorga."

"We are all in your debt, Tondo," Tzeecha said with a lump in her throat, as she looked lovingly at her husband.

"Yes, that is true. I think the gorga would have killed us all," Tzeechoe chimed in.

"Why gorga kill entire hunt party? Is it not just hunting for food?" Coleman asked.

"No," Atura snarled. "A gorga will kill anything or anyone who threatens its hunting area. That's its nature; influenced by the Tempter."

"She's right, Tondo. A gorga will kill anything it sees as a threat. And now that you have killed the gorga, our hunting parties will be safer and find more food. You have done a great thing for the village," Tzeechoe advised.

Coleman smiled and then noticed a sweet odor in the lodge. "What I smell?" He looked down at the fire and saw four large banana-like fruit pods cooking on the coals. "What that?" he asked while pointing.

"We must celebrate," Tzeecha said smiling. She reached down, skewered one of the baking fruits with a stick and gingerly pulled it from the coals. "Here, eat this."

Coleman warily looked at it and then took a nibble, not sure of how hot it was. "Wow, this great! I never taste anything like it. What is it?"

"It is the habaga fruit. It is hard to get. It grows very high in the trees so we must pick it before the monkeys get them. They like it as much as we do," Atura instructed. The others each took one habaga and all ate, quietly repeating oohs and aahs as they slowly consumed the treat.

"That wonderful. How you get it?" Coleman finally asked.

"Atura got them. She is very good at finding the green bunches and hiding them from the monkeys until they become ripe. She climbs a tree, covers the habagas with leaves, and the monkeys don't know they are there," Tzeecha said in an admiring voice.

"Good, Atura. You very brave to climb so high," Coleman said as he took the measure of the woman's athletic build. For the first time since he'd known her, Coleman watched as Atura blushed. She hid her face in her hands and turned away. Coleman stepped next to her and wrapped an arm around her shoulders. "I not know you so skilled and brave. You get more, tonight?"

Atura pulled away from him and exclaimed, "Todo!" The

small group began to chuckle and then the chuckles turned to laughter. Atura, too, began to laugh.

Tzeechoe, Tzeecha, and Atura started telling stories of village life and great hunts of the past. Coleman intently listened until weariness overcame him and he began to yawn. The others were becoming weary, as well; soon all retired for a good night's rest.

However tired he was, Coleman still found it hard to fall asleep. The vision of the young girl returned to him as he strained to recall the words he had heard in the vision. *What was it all about? Was it a message from the gods? Was he indeed favored by them?*

Suddenly, he cleared his mind. *Am I turning native? Am I getting sucked into this tribal hocus-pocus? Is my mind just playing tricks on me? There are too many questions and too few answers. Is my new life to be like this for the remainder of my days? What new surprises are in store for me, Tondo the visitor, the Sutro P'oez?*

CHAPTER 8

THE POWER OF TAAH

Morning came too early and Coleman found the others busily working around him. "Good morning, Tondo," Tzeecha cheerfully called when she noticed him stir.

"I not know why I wake up late. It feel like I just went to sleep. Are the nights shorter?"

"Tondo, you're just lazy. Get up so we can put away your bed," scolded Atura.

"Yes, habaga girl," Coleman teased and then exited the lodge.

Shortly after he left the hut, he met the shaman. "Good morning, Taahso. I like what you said last night."

"If you liked it so well, why did you fall asleep?"

"I not asleep. I had vision, like the one when I sick."

"Ha, I see. Tondo, you are favored by the gods, but their favor always requires great sacrifice."

"Is that so? Tell me, Taahso, how did you make fire start? I never see anything like it. It was like magic. Tell me, what is the trick? I promise not tell."

"What does trehg mean?"

"It mean to fool someone."

Taahso recoiled at Coleman's words. "What do you mean? I am taahso. I have the power of taah. This is not a lie!"

"I sorry I offend you. I mean no harm. Tell me then, how do you start fire?"

"I used the power of taah. That is how you were healed. That is how you have learned to speak with us so quickly. That is what makes our hunters successful."

"Does everyone have taah?" Coleman asked.

"No, just the taahso. It is through him that the village is blessed by the power of the gods."

"So, how do person get this power?"

"Only the gods choose those who can use taah."

"How you know who is chosen? Could I have taah? Could I be chosen?"

"No, you are not even Batru! Only Batru can have taah."

"Are you sure? You see someone other than Batru people, someone like me? You see Anterran?"

"No, I have only seen people in this village," Taahso admitted reluctantly.

"Then how you know only Batru have taah? Is there a test? I need to know. Too many strange things happen to me since I come. I need to learn why," Coleman told him.

"I have felt an unusual power within you, Tondo. It could be taah, or it may be something evil. Only time will tell. When you were brought before the village, it was discussed whether to let you live or send you into the trees to die. I warned the chief that there was great power within you, but I could not tell whether it was of Munnari or Munnevo. It was your Munnari eyes that saved you that night. Yet, I am not convinced. The followers of Munnevo can be very cunning."

"I swear, Taahso, I love the Batru."

"Yes, you have proven yourself worthy to remain with the People, and yet there is danger within you."

"Danger? What danger? What have I done to make you feel this way?"

"My taah feels it. I can sense your power. I do not know how powerful you may become, but you may become a threat to this village."

"Taahso, the Batru are my friends. I could never hurt them."

"Tondo, taah is the inner-power and it may be in you. The gods grant us the right to choose which seeds we wish to nurture. The Tempter and the Whisperer influence our choices. You may be a good person, but you may surrender to evil. The Tempter is very cunning. Only time will tell how strong you are."

"If that so, should we not learn quickly? I only want do good for the Batru and the others in my vision. Help me, Taahso, to learn if this power I may have will be used for good."

"Yes, that is wise. This could be a very dangerous time for us all."

"If I can do some of the things you do, would that mean the power is for good? If I could start a fire like you did, would that mean the power is for good?"

"No, but there is one simple way to find out if the power I sense is taah. I must discuss this with the chief. Come to my lodge this afternoon, and I will tell you what he decides."

When Coleman returned to Tzeechoe's dwelling, he found Atura tidying up the space. "Atura, I will visit Taahso this afternoon. I wish to bring him a gift. Can you get habaga?"

"That will be very difficult. Do you know how high I must climb to get them?"

"No, but if you do, you come with me when I visit him."

A trace of a smile crossed Atura's lips and then quickly disappeared. "I will try," she snapped.

Coleman exited the lodge and found Tzeechoe standing near the entryway with Coleman's broken club in his hand. "Tondo, you must make a new one. This time, we will make it stronger."

"I not plan to break it over ugly gorga head but yes, let us go find perfect rock."

After a short walk, the two found themselves at the creek. For the next few minutes, the men searched for a suitable stone. Several were lifted from the water and examined, only to be discarded as unusable for one reason or another. Finally, Tzeechoe lifted a nearly spherical rock of the right size and composition. "Look, Tondo. I think this will do very well."

"Ha, yes. It looks perfect." Just then, Coleman caught the glint of a shiny object in the water. He reached down and pulled out a yellow pebble the size of his thumbnail. "Could this be what I think it is?" Coleman muttered in English.

"What did you say, Tondo?"

"Tzeechoe! Look at this. It looks like gold."

"Gor-duh? What is gor-duh? It's just a yellow rock. It is worthless. Here let me see it." Tzeechoe took the nugget from Coleman and bit into it, and then he showed it to Coleman. "See, teeth marks. It is too soft to be good for anything."

"Are there many of these rocks around here?" Coleman questioned, still excited about his discovery.

"Oy, you will find many of these little yellow rocks in the water. They are not good for anything, so we just leave them there."

"Okay. Where I come from, these rocks are worth a lot of money. A man could become rich if he finds enough of these."

"Tondo, what are you talking about? What is mhun-nay? What does reetz mean?"

Coleman just stared at Tzeechoe and didn't answer. He considered the implications of Tzeechoe's words for a few moments. Finally, it struck him that these people had no concept of money or personal riches. Their village survived day-to-day by each member's efforts. No one was rich and no one lorded over another with arrogance or hubris. Every villager had their own duties, and only the chief, taahso, and tusk-men had special authority, but there were no class distinctions.

"It is best you do not know what money is. In my world, it is sometimes called evil. Too often, men lust after it and kill one another to get it. Long ago, in my homeland, people like the Batru were chased from their lands when greedy men found gold there."

"How can a little, worthless rock cause men to act so terribly? Did Munnevo teach your people?"

"They seek power over others and they think money will help them get it. Money can also make life easier. If you have a lot of it, you do not have to make your own club. You can trade money for the very best club ever made. One that will never break."

A puzzled look crossed Tzeechoe's face as he stared at the yellow nugget. "Tondo, you are very funny. Here, take your mhun-nay and let us return to the village. You could offer me all the yellow rocks in the water and I would never trade my club or anything else I have for it." With that, Tzeechoe handed the nugget back to Coleman and headed toward the village.

When the men arrived, Coleman stored the nugget with his other items in a wicker basket Tzeechoe had given him. His personal items included the material from his environmental suit. For the rest of the morning, he and Tzeechoe worked on his new club.

Shortly after midday, Atura reappeared with half a dozen habaga. She had a nasty scratch on her left shoulder and what appeared to be bite marks on her left forearm.

"What happen to you?" Coleman asked.

"One of the monkeys tried to take the habaga from me."

"What did you do? I hope you were not seriously injured."

"It scratched me, and then it bit me, so I hit it in the nose with my fist. It ran away making noises."

"I bet it did! I am sure you would do the same thing to a gorga," Coleman said with a broad smile. Atura looked into his blue eyes and offered a weak but proud smile in return. He then washed her wounds with water and examined them carefully. "If the monkey does not have rabies you will be okay," Coleman said lightheartedly.

A look of surprise and fear crossed Atura's face. "What is ray-beez?" she questioned in a concerned voice.

"Oh, nothing. I try to be funny."

"Todo!" Atura stammered and then she stormed out of the lodge.

"I sorry," Coleman shouted as she left. He then turned to Tzeechoe and shrugged his shoulders. "Why does Atura get so angry with me? Is it because I am not Batru?"

"Maybe, Tondo, maybe. Atura is very difficult."

"Has she always been this way?"

"She has always been strong-willed, but when her father died, she became angry and has been that way ever since. I liked the old Atura better," Tzeechoe admitted. "She was about to be banished from the village, but then you came and the chief gave her to you."

"So, what am I? I know I am not her mate, thank the gods. Am I her father?"

"No."

"Am I her brother?"

"No."

"Then, who am I?"

"Tondo, you are her . . ." Tzeechoe paused for a few seconds as his face lit up and a broad smile crossed his lips. "You are her . . . Todo!" He began laughing uncontrollably. Coleman was still holding the fur skin he'd been using to cleanse Atura's wounds, and he flung it at Tzeechoe. The sopping wet fur hit his head, made a loud splat, stifling the laughter.

By mid afternoon, Coleman felt it was time to see Taahso and find out what the chief had decided. He found Atura stacking firewood and told her to fetch the habaga and follow him to Taahso's lodge.

"Why are you going to Taahso? What is this all about?" she

asked as they tramped through the village.

"We will see."

"See what?" Atura then began badgering Coleman with an endless volley of questions.

He continued walking, lost in thought, and ignoring her questions. He wondered what the chief and Taahso had decided. Would he be tested? Would they determine that the risk was too high? What would happen to him if they decided he was a threat? The cold memory of hanging in the balance returned, causing him to shudder. He took a deep breath and became aware of Atura's constant chatter. "What? What you say, Atura?"

"Does this visit have anything to do with me?"

"No. It has to do with me."

"Oy," Atura muttered in a disappointed tone. Coleman just smiled and continued his brisk pace.

A few minutes later they arrived. Taahso's home was located on the edge of the village near the main entryway. It was a typical Batru lodge with one noticeable difference—hanging on poles near the doorway were feathers, various animal furs, the bones of different animals, and small creature skulls.

"Taahso, are you there?" Coleman called.

"Yes, Tondo, you may enter," came the reply from inside.

Coleman and Atura entered the dwelling and found only Taahso standing next to a stack of unlit wood. "The chief has decided you are to be tested. He wants me to learn if the power within you is taah."

"That good, I hope," Coleman replied. "Before we begin, I would like to give you a gift. Atura, give Taahso the gift."

Atura stepped forward and handed Taahso the six habaga pods she had carried with her. Taahso's eyes lit up when he saw the fruit and he took them from her.

"This is a fine gift indeed. Thank you, Tondo."

"You can thank Atura, too. She the one who got them. She is very good at it. A monkey tried to take them from her when she was high in the tree, and she hit it in the nose." Taahso stared into Atura's eyes and then glanced at her scratched shoulder. He then examined the bite marks on her forearm. "She is very brave, Taahso, and the habaga are good."

"Yes, yes," he said trying to refocus on the business at hand. "As I said, the chief wants me to test you for taah. Since you think I fooled the People, I will show you how it is done, and then you will do it if you can."

"Okay. Show me how to do it," Coleman said as he turned and gave Atura a wink. He saw a flash of anger cross her face followed by an audible harrumph. "What is it, Atura? Tell me your thoughts," Coleman chided.

"Only the taahso has the power of taah. You cannot have it. Only a great man can. You are not even Batru." Coleman grinned as he watched Taahso straighten while his ego was puffed up by Atura's words.

"But, Atura, I have been told that the gods favor me. Can I not also have taah?"

"Yes, Tondo, the gods favor you, but only a great and special man can be a taahso."

Coleman watched as Taahso's gaze seemed to express a newfound feeling for and a deeper appreciation of Atura. A smile crossed Coleman's lips as he watched his Cupid's ploy scoring points. "This may be easier than I thought," he muttered to himself in English.

"What did you say, Tondo?" Taahso asked.

"Oh, nothing. I was just wondering if we could start." He didn't want to overreach the great beginning his matchmaking was already scoring.

"Yes, yes. Let me show you how it's done. Sit and observe." All three sat around the unlit stack of wood. "You must feel the power of taah within you, here," Taahso instructed as he tapped his solar plexus and then did the same to Coleman. "This is the center of taah. You then think about the fire, here." He tapped his forehead and then Coleman's forehead. "You must see an image of the fire in your mind, then feel the taah and focus on the wood. Like this."

Taahso took a deep breath, closed his eyes, and suddenly the wood burst into flame. Not nearly as dramatically as the night before, but nevertheless, it was awe-inspiring to both Coleman and Atura. Coleman saw the same look of adoration on Atura's face that he had noticed the night before.

"That is how one with taah can make fire." Now, let's see if you have the power of taah."

Coleman looked at Taahso and then over to Atura. She leaned back, crossed her arms over her chest and hardened her countenance. Coleman gave her a smile as Taahso put out the fire by smothering it with an animal hide.

"Tondo, prepare yourself. Take a deep breath, feel the taah, and think of the fire."

Coleman looked at Atura and then Taahso. He took a deep breath and tried to feel the power of taah, but he felt nothing.

"I do not feel anything."

"Relax, Tondo, you're too tense. Calm your mind and find inner peace."

Coleman closed his eyes and cleared his mind. As he relaxed, he felt a tingling sensation beginning to grow within his chest. The tingling slowly changed to a warming sensation as the intensity increased. Through a fog of thought, Coleman could hear Taahso's instructions.

"As the power of taah grows, you must bring an image of fire into your mind." Coleman continued to let the warmth build within himself, and he began to visualize a fire in his thoughts. "You must bring the taah and the image together and focus them into a point. It is then that the fire will ignite the wood."

The warmth within Coleman continued to grow, and the image of fire began to brighten in his mind, as well. He felt a trickle of sweat slide down the side of his face, and then suddenly, a flash of light burst through his mind. He felt a gush of energy being expelled from his body and the image in his mind exploded into a sheet of flame. He opened his eyes and there, before him, the wood had ignited, fully engulfed in flames. As he watched the blaze, he felt himself returning from a trance-like state, only to hear Atura's screams and Taahso's yells of panic. Coleman shook his head, and as he became semi-aware of his surroundings, he could see that not only was there a fire in the pit, but the entire lodge was smoldering, and flames could be seen in many of its sections. Taahso and Atura were running around beating the flames with animal hides. Coleman calmly sat watching the chaos around him.

"I think it worked," he mumbled, still not fully cognizant of what was going on.

"Stop, Tondo, stop!" he clearly heard Atura yell.

He casually turned his head from side to side and saw flames everywhere. He felt Taahso grab him and literally throw him through the structure's doorway. Coleman landed with a thud and slowly came to his senses. "What happened? Taahso, why did you throw me out?" Then he realized the hut was burning, so he pulled open the door skins and ran back into the lodge.

Obviously, there was no hope of saving the dwelling. The flames were growing and there was no way to extinguish them. Taahso, Atura, and Coleman began tossing items out of the hut in an effort to save as many things as they could from the flames. Finally, when it was too dangerous to remain, all three dashed through the doorway, stood back, and watched Taahso's home burn to the ground.

"Does this mean I have the power of taah?" Coleman shouted to Taahso over the roar of the flames.

Atura gave Coleman a shove and roared, "Todo!"

Taahso just glared at Coleman and said nothing. Atura calmed down, stepped away from Coleman as fear gripped her, and then she ran toward Tzeechoe's lodge. Other villagers began to congregate near the burning rubble. At this point, there was nothing that could be done to save the dwelling. As the last pole collapsed into the ash and charred remnants of poor Taahso's home, a flash of lightning lit the sky, and the village was drenched in another downpour. Coleman stood in the rain, ashamed of what he had just caused, yet almost giddy about his newly discovered inner-power.

"Now, what we do, Taahso?" he asked.

"I must go and talk with the chief. You are very powerful, Tondo. You are also very dangerous."

Taahso turned and trudged off through the rain. Coleman remained for a few minutes more and watched as the last lick of flames was extinguished by the falling rain. Only smoke and steam rose from the smoldering remains of Taahso's home. He turned and slowly lumbered back to Tzeechoe's lodge where he was met by Tzeechoe and the two women, staring in awed reverence. Coleman seated himself by the fire and felt its warmth as the water on his skin turned to steam and swirled into the air. No one said a word. The three villagers just stared at Coleman as he bowed his head and contemplated what had just happened.

Quite a bit of time passed, and everyone was still silent. The rain stopped soon after it had begun. The steady drip, drip, drip of water was the only sound heard in the lodge. From outside, a shout marked the return of the hunters. No one in the dwelling moved.

Finally, Coleman stood and gave the others a smile. "It is okay. Let us find out what the hunters have brought us."

The three villagers stood and exited the hut; no one uttered a word. Other villagers gathered near the village entrance to see what the hunters had brought. Coleman wasn't sure, but he thought they had killed a couple of ghees. As Coleman approached, the other villagers stepped aside and gave him a clear path.

"It seems the word has gotten around the village, Tzeechoe,"

Coleman finally said.

"Yes, Tondo, the People are not sure what you are."

"I am the same person I was this morning. Who do you think I am?"

"You are my friend, Tondo, but I'm afraid."

"Afraid? Afraid of me? What have I done to scare you?"

"I think you are one of the gods, Tondo. You are much different and much more powerful than anyone I've ever met. Have you come to help us or punish us?"

"What? Tzeechoe, I am not one of the gods. I am just a man, like you."

"No, you aren't. You are not like me. You kill the gorga. You have the power of taah. You have the eyes of Munnari."

"Would a god get sick and nearly die? I do not think so, Tzeechoe."

Coleman noticed other villagers were intently listening to their conversation. He heard some whisper in reverence the words taahso and Munnari. The hunting party proudly marched past the gathered throng near Coleman, unaware of the turmoil he had caused earlier; however, the leader pointed to the charred remains of Taahso's home and brought it to the attention of the other hunters. They traded a few comments but did not stop as they proudly marched into the center of the village.

Coleman turned and walked back to the lodge, followed by Tzeechoe, but before he entered the hut, Coleman turned and walked to Chashutzo's place to examine his wounds.

"Chashutzo, may I enter," Coleman called.

For a long and uncomfortable moment, there was no answer.

Finally, Chashutzo responded, and Coleman was allowed to enter. Chashutza and the children were huddled together in the shadows. Coleman could only see their wide eyes staring at him from the darkness. Chashutzo looked fearful, but then greeted Coleman with a smile.

"Chashutzo, how are you feeling? Does the leg hurt much?"

"The pain is lessening. I try not to move much, but I can't stay still all day. I have to move around a little."

"That is okay, just do not stand up. You need to let your leg heal and that will take time. The more you move, the longer it will take. Let me look at skin. I must see if there be infection."

"What is infeg-shone?" Chashutzo asked.

"It is a bad thing if the skin turns red and begins to burn. Does your leg feel like it is burning?"

"No, it just aches."

"That is good. The skin looks healthy and I think there will be no infection. You will be as good as new in a few Munnoga moons."

"We call it the scourge. Those who get it die a horrible death. Are you sure I won't get it?"

"I do not see any signs of it. You should be okay. Anyway, Taahso should be able to help you."

"You can help me. I heard you are taahso, too."

"Chashutzo, I am Tondo. The village has only one taahso and he will take care of you. I can help him, that is all," Coleman counseled as he looked deeply into Chashutzo's eyes. Chashutzo swallowed hard and returned a weak smile.

"Tondo, do you think I will ever be able to lead the hunt again."

"Oh yes, Chashutzo. You will again lead the hunt for bataro and I will follow you." Chashutzo's smile broadened, and a whimper escaped the mouth of Chashutza, still hiding in the shadows. Coleman turned and opened his arms. The two young boys ran to him and he embraced them. Soon, Chashutza left the shadows and kneeled at her husband's side, still not speaking. Coleman watched as husband and wife clasped arms and exchanged looks of devotion. The boys pulled away from his embrace and sat beside their father. This brought a smile to Coleman's face.

They respect you and they fear you. You can be their god, Coleman's inner voice counseled.

A flash of lightning and the rumble of thunder announced another approaching downpour. "Chashutzo, I will return tomorrow and visit you. Rest well, my friend." Coleman then exited and returned to Tzeechoe's lodge.

CHAPTER 9

BREAKING TRADITION

When Coleman entered the lodge, he found Tzeechoe weaving a fine, sturdy wicker and reed basket. His host looked up, smiled, and returned to his work. Heavy drops of rain began to pelt the roof and sides of the lodge. Coleman sat near the fire and became lost in thought as he reviewed the events of the day.

The women soon entered carrying dinner. The smell made Coleman's mouth water. When he tasted the roasted meat, he found it a little tough and with the flavor of turkey. The four ate silently throughout the meal. When all had finished, Coleman asked Tzeechoe when it would be their turn to hunt again.

"There are now eleven hunting parties, so it will be a few more days before we go out again. Do you think Chashutzo will be well enough to go with us?"

"No, it will take him several weeks to recover from his injury," Coleman advised.

"What is weet´se?" Tzeechoe asked.

Coleman pondered how to answer. He wondered if the Batru had a calendar. No one in the village had ever concerned themselves with dates. One day seemed to be the same as the next.

"Where I am from, a week is seven days," Coleman finally said. "Do the Batru keep track of time?"

"I don't know what you mean, Tondo. Taahso tells us when it is time to do things, like adding a line," Tzeechoe said as he drew his hand over the tattoo lines down his cheek.

"You must have some kind of calendar. I'll ask Taahso."

Just then, Taahso gave a call from near the entryway of the hut. "Tzeechoe, may I enter. I must speak with Tondo."

"Yes, Taahso, please join us," Tzeechoe quickly responded. When he entered, all could see that Taahso was drenched, and he looked miserable.

"Tondo, I have no home and I am cold and wet. May I use your lodge until I can rebuild my own?"

Coleman looked surprised. "This Tzeechoe's home. Ask him."

Taahso stiffened. "Yes, I know this is Tzeechoe's. I am talking about your lodge. It has been empty since you arrived. Hasn't Atura told you about it?" Coleman looked at Atura and watched as her face turned to stone and the look of outrage filled her countenance. He had seen that look before and he realized she had become very irritated.

"No, she has not. Atura, what is Taahso talking about?"

"It was my father's lodge," she replied.

"All this time we have been living here with Tzeechoe and Tzeecha when we could have been living in our own place."

Atura lowered her head as if ashamed. "I did not want the People to talk. I'm not your daughter and I'm certainly not your woman!"

"Tzeechoe, why did not you tell me? I feel like a guest who has overstayed his welcome."

"I am honored you live here. You are chosen by the gods and you bless my home. You can stay here for as long as you wish."

"Thank you, my friend," Coleman said and then turned and addressed the woman. "Atura, I understand. We certainly do not want the village to think the wrong thing. Can Taahso use your lodge until we build a new one for him?"

"It is not my home. It belongs to you now. Do with it as you wish, but I will not live there ever again," Atura answered and then moved into the shadows and began wiping her eyes.

"Yes, Taahso, you may use the lodge. We will start building a new one for you tomorrow."

"You will help me? Don't you think I can do it myself? It has always been a man's duty to make it by himself. No one ever helps. You destroy my home, and now you wish to shame me, too?" Taahso grouched, obviously upset by Coleman's offer.

"It certainly seems odd to me that no one would help. Your lodge is not the first home to be destroyed by fire or some other tragedy, is it?"

"True, but such things are by the will of the gods," Taahso stated bluntly. "If it is the will of the gods, others should not interfere with their judgments."

"Maybe the gods want us to help one another. Tragedy could be the way they encourage us. The hunters share the food they hunt. Why not share in the labor of building a lodge or, for that matter, everything else?" Coleman argued. "I must help you. I am responsible for your home burning down. It is my duty. It is I who will be shamed if you will not allow me to help."

"You do not understand the Batru Code," Taahso said, his voice hardening. "I do not understand your words, but I know our Code, which says that each man must grow his own strength and not allow others to weaken him. How can a man grow strong if others are helping him?" Taahso's eyes had narrowed to a glare.

Coleman looked around the hut and saw that everyone was looking at him with a mixture of pity and horror.

Atura stood a little closer to Taahso. "Do not do this," she said, cold as ice. "Do not be todo and try to help."

He had obviously missed something. It seemed like the very idea of helping was offensive. He wasn't going to win this argument by force of character. It was him against the entire history of the Batru. It was a history that Taahso had committed entirely to memory. He needed to attack this issue in a different way.

"What if Tzeechoe came while you were away and broke all your baskets?" he said, turning to point at Tzeechoe.

Taahso looked confused at the sudden turn in the conversation. "He would be punished by the People according to his crime."

"Could his punishment be that he make you new baskets?" Coleman asked.

"Of course. He would have to right his wrong," Taahso said.

"So, you mean that Tzeechoe would get stronger for destroying your things?"

Taahso looked startled. "I have never thought of it that way before," he said, visibly shaken by the idea.

Coleman let his voice become gentle and said, "Bad things happen to all people, Taahso. That is just the way it is. It is how we deal with the will of the gods that sets us apart. When we see a friend made weak by their will, we are made weak, too, because they cannot hunt or do their work for the People. But, if we all help him, then all of the Batru can grow stronger together."

Taahso looked deep in thought. Everyone in the hut waited for him to make up his mind. Finally, he said, "Your words are right, Tondo. This way of thinking will be uncomfortable for many to understand and some may think them from Munnevo. But I feel the Whisperer in your words. I will let you help me." He said the last words with a grimace.

Coleman turned to Tzeechoe and asked, "Will you take this chance to grow stronger with me? Will you also help?"

"Yes, Tondo, I will help." Obviously, he was uncomfortable with breaking the village traditions, but his friendship and the respect he'd gained for the visitor swayed him enough to acquiesce.

"Tzeecha, will you help?"

Tzeecha looked at her husband and he nodded his head in permission. "Yes, Tondo, I will help, but I don't know what I can do."

"Do not worry about that. I do not know what to do either. I am sure Taahso and Tzeechoe will guide us. Atura, will you help?" A startled look crossed her face and was quickly replaced with a look of stern annoyance. It was the look that Coleman had seen many times in the past as she tutored him. "Will you stay weak or grow with us? Do you see Taahso as a house builder or as the taahso of the Batru?" Coleman queried, already aware of her answer.

"Yes, I will help Taahso. This is not the Peoples' way. The others will not like it."

"When the others come to watch, we will put them to work. Taahso's lodge will be done very quickly, I think," Coleman postulated.

"And if they come, they will call all of us todo!" Atura blustered.

"Better todo than weak!" Coleman barked back and roared with laughter. Tzeechoe and Tzeecha shortly joined him. Taahso looked puzzled, then he too began to chuckle. Atura shook her head and began to snicker.

Taahso, Atura, and Coleman exited Tzeecho's home and quickly marched to the lodge of Atura's father, Tumtuo, as the rain pelted them. Taahso pulled aside the doorway cover and all quickly filed into the deserted dwelling. Coleman felt his foot kick a solid object on the dirt floor. In the meager light, he saw a stone and picked it up. It was a flint used to spark a fire.

"I will start the fire," he said.

"No!" shouted Taahso and Atura simultaneously.

"With this," Coleman said as he held up the flint stone, revealing it in the subdued light filtering through the hole in the roof.

Atura quickly snatched the stone from Coleman's hand and curtly stated, "I'll do it."

While Atura lit a fire, the men carried in Taahso's belongings. Most of his things had been saved from the inferno, mainly because he had very few possessions. Coleman expected a man of his importance to have more belongings, but he realized that this society wasn't based on the accumulation of things. Taahso owned little. He seemed only to favor his staff and the animal bones and skulls that had hung near the entrance of his old lodge.

Coleman felt it was time to delve more deeply into the history and culture of this tribe. From what he could tell, the tribe was barely hanging on. There were few children in the village and nearly no elderly. *Could disease or plague have decimated their number or was there a more sinister shadow in their history? Could the gorga have weakened the tribe?* He felt he needed to learn more and tried to think of ways to invigorate the tribe that had welcomed him as one of their own.

Yes, you can do it. You'll become their greatest leader and the example for all to follow, his inner voice advised.

After all Taahso's belongings were stored and a fire lit, Coleman suggested that the surviving habaga fruit be prepared. Taahso's eyes lit up and a smile crossed his face. "Yes, yes, that is a good idea. It has been a hard day and habaga would make it end better." Coleman noticed Atura's smile when Taahso uttered these words.

"Ah yes, thanks to Atura we have this great treat," Coleman reminded him. Atura lowered her head, somewhat embarrassed by the attention. She continued preparing the fruit, occasionally glancing toward Taahso.

Taahso walked around the lodge examining the few items remaining of Atura's family: a spear, a knife, and a bolo were stored near the doorway; bedding near the fire; a few articles of clothing and a string of bones in another out of the way place. Atura's gaze followed Taahso as he made his way around the room. Coleman studied them both and thought he saw tears forming in Atura's eyes. She finally noticed him watching her and turned away, wiping her face with her forearm.

"The habaga are ready," she muttered as her voice broke just a little. She handed each of the men a portion and waited.

"Please, Atura, help yourself," Coleman said politely. Atura looked at Taahso, and he nodded.

"We have you to thank for this treat, Atura. Tell me again how you got these?" Coleman asked, encouraging her.

Atura related for the two men how she had climbed to the top of the jungle canopy many days ago and had hidden a green habaga bunch in the leaves. The monkeys seldom climbed that high and, unless they could see the fruit, they would not venture so high. She told the men how, when the monkeys saw her retrieve the habaga fruit and begin to descend with it, they howled in anger and one of the bolder ones attacked her, clawing at the fruit and biting her arm.

"And when it bit me, I hit it in the nose with my fist," she said.

Both Coleman and Taahso laughed, and Coleman slammed a fist into an open palm, producing a loud smack. "That is one monkey who will not touch you again," he gleefully declared as Taahso nodded in agreement. Atura couldn't help herself and began smiling proudly.

The small gathering chitchatted about various things for the next few minutes. Then Coleman asked, "Taahso, may I hold your staff?"

"No one but the taahso is to touch his staff," Atura barked.

"Oh, sorry. I hope I did not offend you," Coleman said coyly.

"You are still new here and you don't understand all of our ways. The taahso's staff is the symbol of his power and only he can touch it," Taahso explained.

"Can you tell me about it? Is it passed from father to son?"

"It was given to my family at the time of the Great Separation. Since then, the staff has been handed down from taahso to taahso. It is now my honor to keep it as a warning to those who would disobey the law."

"You said the 'Great Separation.' What is that?"

"Our old village had become very large and the land could no longer support all the People. It was decided that many of the village families should move to a distant place and start anew. In my fathers' line was a second son of the taahso. Under normal circumstances, he would not become taahso unless the older brother died without bearing a son. But in this case, the taahso created a new staff and made him taahso of the new tribe. The leader of the new tribe was appointed by the old village chief. Some families volunteered to leave. Some were chosen by lot. For many, it was a sad time, for others, it was a time of opportunity. The new tribe left and traveled for many days until they found this place and built a new village."

"How many started this new tribe?" Coleman asked.

"There were about as many as there are today. Life was hard at first and many died. Many rains later, a gorga came and did not like us living in his territory. Many of the People were slaughtered by the beast."

"How long ago did this happen?"

"Many rains."

Coleman pondered the phrase 'many rains.' *Could this be the way the Batru measured their year, by the rainy season?* "What do many rains mean?"

"When the rains end, we celebrate a new beginning. The time of the rains is followed by the New Birth, Matti-mas. That is when Nature renews itself. This lasts until the rains come again."

"It seems to rain every day. Will the rains end soon?"

"We will have rain almost every day, but there will be clouds and blue sky most of the time, soon. During the rains, it rains all day long, day after day."

"Oh, like the monsoons."

"What is that?" Taahso asked as he scratched his head.

"In my homeland, there are places where it rains for days and days, just like here. It is called the monsoon season," Coleman explained and then asked, "Do you ever visit the old tribe?"

"No. The old village is a long walk and it would be a perilous journey. It was decided long ago no one would ever return. We needed to grow in our own strength. It is the Batru way. With the blessings of the gods, we have." Taahso proudly smiled and leaned back. "Tell me about your land, Tondo. Tell me about your people."

Coleman noticed Atura turned and looked at him. Not once had she ever asked him about how he arrived here. Yet there was curiosity etched on her face and questions she wanted answered.

"Tzeechoe told me and Tzeecha that you come from a land where people ride inside big birds. That is not possible.

Were you telling Tzeechoe a funny story?" Atura asked with a disbelieving air.

Coleman chuckled and said, "That is not exactly what I told Tzeechoe. I said it was like a big bird. It is a machine that looks like a big bird, but people build it. People can ride inside it as it fly across the sky." Taahso stared at Coleman in wonder and began shaking his head.

Atura's countenance hardened and she spouted, "Do you think I'm a fool? I don't believe a word of this!"

Coleman didn't know what more he could do to convince them. He merely stuttered, "But . . . but, it is the truth. Why would I make up such a story?"

Taahso thought for a few seconds, then questioned, "If this is so, why have I not seen one of these bird-things? I'm sure I would never forget such a sight. No one here has ever seen anything like that."

A hard smile crossed Atura's lips and her face turned hard as stone. She glared at Coleman as if to say, 'Well, what is your answer to that?'

Coleman pondered Taahso's words for a while. *How could he explain the modern technology of a world they had never even dreamed about? How could he make them believe in aircraft, rip chambers, or even felt-tipped pens?* He began to feel isolated and lonely again. His world was as foreign to them as this world was to him.

Coleman took a deep breath, "The place I am from is very different from this land. Many things there would seem like magic to you: machines that fly; little boxes that allow you to see and talk with someone who lives many days journey away;

tubes that you look through that enable you to see far away things close up. You may think I am todo or I am trying to fool you, but these things and more are part of my homeland."

"You cannot make a decent club, yet you say you can make things that fly? Show me!" Atura bluntly stated in an accusatory tone.

"I did not say I can make things that fly. I said people make them."

"Then what can you make?" Atura challenged.

Coleman could see this conversation was going nowhere in a hurry. How could he explain a world of modern technology to those still living in this world's Stone Age? How was he to explain String Theory, the Ripple Effect, and the unfortunate accident that brought him here? How indeed? Even he didn't understand how he got here. In any case, he wouldn't have believed it possible to be plunked down into this forsaken land. Yet, here he was and now he had to cope with this and more.

"The gods brought me here for some unknown reason," he said, trying not to sound bitter. "I hope to find out what it is. In the meantime, I will struggle with you to make a life for myself."

Taahso grunted in satisfaction and Atura seemed placated with this statement, at least for the moment. These were simple people, educated only in the things that had relevance to their daily struggle to survive in a harsh environment. It made no difference that he was an educated and well-trained citizen from a planet called Earth. He could hunt well and that was what really mattered to them.

The three sat and stared into the fire in silence, each lost in their own thoughts. Finally, Taahso turned to Atura and said,

"Your father was a good man. I was very sad when he crossed-over. It was a great loss to the village." Atura looked at him as tears welled. Just as a tear escaped her large brown eyes, she turned her face from him and continued to stare into the fire. Although Coleman wanted to learn how her father died, he said nothing. He could see the pain was too dear and it was all Atura could do to control her grief.

Finally, he said, "Why is it that the People share in the hunting of food, yet they do not help one another build a lodge?"

"That has been the custom of the People since we came here. Every man and family must survive on their own. That is how we understand the traditions. We have made an exception because of the danger in hunting, but now that the gorga is gone, maybe we should return to the old ways and let each man hunt for himself," Taahso speculated.

"I think working together would strengthen the village. It has worked in hunting. Why not other things, like lodge building?" Coleman questioned.

"It is the Batru Code," Taahso said. "We must not let others make us weak." His voice seemed distant, remembering what had been said earlier that day.

"Are you sure that is what the gods want? Could the traditions be misunderstood?" Coleman wondered.

"You are todo," Atura finally uttered. "The chief and Taahso understand the traditions. You do not!"

"I meant no offense. I am just trying to understand. In the place I come from, people work together, and by doing so, they become stronger. When they do not, they grow weaker. I think if we work together, the village will be made stronger and safer." Atura looked at Coleman and then Taahso, but said nothing.

"Tondo, you ask difficult questions. You challenge our wisdom. But it is true that we struggle much and we lose many of our people." They all sat in silence around the fire for a few moments. "We call it the will of Batru, but we know that the Tempter works by changing the meaning of our beliefs. He twists our words. Maybe you bring a message from the Whisperer to restore us to the true Batru Code."

"How long does it take one man to build a lodge?" Coleman asked.

"It takes many days. It depends on how hard he works and if he has sons old enough to work with him."

"I think if several men and women cooperate to build your new home, we can have it finished in one day," Coleman assured him.

Taahso looked at him in disbelief, "No lodge has ever been built in just one day; never since our people came to this place."

"Tomorrow will be eye-opener for everyone. Perhaps it is time to change how things are done from now on. The village will become stronger when everyone shares in the work," Coleman persuaded.

Taahso grunted in agreement and smiled in a way that made Coleman grin. Although, under his air of confidence, he was a bit worried. How difficult was it to build a lodge? He had no idea, but guessed that it couldn't be too hard. It would all depend on how many other villagers he could persuade to join the effort.

Don't concern yourself with these doubts. You'll master all these things just like everything else. You're better than they are. It's your duty to show them the way. Just think how much they'll love you then, his inner voice lauded.

As the fire burned down, Taahso and Atura chitchatted about village life and the upcoming Matti-mas. Coleman deduced that it was some form of celebration. He wanted to inject his own questions every now and then, but he let the two carry on their conversation without interruption. He sensed that they had never sat like this and talked, so he didn't want to interfere. Coleman listened quietly and felt that the two were starting to appreciate one another. He already knew how Atura felt about Taahso. Now, he was beginning to think the feeling was becoming mutual.

Eventually, Taahso gave a loud yawn. Coleman took it as a cue that he and Atura should politely dismiss themselves. He was exhausted and knew the morning would be arriving much too soon.

The other three were up and working by the time he awoke. "The nights feel about four hours long," Coleman muttered to himself in English.

"What did you say?" asked Tzeecha.

"Oh, nothing. It just seems that the night passes so quickly."

"You're just lazy," Atura scolded, as usual.

"I am hungry. Is there any food?" Coleman wondered.

"You will eat after the hunters return, just like the rest of us," Atura told him, a bit perturbed by his question.

"Yes, yes, you are right. I would sure feel a lot better if I had some food in me to start the day. And it is going to be a busy one. We have a lot of work to do."

"Oy, the sooner you start, the better. Now, go and let me put away your bed," Atura chided as she grabbed his furry blanket and folded it.

"Yes, my habaga girl," Coleman teased. Atura would have none of this foolishness. She shooed him out of the lodge and went about her other tasks. Coleman found Tzeechoe waiting for him near the doorway.

"I am here, Tondo. Are you ready to meet with Taahso?"

"Yes. Today we will help him and teach the village that by helping one another we will all be stronger."

"The chief will not like it, Tondo. This has never been done before and he may order us to stop."

"I have always believed it is better to ask for forgiveness rather than permission. Let us get to work."

Coleman and Tzeechoe hurried to the remains of Taahso's lodge and found him rummaging through the charred pieces. The three men chatted for a few minutes and then began clearing the site. They carried the burned remnants of Taahso's home out of the village and dumped them out of the way. It took several trips. By midmorning, they had removed about half of it.

While this work was going on, a small gathering of village children watched the men working. This was the first time

Coleman had seen such a large collection of young ones and he was shocked at how thin they all were. They were not emaciated, but all were underweight. Maybe he wasn't the only one who would benefit from eating a daily breakfast.

Soon, about a dozen older boys without tattoo lines were watching the cleanup. In a short time, many village men also gathered and were watching the trio work. Coleman kept glancing over at the growing crowd of men and boys. "Hoy! We could use a little help. Grab something and take it out," he shouted. No one moved; they just stood where they were and watched. After another trip, Coleman noticed the village chief had joined the crowd. He, too, stood watching with no apparent inclination to help.

Coleman walked to him and respectfully said, "We could use a little help here. Many hands make light work." Apparently, it wasn't a saying in their language, judging by the chief's stare.

The chief pondered Coleman's words for a few seconds and then stated, "Tradition says a man is responsible for his own affairs. It is not the duty of others to interfere with the gods' rulings."

"I am not interfering; I am helping. Taahso can strengthen the People better when he has a lodge, and Tzeechoe and I grow stronger through the work. I think we can build a new structure in a day if others join us. Does tradition say a man must do it by himself?"

"This is not the way things are done here, Tondo. I forgive you for your lack of knowledge of our ways, but Tzeechoe and especially Taahso know better."

"So, you are saying the People must be weak while we wait for Taahso to do this alone?"

"No, I'm not, but never before has it been done this way."

"Maybe it is time to grow as a people. The more men who help, the stronger we will become together."

The chief thought for a while and continued observing but not helping nor interfering. Coleman persuaded members of his and Tzeechoe's hunt team to join the effort. Ayascho alone stood next to the chief shaking his head.

After the rubble was cleared, the men divided into two groups. While one team left the village to find poles, the other group went to find vines that would serve as bindings. Coleman followed Taahso and Tzeechoe to the tree line and watched as they selected and chopped down a bamboo-like plant of forty or more feet in length. As the men carried back many light and flexible poles, Coleman noticed they passed through a field of ground plants, some with purple flowers. The plants rested atop a small raised area.

"Stop!" Coleman ordered the men. Surprised and confused, they came to a halt. He then dropped to his knees and began digging while Taahso and Tzeechoe stared at him as though he had lost his mind. Coleman pulled up a round, red tuber from the soil the size of his fist and held it up for the other men to see as he admired it. "It is a red potato. My family used to grow these at my lodge when I was a boy."

"What is rud-bo-t´a-tzo?" Taahso asked.

"It is food. You can eat them raw, or you can cook them. Potatoes are good." Coleman cut the tuber open and took a bite. "It tastes just like a potato. Here, take a bite," he said excitedly. Taahso and Tzeechoe both took bites, and Coleman chuckled as they responded with sour expressions. Both spat out what they had bitten off.

"It will taste better after it is cooked. Tonight, we will have baked potatoes with dinner." The men laughed and shook their heads before gathering up their poles and continuing back to the village.

Back at the lodge site, holes were dug in the ground as deep as a man's arm, from fingertip to elbow. The poles were lashed together with the vines and set in the holes. The lengthened poles were placed in a circle about twenty feet in diameter and then bent into an arch with the top of the pole being sunk into the hole of the pole on the opposite side of the circle. The holes were then filled with dirt and tamped down with logs. The men then began weaving the vines through the poles, starting at ground level and working their way around the circle.

A steady stream of team members and their sons returned with more vines as a couple of weavers continued their work. Coleman stepped back and admired what had already been accomplished, not so much for the progress being made on the lodge, but how quickly the men and boys divided the responsibilities and coordinated their tasks.

The chief also continued watching, apparently amazed by how quickly the new home was coming together. After a few minutes, he eased his way over to where Coleman was standing. "Tondo, this is impressive! Your words have obviously swayed Taahso, and I can see how we are all stronger from them. The gods seem to work through you."

Coleman bowed his head. He wondered how such a trivial thing as helping one's neighbor was such a new concept for these villagers. "I do not think the gods had anything to do with this. Where I am from, this is called being a good neighbor."

"Tondo, if the gods have nothing to do with it, tell me how you got here."

Coleman was stunned by the chief's remarks. He had no answer for him. He only stood in silence and continued watching the men as they hustled around the quickly forming lodge. He soon felt someone touch his elbow. It was Atura, and she offered him a waterskin. He drank and thanked her for it. She then went to Taahso and offered him a drink. He also drank and soon the two were engaged in conversation. Coleman couldn't tell what they were talking about, but their smiles seemed to indicate that things looked promising for his Cupid's stratagem.

By the time the hunters returned late in the afternoon, Taahso's new home was completed. Coleman could see, the hunters were surprised and confused by how quickly the dwelling was rebuilt. When they had left early in the morning, Taahso's lodge was just a pile of charred fronds and poles. To the hunters, it was as though the structure had risen from the ashes by some magical power. Coleman smiled to himself as the hunters filed past, gawking and commenting about what they beheld.

After a hard day's labor without a single meal, Coleman was famished. He was gratified to see that the hunters had been successful and were lugging back to the village two large carcasses that resembled beef.

Don't forget about the potatoes. There's enough to feed the whole village. These people will love you even more, Coleman's inner voice chimed.

He quickly ran to the potato patch. When he found it, he realized he didn't have anything to carry them back to camp in, but as fortune would have it, Tzeechoe had seen him leave the village and had followed him.

"Tondo, it is not safe to leave the village alone. There are many dangerous creatures out here and it will soon be dark."

"Yes, you are right, my friend, but I needed to get some potatoes for our meal tonight. I do not have anything to carry them in. Can you make a basket?"

Tzeechoe went into the trees and returned a few minutes later with a large woven basket quickly assembled from green leaves and vines. While he was doing that, Coleman began digging up the tubers. He had a nice collection by the time Tzeechoe returned.

"I think we will need another basket," Coleman told him. Tzeechoe scurried back into the trees and returned with another freshly woven basket. By then, he had a collection of fifty or more potatoes. Coleman gave him a thumbs up upon his return and watched as Tzeechoe examined Coleman's thumb for wounds. "Thumbs up means excellent. We now have a beautiful collection of red potatoes. We need to get them into the fire as soon as possible."

The two men quickly returned to the village and caused quite a stir as Tzeechoe handed the potatoes one-by-one to Coleman. He carefully placed each on the coals. He then covered them with more coals, watching as the meat sizzled and the potatoes steamed.

In about an hour, the meal was ready. Coleman carefully extracted one of the potatoes and split it open with his knife. He let Tzeechoe take the first bite and watched as his friend made a face because it was hot and then struggled to swallow. Coleman grabbed a couple more potatoes from the fire and invited the villagers to help themselves as the women began to divide the meat.

Coleman feasted that night in a way he hadn't since he'd arrived. A meal of meat and potatoes lifted his spirits more than anything he'd done or seen since he arrived. "The only thing we are missing is bread," he said to the others.

"What is b´ud?" asked Tzeecha.

"Did you like the potato?"

"I have never tasted anything like it. It taste . . . strange."

"If you like potato, you will love bread."

That evening, Coleman spent some time gazing at the stars and moons. He thought he could make out a constellation that resembled the Big Dipper, but then let out a sigh. *If only.* he mused to himself. *Nothing up there is in the right place.* He took a deep breath and felt his exhaustion. It had been another tiring day, but it had been a good day. No need to think about how to get home. He had helped the village and had introduced them to a new food source. Now, if he could only convince them to eat more meals in a day. The children, in particular, needed the additional nourishment. That was his next challenge. When he got back to Tzeechoe's lodge, he went straight to bed and was soon fast asleep.

CHAPTER 10

FULL BELLIES

Coleman awoke after dawn and found Atura already busy with her daily duties. He had always considered himself to be an early riser, but lately, he found himself waking well after the day had begun. As he pondered this, he felt a hunger pang.

"I am hungry. Would anyone like some breakfast this morning?" he asked the others.

"What is b´ug-fest?" Atura wondered.

"It is a morning meal. Food helps you get started when the day begins," Coleman advised.

She gave him another look and chided, "You must wait until the hunters return."

"Not this morning. I am going to get some potatoes. Who would like one?" Atura simply scowled because she hated their taste and refused to eat them.

It was then he noticed that Tzeechoe and Tzeecha were still under their furry blanket. *That's unusual*, he thought. "Tzeechoe, are you awake?"

Tzeechoe stirred and groaned. In a labored tone, he responded, "Tondo, I don't feel well; I'm sick. Tzeecha is sick, too."

"What is the matter?" Coleman asked.

"My stomach hurts and so does Tzeecha's."

"Atura, see if there is anything you can do for them. I will fetch Taahso."

Coleman exited the lodge and briskly stepped toward Taahso's newly constructed home. Before he got there, the village shaman came out of a different hut and stormed over to Coleman, obviously upset and angry.

Coleman warily greeted him, "Good morning, Taahso. Tzeechoe and Tzeecha need your help. They are sick."

"Tondo, what have you done? I've been summoned throughout the night by sick brothers and sisters. Every one of them ate your bot´ay-tzo. You've poisoned half the village!"

"That cannot be. I ate twice as many potatoes as anyone else did. I feel fine. How bad is the sickness? Will they recover?"

"I have seen the effects of bad food before. It is like that. Pray to the gods everyone survives, especially the little ones. I will go to Tzeechoe now." Taahso turned and rushed toward Tzeechoe's lodge.

Coleman hung his head in shame. He was expecting to increase his status in the tribe, adding to his esteem as the Sutro P´oez. "Now, look what you have done," he grumbled. *Will I also get sick?* he wondered. Coleman went to the village fire and collected the remaining potatoes and put them in one of Tzeechoe's leafy baskets. Fortunately, many villagers didn't like them and had abstained. Coleman dumped the remaining potatoes in the village latrine.

Several days passed before the stricken villagers recovered. During this time, Coleman laid low, spending most of his time in and around Tzeechoe's lodge, doing what he could to help his hosts in their recovery. It remained a mystery to him why the villagers became ill and he hadn't. *Could there be a difference in mine and the villagers' physiology?* he wondered.

Several more days passed. The day after Coleman's hunt team had performed their duty and fed the village, Coleman was relaxing near Tzeechoe's lodge watching his host, now fully recovered, weave an intricate design in a sturdy wicker and reed basket. The shout of the day's returning hunters was heard, so Coleman and Tzeechoe quickly jogged to the village entrance to see what they had brought. It was quickly learned that one of the hunters, Dubo, had been killed. The hunting party had been stalking a tuntro and her youngling, creatures that Coleman had learned were like giant water buffalo. The beast turned and charged the hunters. Poor Dubo slipped in the mud and was gored. The hunters had managed to kill the creature and its young, but Dubo died shortly afterward. Coleman found Dubo's wife and three young sons sprawled across his bloody and lifeless body, wailing in grief and horror.

Tzeechoe turned to Coleman and asked, "Tondo, is there anything you can do to save him like you did Chashutzo?"

Coleman kneeled and felt for Dubo's pulse. He couldn't find one. He examined the gaping wound in Dubo's torso and realized that the wound had done mortal damage to the young man's internal organs. He looked into the pleading eyes of the young woman, but there was nothing he could do. He felt helpless as he reached out to her and cradled her in his arms. Sadness welled in his eyes as he felt Duba convulse in spasms of emotional pain and suffering.

Taahso and the chief soon arrived and surveyed the situation. Coleman noticed when Taahso saw Dubo's lifeless body and the wound, a look of panic crossed his face. He started breathing heavily, but slowly regained his composure. When the chief and Taahso realized there was nothing that could be done, they turned and walked away without uttering a word. Coleman looked to Atura and Tzeecha and motioned for them to come and comfort the woman and her children. At first, they were reluctant, but when Tzeechoe motioned for his wife to do as Coleman requested, she acted and Atura quickly followed. Coleman stood, wiping Dubo's blood from his arms, realizing that it had come from his embrace with the young woman.

"Does this mean what I think it does? Will this woman and her children be banished from the village?" Coleman asked Tzeechoe.

"Yes, it is our way. The man must provide for his family. If he is unable to do so, no one else will," Tzeechoe said.

Coleman felt anger burning at his center. He turned toward the chief and shouted at his retreating figure, "This village is dying! If the beasts do not kill you, you kill each other. This must end!"

Both Taahso and the chief stopped in their tracks and turned around. The chief began to speak. "This woman has no keeper. It is not the village's responsibility to care for her and the children. That is the way it has been done by our fathers and that is the way we will continue to do it." The woman began to wail even louder, frightening her children even more.

Coleman angrily strode to the chief and confronted him.

"This is todo! It is time to put away such an awful tradition. This woman and these children have done nothing to harm the village. The young boys will grow and become hunters, strengthening the village. Sending them and their mother away to die is foolishness. I will not allow it!" Coleman was beginning to lose his temper and the two men he confronted could see in his blazing blue eyes the anger he was only barely able to control. But there was more to his anger; they could feel it like the heat radiating from a fire.

The chief looked into Coleman's eyes and then to the scene of horror and anguish behind him. "Tondo, we will talk. After today's meal, you will come to my lodge." With those stern words, the chief turned and walked away with Taahso still at his side.

The evening meal was taken in an air of solemnity. The loss of a hunter lay heavily upon the entire village. Coleman ate his evening meal while lost in thought. No one disturbed him. In his anger, he had challenged the chief's authority publicly and he knew he had overstepped his bounds. The chief was not used to such insolence by a villager, let alone a visitor.

Even so, Coleman could not abide a village tradition that was so heartless, and to his way of thinking, damaging to the welfare of this small community. As he searched for ways to reason with the village leader, his resolve strengthened. He could not allow an innocent and grieving woman and her young sons to be banished from the village and consigned to what was nothing less than a death sentence.

Leave it alone, his inner voice hissed. *You've already made a fool of yourself. The chief knows best.* He shook his head, trying to chase away the thought. *What is wrong with these people?* he wondered. *Have they no compassion?*

He could see in the expressions of his lodge mates the sadness they felt for the coming loss. Why then didn't they stand up and defend the young woman? Why did he have to encourage the two women to comfort the grieving family? He could tell the feelings were there. It took only a little coaxing to get them involved. All he could do was hope the chief would understand when he said it was time to change yet another misunderstood tradition.

When Coleman finished his meal, he continued staring into the fire. No one said a word, but all eyes were on him as he seemed to project an aura that made his companions tremble. After a while, he stood and turned to Atura, "I want you to come with me when I talk with the chief."

"You can't take me to the chief's lodge. I was not invited," she protested.

"Invited or not, you are coming with me. Would you not be dead if I had not come here?"

"Yes, that is true, but what has that to do with you talking with the chief?"

"Do not you see, Atura? You are a strong woman and you have many things to offer this village. If you had been banished, your life would have been ended and the village would be the worse for it. This tradition of banishment must stop now. It is inhumane and evil," Coleman growled, using the English words.

"I don't understand. What does that mean?"

"It means you let innocent people die and do nothing to stop it. It is from Munnevo. Does it not make you feel bad when people are banished from the village?"

"Yes, but it is the will of the gods. It is what we have done in the past. Our fathers' fathers have taught us these things. We must continue in the ways we have been taught. It is all we have. Without it, the People will perish," she explained.

"Justice may be blind, but she is not stupid. These traditions are todo and must be changed." Tzeechoe grunted in agreement but said nothing.

Coleman left the lodge with Atura trailing after him. He could tell she was fearful and worried, but he didn't care. He expected a battle of wills with the chief and Taahso, so he was preparing himself for a significant confrontation. He was in no mood for Atura's protestations and she knew it. No one had ever seen him like this. It was as if anger radiated from his very core. The villagers he passed stepped aside and stared. No one greeted him nor tried to deter him.

When he arrived at the chief's lodge, he shouted a greeting. The tone of his voice clearly expressed his antagonism. The chief grunted in reply, so Coleman and Atura entered the dwelling. The chief and Taahso were seated on stools and leaned back as if hit by a wave of unseen energy. They were shocked when Atura stepped from behind Coleman.

"What is this woman doing here? I did not invite her," the chief bluntly stated.

"I invited her! I want you to look at her and remember, if not for me, she would be dead. Yet she lives and contributes to the village. She is full of life and, in time, she may bear children and the village will be strengthened." He softened his tone a bit and asked, "Is that not so, Taahso, my friend?"

Taahso looked as though he'd been slapped across the face. His gaze fell upon Atura and Coleman could see his expression soften. The taahso took a deep breath and said, "Our leader is very wise and he knows what is best for the village. We must follow his counsel."

"In my homeland, people would call that a well-practiced and politically neutral answer, Taahso."

Taahso attempted to repeat the words and gave up. "What do your words mean," he stammered.

"It means you are hiding your true feelings. Tell me, Taahso, shall I send Atura into the night and let some creature kill her?" Coleman could see that the chief was perplexed by this confrontation. He was planning to chastise the visitor, but the table had been turned, and the visitor was chastising them. "Well, Taahso, what does your heart say?"

Taahso's discomfort grew and he shifted on his stool. Finally, he gathered his composure and spoke from the heart. "I will talk with you later concerning Atura," he said. The chief turned and stared at Taahso. Atura's head snapped back as she heard the words pass Taahso's lips. Coleman watched as Atura's shocked expression changed to a broad smile of joy. By the reaction of the others, he assumed Taahso had just offered a proposal of marriage or something akin to it.

Finally, Coleman continued. "Go on. What were you about to say?"

"It is true; this woman would be dead. Yet she has many things to offer." Taahso turned his head and spoke to the chief. "Tondo has given us good counsel in the past. We should reconsider our interpretation of the traditions."

"He poisoned half the village. Was that wise?" the chief growled.

"He ate more bot´ay-tzo than anyone and didn't get sick. He has taah. He could be a god," Taahso suggested, with a bit of fear in his voice.

"Maybe I should turn the leadership of the village over to this supposed god, then," the chief mused to Taahso. "It seems I am not needed in these affairs anymore."

Coleman's inner voice whispered, *They think you're a god. Now's your chance. You're an educated man; smarter, tougher, and more capable than any of these savages. Take over the tribe and raise them up. Make something of them. Make them better than they are now. You know you can do it.*

Coleman glared at the chief and challenged, "If that is what it takes to save Duba and her children, then that is what I will do."

The chief glared at Tondo. He did not immediately respond but waited and calmed himself before replying to the visitor's threat. "I will give you time to rethink your words, Tondo. I sense the influence of the Tempter is upon you. Leave my lodge and pray to the gods of Munnari. We will continue after you have pondered your challenge. Now, go!" the chief ordered.

Are you going to let that old fool speak to you like that? Coleman's inner voice growled. *Grab him by the neck. Put fear into his heart.*

Then, he'll respect you. Coleman raised his right arm, ready to follow through when he realized what was happening. He closed his fist, turned and walked out. Atura followed him, her emotions jumbled.

Coleman tromped through the darkness, his anger barely under control. Atura followed a couple of steps behind, afraid to say a word to the big man whose anger she could literally feel. *What was he? How dare he challenge the chief? Taahso thinks he may be a god,* she thought. A smile slowly crept across her face. *Taahso will speak to Tondo about me. That is thrilling.*

"Atura," Coleman snapped as he halted, "I'm going to stay out for a while. You may return to the lodge." Atura nodded and walked past him.

He stood staring into the night sky, not really observing anything in the heavens. His mind was reeling.

"Why did I challenge the chief's position?" he wondered aloud.

You deserved it. You know more than that old man does, his inner voice counseled.

"That's foolishness. The last thing I want is to be tied down to this place."

Remember the vision. You must help these people. Something awful is going to happen. It's up to you to save them.

"Yes, but I'm not going to become their chief, and certainly not their god."

You must take over the tribe or poor Duba and her boys will die.

Coleman ran his fingers through his long hair like a comb. "That's not going to happen. I'll take care of her and the boys myself if I must."

That's foolish. You'd be tied down and stuck here. You don't want that. There's a big world out there to explore.

"I'll care for them until the oldest boy can hunt."

Don't be a fool. When you become their god, you'll be able to do whatever you want. Saving Duba is only the beginning, and you'd be able to leave anytime you wish.

Coleman gave an audible sigh. "Stop thinking like that. What's wrong with me?" He'd had enough. It was like his thoughts were trying to coerce him into becoming someone else. He shuddered and returned to Tzeechoe's lodge.

He entered the dwelling and, in the dim light of the fire, noticed the worried faces staring back at him. "It is alright; I will apologize to the chief and ask him to forgive me. I should not have challenged him, but I will not allow Duba to be banished. I will become her keeper. Tomorrow evening, I will talk to the chief, again."

Tzeecha smiled broadly, but Tzeechoe looked perplexed. "What will you do with Atura?" he wondered.

"I will speak with Taahso. He has something he wishes to say to me."

"What is this you say?" Tzeechoe wondered as all eyes fell upon Atura.

"We will see after Tondo meets with him," Atura answered, attempting to stifle a smile.

The following morning, Coleman asked Tzeechoe to relay a request that the visitor would like to meet with the chief in his home that evening. The chief acquiesced. After the evening meal, Coleman went to the chief's lodge and announced his presence respectfully. After a short delay, he was allowed to enter. He found the chief and Taahso sitting on stools.

"Have you considered my counsel?" the chief began. "Have you prayed to the gods of Munnari?"

"No, I have not, but I have come to express my regrets for what I said last night. I was wrong and it will not happen again."

The chief crossed his arms over his chest and thought for a few moments before responding. "Tondo, I cannot force you to pray, and I think you should, but I do accept your apology. I can see it comes from the heart." Coleman nodded his thanks and bowed in submission. "Tondo, you don't know our ways. Yet, you do sometimes bring wise counsel. Taahso and I know you have a good heart. You must learn to listen to the Whisperer and ignore the promptings of the Tempter." Coleman simply nodded and said nothing; he didn't want to comment on the village religion. "Is there anything else you wish to say?" the chief asked.

Coleman absentmindedly cleared his throat. "Yes, we still have the issue of Duba and the boys. I will not let them die. I will become their keeper until the oldest boy can hunt."

"And will you be the keeper of all future women and children who face the same tragedy?" the chief asked.

"If I must, I will. I still think this awful tradition of banishing a grief-stricken family is todo. Anyway, hunting is less dangerous now that the gorga is dead."

"Tondo, you may not have spent the night in prayer, but I have. I believe that you are a messenger from the gods. You are not one of them, but we will give heed to your words. We will not banish Duba and her sons. The village will feed them. We will learn if that is the better way. We will all be their keeper," the chief decreed. Coleman smiled and bowed again.

The chief studied the visitor's face. "Do you have more to say?" he finally asked.

"Yes, I think you should send out all the hunting parties each day. Gather more food from the trees and bushes. Then, we can store some of what is collected for hard times. There are many more things the village can do. Now that the gorga is dead, the risk for everyone is lessened."

"I will think on your words, Tondo," the chief said in a non-committal tone.

Coleman was not finished, so he continued, "Also, the village should have at least two meals a day. We could eat an early one and one later in the day, as usual. The children need more food and should eat more often. In time, they could even eat three or four times a day. They need more food to grow strong and healthy."

"You have given me much to think about," the chief said with obvious annoyance.

Coleman realized he had pushed the chief to the limit. He had willingly humbled himself, accepting the chief's chastening, but change needed to be slow or it might not happen. He would have to be satisfied with the possibility that he may have provided the village with a brighter future.

Good going, he thought. *You're now a messenger from the gods. You can use that to your benefit.*

Late in the evening, the word went out to all the tusk-men that the chief wanted to meet with them for a special council in the great lodge after tomorrow's meal. Only tusk-men were invited, which now included Coleman with the gorga tooth hanging from his neck. Tzeechoe advised him that the invitation was a great honor.

Chashutzo, a tusk-man, protested Coleman's insistence that he remain in his lodge and heal. Taahso finally had to intervene and ordered him to follow the visitor's counsel. He reluctantly submitted and pouted the remainder of the evening, much to Chashutza's dismay.

Coleman and Taahso made their way to the great lodge and entered. The chief was sitting on his stool in front of the tusk-men, a fire burning in the pit. The chief motioned with his arm, indicating he wanted Coleman to take his place on the chief's left side. Coleman took the designated seat and sat on the ground mat next to the chief. Taahso sat on a stool to the chief's right and crossed his arms over his chest.

The village leader stood and began to speak, "My brothers, the gorga is dead, and we have been freed from its dread. Our fathers chose to use large hunting parties to feed the village and protect the hunters. We now can hunt in smaller groups. We can send out more men and bring back more food. If we do this, we can eat twice a day and gain strength from it. The hunters must go out every day to make this possible, and there are still great dangers to be faced. What think you, my brothers?"

None of the tusk-men said anything at first. They looked at each other in silence and after several seconds, Dondi, the senior tusk-man, stood and spoke. "Sometimes, my children tell me they are hungry even after they have eaten. If we have no tree food to give them, they cry. I want to have enough food so my children will cry no more for food."

Several tusk-men grunted in agreement. Another tusk-man stood. "There are still many dangers in the wilderness. If we send out more hunters, there is a greater chance that hunters will die, and we all know what that means for their families."

Taahso stood, "Our ancestors began the law of banishment in the days when we couldn't help one another; in the days of our suffering. Now that the gorga is no more, we have already seen that hunting has improved. It is time to change our traditions. Your families will not suffer because you seek to help the village. We will all be their keepers." With Taahso's endorsement of the new plan, all the tusk-men grunted their approval.

The chief stood and said, "Let me see your choice." All ten of the present tusk-men raised their tusks with the tip pointing up. Coleman remained seated, simply watching and listening. The chief turned and looked down at him, waiting. Coleman quickly realized he had a vote in this matter, too, and he lifted the gorga tooth with its point turned upward. "Then it is decided. A new time is upon us and, with the help of the gods, we will increase in strength. I want Taahso and Tondo to go to Dubo's lodge and tell Duba and her children of our decision. Tell them, from now on all the People will help them. After that, I want you to plan the hunting parties.

I want the rest of you to pass the word to the People. Let them know that no one will be banished unless they transgress the Batru Code."

The tusk-men stood in unison and began shouting their affirmation. Coleman also stood and smiled broadly. *These poor people have had a huge burden lifted from their shoulders. They are ready to help each other and escape the bonds of the past.* He held high hopes for their future. He could see himself showing them many ways to improve their lives. Although he had limited skills when it came to the hunter-gatherer lifestyle, he knew enough to get them started on the right foot.

Excellent! The chief and Taahso trust you. Soon, the whole village will follow your every wish, Coleman's inner voice harped.

Taahso and Coleman went directly to Dubo's lodge and entered without warning. Duba shrieked in terror, fearing the worse at the sudden intrusion. Her three young sons jumped from their beds and clutched their mother's legs. Coleman reached out to her and attempted to ease her fears, while Taahso told her of the council's decision. As Taahso continued his explanation, tears welled in Duba's eyes and Coleman could feel her legs lose their strength. He gripped her tightly and kept her from falling to the ground. She quickly regained her strength and slowly composed herself.

Coleman could see the recent loss of her husband and the burden of dread that she had suffered under since her husband's death was more than the poor woman could bear. At least now she would no longer fear for her life and the lives of her children. He could not remove the terrible hole that had been seared through her life, but at least she would now have time to recover and raise her children in the legacy of their father.

After comforting Duba for a few more minutes, Taahso and Coleman exited and found the entire village surrounding Dubo's home. The people began to sing, and soon Duba and the children stepped through the doorway and joined in the singing. It was entirely clear to Coleman that this course of action had been the correct one. He felt justified and proud of what he had accomplished. He joined in the singing although he did not know the words. He only hummed the tune while he stared at the night sky and watched the blue moon slowly eclipsing the red moon.

Long after the villagers had left and gone to their homes, Coleman remained and watched the eclipse. It had become obvious to him that the blue and red moons orbited each other as they circled the planet. Therefore, he reasoned, an eclipse by one or the other was not that uncommon an event.

Tzeechoe approached and stood beside him, also watching the two moons. "This is an excellent omen. It is said, when the good moon eats the evil moon, good has more power over the land of the Batru."

"I enjoy watching the moons in their orbits. I am used to only one moon, but to have three is a real delight."

"Tondo, when you use godspeak words, I cannot understand what you say."

"Godspeak? What is that?" Coleman asked.

"Our leader says you are the Messenger sent by the Great Batru. Your other tongue must be godspeak," Tzeechoe reasoned.

Coleman watched as the red moon slowly began to reveal itself from behind the blue moon. He figured a long explanation of the orbits of the moons and planet would be more than

Tzeechoe bargained for. How could he explain such things to his friend? Coleman had no desire to sully the moment. He was enjoying the spectacle and only wanted to observe.

When the red moon was in full view again, Coleman told his friend he needed to talk with Taahso about an urgent matter. He turned and walked to the shaman's new lodge as Tzeechoe returned to his. Coleman pondered the important duty the chief had charged them with; a task which needed to be addressed as soon as possible. Coleman was not one to dawdle, so off to work he headed.

"Taahso, may I enter?"

"Yes, Tondo, you may," came Taahso's quick reply.

"Why do we need to choose hunting parties? Why cannot the men decide whom they want to hunt with?" Coleman asked.

"Our fathers guided us in this way. The taahso decides which men are in the hunting parties. It is our tradition."

"I think we should let the men choose their own groups. Let them think for themselves," Coleman advised.

"Again, you want change. I am having a hard time adjusting and I am not alone."

"The People seem to welcome the changes. I think the traditions have served you well in the past, but they have also restricted the People and kept them from reaching their full potential. Give the People freedom to choose and they will surprise you with their ability to make good choices that serve the village well. They will come up with many new ideas and solutions to problems that neither one of us can even imagine," Coleman counseled.

"Tondo, are all your people wise? Our people know the traditions, but we struggle, nevertheless. Are your people gods that do not err?"

"They are not gods. Some are wise and some are not. When given the opportunity, all men will struggle to do what they can with what they have. It makes no difference if they are Batru or visitors."

Taahso thought for a few moments, then said, "I will tell the hunters in the morning what your counsel is. We will then decide together what is to be done. I would like you to be there with me."

"I will be there."

"Before you go, I wish to talk to you about . . ." Taahso paused as he worked up enough courage to go on.

"Yes, what is it, Taahso?" Coleman teased.

"I must speak with you tomorrow night. I will see you in Tzeechoe's lodge. I must tell you of my intentions."

It was all Coleman could do to contain himself. He wanted to jump for joy and high-five Taahso, but he didn't. He only lowered his head and said in a stern voice, "I see. I will speak with you then."

Taahso grunted, ending their conversation. Coleman exited the hut and returned to Tzeechoe's lodge. When he entered, he found the others waiting for him with bated breath. He looked into each face and stifled a smile. He slowly and deliberately walked to the waterskin hanging on a lodge pole, took it down, uncapped it, and enjoyed a long draft. He spied Atura anxiously waiting. She was watching his every move, wanting him to speak, yet afraid of what might be said.

Finally, after the tension in the room had reached an unbearable climax, he spoke. "Taahso will come here and speak with me tomorrow night. Do any of you have the slightest idea why?"

Tzeechoe grunted and slapped his chest. Tzeecha let loose with the village women's wavering shriek, and Atura blushed.

"I bet he wants some more habaga. What do you think, Atura?"

"I think you tease me. I think you are todo," she quipped.

Coleman and the others laughed. "Maybe I am todo. Maybe I will get lost in the wilderness tomorrow. Maybe I will stay out all night and watch the moons." Atura's eyes widened. Coleman sat beside Atura and put his arm around her shoulders. "Maybe I will meet with Taahso and find out what he really wants." Atura blushed even more and attempted to hide her smile.

Coleman awoke as Tzeechoe shook his shoulder. "It is time to meet with the other hunters," he said, a bit annoyed. Coleman rubbed the sleep from his eyes and arose. "The light of day will soon be upon us. It is time to find food for the village. Let us hurry or we'll be late," Tzeechoe scolded as the two men rushed to the center of the village.

They found the other hunters gathered in a circle around

the chief and Taahso. The others made room for the two late arrivals as Taahso began speaking.

"My brothers, the gorga no longer threatens us. There is not a need to hunt in large parties anymore, thanks to Tondo. Starting today, we will hunt in smaller groups and more often. Our families will have more to eat and our children will no longer cry for food." The men in the circle grunted in satisfaction. Taahso continued, "You are to choose four or five hunters from your hunting party and they will hunt today. The remaining hunters will hunt tomorrow. Those who don't hunt today will go out and find other food from the plants and trees. This is how it will be done from now on."

The men nodded their heads in agreement and waited for further instructions as the chief began to speak. "Now, select your hunting parties and do your duty. Bring back what you find as soon as you can. We will have our first meal when p´atezas is at its height. We will have a second meal at the end of the day, as usual. Now, go in haste, my brothers."

The men milled around for a while as hunt leaders took charge and divided their teams into the most efficient groups. Soon, parties of four and five hunters had been selected, were blessed by Taahso, and disappeared into the jungle. Because of Chashutzo's injury, Coleman, the bearer of the famed gorga fang, became the de facto leader of his group. He oversaw the discussion as the other eight men chose the best groupings. He could tell Ayascho was not pleased with the changes taking place.

"This man is evil. His influence is from the Tempter. Cast him out before all is lost," Ayascho shouted. The other men let him rant but ignored his protests. It was apparent to Coleman he had won the confidence of all the other men in his hunting party.

When all was decided, there were five in his group. Tzeechoe was the spearman and bolo-man. Icee was lead spearman. Namad was the tracker. And Shadi was the scent-man. Coleman was their leader and a club-man. The others were to search for edible plant food in the jungle. After receiving their blessings, the two teams marched off in different directions, disappearing into the thick underbrush.

Namad seemed to be following indistinct tracks when he stopped and kneeled. "A pack of betzoes came through this area early today," he finally said.

"What is a betzoe?" Coleman whispered to Tzeechoe.

"They are four-legged animals whose heads are as high as a man's. They have sharp teeth and hunt in packs. The males have a bony plate on their heads. The males knock down the prey and the females kill it. We must be cautious," Tzeechoe explained.

"How many do you think there are?" he asked Namad.

"I can see at least four different sets of tracks. They go off in that direction," Namad said as he pointed to a cluster of large boulders about one-hundred yards away.

The men shifted into their attack formation with Namad in the lead; Tzeechoe and Icee to either side; Shadi and Coleman brought up the rear. The men stealthily moved forward from downwind. Soon, they could hear growls and yips coming from the boulder-studded area. Coleman watched as the two spearmen silently stepped closer to the boulders, their spears set in the levers ready for launching. Quickly and without a signal, both men hurled their spears and prepared for a second throw. Shadi charged forward with Coleman closely on his heels. The club-men burst past the spearmen just as they let their spears loose again and watched as they found their marks on two more large creatures. There was little work for the club-men to do because of the deadly effects of Tzeechoe's and Icee's aim.

Coleman found their spears sticking out of four huge black animals. They were like mastiffs, and the males' heads had a boney headplate. Shadi went around and gave each one a coup de grace. Yips were heard coming from the boulders. Coleman ran to see what was making the noise. He found two very young pups, about four or five weeks old, hidden under a stone ledge. He pulled one out and dropped it behind himself and went for the other one. As he pulled out the second pup, Shadi dashed to Coleman's side and struck the first pup a killing blow.

"Stop!" Coleman shouted, but it was too late. The young betzoe was dead. Coleman held the remaining pup tightly against his chest and protected it. "Do not strike this one. I will keep it and raise it," he told the others.

"The young ones are the best to eat. They have tender meat and taste good," Tzeechoe advised.

"I will keep this one as a pet," Coleman said.

"What is that?" Tzeechoe asked as the other men drew near.

"A pet is an animal friend. It will help me hunt when it grows up," Coleman instructed.

"Tondo, you do strange things. I think this p´ut will try to eat you when it grows up," Shadi warned.

"We will see, my friend, we will see," Coleman said.

The men then skinned the dead betzoes and made baskets for their entrails. Coleman attempted to make a basket for carrying the pup but failed miserably. Tzeechoe finally came to his aid and finished a leafy one with shoulder straps in minutes. The men then gathered up the various skins and parts and carried them back to the village.

They arrived a little before midday, just in time to add the betzoe meat to the cooking fire for the first meal of the day. Two other groups had already returned and it looked like the village would have quite a feast. When Coleman reached into his basket and pulled out the betzoe puppy, every child within sight ran to his side and wanted to see what he had. Some of the parents pulled their children away, fearing they would be attacked. Quickly, they realized the pup was too small to hurt anyone and appeared to be frightened out of its wits. Coleman held the puppy against his chest and let the bolder children touch it.

After each child who wanted had a turn, he put the pup back in the basket, placed the basket on his back, and wore it like a backpack. He then talked for a while with the men of the other hunting teams and traded stories about the day's hunts. While so engaged, many teams of gatherers returned to the village with baskets full of food pods from the trees and bushes.

When Coleman had finished conversing with the others, he went to Tzeechoe's lodge and showed the pup to Tzeecha and Atura. Tzeecha hugged the little creature while Atura wondered aloud why anyone would keep it alive.

"It is a beast from the trees. It will grow big and become a threat. It is dangerous," she warned.

"If I cannot teach it to be good, I will kill it myself," he told them. He asked Tzeecha to watch the little betzoe while he checked on Chashutzo. He returned a little later and gave a thumbs up to Tzeechoe. The women looked a bit confused, so Tzeechoe told them that it meant Chashutzo was doing well. The revelation brought smiles to their faces.

The midday meal was shared around the communal fire. About a half-dozen hunting teams and a couple of gathering teams had yet to return, so their families saved a portion of the food for their men to eat upon their return. It was evident the meal was very welcome by the villagers. The chief joined the party and spoke with many of the families, moving from group to group like a host at a social gathering. Coleman could tell he was checking to learn how the villagers felt about the new way of doing things.

As Coleman waited for the other teams to return. He squinted at p´atezas, this world's sun. It was the first time he had stopped to examine it closely. To Coleman, it appeared to have a red tint. Could it be the planet's atmosphere causing an illusion? Earth's sun appeared in many colors: white, yellow, orange, and red. Coleman knew that the sun was a white dwarf star. *Could p´atezas be a red dwarf?* It was another mystery to the visitor.

Coleman had a nagging fear in the back of his mind as he worried about the hunters and gatherers still in the wild. He hoped everyone would return safely whether they succeeded in their tasks or not. He closed his eyes and offered a silent prayer for the welfare of the remaining hunters. As the shadows grew longer, the other teams trickled back to the village. It was late in the day by the time the last hunting party returned. Every team had returned with food. Coleman was relieved that no hunter or gatherer was injured. The day had been a great success. The people were obviously happy and the children were well fed. In fact, they had full bellies for the first time in a long time. He took a few scraps of meat and fed them to the betzoe pup as many children watched. He let them take turns holding the puppy and watched as their parents observed with worried expressions. They soon relaxed when they saw the pup licking the faces of the children as they giggled and laughed.

You've overcome the potato incident. The People love you; they revere you. It won't be long before they worship you. Coleman shook his head, attempting to chase away such arrogant thoughts, nevertheless, he was feeling very self-satisfied with his efforts to date.

CHAPTER 11

STRANGE POWERS STIRRING

The boy, Nevesant, and his odd-looking companion had become close friends during the many days they had been together. Upon Nevesant's suggestion, Tangundo had taken to wearing a kerchief across his face to hide his growing beard. The outsider could tell it made Nevesant more comfortable for the boy still was not fully accepting of his hairy face.

The two had built a relatively comfortable lean-to that was closed on three sides. The boy had managed to steal a hand ax from a farmer and Tangundo had put it to good use in designing and building their makeshift home. Fair-sized logs were used, making the structure semi-permanent and requiring many days of effort. During the project, Tangundo began learning Nevesant's strange language, and by the time the lean-to was completed, the outsider could communicate well enough to convey his points.

Nevesant avoided his home hamlet most of the time because of what the townsfolk had done to his outsider friend, the only friend he had. They had driven the stranger into the mist, expecting him to die there, but he hadn't, much to Nevesant's surprise. The boy's curiosity drove him to badger Tangundo with questions about what lurked inside the mist, but the outsider had never given him a clear answer. Nevesant quit asking about it when his incessant questions drove Tangundo into a fury. The outsider threatened to thrash the boy if he didn't stop pestering him about it.

The two survived by hunting small animals. Tangundo had become proficient with a sling he had made and a spear he had fashioned from hardwood. Nevesant continued to set snares. Tangundo had also become skilled at spearing fish. At first, Nevesant had warned him not to stand in the water, but the outsider either didn't understand or only scoffed at the boy's warning. Consequently, he received a nasty bite on his left leg and quickly scrambled out of the water. He had since learned that every nearby body of water in the area that was able to support fish also contained creatures with sharp teeth.

Occasionally, when hunting went poorly, Nevesant would disappear, returning at night with something he had pilfered from a farm or even from the town. It was risky, and he knew the consequences of being caught would be dire, but the choice was between taking the risk or facing a night of hunger pangs. Tangundo had warned the boy that eventually someone was going to come looking for him.

Tangundo had failed in his hunt and Nevesant's snare was empty. Late in the afternoon, Nevesant slipped away, returning that night with a couple of feathered creatures he'd snatched from a farmer's coop. Man and boy ate late and slept late the next day. The two had just arisen from their beds, a few blankets the boy had illicitly appropriated long ago, and were sitting on logs when three men burst into their camp.

"Stay where you are, Creeper!" one of the men ordered as he brandished his quarterstaff menacingly. "Who are you?"

the intruder growled at the tall Tangundo. He didn't answer. "Why is your face covered? You been helping this little thief steal from me?"

"Look!" another of the trio said, pointing to the hand ax protruding from a nearby log.

The man with the quarterstaff quickly glanced at it and when he looked back at Nevesant, his eyes filled with hate. "That's mine! I'm tired of your thieving ways, Creeper. I'm taking you back to Purrant Grazius. He'll know what to do with you," the man threatened.

"No, I won't go!" Nevesant cried.

"Yes, you will, and it will be the end for you," the man chuckled.

"Who be Purrant Grazius, and what he do with boy?" Tangundo haltingly asked.

"He rules this province and reports to King Ben-do-teg. The purrant has already warned the boy that if he didn't change his ways, he'd be given to the slave traders. Who are you?"

"Tangundo."

"Remove that scarf and let me see your face," the man ordered. Tangundo didn't move. "Gund, take the boy. Fino, remove the man's kerchief," the man with the quarterstaff ordered.

As the two men advanced, Nevesant cried, "No!" and moved behind Tangundo. The outsider pushed Gund back, and that started a struggle between Tangundo, Gund, and Fino. Tangundo was taller and stronger than either of the other two men, and he was getting the better of them when the third intruder's quarterstaff crashed down on the outsider's back, stunning him and causing him to cry out in pain. In the ensuing scuffle, Tangundo's face was revealed, causing the three intruders to recoil in surprise and fear.

"By the gods, it's the crazed beast! The one we drove into the mist!" Fino shouted.

The man with the quarterstaff quickly recovered and grabbed the boy. The other two men jumped on the outsider, attempting to subdue him. Tangundo roared in anger and began glowing with a purple aura. Gund and Fino screamed in pain as Nevesant and his captor tried to shield themselves from the burning purple rays. Tangundo pounded his fists into Gund and Fino until the two were no longer able to fight back. He then turned on the one holding Nevesant. The boy broke free of the man's grip and dashed into the brush. The intruder attempted to defend himself with his quarterstaff, but he was too frightened to mount much of a defense. Tangundo tore into him as he had the other two, leaving him bloody and nearly unconscious.

When the noises coming from the camp ended, Nevesant cautiously returned and looked around. The three intruders were vanquished and Tangundo stood over their bleeding bodies. The outsider's aura was fading but still clearly visible.

"Tangundo, what did you do? Are you one of the gods?" the boy asked nervously. The outsider didn't answer. He simply stood, examining his arms and body as the purple aura slowly faded away. "You're a god!" Nevesant exclaimed. Then he dropped to his knees and prostrated himself before the outsider. "Please master, let me serve you," the boy offered.

The outsider thought for a few moments before responding.

"Alright, Nevesant. I want you tie hands and feet," Tangundo ordered, pointing at the intruders.

"Yes master, but what shall I use to tie them?"

"Use what they got."

"Yes, master."

Nevesant did as he was commanded. Tangundo sat on a log and watched the boy complete his task. Ever since being driven into the mist and experiencing the wonder and horror dwelling there, he had felt different. It was as though strange powers were stirring within his core. And now, these powers had been manifested in his anger and fear. The mist dwellers had spared him and infused him with their strength, but he didn't know what that was until now. The gods of the mist had demanded a payment for empowering him, but it was a ghastly price to pay. Nevertheless, he wanted more of this incredible power. He stared at the three intruders, wondering what he should do with them.

As he sat contemplating, he felt an unseen presence enter the camp and envelope him. It whispered enticing things and stroked his ego. It reminded him of how he easily defeated the three intruders and how the boy now revered him as a god. This was only the beginning, he was told. He was tempted with promises of power, fame, and fortune, and as the quiet voice in his head hissed its message, a smile slowly crept across his face. The thought of becoming someone of high stature had never before entered into his thinking, but now, because of this new power, he could become whatever he wished.

His decision—his choice—having been made, the unseen

entity departed. Nevesant went to the outsider and waited. "They hope I die in mist. Now, I send them into mist," Tangundo said with an evil smile.

Nevesant grimaced. "You are the only one I know who has ever returned after entering. What lives there?" the boy dared to ask.

"You not want see, Nevesant. They horrible, powerful. I must feed them."

"With what are they to be fed?" the boy asked. The outsider didn't respond, but his cold red eyes shifted to the three intruders lying in the dirt.

CHAPTER 12

CITY OF THE ANCIENTS

At the Batru village, the evening meal was taken to the lodges as usual. There was a huge selection of foods from which to choose. The women smiled and laughed as they made their selections. Tzeechoe and Coleman waited near the hut's entrance for their women to return with the food they had chosen. The betzoe pup was asleep on Coleman's foot. Soon, the women arrived and the four ate a substantial meal in the dwindling twilight. Coleman dangled a piece of cooked meat in front of the sleeping pup, which caused it to awaken and snatch the food, swallowing it in one gulp. Coleman continued feeding the pup until its belly bulged. Darkness had fallen by the time they finished, and in the glow of the silvery moon they could see Taahso, dressed in all his regalia, heading their way. Quickly, the women retreated into the lodge while the men waited to greet him.

"Good evening, Taahso. I greet you with friendship. What brings you here?" Tzeechoe knowingly chimed.

"I will speak with Tondo on a most important matter," he replied.

"Then we will discuss it in my home. Please enter," Tzeechoe continued.

The three men entered the dwelling and Coleman put the

pup in its basket. They found the women sitting a respectful distance from the central fire. Tzeecha wore a big smile and it was evident Atura was barely able to contain her excitement. The men sat and chatted for a few minutes discussing the affairs of the day. Finally, much to the relief of the women, Taahso slapped his knees, turned to Coleman, and said in a formal tone, "Atura has caught my eye. I would like your blessing to talk with her more often."

Tzeechoe had taught Coleman the correct procedure to follow in this matter and he said, "Are your intentions honorable?"

"I only wish to honor your family. May I speak with Atura?" Taahso requested.

Coleman continued with his portion of the protocol. "You are to honor my daughter. Are you an honorable man, Taahso?" Coleman forcefully asked, a bit uncomfortable with the term daughter, but the ritual had to be repeated in this manner.

"I will honor your daughter as I honor you," Taahso said as he bowed.

"I know you to be an honorable man, Taahso. You have my blessing to speak with Atura. I will ask Tzeecha to be the observer of these meetings," and he bowed to Taahso.

All eyes turned to Tzeecha. She bowed and said, "It is an honor for me to serve these two." Taahso, Tzeechoe, Atura, and Coleman then bowed to her.

"Tondo, I want to speak with Atura this evening. Do I have your blessing?" Taahso continued in his formal tone.

"Yes, you have my blessing, but do not make the observer late for bed," Coleman formally answered.

That ended the dialog and Taahso retired from the lodge with Atura and Tzeecha following closely behind. When he could no longer hear the trio's footsteps, Coleman leaned back and smiled broadly, clasping his hands behind his head. "Tzeechoe, give me high-five!" he erupted. Tzeechoe stared at Coleman, bewildered at what he had just said. Coleman then raised Tzeechoe's right arm and slapped their hands together. "High-five, my friend. It means everything went very well."

Tzeechoe raised his left arm and shouted, "Hi-feeva! Everything went very well!" They high-fived each other again and Tzeechoe began slapping his chest. Coleman also started slapping his own chest, his skin turning a brilliant red.

An hour or so later, the two women returned. Atura was almost giddy with delight as she glided into the lodge. Coleman smiled as she drifted past him. The sleeping mats were laid out and the four retired for the night. The pup fussed a bit, so Coleman pulled the basket closer. Soon, all was quiet and Coleman fell asleep.

He awakened with Tzeechoe shaking his shoulders. "It is time to meet with the other hunters," he whispered.

He got up quickly and rubbed the sleep from his eyes. He lifted the pup from its basket and took it outside, returning a few minutes later and placing the betzoe back in its basket. The two men trotted off to the center of the village. Most of the hunters were already there. Only a couple of stragglers arrived after Tzeechoe and Coleman. The teams divided into hunters and gatherers, received their blessings from Taahso, then darted into the jungle. Coleman's team chose to look for plant food this day. As soon as they entered the jungle, men began weaving baskets of green leaves and flexible vines as they walked. Tzeechoe took some time to teach Coleman, again, how to quickly assemble and weave a strong basket for temporary use. He was getting better at it, although he was much slower than the others and doubted his finished product would hold up to much abuse. Nevertheless, Tzeechoe slapped him on the back and congratulated him on his attempt while the other men chuckled to themselves.

The group had traveled for about an hour before they began looking for food. Some of the men scanned the trees for fruit pods while the others examined the bushes. Unlike the villagers, Coleman spent his time looking for signs of food growing underground. He noticed the men always looked up, but they never examined the ground. After a while, he found a patch of wild onions and attempted to pull one up but failed. With Tzeechoe's help, they were able to extract one, a bulb nearly as big as a man's fist. Tzeechoe puzzled in wonder at what they had discovered.

Coleman cut a piece and tasted it. "Umm, that is good. It is sweet and has a bit of a bite to it. Have you ever tried one of these before?" Coleman wondered as Tzeechoe examined the round bulb.

"What is it, Tondo?"

"It is onion,"

Tzeechoe sniffed it and immediately his eyes began to water. "Tondo, it's killing me. It hurt my eyes. I can't see."

"Stop it, you big baby. It will not hurt you." Tzeechoe warily looked at the onion, but after his sad experience with rud-bo-t´a-tzo, he refused to taste it. Coleman wasn't about to risk causing another sickness in the village, so he didn't press the issue and only took the one onion with him. He knew he'd enjoy his new discovery. He returned to the potato patch he found days earlier and pulled out a tuber, adding it to his collection.

It was only midmorning and Coleman wanted to look around some more before the team returned to the village. He was sure there were other foods he could find that the Batru had never noticed before. The other men only watched him as he rambled around a large area for another hour but he came up empty-handed. He examined the fruit pods, berries, and nuts his team had collected.

"I think we have done well enough for today. We should return to the village for the midday meal," he finally told them.

By the time they got back to the village, most of the other hunters and gatherers had already returned. It was evident they had hurried back, not wanting to miss the midday meal. Coleman found four green branches and made skewers. Then he cut up some meat, the potato and onion, and made a shish kabob for himself. He made shish kabobs for his three lodge mates, except for theirs' he used meat and fruit from a pink pod the villagers favored called ghim. Coleman didn't like it. It tasted bitter and left an awful aftertaste in his mouth; however, the villagers loved it. He wondered why. As he assembled the four shish kabobs, the other villagers watched him, mesmerized by what he was doing.

When the kabobs were cooked, he gave them to Tzeechoe, Tzeecha, and Atura. The four feasted while the other villagers watched in envy. It wasn't long before several other skewers were fashioned by the villagers and more shish kabobs were created. Coleman smiled to himself as he watched the People breaking away from their self-imposed traditions that had restricted their growth and culture. He felt he had improved their lives and was gratified, but he began to worry about the speed of change, just as Taahso had warned. Maybe he should step back for a while and let things develop naturally from here.

His inner voice counseled, *In time, you can become a master over these people. You can manipulate them and bend them to your will. They are so naive and trusting of you.* He contemplated his thoughts and pondered how to proceed. He literally shook his head, as if coming out of a daydream.

"Did you say something, Tondo?" Tzeechoe asked.

Coleman looked into Tzeechoe's trusting face and replied, "No, my friend, I did not. I was just thinking about how lucky I am to have you and the People as my friends."

Tzeecha left the gathering and returned a few minutes later leading the betzoe pup on a braided leather cord. "It has been crying since early this morning. I think it misses you." Coleman gave the betzoe a good rubbing and then started feeding it scraps of meat.

"When he gets bigger, I will take him on our hunts and see how he does," Coleman told the people near him. He could tell by their skeptical expressions that they doubted the betzoe would be helpful on a hunt. A few quiet comments could be heard wondering if the pup wouldn't eat the gods' messenger. Coleman smiled and continued feeding his new pet.

A warning shout was heard coming from the village entrance. The men grabbed their weapons and rushed to get there. Coleman quickly gave the pup's leash to Atura and dashed off. As he approached the village entrance, he could see in the distance a line of three odd-looking animals marching one behind the other, moving toward the village. As they drew closer, he saw a man riding the lead animal and another man mounted on the last one. The men were dressed in brown robes. The animals appeared to be carrying heavy loads wrapped in tarps well secured by ropes. The creatures reminded Coleman of camels, but as they moved out of the tall grass, he noticed that each creature not only had a pair of legs in front and a pair of legs in the rear, they also had a pair of legs in the center of their bodies. The closer they got, the bigger the creatures appeared. These were huge animals, ten or twelve feet tall at the shoulder.

When the lead mount neared the village entrance, the procession stopped. The lead rider kicked his mount's neck and it kneeled on the ground. The following two creatures did the same. The man in front stepped off his beast and walked toward the gathered villagers. The chief and Taahso stepped

forward and waited for the man to reach them. Coleman could tell the visitor was a bit concerned about the greeting he would receive by the way he scanned the villagers. It was as if he were looking for signs of hostility. His eyes fell upon Coleman and he stopped dead in his tracks and stared. Coleman noted that he was just out of range of a spear's throw.

The man shouted in Coleman's direction, "Are you the chief?" He had a strong accent that caused Coleman to struggle in understanding what he had said.

Coleman quickly walked over to where the chief and Taahso were standing and shouted back, "No, you must talk to this man. He is the leader of the village."

"I have come to trade. May I enter your village?" the stranger called back.

The chief looked to Coleman for advice. "He's difficult to understand. What does he want? Why has he come here?" the chief asked.

"I think he wants to trade with the villagers. He looks harmless. You should let him enter. He may have some things the People can trade for. That is how he makes his living; trading things," Coleman guessed.

"Yes, you may enter," the chief shouted to the foreigner.

The man waved to his companion and walked into the village on foot, leading his beast while the other man stepped off his mount and followed his leader with the other two pack animals right behind him. Their intimidating size made the villagers step back as the animals neared. The ground vibrated as the beasts marched past. The handler, who looked much like the leader, only younger, found an open area near Taahso's lodge and commanded the animals to kneel and rest on their bellies. He began unloading the merchandise.

Coleman examined the leader as he approached the chief. He stood well under six feet tall and was a little overweight. He had brown eyes and dark-brown hair graying at the temples. The light-colored skin of his face and hands was tanned and wrinkled. He wore a brown robe over shirt and trousers. His feet were protected by leather sandals and his legs sported long stockings. The stockings disappeared under pants that came down to mid-calf.

The leader introduced himself. "I am Myron. I've traveled far to trade my goods. Examine my wares and let us trade."

Coleman continued to struggle with the man's accent that required him to listen carefully to decipher his words. The chief cocked his head as if he too were trying to figure out what was just said. Myron could tell that the chief either didn't understand him or had no idea what trading meant. He pulled a brightly polished, palm-sized piece of metal from his robe and held it before the chief. "Let me present you with a gift, Your Highness. I have more and I will trade for hides. You do have hides, don't you?"

The chief took the metal piece and examined it. He turned to Coleman. "What is this thing?"

"It looks like a mirror," Coleman answered. "Look into it." Tondo took the chief's hand and moved the mirror in front of his face.

The chief gasped, "There is someone in this!" He then turned it and examined its back and edges.

"No one is in there, Your Highness. It is your reflection, just like in a pool of water," Myron instructed.

The chief looked into the mirror again and, with a smile, he said to Myron, "You may talk with the People."

"Excellent, Your Highness. You will not regret your decision," he responded.

"As long as you treat the People fairly, there will be no problems. If you try to take advantage of them, I will be very unhappy," Coleman warned.

Myron's head snapped in Coleman's direction and the trader glared at him for a moment. Quickly, his expression changed from anger to amazement as his gaze scanned Coleman's tall, tanned body from head to foot and back again. His gaze became transfixed on Coleman's eyes. "You are not from this tribe, are you? At first, I thought you were a light-skinned native, but you are much different. You have the eyes of Munnari. I have never seen this before. I have traveled all my life, but I have never seen anyone with eyes the color of the blue moon. Tell me, where are you from?"

Coleman pondered the merchant's words for a moment, trying to interpret his message. "I am from a place you have never visited. You could travel all your days and never find it," Coleman told him.

"Ha! A mystery. What brings you here?" Myron asked.

"An accident brought me here and the People saved my life. I am in their debt."

"I knew these were good people," Myron said and turned back to the chief. "Come, Your Highness, and I will show you things you have never even imagined before. These are goods from all over the known world. They can be yours for the right price."

It didn't take Coleman long to realize that Myron was a bit of a con artist, and possibly a rogue, but he would let the man deal his wares so long as he didn't abuse his invitation. He thought it might be an excellent opportunity for himself and the villagers to see that there is a much larger world out there. Also, he wanted to learn from these traders about the world he was on. They had clothes of woven cloth and they wore quality sandals. Coleman thought he saw the hilt of a sword or long knife under Myron's robe. These items told him there were some advanced societies beyond the boundaries of this wilderness he now found himself in.

Myron's companion had already laid several woven blankets on the ground and covered them with merchandise. Coleman took a second look at the young man and noticed he had a tattoo of a circle with an 'X' in it etched into the center of his forehead. Coleman looked down at the merchandise and his eyes were immediately drawn to what appeared to be a shiny brass-colored short sword lying next to its scabbard.

He knelt on one knee and reached for the sword, "May I?" he asked Myron's assistant before he touched it.

"Yes. My master does not mind if you handle the wares. Don't cut yourself; it's very sharp," he warned.

Coleman hefted the piece and moved it in the air. "This is unbelievable! I have never seen a brass sword before and it is in such beautiful condition," Coleman declared to Myron.

"Brazz? I don't know what brazz is, but this fine blade is made of gravetum. The only thing better you can find in all the world is a sutro gravetum blade, but only a very few can afford such a masterpiece. You will find that this one will meet your needs quite well. Its edge will remain sharp under normal use and it will never lose its gleam. You can have this excellent blade for only two-hundred large skins," proclaimed Myron.

"Did you say two-hundred?" Coleman thought he misunderstood the offer. The merchant simply nodded. Myron's proclamation started a murmur of surprise and discontent among the villagers standing nearby. "I am sorry, Myron, but no one in this village has that many large skins to trade," Coleman informed him as he placed the sword back on the blanket. "What about this?" he asked as he pointed to a heavy pot and lid that looked like a Dutch oven.

"Ha, that gravetro pot will only cost you fifty large skins."

Coleman rubbed his head and replied, "I doubt you will make many trades today. The People use their skins for clothes, shelter, and daily needs. We are a poor village."

"I notice your people make wicker baskets. I see one over there and another over there. I might be enticed to part with some of my other goods for them," Myron suggested.

"Tzeechoe is an excellent basket weaver. Maybe he would be willing to trade," Coleman said as he faced his friend. "Is there anything here that catches your eye?" he asked Tzeechoe. Coleman could see he was drawn to the sparkling, beaded necklaces on display on another blanket.

"I think Tzeecha would like that one," Tzeechoe said as he pointed to a multicolored necklace. Coleman thought it was the gaudiest thing he'd ever seen, but he said nothing.

"Ha, I'm sure your Tzeecha would love to possess such a beautiful trinket. What do you have in trade?" Myron asked.

"The basket you finished a couple of days ago, are you willing to give it to Myron for the necklace?" Coleman asked Tzeechoe.

"Yes," Tzeechoe replied and trotted off to his lodge. A few minutes later, he returned with a large basket about three feet tall and eighteen inches in diameter. Woven into the basket was an intricate design of dark-brown reeds in the shape of diamonds that contrasted handsomely with the light-colored wicker. "I will give you this if I can have that," Tzeechoe said as he pointed to the gaudy necklace. The young merchant looked to his senior for guidance and waited.

"Tzeechoe, ha? Oy, let me examine this beautiful basket," Myron said as he was handed the basket and studied it with a trained eye. "This is exquisite work; yes, a real craftsman made this. Tell me Tzeechoe, did you weave this yourself?"

Tzeechoe proudly smiled and replied, "Yes, I have made baskets since I was a boy. My father's father taught me how. Many others in the village can do it, but everyone says mine are the best."

"I think this one is worthy of that necklace you have your eye on." Myron reached down, grabbed the necklace, and held it high above his head. He then turned and faced the gathered villagers. "Tzeechoe has just traded one basket for this beautiful necklace. You can do the same. Bring me your skins and baskets. Bring anything of value and maybe we can trade." He then handed the necklace to Tzeechoe and slapped him on the shoulder. "Take this with my blessing, young man. I'm sure your Tzeecha will love you all the more for such a special gift."

Coleman shook his head and leaned over to Tzeechoe and whispered, "I wonder if he has any snake oil in his kit." Tzeechoe looked at Coleman with a confused expression and then smiled when Coleman started to chuckle.

For the remainder of the afternoon, Myron plied his wares as the villagers gathered around the displayed merchandise in awe at what they saw. Many asked Coleman questions about the unusual items the merchants had displayed. The villagers milled around the offerings the remainder of the day but there was little trading. A few small skins were traded for loose beads and another basket was traded for a metal comb. All in all, it had been a disappointing afternoon for the merchants. The villagers had little they wanted to trade, therefore, as the shadows grew long, Myron and his companion started packing up.

Coleman had spent the afternoon observing the goings-on. He wanted to make sure that Myron didn't cheat the villagers and, though he always traded to his benefit, his offers were generally fair. During this time, he had noticed that Myron's companion was subservient to his 'master,' as the young man called him. Coleman thought this a little strange but kept his concerns to himself.

When all was packed, Myron strode over to Coleman and said, "We will leave at first light tomorrow. I must say, of all the places I've visited, this is the poorest and the most isolated."

"They may be poor in goods, but they will learn and grow. I am sure by the next time you come this way, they will have more worthwhile things to trade," Coleman replied. Then he offered, "Would you and your helper join us for our meal tonight? I would like to learn more about your travels and the places you have been."

"I am hungry and tired of dried meat. I would be pleased to join you," Myron answered. "What will you be serving?"

"We will have shish kabobs. Have you ever had shish kabob?"

"I have no idea what that is, but I'm sure it will be delicious."

"When the meal is ready, I will get you," Coleman told him, and then he walked back to the lodge.

CHAPTER 13

DINNER GUESTS

Coleman broke tradition again by collecting several cuts of raw meat that he took to Tzeechoe's home. He gave them to the women and instructed them to make shish kabobs for six. When asked, he told them that they would sit around the lodge fire and enjoy their meal with the merchants.

"I want to learn about all the places they have been," he told his companions. "This is a great opportunity for all of us to learn about the world beyond the trees." No one disagreed or argued with him. Even Atura was curious about what these strange looking men could tell them. Although tradition would be broken again, she made no protest.

When all was ready, Coleman went to the traders' camp and invited them back to the lodge; however, he was surprised when only Myron followed him. "What about your helper? Is he not hungry, too?" Coleman asked.

"He must stay with the animals. They get restless when left by themselves," Myron told him, though Coleman could discern it was for a different reason that the young man remained with the goods. Coleman suspected he remained as a guard to protect the merchandise.

"The food is ready, and I will bring him some," Coleman offered.

"Don't worry about him. He will be all right," Myron said with an air of indifference.

"I will make sure he gets a warm meal," Coleman said somewhat irritated at Myron's laissez-faire attitude toward his young helper.

When they reached the lodge, Coleman introduced Myron to Tzeecha and Atura. "Ha, the beautiful Tzeecha. I see you are wearing the necklace your bondmate got for you. It shows your beauty even more," Myron puffed with such zeal that it made Coleman cringe. Nevertheless, Tzeecha was eating it up. Coleman noticed something in her countenance that he had never seen before: conceit. She seemed to assume an air of haughtiness. Coleman was very disappointed in her, yet he said nothing.

He saw the shish kabobs roasting over the fire and bent down and grabbed one. "I will take this to your helper while it is still hot. Tzeechoe, make Myron comfortable and tell him about your most exciting hunt. I will be back soon." Coleman exited the lodge and briskly walked to the merchant's camp. He found Myron's assistant sitting on the ground, his back resting against the side of one of the six-legged beasts.

"Here is some warm food for you. I understand you must remain with the animals," Coleman said as he handed the young man the skewer. The young man quickly jumped to his feet and bowed.

"Thank you, my liege. I'm starved and this smells splendid," he replied.

"The People call me Tondo. What is your name?"

"I am Zoseemo, the beastmaster."

"I have never seen such creatures. What are they called?" Coleman asked as the young man began nibbling at the food.

"They are rasters. Most of the time they are gentle, but if they get scared, they can be hard to control. Their hearing is excellent and so is their sense of smell. They warn us when dangerous creatures are about. They caught scent of the village two days ago. That's how we found you. I am the raster master and they obey my wishes," he proudly declared.

"Yes, I'm sure they do. Tell me, why do you have a mark on your forehead? Is it a tribal sign?" Coleman asked.

The young man lowered his head and spoke to the ground. "It's the mark of a slave. I was given this mark shortly after I was born. My mother was a slave. My father was a slave. I will be a slave all the days of my life. If my master allows me to have a woman, all my children will be slaves, too."

Having watched Myron and Zoseemo all afternoon, Coleman feared that was the case. "Does your master treat you well? Does he beat you or abuse you in any way?"

"Master Myron is good to me."

"Is that so? What do you think about being a slave?"

"It's all I've known for all my life."

"Do you wish to have your freedom," Coleman asked.

"Slaves do not talk about freedom; it is not permitted. I am what I am. May the gods be praised. This is magnificent," he said as he took another bite of meat from the shish kabob.

"Tell me about the City of the Ancients," Coleman eagerly asked.

Just then, Atura approached and asked, "Tondo, will you be returning to the lodge soon? Myron is worried one of the animals stepped on you."

"I am okay. I was just talking with Zoseemo. Zoseemo, this is Atura."

"I am honored to meet you, Atura," he said as he bowed deeply. "Is she your bondmate?"

"Bondmate?" Coleman wondered.

"Is she your woman?"

"No, she is my daughter," Coleman mused as Atura took affront and Zoseemo looked perplexed.

"I hope to talk with you again before you leave in the morning," Coleman continued. "Enjoy your meal. I must return to the others." With that, he departed with Atura following close behind.

He apologized when he got back to the lodge. "I am sorry I took so long. I spent some time talking with Zoseemo," Coleman told the others. "I am hungry. How about the rest of you?" Tzeechoe just grunted, grabbed one of the skewers, and began eating.

"Help yourself, Myron," Coleman told him as he pointed to the cooking food.

"I thought you would never ask. The wonderful smell has been making me Munnoga-touched," he said in a loud and boisterous voice as he reached for one of the skewers. He reached for the one Coleman had made for himself, which included chunks of potato and onion.

"Don't take that one," Tzeechoe warned.

"Oh, my apologies. Is it for you?" Myron asked.

"No, it's Tondo's. Only he can eat rud-bo-t´a-tzo. The People are afraid to eat hunion."

"Why is that?" Myron wondered.

"Rud-bo-t´a-tzo is poison to everyone but Tondo. He loves them and eats them all the time. Hunion could be poison to us, too," Tzeechoe explained as he pointed to another shish kabob. "Take that one."

"Ho-ho, it's hot!" Myron exclaimed after grabbing it. He took a few tentative bites and smiled. This is excellent!" he exclaimed. He watched as Coleman took a few bites of his. "How is it possible for you to eat poison?" he wondered.

"He's a messenger from the gods," Tzeechoe declared.

Coleman quickly changed the topic. "Zoseemo told me your animals are called rasters. They are the most amazing creatures I have ever seen. Tell me about them," Coleman asked, as he took another bite from his skewer. Tzeechoe indicated for the women to take their turn and they, too, started eating.

"Rasters are filthy beasts, but they can carry more than any other creature I know of. It's because they have six legs to support the weight. They are dumb and only need to be pointed in the direction you want them to go. And they won't stop until you tell them to. I've heard of rasters walking right over a cliff, one after the other. Can you imagine that?"

"Really? They are that dumb?" Coleman wondered in amazement.

"Yes! They don't know what's good for themselves. It takes a savvy beastmaster to keep them safe."

"I understand Zoseemo is the raster master."

"He said that, did he? He's very good. He thinks like a raster and sometimes acts like one, too, but he is a good boy," Myron continued.

"What is that mark on his forehead? Is that something special? I do not see one on you," Coleman said trying to temper his sarcasm.

"Ha, that is the mark of a slave. The City of the Ancients has many slaves and we freemen take good care of them. They are quite valuable, don't you know," Myron explained. "If I ever return to the city, I may sell him and rest in comfort the remainder of my days. He's young and strong; he will bring a good price, I think," Myron continued, not realizing how offensive his words were to Coleman's sensibilities. The others listened intently, though they had no idea what Myron was talking about.

"You say he is a young man. How old is he?" Coleman asked.

"I guess he's about seventy spans. I think your friends here would say he's seventy rains or lines," Myron answered as he took another bite."

"Seventy spans? He does not look that old!" Coleman exclaimed. "If I may ask, how old are you?"

"I will be five-hundred and seventy-two spans in another detz, and I'm beginning to feel my age," Myron responded.

Coleman was amazed. *Could this man really be that old? He looked to be in his late forties or early fifties and quite vigorous.* Then he thought, *Maybe a span is less than a year,* so he asked, "How many days are there in a span?"

Myron looked at Coleman in wonder and then answered like a school teacher, "Four-hundred days in a span, ten detzamars or detzs to a span, and forty days to a detz. Where did you say you were from?"

"My people use a different way of keeping track of time," Coleman told him as he calculated Myron's age in Earth years and marveled in English, "You're over six-hundred Earth years old!"

"What did you say," Myron asked.

"Tondo says things in godspeak sometimes. He forgets himself and no one can understand him," Tzeechoe explained to Myron.

"Those are strange words. I have traveled many marches from Anterra and all people use world-speak. This is the first time I have heard such incomprehensible words. Where did you say you were from?" Myron asked again.

Coleman looked at Myron, "Anterra? Anterra! Is that what this world is called?"

"This world's name?" Myron looked confused. "We Anterrans call the land around our city the Teg-ar-mos Kingdom. The city I'm from is called Anterra; some call it the City of Ancients or the Ancient City. What is this land called?"

"The People call it the land of the Batru or The-Land-We-Live-On," Coleman told him. "I only know it by their names."

"You are a mystery and a riddle to me, Master Tondo. Where did you say you were from?" Myron questioned for the third time.

Coleman thought for a few seconds and then responded, "I am from a place that has been hidden. I was the first to leave that place and I got lost in a dream and found myself here."

"Our legends tell of a city hidden in the Dark Forest, very

far from here. They say the streets are paved in zanth and the people are magical. I always thought it was a child's story, but now, I have my doubts. Are the streets really paved in shiny zanth?"

"Zanth? What is that?" Coleman asked.

Myron pulled a pouch from his belt and opened it. He quickly pulled out a large gold coin an inch and a half in diameter.

"This is called a regum and it is made of pure zanth," Myron told him.

"May I see it?" Coleman asked. Myron handed the heavy coin to him and he examined it.

"Whose image is this on the coin?"

"That is King Teg-ar-mos. He has ruled Anterra for over three-hundred and fifty spans."

"This is called gold where I am from," Coleman explained.

"Gor-duh," Tzeechoe interjected. "Tondo warned me about gor-duh. He says men do crazy things to get it."

"Yes, Tzeechoe, my friend, Tondo is right. The shiny metal, gor-duh you call it, drives men to do strange things sometimes. Do you have any gor-duh here?" Myron asked.

"Little yellow rocks . . ." Tzeechoe began to say, but Coleman rudely interrupted.

"The Batru have no need of gold. They put their faith in a good spear and club. Is that not true, Tzeechoe?"

"A good spear has a purpose. Gor-duh is good for nothing," Tzeechoe replied.

"Now, Tzeechoe, you would tell 'ol Myron if you had gor-duh, now wouldn't you?" Myron prodded.

"Tzeechoe has no gor-duh and I want no gor-duh," Tzeechoe emphasized.

"If you knew where to find gor-duh, you'd tell your friend Myron, wouldn't you?" Myron continued.

"Myron, stop! You are confusing him. He has no idea what gold is. He spends his time making baskets and spears and hunting for food to feed the village. These are simple people with no understanding of such things," Coleman interjected, showing his irritation with Myron's pressing questions and fearing that the knowledge of the Batru's cache of riches could cause a gold rush that would destroy their peaceful lives.

"Yes, yes, Master Tondo. No need to raise your hackles. I'm just curious. I always like to look for possible fortune, don't you know? That's why I travel far and wide," Myron instructed as his eyes strained to pierce Coleman's inner thoughts. Coleman felt uncomfortable under Myron's scrutinizing gaze.

"What is the City of the Ancients like?" Coleman finally asked as he tried to ease the rising tension.

"It is a marvelous place, a magical city to behold. The city gates are as high as ten men are tall, and the whole city is surrounded by a stone wall higher than the gates. The entire world comes to the City of the Ancients to learn from the scholars and study the gods' precepts. It is rumored that some of the masters of the Great Temple are nearly a thousand spans old."

"A thousand years . . . I mean spans? How is that possible?" Coleman asked in amazement. Myron simply shrugged. "How is the city ruled?" Coleman asked.

"By a king, just like all the other cities; except for the City of Women; it is ruled by a queen. The king has his guards, the Panerra, who protect him and his subjects."

"Do the cities fight with one another?" Coleman asked as he was beginning to suppose that the cultures Myron was describing resembled city-states of Earth's ancient past.

Myron looked at Coleman with a studied eye, wondering how this guest of the villagers knew of such things. "Oy, they war with one another, but war is expensive, and the people grumble if there's too much of it. Mostly, the kings threaten and posture and put on a good show for the people, but seldom do they draw blood."

"This is fascinating. Go on, tell me more," Coleman urged.

"The City of the Ancients is the cultural center of all the kingdoms in the area. The Great Temple of the Unnamed God is found there and scholars from the other kingdoms go to it so they can learn and debate. It is quite marvelous."

"How far away is this City of the Ancients?"

"It's hard to say. I would guess more than half a span's journey by raster. It all depends on how many stops I make. It could be less if one traveled directly there," Myron advised.

Myron noticed the other three villagers were getting tired of listening to the conversation. It was evident they didn't understand much of what was being discussed, so he changed the topic. "Tell me Tzeechoe, how long does it take for you to weave a basket like the one you traded today?"

"If I work on it steadily between hunts, it takes three days to make one like the one I traded to you."

"An excellent piece of craftsmanship, if I ever saw one. If you lived closer to the kingdoms, I would contract with you to produce more," Myron said as Tzeechoe looked first to their guest and then to Coleman.

"He means, he would have you make more and he would trade things for what you make," Coleman interjected.

"Ha, I see," Tzeechoe said as he rubbed his head.

Just then, a raster bellowed; then the other two added to the racket. "This has been an enjoyable evening," Myron told his hosts as he stood. "I wish I could stay longer, but as you can hear, the beasts are restless. I must find out what has upset them." He turned to Coleman and said, "Master Tondo, I would like to learn more about your home. I hope to come this way again, and if I do, we can talk some more."

"Can you not stay a few more days?" Coleman nearly pleaded.

"I must be on my way. I cannot tarry long in one place. I don't want time to catch me," Myron replied mystically.

"Why, what do you mean?" Coleman stuttered, just as all three rasters began bellowing even louder.

"I must hurry. I fear Zoseemo is losing control. Thank you for a wonderful evening, my friends." With those parting words, Myron bowed and exited the lodge, leaving the three villagers and Coleman looking one to another.

"He is a very strange man," Tzeecha finally said. "I had no idea what he was talking about half of the time, and you too, Tondo."

"I agree," Atura interjected. "What was he wearing? They didn't look like skins."

"That is cloth. His people make it from animal fur and plants, I think," Coleman told her.

"Really? I like them. Can you show me how to make got´e?'" she asked.

"I wish I knew how, but I do not. It is complicated," Coleman admitted.

"What we have has served us well. I don't think we need to make those kinds of clothes. Animal skins do just fine," Tzeechoe told her.

Coleman couldn't help but notice that Tzeecha was sitting with her head bent down, admiring her garish necklace.

"Tzeecha, if you keep looking at your necklace that way, you will get a stiff neck," Coleman warned whimsically.

"It's very beautiful. I like it very much," she told him as she smiled at Tzeechoe.

"Yes, I can tell," Coleman said even more concerned about the change in her demeanor.

"It is beautiful, Tzeecha," Atura said in admiration. "I wish I had one like it."

Coleman didn't say anything in response but just rubbed his temple as he moved his head from side to side. In the distance, they could hear Myron yelling something and then the rasters seemed to calm down.

"I wonder what that was all about?" Coleman quipped. He heard the betzoe pup whimper and then yip. Coleman reached into its basket and pulled it out, giving it a good rubbing. He then took some cooked meat and started feeding it. The others just watched as the pup gulped down its food.

"He is a hungry little guy. Look at those huge paws. He is going to be big when fully grown," Coleman told the others.

"I still think he will eat you when he gets big," Atura warned as they all laughed.

Coleman sat in thought as the other three talked about the rasters. Apparently, they had never seen such amazing animals either, and they were awestruck by their huge size, their six legs, and the two odd men's power over them. While they carried on their conversation, Coleman analyzed what he had learned that night about the city-states in a faraway land. He wanted to join with Myron and go exploring, but he wasn't sure that would be a good idea. After some thought and a review of his previous visions, he thought it best to remain here and protect the village from the coming catastrophe. At least he now knew there was a much larger world out there awaiting him; a world seemingly without a name.

Coleman left the lodge and watched the moons for a while. Munnari and Munnevo wrestled with each other in the east while lonesome Munnoga rose in the west, barren and alone. He marveled at their motions. He was now certain that the blue and red moons orbited each other as they circled about the planet. Coleman thought about the story of creation Taahso had shared and wondered if it was all myth or based on some event from the distant past. He recalled Myron's words about the City of the Ancients and how it was the center of culture.

"That is a place I must see someday," he muttered to himself in English.

His thoughts turned to taah and the power he had discovered within himself on this alien world. He must learn to control it. Taahso was right; he was dangerous and, until he gained control, he would remain so; however, if he could control fire, what else may this inner-power offer? He looked at his hands and wondered what astounding powers were hidden within himself. This new world held wonders beyond his imagination and yet he knew very little about it.

Coleman sighed as he realized he would never return to his home. Feelings of loneliness and despair began to creep into his thoughts. He gritted his teeth and shook his head as if to chase these thoughts from his mind. "There is much to do and many places to go. There is no time to feel sorry for myself," he uttered out loud.

"What did you say?" he heard Taahso ask. So near was his voice, Coleman was startled and jumped at the sound.

"I was lost in thought, Taahso. I did not hear you approach."

"I heard you say something, but I wasn't sure if you were talking to me."

"I was just thinking out loud. I do that sometimes when I am trying to understand things," he told the shaman.

"I have come to ask for your blessing to speak with Atura this evening," he intimated.

"Oh yes, go with my blessing," Coleman told him.

Taahso then announced his presence to Tzeechoe and was welcomed into the lodge. A few minutes later, he and Atura exited and walked to the entrance of the village with Tzeecha a discrete distance behind. Coleman smiled and told himself it had been another good day. He then turned his face upward and watched the moons in their motions once again.

After another half-hour or so, Coleman returned to the hut and went to bed. He quickly fell asleep and never heard the women when they returned.

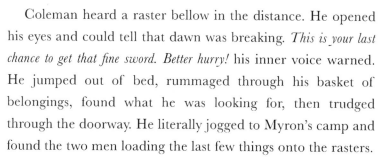

Coleman heard a raster bellow in the distance. He opened his eyes and could tell that dawn was breaking. *This is your last chance to get that fine sword. Better hurry!* his inner voice warned. He jumped out of bed, rummaged through his basket of belongings, found what he was looking for, then trudged through the doorway. He literally jogged to Myron's camp and found the two men loading the last few things onto the rasters.

"Good morning, Myron, Zoseemo," he called. The two men stopped what they were doing and greeted him. Then Zoseemo continued with his work while Myron turned to talk with Coleman.

"Good day, Master Tondo. What can I do for you this beautiful morning?"

"I would like to make a trade with you before you leave."

"Yes, yes, I'm always ready to do business. How may I help you?"

"There are a few items I would like to purchase from you: the sword and the metal pot. Also, a few wooden bowls and a knife."

"Ha, those are fine items. The sword is the best of all the weapons I carry, but it is very expensive. What do you have to trade for it?" Myron asked in a condescending tone, knowing that Coleman had nothing of value to trade the day before.

"I think this should cover the price," he said as he extended his cupped palm before Myron and dropped the gold nugget into the merchant's waiting hand.

Myron's amused look turned into a broad smile and his eyes widened. "Where did you get this?" he said in amazement as he stared at a zanth nugget he now held between finger and thumb.

"It is a little thing I brought with me from the City of Gold," he lied with a roguish grin.

"And you told me the city's streets are not paved in shiny zanth. Now tell me Tondo, who is fooling who?" Myron quipped.

Coleman laughed and said, "Are you interested in doing business or shall I take it back?"

"Zoseemo, get the gravetum sword, the gravetro pot, a knife, and the wooden bowls," he yelled over his shoulder. "Yes, my good friend, we have a trade. And I thought this had been a wasted visit. Do you have any more?"

"It is not polite to ask about a man's wealth, now is it, my friend?" Coleman scolded.

Myron bit into the nugget, looked at the teeth marks, and he smiled even more broadly. "Of course, of course! I'm just surprised to see something like this way out here in the Wilderness. I thought I would never come this way again, but you have given me a new incentive to return. I just might put this village on my regular rounds from now on," Myron declared as he slipped the nugget into a pocket of his robe.

In a few minutes, Zoseemo handed the shiny gravetum short sword, the gravetro pot, a gravetrum knife, and six wooden bowls to Coleman.

Coleman had a million questions he wanted to ask Myron. He begged him to stay, 'Just a few more days,' but Myron would not hear of it. He was in a hurry and he would not delay nor explain why. Coleman could sense a hidden purpose in the merchant's haste, but Myron would not elaborate enough to clarify his suspicions. Coleman and Myron exchanged a few pleasantries. Then the two merchants mounted up and, with bellows and grunts of annoyance by the rasters, the little caravan was off, quickly disappearing into the trees. Coleman heard footsteps approaching and turned to see Tzeechoe.

"What have you there, Tondo?" he asked.

"Here, my dear friend, this is a gift for you and Tzeecha," Coleman said as he handed Tzeechoe the pot and two wooden bowls.

"What is this thing?" Tzeechoe asked.

"It will cook food and make it taste even better than shish kabobs. Tonight, I will introduce you to stew."

"Stee-woo? Tondo, I don't know what that is, but I know it will be good," Tzeechoe said with a smile.

The two men walked back to the lodge and Tzeechoe handed the pot and the two bowls to Tzeecha while Coleman gave the remaining bowls and the knife to Atura. He then began adjusting his new sword's harnessed scabbard to fit his back. The sword pommel rested just above his right shoulder and he pulled the sword out. He returned it to the scabbard several times, testing its utility.

"Ah, that will work just fine," he said. "Atura, the knife is for you. Please take the betzoe for a walk, and give him some of the meat I left for him." Atura initially smiled when Tondo told her the knife was hers, but her smile quickly turned into a scowl at her assignment, yet she said nothing. Coleman then placed his hand on Tzeechoe's shoulder and said, "Let us hurry to the meeting."

CHAPTER 14

A NEW POWER

Tondo had just completed his transaction with Myron, causing Tzeechoe and himself to get a late start on their duties. They trotted to the center of the village, leaving Tzeecha holding the heavy metal pot with an expression of confusion. When they arrived, they found that Taahso had already blessed most of the hunters. The chief was standing at Taahso's side and Coleman couldn't help but notice that he was wearing the mirror Myron had given him as a necklace. Coleman could tell by the expressions on the faces of his team members that they were annoyed at having to wait so long and be the last ones to leave the village.

He gave them a sheepish grin and said, "I am sorry. It is my fault we are late. I had to visit the traders before they left this morning."

Most of the men accepted his excuse, but Ayascho gave an exaggerated grunt of annoyance, which he made sure all could hear. The men then divided into their usual teams, received their blessings, and departed. It was Coleman's team's turn to hunt for meat. The five men quickly dashed across the creek and continued heading toward the Sweet Waters spring.

As they crossed the creek, Tzeechoe noticed Coleman staring at a shiny yellow pebble in the water, but he didn't stop.

As the men continued moving onward, Tzeechoe asked, "Tondo, did you trade your little yellow rock for that big knife on your back and the other things."

"Yes, I did."

"You said gor-duh had power. Now, I understand."

"Gold can make men go crazy. I do not worry so much about the People as I do about men like Myron. If they learn this creek is full of gold, they will come here and destroy The-Land-We-Live-On," Coleman warned.

"You didn't tell him where you found it?"

"No, Tzeechoe. I said I brought it with me from my home."

"Do you think he believed you?"

"Maybe he did, but he does not know where I found it and that is the way it should remain." Tzeechoe was out of breath and quit asking questions. Coleman wondered if his lust for the sword would cause the village and himself grief in the future. He decided it was time to visit the chief and tell him about the riches lying in the creek.

"I must visit the chief and tell him about gold," Coleman said to him.

"I will go with you." The two men quickly informed the other hunters where they were going and departed.

Coleman called a greeting when they reached the chief's lodge. He immediately welcomed them in and motioned for them to join him as he sat on his stool near the fire.

"I must tell you something important," Coleman began.

"What is it, my son? You have the look of a worried man," the chief responded.

"The yellow rocks we find in the water have value to people like Myron, and me for that matter," Coleman admitted.

"The yellow rocks are of no use to us," the chief noted.

"That is true, but other men find the yellow rock to be extraordinary and very rare. I traded one little pebble for this big knife, a cooking pot, a knife, and some wooden bowls. I did not tell the man where I found the gold, the yellow rock, but I worry he may send others to look for it. If that happens, it will destroy the People's peace," Coleman warned.

"The Great Batru will protect his children," the chief advised with confidence.

Coleman could see that there would be no countering the chief's faith. "Then prepare yourselves for the worst if outsiders come looking for it."

"We will trust in our god. If you find benefit in collecting the yellow rocks, then you can have them. We have no need of them," the village leader declared. The chief waved his arm, indicating the conversation was over. Coleman and Tzeechoe exited his lodge and quickly left the village in search of their hunt team.

In a couple of hours, the men returned to the village with two gazelle-like creatures hanging from poles. Coleman looked for edible ground plants on the way back to the village. He didn't identify any, but didn't expect to. The men were in a hurry to get back for the midday meal and didn't want to be delayed by Coleman.

When they got to the village, they found most of the other teams had already returned with a huge collection of meat and other foods. Every villager Coleman saw was smiling and acting joyfully. It was as though a heavy burden had been lifted from everyone. The children were more active and played much more than he had ever seen them do before. The chief was much happier and talked more often with his people.

It's amazing how a full stomach improves morale, Coleman thought.

When his team had delivered their food, he and Tzeechoe went to the lodge. Coleman found the betzoe tied to a stake near the structure's doorway. The pup greeted its master with yips and licks while Coleman untied it and let it run free for a few minutes.

"I think it is time I gave him a name," Coleman told Tzeechoe, who was warily watching the pup romp around the village.

"A name? You will give it a name? Why? It's just a wild beast?"

"I think he is smart enough to learn his name. Once he gets used to it, he will come when I call him," Coleman advised.

"Do you really think so? It is just a wild beast and one day it will try to eat you just like Atura says," Tzeechoe warned him.

"I do not think so. Has he done anything to make you think he will eat me or anyone else?" was his riposte.

Coleman enjoyed the midday meal with the other villagers. He noticed several of the People were referring to this meal as Tondo-measha, which means Tondo's food or Tondo's meal.

Coleman took it as a confirmation of what he had done, feeling happiness and joy for the relief he had brought the villagers.

After the meal, he and Tzeechoe left the village with the betzoe pup trailing them, sniffing the ground. After a short walk, they found an open area out of view of the village. Coleman then began to practice starting and controlling fire. He knew he had to master this power if he were ever to use it in any way. As he practiced, he couldn't help but wonder what other powers he may possess. This world must be a marvelous place. He had already seen extraordinary powers and creatures, and if the things Myron said were accurate, incredibly long-lived people, as well.

As he continued to work on his taah control, his mind drifted to the day he entered the rip chamber and started on this unexpected adventure. Where had he gone? Was this world in his universe or had he escaped the bounds of his old reality to make a dimensional jump into an alternate universe? These ideas excited him, but suddenly he was shaken out of his introspection by Tzeechoe's frantic shouts. Coleman opened his eyes to find the grass surrounding him ablaze.

"Oh nuts, I've done it again," he said in godspeak.

He and Tzeechoe quickly put out the fire while the pup whimpered in fear. After the fire had been extinguished, Coleman tried again. This time, he forced himself to remain focused on the task at hand. He practiced for the next two to three hours and was able to improve his control with each attempt. Every time the fire was put out and the wood re-stacked, Coleman would sit and clear his mind. The poor betzoe pup would try to bury its head under Coleman's leg because it knew what was coming next. The creature was very much afraid of fire, and to be at the center of what it considered a firestorm was more than it could endure. Nevertheless, Coleman continued his practice, but he comforted the pup with a good belly rub after each attempt.

When the shadows began to grow long, they walked back to the village. Coleman was happy with his progress, though he felt he had a long way to go before he gained the control he sought. Coleman's efforts had only underlined Tzeechoe's awe. Without a doubt, he was sure Tondo had been sent by the gods, or even more exciting and terrifying, he was a god.

The men went directly to Tzeechoe's lodge and Coleman erected a tripod of green wooden poles, then he hung the gravetro pot over the lodge fire. He sent the women to the center of the village to retrieve their portion of food. He noticed that Tzeecha always wore her new necklace and seemed to lord over the other women she interacted with, much to his disappointment. A little later, the women returned with raw meat. Coleman taught his companions how to make stew. He melted fat in the pot and cut the meat into chunks using his new bright and shiny sword. He then braised the meat, added water to the pot, and a couple of sliced fruit pods he could tolerate. He then sat back and mused to himself as he watched the others examining what he had made and the bubbling stew.

After a while, the aroma permeated the lodge and Coleman could hear Tzeechoe's stomach growling. From time to time, Coleman would stir the stew with a wooden stick.

"How long do we have to wait?" Tzeechoe anxiously asked.

"Just let it cook. I will tell you when it is ready," Coleman said. He pulled out his obsidian dagger and began fashioning a spoon with tines from a flat piece of wood he found near the fire. He chuckled as he watched the eyes of the others shift from his work, then to the pot, and back again, over and over.

"While you are waiting, you should make one of these, too," he said as he held up his finished spork utensil.

"What is that for?" Atura asked.

Coleman dipped it into the stew and scooped up a piece of meat and some broth. He then tasted it. "Not quite ready. We need to let it cook a little longer," he advised. The little betzoe sniffed the air and headed for the pot. He danced back and forth in front of the fire, trying to get to the cooking meal, but finally gave up and returned to Coleman's side.

The stew bubbled for a few more minutes. Finally, Coleman told them it was ready. He served the others first. They held their bowls in both hands, sniffing the aroma. All three had big smiles on their faces, but no one took a taste. They were waiting for Coleman. When he had served himself, he took his spork and tasted the broth.

"Mmm, this is fabulous. Go ahead, taste it. Be careful. It is hot," he warned.

He chuckled to himself as the three villagers struggled with their newly fashioned utensils. Clearly, they had no experience with such a thing and their control and movements were awkward. After several frustrating minutes, Tzeechoe gave up and dipped his fingers into his bowl pulling out a chunk of meat and began eating. The women soon followed his lead.

Coleman couldn't help but chuckle to himself as he continued eating. Tzeechoe finished his serving quickly and then dipped his bowl into the pot and refilled it.

"This is very good, Tondo. You call this stee-woo?" he asked.

"Stew, it is called stew."

"Stooo," Tzeechoe repeated slowly. He then tipped his bowl and drank the broth, slurping as he ate the remaining meat and fruit pieces. The women followed suit and ignored Coleman's cringe as they continued slurping their meal.

"We are going to have to work on our manners," he told them. Their brown eyes looked at him over the rims of their bowls while they continued to slurp and chew.

Tzeechoe lowered his bowl and said, "Man-norz? What is man-norz?" he asked.

"Oh, never mind. Enjoy your meal," Coleman said. He picked up another bowl, dipped it into the stew, and let it cool for a while. He then placed it on the ground in front of the pup. The betzoe quickly gulped down its contents and licked the bowl clean, pushing it around the lodge floor as he licked every morsel from it. Coleman and his companions laughed as they watched.

"What should we name the puppy?" Coleman asked them.

They looked at him with puzzlement. "It's a wild beast. You treat it like it was a child. What's wrong with you?" Atura grumbled.

Coleman snatched up the pup and began rubbing its ears. "Yes, you are my baby," he said to it as he continued to pet the betzoe, to its utter delight. Atura expelled a loud 'harrumph' while Tzeechoe and Tzeecha smiled at what they considered Coleman's silly antics and speech.

"Well, any suggestions?" Coleman asked again.

"Todo," Atura spouted in her most aggravated tone.

"Ah, that is it!" Coleman shouted with glee. "I will call him Toto because I am not in Kansas anymore!"

"Todo? You will call it dumb?" Tzeecha asked.

"No, Toto . . . To-To," he repeated.

"Toto? What does it mean?" Tzeechoe asked.

"It is just a name from my homeland. It reminds me that I am far away from home," Coleman explained.

"Is gan-t'iz the name of your home?" Tzeechoe asked.

"No, but if I click my heels together three times, maybe I can go there," Coleman mused. The others looked at him with quizzical expressions and looked down and watched his feet. Coleman laughed out loud while the others exchanged perplexed glances with one another. *Has the visitor lost his mind completely?* they seemed to be communicating. As their confusion increased, Coleman's laughter grew, and he grabbed his stomach.

"I have not had such a good laugh in a long time," he finally told them.

"I think you've lost your mind," Atura grumbled. "What's wrong with you?"

"I am just having a little fun with my friends," he admitted as he calmed down and rubbed Toto all over some more. Coleman finally regained control of himself and instructed the other three on how to clean their bowls with water. Although they didn't understand the purpose, they did what he said, a little concerned that he really had lost his mind.

Coleman then turned to Atura and asked whimsically, "Do you think Taahso will visit tonight?" Atura gave him a coy smile but didn't respond.

"Ha, Taahso has the fire," Tzeechoe chortled as Atura blushed, covered her face with her hands, and turned her back to the men.

"Now stop it, you two," Tzeecha quipped. Just then, they heard Taahso announce his arrival.

"Speak of the devil. Here he is," Coleman cracked.

"Come into my home, Taahso," Tzeechoe called.

Taahso stepped through the doorway and asked Coleman, "What is dee-vahr?" Coleman's shocked expression told him all he needed to know. "Humph," was Taahso's reaction. Then he said, "May I speak with Atura?"

"Yes . . . yes, of course, you may," Coleman stuttered. Taahso quickly turned around and exited with Atura following, her new metal knife in a leather sheath at her hip. Tzeecha walked to the doorway, ran her fingers through her hair like a comb, straightened her necklace, and stepped out of the lodge.

Coleman turned to Tzeechoe and said, "I think she likes that necklace too much."

Tzeechoe had followed his wife with his eyes as she exited and he continued staring at the doorway. "What did you say, Tondo?"

"Never mind."

Coleman then decided to visit Chashutzo and check on his condition.

"Chashutzo, I am here. May I enter?" he called when he arrived at Chashutzo's home.

After a short delay, Chashutzo replied in a strained voice, "Enter, Tondo,"

Coleman entered and asked, "What is the problem?" Chashutzo didn't say a word but lowered his eyes.

"He tried to stand up and hurt himself," Chashutza admitted.

"I warned you it will take time for this to heal properly. Let me take a look."

Coleman examined the injury but couldn't see any noticeable damage. All of a sudden, a thought, but not really a thought, more like a feeling from his core, told him he could relieve Chashutzo's pain. Coleman pondered for a moment and wondered if it were possible for him to use taah to reduce the pain. He rubbed his hands together until the friction warmed them. Then he placed his hands on Chashutzo's wound. He felt the taah in his chest. Then he focused the energy in his mind. His hands warmed and glowed a dim red. He felt power pass to Chashutzo's body.

"Tondo, what did you do? It doesn't hurt anymore," Chashutzo told him.

"I think I helped remove the pain."

"Is my wound healed?"

"I do not think so. I think all I did was relieve the pain. You must not stand up until I tell you it is okay. Do you understand?"

"Yes, Tondo. I understand. I promise I will not stand up again."

Coleman was amazed that he had found a new taah power. He wondered how many more powers he would discover. Coleman and Chashutzo talked for a while about the latest hunts and the changes to the village traditions. Chashutzo couldn't wait to get moving again, but he agreed to do what he'd been told.

After about an hour, Coleman excused himself and walked back to Tzeechoe's lodge. Before he went to bed, he took Toto for a short walk. Then both retired for the night. Just before he fell asleep, he heard Atura and Tzeecha return. For the next several minutes, he listened as Tzeechoe and Tzeecha whispered quietly. Soon, the others heard his heavy breathing as he slipped into an untroubled sleep.

In the middle of the night, Coleman awoke to the sound of thunder rumbling overhead. Rain began pelting the outer walls of the lodge as a flash of lightning illuminated the room with white light. Toto rustled in his basket and began to whimper. Coleman tipped the basket and the little betzoe crawled to his side, attempting to bury its nose under Coleman's arm. It wasn't long before both man and beast were sound asleep again.

For the next several days, Coleman's activities settled into a regular routine, although a steady drizzle fell during this time. He usually spent half a day obtaining food, either by hunting wild animals or searching for plant food with his hunt team.

While the other men continued to scan the trees and bushes for plant food, he examined the ground.

He found a root plant that was very similar to a carrot, except in color, which was green. He also found mushrooms; however, he wasn't sure if they were safe to eat. He decided the risk was too great and struck them off his list.

In the afternoons, Coleman continued practicing his taah control, and he felt confident he had mastered what was fast becoming a simple task. Chashutzo continued to heal, as well. After his recent painful experience, he followed Coleman's advice closely and remained as still as he possibly could. Coleman even brought Toto into Chashutzo's lodge to give him comfort. Although Chashutzo was a bit uncomfortable with the creature at first, they became good buddies in short order. After the pup had a couple of accidents in the dwelling, Chashutza lost any fondness she might have had for the beast. Nevertheless, it had been a relaxing and productive few days, and Coleman was feeling very pleased with himself about the progress the village was making. The children seemed happier; their singing and laughter was heard more often throughout the village. Coleman had even found a stone near the creek that he could use to sharpen his newly purchased short sword. In the quiet evening hours, he would sit near the lodge fire and sharpen his blade while Tzeechoe wove a new basket. Taahso continued to visit with Atura and they went on evening walks. Even the continuing rain never dampened their spirits.

Tzeecha became more and more enamored with her new necklace, wearing it all day long, every day. If Tzeechoe had allowed it, she would have worn it at night, as well. While this worried Coleman, he said nothing about it, except to tease her occasionally. One day Tzeecha and Atura left the village and climbed trees nearby to gather fruit pods. It was on this day that she left her necklace in the lodge, not wanting it to be lost or damaged while she was climbing. On that day, Coleman's team returned from the hunt earlier than usual and as he approached Tzeechoe's home, he noticed Nita, Namad's teenage daughter, leaving Tzeechoe's lodge. She trotted off toward her home and didn't see Coleman approaching. He was surprised to find the dwelling empty, except for the napping betzo in his basket. He wondered what Nita was up to but dismissed it at the time as unimportant.

Later that day, when Tzeecha and Atura returned with their baskets of fruit, Tzeecha discovered her necklace was missing. She searched every nook and cranny of the lodge and couldn't find it. At the time, Coleman was outside the village practicing his fire-starting power. It wasn't until nearly dusk when he returned and learned about the missing necklace.

Coleman quickly deduced that Nita might have something

to do with its disappearance, so he and Tzeechoe trudged through the rain to make a visit to Namad's home. They wanted to learn what Nita had been doing in Tzeechoe's lodge earlier in the day.

"Namad, Tondo and I wish to speak with you," Tzeechoe called.

"Yes, my friends, come in from the rain," Namad called in response. The two men stepped into the hut and felt the warmth of the fire on their wet skin.

"It was a good hunt today. Sit by the fire and let us talk about it," Namad began.

The visitors sat and politely discussed the day's hunt for a few minutes while Coleman and Tzeechoe watched Nita shift uncomfortably, her worried gaze moving from one man to the other.

After a respectable period, Tzeechoe got to the point of their visit. "Namad, Tzeecha is missing her necklace."

"What has that to do with me?" Namad asked.

"We have looked everywhere for it, and it is not to be found," Tzeechoe continued, "I must ask you to question Nita about it. Tondo saw her leaving my lodge when he was returning from the hunt. No one else was in my home." Nita's eyes widened and fear was etched across her face as an audible gasp escaped her mouth.

"This cannot be," Namad exploded. "She would not have entered your home without your blessing." He looked at his daughter and the guilt she exuded was all that was needed to confirm his worst fears. "What have you done, my daughter? Did you enter Tzeechoe's lodge without permission?" She didn't answer and only bowed her head in shame. Namad jumped to his feet and slapped her across the top of her head. "Did you take Tzeecha's necklace?" he shouted. The poor girl began to whimper, and suddenly, she broke into gasping sobs, covering her face with her hands while rocking back and forth. Namada rushed to her daughter's side and embraced her, attempting to comfort the panic-stricken girl.

"How could you shame me like this? Tzeechoe is my friend. We have hunted together for many rains," he growled and slapped the trembling girl again. "Give me the necklace!" he yelled. Nita scrambled to a dark corner of the lodge and rummaged through a collection of furs and baskets. She stopped and slowly raised the stolen necklace above her head, unable to look into her father's enraged face. Namada gave a cry as if she had been pierced by a knife and fell to her face, clutching at the mats and skins on the floor. Namad carefully grasped the necklace and took it from Nita's hand. He slapped her a third time. She shrieked, sprawled at her father's feet, and continued sobbing uncontrollably.

Namad turned and knelt before the squatting Tzeechoe, holding the necklace with both hands. He bowed lowly while speaking to the floor, "Tzeechoe, I am ashamed. Please take this and forgive me."

Tzeechoe took the necklace and said, "You are still my friend, Namad. I forgive you."

Tzeechoe stood and exited the lodge leaving Coleman sitting on the floor mat. He looked at the bowing and humiliated Namad, then to the pain wracked Namada, and finally to the sobbing Nita. Realizing this injured family needed privacy to come to terms with what had just happened, he stood and left the hut without speaking a word.

As he was walking back to Tzeechoe's dwelling, he saw Namad exit his home with Nita firmly held by the upper arm. They marched off in the direction of the chief's lodge. Suddenly, Coleman's heart sank. He realized that this matter was not yet fully resolved and Nita's life could be in jeopardy.

Coleman entered Tzeechoe's home just as Tzeecha was placing the necklace around her neck. She had a bright, toothy smile, beaming with renewed joy. Coleman turned to Tzeechoe and asked, "I saw Namad and Nita heading toward the chief's lodge. What is happening?"

"Namad must tell the chief of his daughter's transgression. Nothing like this has happened in the village in all my days. I think Nita will be banished for her misdeed."

Tzeecha's expression quickly changed from happiness to worry and burden. She covered her mouth with her hand and her eyes widened. "Oy!" she gasped.

Coleman plopped himself on the floor of the dwelling and began rubbing his forehead. Banishment seemed to be the only way the village elders dealt with problems. "I hardly think a string of beads is worth someone's life," he finally grumbled.

"It is our law; the traditions keep us safe. Without them, all would be chaos and confusion. Either one follows the path of Batru and nurtures the good seeds or one falls into the grasp of the Tempter. Nita chose her path and now she must suffer the consequences," Atura said in a matter of fact tone.

"But the consequences are always so harsh. Is there no

sense of a measured response in such matters?" Coleman asked.

"We must purge our village of all evil before it becomes a threat to the welfare of the People," Tzeechoe firmly stated.

"Are you telling me Nita is evil and a threat to the People? Do you really believe that, Tzeechoe?" Coleman questioned.

Tzeechoe looked into Coleman's blue eyes and stared transfixed for several seconds. He lowered his gaze and whispered, "No, Nita has always been a good girl. I see no evil in her." Coleman looked at Atura and she, too, lowered her gaze.

The evening meal was eaten in silence as all four companions contemplated Nita's fate. Later that night, Taahso made his usual visit and explained that there would be a special meeting of the whole village in the great lodge the next evening. Taahso also instructed Coleman that he was considered a witness to the worrisome transgression and would be expected to tell what he had seen. The adult males would then discuss what should be done with Nita and the chief would make the final decision. To Coleman, it sounded all too ominous. The girl had given in to temptation, and now she would pay for this infraction with her life. It pained Coleman to contemplate her doom, and he wondered if there was anything he could do to save her and yet allow justice to be served.

Stay out of this affair. The village leaders know what's best. If you get involved, you'll make a fool of yourself, Coleman's inner voice whispered.

The next morning found the village under a depressing pall of dampness no less thick than the gloom that enveloped the spirit of the People. A great transgression had been committed; one that had never been seen by even the most elderly: theft. The hunters departed the village as usual but their steps were heavy-laden. The gatherers also felt the burden of what was to take place in the evening. Namad assumed his duties as the tracker but said nothing. Not only was he suffering under despair for his daughter's wrongdoing, but he also burned within by the shame she had brought upon his name. He spoke to no one and no one spoke to him. Coleman wanted to, but Tzeechoe counseled him to hold back.

"He must be left alone with his thoughts and his prayers," Tzeechoe advised.

The hunt went poorly at first. The men didn't focus well and many prey fled before the party could get within range. After midday, they reached a swampy area and found a saptur, a giant turtle-like creature with a shell two feet wide and four feet long. The biggest problem the men had was getting the large and heavy carcass back to the village. Coleman instructed the men on the building of a sled and the men struggled mightily as they dragged the heavy creature home. It was late in the day by the time they got back, and they were all ravenous with hunger from their exertions; however, the effort made them forget their troubles. But when the task was completed, their thoughts turned again to the evening's meeting in the great lodge.

To make matters worse, Atura angrily confronted Coleman and told him she was tired of caring for Toto all day; she'd had enough of watching 'that dumb beast,' as she put it. He released her from this assignment, and he told her that from now on he would take the young betzoe with him when he went hunting. She handed him the leather cord she had been using as a leash and marched off to the center of the village to assist with the evening meal.

As the red disk of p´atezas set, the evening meal was taken in silence. Very little conversation could be heard in any part of the village. A short time later, the monotonous beat of the drums sounded and the villagers slowly walked to the great lodge, mostly in silence. Only the smallest children uttered sounds. Taahso had informed Tzeechoe that his wife was to bring the necklace with her. She had not worn it all day and was reluctant to, but Tzeechoe insisted and she complied.

The villagers took their usual places and soon after all had arrived, the chief and Taahso entered and sat on their stools. Taahso pointed his staff at the stack of wood in the fire pit and it burst into flame, sending flickering light throughout the structure. The chief stood, indicating the beginning of the meeting and the drumming abruptly stopped.

"My children, we are gathered together this night on a matter of burning concern. Tzeecha, come forth with the necklace," the chief commanded. Tzeecha slowly rose from her place and with distinct, self-conscious steps, made her way to the chief. She stopped and faced him. He grabbed her shoulders and turned her until she faced the gathering.

"Tzeecha, is this your necklace?" he asked.

"Yes, Tzeechoe gave it to me," she replied.

"Was it missing yesterday?" the chief questioned.

"Yes," she meekly answered.

"Tondo, come forth." Coleman rose from his place and moved silently to the chief's side. "Tondo, did you see someone leaving Tzeechoe's home when you returned from the hunt yesterday?"

"Yes."

"Who was it?"

"I saw Nita leaving the lodge."

"Was anyone in there when you entered?"

"No." A murmur of whispers could be heard as it became apparent Nita had entered Tzeechoe's domicile without permission, which by itself was a serious transgression.

"Tzeechoe, come forward," the chief ordered. Tzeechoe rose and quickly moved to Tzeecha's side and then turned toward the array of faces. "Tzeechoe, when you were told the necklace was missing, what did you do?" the chief questioned.

"Tondo and I went to Namad's lodge to ask about the necklace. Nita confessed to her father that she had taken it. Then the necklace was returned."

The chief scanned the faces of the villagers until he found Nita. In a loud and stern voice, he commanded, "Nita, stand!" The young woman did as she was ordered. "Did you take the necklace?" the chief asked. Every eye was upon the young woman. Not a sound was heard; even the little ones felt the gravity of the moment and fell silent. The chief repeated his question, "Did you take the necklace?"

Nita's eyes widened and she lowered her head. In a tremulous voice, she whispered, "Yes."

"Nita, come to me! The rest of you may return to your places," the chief said. The girl came forward and kneeled at the chief's feet, her eyes staring at the floor mat. "This is an evil moment for our village. I have served as your leader for many rains, and never has such a thing happened before. We must now determine the punishment for such an offense. Taahso, tell us what the law has to say about such things," the chief ordered.

Taahso stood and spoke to the gathering in a loud and commanding voice. "Those who commit a great offense against the People, such as theft, will be sent away." Nita put her hands over her face and began to sob.

"What is to be done with her?" the chief asked the men seated before him.

Namad stood and declared in a loud voice, "The law is clear . . ." He ended his declaration before finishing his statement, having been overcome by emotion. He sat. A cry of anguish escaped Namada's lips and she began sobbing in the shadows. Namad didn't move, but Coleman could see tears rolling down his cheeks.

Ayascho was the next to stand. He turned and pointed at Coleman. "It's his fault! We have never seen trouble like this until he came. If anyone should be removed from the People, it is Tondo. He burns down Taahso's home and we forgive him. He breaks all the traditions and we follow him. After he came here, other outsiders arrived and brought their evil things. He is the Tempter's tool. Remove him, not Nita."

A loud murmuring suddenly erupted in the lodge as the villagers discussed among themselves the meaning of Ayascho's words. Coleman crossed his arms over his chest but said nothing. Although his anger boiled, he presented an outwardly calm demeanor. Those seated next to him, including Tzeechoe, began to feel heat radiating from the gods' messenger and leaned away from him.

Ayascho finished his statement and sat down. Tzeechoe quickly stood and began speaking, "Ayascho has always spoken against Tondo, and he has always been wrong. This matter is not about Tondo. Tonight, we must decide what to do with Nita." He then sat and said no more.

It wasn't long before Shadi stood and began speaking, "The law is clear; she must be separated from the People. Send her away." He then sat.

Many other men took their turns and voiced their opinions. Every one of them advocated banishment of the young woman. Throughout this discussion, Nita's whimpering could be heard as she remained kneeling before the chief.

As each man stood and condemned her, the whimpering grew louder, and it stabbed at Coleman's heart. *She's a thief. She gets what she deserves,* Coleman's inner voice grumbled. This was too serious a matter to remain silent. He pushed away his heartless thoughts and pondered. Finally, he realized he could remain silent no longer, so he stood and took his turn to speak to the People.

"This young woman has lived with you all her life. You know her. You know what kind of person she is. All of you know she is not evil; neither is she a threat to the village. She was tempted by the glitter of a shiny thing and committed a very foolish act, but how serious is her transgression? Did she kill someone? No! Did she hurt someone? No! Did she lie to anyone? No! The law says she must suffer a fate that will lead to her death. Is this justice? Is this what the gods desire? I say no, it is not! A just god would not want to take this child's life over a trinket. Nita, look at me." The girl turned her face toward Coleman but continued crying softly, her cheeks streaked with tears. Namada's sobs could be heard clearly coming from the shadows. "What have you learned from your transgression?" Coleman asked in a stern voice? The girl did not answer. "What have you learned?" he repeated.

Nita turned her face to the floor again and weakly said, "I did a bad thing. I shamed my father and my mother. I hate myself for what I did."

Coleman moved to the young woman, kneeled, and lifted her chin until she was looking him in the eyes. In a gentle voice, he asked, "Will you ever do anything like that again?"

"No, never again. I'm ashamed of myself," came her quick and sincere reply.

"I am sure you speak the truth." Coleman stood and turned to the chief and Taahso. "She has indeed broken the law and deserves punishment, but a punishment that fits her transgression. Condemning this girl to death would be an even greater offense. You are the father of the village and you, Taahso, are the keeper of the Law. I look to both of you for justice and mercy for this child."

Coleman finished speaking and looked deeply into the chief's eyes and then into Taahso's. He returned to his place and sat. The room was silent except for the soft sobs coming from Namada and Nita's heavy breathing.

The chief stood in silence for a very long time and waited for someone else to rise and have his say, but no one else stood. Finally, he asked, "Is there anyone who wishes to speak?" No one stood. He then sat on his stool while he and Taahso quietly spoke between themselves. After several minutes, the chief took a deep breath and stood again. Coleman held his breath as the chief began to speak.

"This girl has committed an evil act. It cannot and will not be ignored. Since her crime did not cause death, she will not die, but it was her hand that took that which did not belong to her. That hand will carry the mark of her offense for the rest of her days as a reminder to never again follow the Tempter's ways. Nita, stand. Namad, come forth and hold your daughter's arm." Both father and daughter did as they were commanded. The chief firmly took Nita's right hand and held her palm upwards. Taahso drew his obsidian knife and stabbed the girl's open palm, dragging the knife point across it. Nita screamed in agonizing pain; a wail that bore into the heart and soul of everyone in the great lodge. Little children began crying, and Namada shrieked as though she, herself, had been wounded. The punishment was done in an instant, and the girl was released. Her left hand held her bleeding right hand by the wrist as she continued to wail in pain. Coleman wanted to help her but thought better of it. This punishment's purpose was to dissuade any future acts of theft, and he felt he needed to let it play through. Namad led his crying daughter to her mother. Then he returned to his place among the men.

The chief began speaking again. "The punishment is fair and justice has been served. We will speak no more of this." His eye caught movement coming out of the shadows. As he watched, Tzeecha approached as all eyes turned to her.

When she reached the center of the lodge, she stopped, lifted the necklace from around her neck, and said in a loud and clear voice, "This is a wicked thing and not worth the life of a young woman. I will not allow it to tempt another." She dropped it into the fire, turned, and glided back to her place with the women. Everyone sat in silence as they contemplated what they had just witnessed.

The chief dismissed the meeting and everyone quietly departed. When Tzeechoe and Coleman exited the lodge, they saw Ayascho standing near the entrance. He said nothing, but his angry eyes were fixed on Coleman as he walked past.

After they had passed him, Coleman began speaking to Tzeechoe, "I still do not understand why Ayascho hates me so much."

"He favors Nita," Tzeechoe merely commented.

Coleman turned and looked at Ayascho and saw he was still following him with his eyes. "Then he should thank me, not hate me."

"He doesn't know what to think anymore. You saved Nita, and for that, I'm sure he is grateful, yet he still hates you because you're not Batru," Tzeechoe advised.

"Why is that," Coleman asked.

"Others have told me he thinks the Batru people have been chosen by the gods for a special purpose. The changes you are making with the traditions have upset him, even though we are better now than before you came. He thinks these changes will lead to our destruction in the future. There is something else; he feels he is in your debt. No one knows why. It has to do with the day you killed the gorga. Do you know why he feels that way?"

Coleman pondered his answer carefully and then said, "It may have something to do with his code of honor."

Tzeechoe looked into Coleman's face, attempting to read his thoughts and then said, "I think there is a secret between the two of you. I don't know what it is, and I will not ask. But be careful, Tondo. He is a foolish boy and very angry. I wouldn't want him to hurt you."

"Do not worry about me, my friend. He may be angry and foolish, but he is not todo." The two men laughed and continued toward Tzeechoe's home. A flash of lightning warned of the start of another downpour. The men rushed back to the hut and entered just as the rain began to fall again.

CHAPTER 16

FOLLOWERS OF MUNNEVO

Tangundo and Nevesant had securely bound the intruders; Gund, Fino, and their leader, Turvy. A long, straight branch had been cut down and rested across the three men's right shoulders. Their necks were tied to the pole, and each man's hands were tied together at the wrists. Every sign of resistance was met with a severe beating by Tangundo, using Turvy's quarterstaff as his weapon. The three prisoners were still reeling from the outsider's painful aura and all three began lamenting the gods' punishment.

"You go with me into mist," Tangundo ordered.

"No!" Gund yelled in fear.

"It will be the death of us all," Fino wailed.

Tangundo's purple aura ignited again and he slammed his quarterstaff onto each man's head, drawing more blood. "Mist or purple fire?" he threatened. He then pushed the rear end of the pole linking the men together and they stumbled forward.

As they approached the edge of the mist, Nevesant stopped. He would go no further; the gods of the mist were ruthless. Only Tangundo had ever returned after entering their domain. Nevesant would remain at least a stone's throw from the mist. Although he had heard the gods' names whispered in quiet conversation by village folk, he dared not even repeat them here for fear of summoning one.

Tangundo turned his head and saw that Nevesant had stopped. The tall man with the red Munnevo eyes simply nodded and continued his trek into the mist, pushing the pole holding the other men as they woefully advanced. Soon, all four men disappeared into the embracing fog, while Nevesant nervously waited.

The men had entered the mist around midmorning and Nevesant had neither seen nor heard anything from any of them since. Had his new master failed to please the gods? Had the outsider returned to them and abandoned him? He began to worry and despair as tears of grief and sorrow were shed.

In the late afternoon, when the boy was about to give up hope, he saw a shadowy figure moving in the mist. The image drew closer and soon Nevesant could see it was the tall outsider, Tangundo. As he watched, his master stumbled forward. He looked weak and tired. Nevesant rushed to him, helping to steady him as he moved away from the mist. It wasn't long before Tangundo dropped to his knees with an anguished sigh. He fell forward and lost consciousness.

Nevesant built a small fire next to where his master and friend had collapsed. Tangundo awoke and found himself covered by a blanket, a fire nearby, and the boy roasting his snared catch over the flames. The outsider clutched his head, attempting to push away the fierce throbbing pain he felt.

Nevesant looked up and saw his master had awakened. "Master, are you alright? You gave me a big scare."

"Yes, I'm fine. I just have a head-pounder."

"You were gone a long time. I feared you would not return. What happened?" the boy wondered.

"The gods took them and then they turned to me. I thought I was about to face the same fate." Tangundo paused and his Munnevo eyes grew wide as he recalled the terrifying memory.

Nevesant stared at Tangundo's fearful expression and asked, "Tell me what they did. What do they look like?"

The outsider refocused. "They are ghastly and hideous. But they were pleased with my offering, so they trained me and increased my inner-power. It was a painful experience and I was overwhelmed. They warned me that too much too fast will cause insanity in a simple Worlder. When they finished, I was undone." He took a deep breath. "What have you there? I'm hungry."

Nevesant took his gravetum knife, cut off a piece of meat, and handed it to the outsider. "Master, what did you learn?" Tangundo swept the air with his free hand and Nevesant's knife sprang from his grip and flew to his master, who snatched it out of the air. Nevesant's eyes widened in awe. Tangundo smiled. "Master, can you teach me what the gods taught you?"

"Maybe, in time, Nevesant. I've learned that all intelligent beings of this world possess the inner-power; however, it must be awakened. Someday, I may be able to awaken yours, but only after you have shown me your full loyalty," Tangundo declared. The boy smiled widely, and the two ate in silence for a while.

Finally, Nevesant spoke. "Master, your speech, it has improved. How is that possible?"

"By the power of the gods of the mist." Tangundo finished

his meal and stood. "We can no longer remain here. The three sacrifices will be missed. Others will soon come looking for them. We must move deeper into the forest."

"But master, no one can contend with you; you're all powerful," Nevesant exclaimed.

"Not yet, boy. In time, I'm sure to be. I cannot yet resist a village. We will move our camp in the morning," the outsider told him.

"Master, if we move deeper into the forest, we will surely run afoul of the marauders who call it their home."

"Who are these marauders? How many are there? Who leads them?" Tangundo wondered.

"They're men who have broken the king's law, and they are hiding in the forest. They pillage and rob; they're dangerous," Nevesant warned.

"How many?" Tangundo asked.

"Ten or twenty. I don't know for sure, master. I've heard they are led by a big man named Buffo. He once lived in my village, at least until he killed a man in a tavern brawl. He fled and the purrant sent men after him, but he was never found."

"What's a purrant?"

"A purrant is the king's representative in the village. He upholds the law and has received a sword of authority from the king," the boy explained.

"We will search out these marauders, and I will speak with their leader, Buffo. Then, we will pay the purrant a visit," Tangundo told the boy. Nevesant's expression soured, displaying his concern. Obviously, the boy wanted nothing to do with either.

The next morning, the two disassembled their camp and moved further into the forest. They traveled for several days and established a new camp near a spring that flowed into a large, green pool of deep water. They continued their daily routine, surviving on creatures they hunted and ate. It wasn't a life either preferred, yet it was one they had to tolerate for the time being.

Many full Munnoga moons passed. Early one afternoon, Tangundo returned to his camp after spending a couple of segments spearing fish that hung from a braided leather cord; enough for a few meals for the two. As he approached, he saw several men milling around the camp. Nevesant was sitting on a log with a large man hovering menacingly over him. The boy looked terrified.

"What's going on here?" Tangundo shouted as he approached, his kerchief veiling the lower half of his face.

The men turned and faced him. Tangundo counted fifteen. "Come on in, we've been waiting for you, outsider," the big man roared with a laugh.

Tangundo stopped at the edge of camp, dropping the string of fish and holding his spear leveled at the nearest intruder. "Are you all right, boy?" he asked. Nevesant responded with a nod but said nothing.

"We're just paying this little creeper a visit," the big man growled. "I'm Buffo and I own these woods. You two are trespassers and must pay a price if you want to remain here. That string of fish is a good start."

"So, you're Buffo. The boy has told me about you. I've wanted to meet you," Tangundo told him.

"Is that so? Remove your kerchief and let me see your face," Buffo ordered. Tangundo pulled the kerchief down, revealing his growing, dark beard. "What kind of creature are you? Men, take him!" Buffo shouted.

Tangundo's aura ignited and its burning rays chased away his assailants. He threw his spear as hard as he could, and it hit Buffo in the abdomen. As the big man staggered, Tangundo charged him and grabbed him by the upper arms, holding him in the purple aura of heat. Buffo screamed in pain and his suffering cries continued for quite a few agonizing moments. When the man's legs gave out, Tangundo pushed him away and he collapsed to the ground whimpering as he clutched the spear's shaft. A few moments later, Buffo became silent and unmoving. One of the marauders, witnessing the demise of his leader at the hands of the sorcerer man-beast, darted away. Before he could take three steps, he fell to the ground. He scrambled to his feet and attempted to continue his dash. He fell again, knocked down by an unseen force.

Tangundo pulled the hand ax from a nearby log and strode to the cowering man. "You cannot escape. I possess power from the gods of the mist," he barked. He turned and faced the others. He passed his left arm through the air and a visible wave of energy crashed into the standing men, knocking them off their feet. Nevesant rolled backward off the log he was sitting on and dropped to the ground, his head slowly peeking over the log again with eyes wide.

"Don't kill me, please!" a marauder cried.

"Spare us," another wailed. The others simply cried in fear.

"Ha, that's better," Tangundo said with satisfaction. "Let me make you an offer. If you follow me, I'll allow you to live. If you refuse, you'll be fed to the gods of the mist." The men whined their dread, all offering allegiance to their new master. "Very good," he said. "Gather around, my fellow followers of Munnevo, and I will tell you what we will do. I'm tired of living like an animal in the wild. That's about to change, and you may become great ones in the eyes of those who have scorned and hunted you. Nevesant, fetch the fish I speared and prepare our meal while I talk with our new friends." Tangundo pulled up his kerchief as the marauders gathered and squatted on the ground in front of him.

Nevesant listened closely as he prepared the meal. Tangundo was speaking of things that boggled the young man's mind. He spoke of conquering villages, then towns and cities, and finally entire kingdoms. Those who followed him would be rewarded with riches, power, and fame. It was a grand dream, one the others had never even imagined, yet this hairy outsider painted a picture that mesmerized all of them, especially the boy. They were caught up in the glory they could all receive and the respect they craved; respect from those who despised them. It was the promise of a life they could only imagine in their wildest dreams. They easily embraced the outsider's call and when he had finished, they re-pledged their allegiance to him and his plan willingly.

The meal was still being cooked when Tangundo finished. He ordered his new followers to dispose of Buffo's body.

They dragged it to a small cave not far away and left it there, unburied. When they returned, the meal was served. As they ate, they shared their dreams of the future and their promised power. Their new master smiled under his kerchief and let them continue with their boasting and blustering.

After they had eaten, Tangundo spoke again. "We will soon pay Purrant Grazius a visit. I will take his sword. It will be the first of our many victories." All of the men and the boy, Nevesant, cheered heartily for their new beginning.

CHAPTER 17

WORTHY GIFTS

A bright dawn broke over the Batru village, lifting the villagers' spirits. Coleman declared it one of the most beautiful mornings he had yet seen. The clean, sweet air had a hint of dampness to it, unlike the oppressive humidity that he had become accustomed to. The members of his hunting party had received their blessings from Taahso and were looking for plant food this day. Namad was silent, but Coleman could tell that the fear of losing his only child was no longer in his thoughts. Though the immediate danger was past, it would take time for him and the village to forget his daughter's transgression. Coleman was interested in watching how he was treated by the other men in the party. So far, nothing had been said to Namad about it, and he continued to keep to himself. About midmorning, Coleman approached him and asked about Nita's wound.

"It hurts her very much, as it should. She will have a scar to remind her of what she did," Namad told him in a matter of fact tone.

Coleman offered to ease her pain, but Namad rejected his offer. "She must suffer the ache of her punishment as I must suffer this humiliation and shame."

There was nothing Coleman could say to change his mind.

Namad was an honorable and proud man, as all his other hunting partners were, and something as grievous as this would leave a deep scar on his honor, just like the one on Nita's palm.

Coleman brought the betzoe pup along for the first time. Toto ran free and often stopped to sniff some exciting smell on the ground. He would disappear into the tall grass for minutes on end, causing Coleman to worry he had run away. After some time passed, the gangly pup would return and look up at Coleman as if to ask, 'Can I do it again?' Coleman would rub his ears and the pup would scamper off, chasing a new smell. The other hunters were concerned to have a wild animal running amok near them, but as they became accustomed to the betzoe's presence, they relaxed. Some even chuckled at the pup's antics. After an hour or so, the pup was completely exhausted and plopped himself down at Coleman's feet. He lifted the tired animal and put him in a wicker basket Tzeechoe had woven for such an occurrence. It had leather straps and he wore it like a backpack. Toto was comfortable and secure in his little mobile den and quickly fell asleep. Coleman knew it wouldn't be long before the pup outgrew the basket, but he figured by then Toto would be large enough to fend for himself.

"Tzeechoe, as we left the village, I noticed Taahso placing a pole on a rock, and he was looking at the rising p´atezas. What was he doing?" Coleman wondered.

"Taahso was checking to see how long before Matti-mas begins. I think it is very close," Tzeechoe answered.

"Do you know how many will be joined at the Matti-mas."

"I don't know for sure, but usually it's one or two. We get another line, too," Tzeechoe told him as he drew a finger across his cheek. "Tondo, how many lines are you?"

"At my homeland, I am about thirty lines, although there are fewer days to a line." Tzeechoe looked at Coleman with wonder but said no more. "How long does the Matti-mas last?" Coleman asked.

"Three days and nights."

For the next several days, life in the village continued in its regular routine. Nature was resplendent with new growth all around. Flowering bushes and trees began to bloom in a dazzling array of colors. Hunting improved and the collection of edible foods expanded as the villagers began searching the ground as well as the trees and bushes. It was a happy time for nearly all in the village. The children played harder and laughed louder than Coleman had seen and heard before, and nearly all the villagers were more willing to leave the village in small groups.

The elimination of the gorga threat had freed them from a anxious life of fear, near starvation, and slavish dread. Coleman often smiled in satisfaction as he saw the good that he had brought to the village; however, one thing did worry him. He had not seen Nita at all since her punishment and very seldom did Namada leave the lodge. During a hunt, Coleman convinced Namad that his daughter needed to stop hiding and come outside, no matter how ashamed she felt. He suggested Namad and Nita meet him near the center of the village to have her wound examined. Namad agreed and, though reluctant, Nita obeyed her father, allowing Coleman to examine the wound. He found it to be healing satisfactorily, but she said it was still painful. Coleman convinced Namad to allow him to use his taah and eliminate her pain, helping Nita relax. After that was done, some of the other young women of the village approached her in conversation, and soon they were talking like typical teenage girls.

It was easy to see that Nita was very self-conscious of the wound on her palm. While Coleman watched and listened, he noticed Ayascho silently observing from a distance, but when their eyes met, the young man quickly retreated and disappeared into the village.

Taahso continued visiting Atura and Tzeechoe told Coleman, it wouldn't be long before Taahso made an offer to take her from him. It was a tradition in the village for the suitor to present the prospective bride's father with a gift, usually of something that the father greatly desired. Since Coleman was not from the village, Taahso was having difficulty determining what a suitable gift would be.

"Taahso has asked me for help. He wants me to find out what would be a proper gift," Tzeechoe had told Coleman. Usually, the gift was a favored hunting weapon, like a well-made spear or knife. Everyone knew Coleman had no skill with a spear. His shiny short sword was the envy of all the hunters in the village, and that made a new knife redundant. This left Taahso in a quandary. Coleman had been pondering this very problem since he had learned from Tzeechoe that a gift was part of the protocol. If he were to be honest, the only thing he really wanted was a rip ticket back home. He knew Taahso wasn't going to be able to get that; however, as he thought about it, he developed a plan.

"Tzeechoe, may I enter," Taahso called.

"Yes, you may come in," Tzeechoe replied.

The evening meal was over and the expected visitor had arrived. Taahso walked through the doorway and immediately Coleman noticed his puzzled expression. He faced toward Tzeechoe and Coleman, giving each a curt bow before he seated himself on a mat that had been prepared for him. After he was seated, he looked at Atura and presented a slight smile before his face became stoic.

Taahso took a deep breath and began speaking. "Tondo, I would like to present you with a gift, but I cannot think of anything that would be appropriate. I have talked with many in the village and those with whom you hunt, but no one knows what you would find acceptable. I come before you this evening to humbly ask what I may present to you."

Coleman took a deep breath, crossed his arms over his chest, and leaned back slightly. "I can see that is a problem. After all, I am a visitor to the village. I have found good men here, and many I can call my friends. To me, that is most important; however, there are some things I favor that I do not yet have." And then he paused. Taahso leaned forward, eyes wide, hanging on Coleman's every word. "I really like habaga," Coleman finally admitted.

"Yes, Tondo, we all do, but as you know, Atura is the best at finding them. Why not ask her?" Taahso questioned.

"She was injured in her last attempt. I want her to heal fully before I ask her to do it again." Atura looked puzzled. The bites and scratches she had suffered many days ago had healed. Coleman continued, "Sometimes I am cold. I need a warm wrap made by the hands of a taahso."

"That's women's work. Anyway, I have no skill at making such things," Taahso said, a bit annoyed.

"It is only a taahso who can infuse it with the power of taah," Coleman continued, doing his best to suppress a smile. He could see Atura was becoming uncomfortable with his odd requests. "Also, I want the horn of the tuntro."

Tzeechoe could no longer contain himself and interjected, "Tondo, no one has ever given such gifts. It is too much."

"I think a woman as special as Atura is worth nothing less. Taahso, is Atura worth these things?"

Taahso cleared his throat, took a deep breath and answered shakily, "If these are the things you desire, I will get them. I do not know how to make a cloak and I have not gone on a hunt since I was a young man."

"I am sure Atura can help you find the habaga, but you must retrieve them yourself. I am certain she can show you how to make a wrap, but it is only by your hand that it will receive the special power that only you can give it. I am sure many hunters in the village will help you hunt the tuntro, but you must strike the killing blow."

"Then it all will be done as you have said. I would like to speak with Atura this evening."

"Of course," Coleman replied as he pointed to Tzeecha with an uplifted open palm. The three immediately left the lodge.

"What is this you have done, Tondo?" Tzeechoe quickly asked. "I know you well enough to see there is a plan somewhere in all of this."

Coleman simply smiled and said nothing.

"Can Taahso really make a warm wrap with special powers?" Tzeechoe asked.

"We will see," Coleman told him with a wry smile.

For the next several days, Coleman heard reports of Taahso's struggles. His first attempt at retrieving habaga ended in near disaster. He had climbed to the top of the jungle canopy and, when a strong gust of wind hit him, he lost his grip, falling into the lower branches. He tried to get the habaga again on the next day, and with Atura's advice was able to cut and bring down a large bunch of the delicious fruit.

His next challenge was to make the wrap that Tondo wanted. Taahso decided to use ghee hides since the soft fur provided the best warmth. Again, he relied on Atura's guidance to soften the tough hides with plant oil. He then cut, formed, and sewed the skins into a cape-like wrap that would fall below the knees on the tall visitor.

Although Atura offered to help, Taahso wouldn't let her do more than give him counsel. "Tondo said I must make it myself, so I will," he told her, obviously annoyed by the project.

His last challenge was the one he dreaded the most. He had not been on a hunt since he became the taahso and even more telling was his fear of the huge creature—the massive water buffalo-like beast.

He had no problem assembling a hunting party. Every hunter in the village considered it a great honor to accompany the taahso on a hunt. It took a few days to locate a tuntro, but eventually, the deed was done and Taahso had obtained the final gift.

After the evening meal, Coleman, Tzeechoe, Tzeecha, and Atura waited for Taahso. Atura was smiling from ear to ear and could hardly contain herself. The others passed coy smiles, watching her nervous antics as they waited.

"Tzeechoe, may I enter?" Taahso finally called.

"Yes, Taahso," came Tzeechoe's quick reply.

Taahso entered the lodge dressed in his finest garb. Coleman hadn't seen him decked out in such finery since the meeting in the great lodge when he gave the oral history of the Batru's beginnings. The only thing absent was his staff because his arms were full of the gifts Coleman had requested.

"Tondo, I wish to take Atura from you," he said bowing before him. "I have brought you these gifts."

Coleman carefully examined each item. He hummed and hawed as he lifted and poked at each offering. He tried on the wrap and then laid it back on the mat. His expression was stern and emotionless. This ritual went on for several minutes until the tension in the lodge was thick enough to cut with a knife. A trickle of sweat slid down Taahso's face as he watched. Atura shifted nervously and waited for Coleman to say something, anything.

Finally, when not even Tzeechoe and Tzeecha could bear it any longer, Coleman spoke. "Tell me, Taahso, how did you come by these fine things?"

Taahso seemed taken aback by the question. His eyes widened and he leaned forward as though he hadn't heard the words correctly. "I . . . I . . . with my own hands," he stuttered, completely flustered by the unexpected question.

"How did you come by these?" Coleman asked as he lifted the habaga bunch off the floor mat.

"I climbed to the tops of the trees and cut them," Taahso replied.

"Had you ever done that before," Coleman asked.

"Never. It is a long way up and I nearly fell to the ground. Atura gave me good advice, and I was able to get them on my second try."

"And this?" Coleman asked as he put down the habaga bunch and lifted the ghee cloak.

"Atura showed me how to make it, but I did it with my own hands," Taahso replied firmly.

"And this?" Coleman asked again, lifting the tuntro horn.

"That was the most difficult. I had not hunted for many rains, and I wasn't sure how I would do it. Many of the hunters in the village helped me prepare. Then we hunted the tuntro and I took its horn."

"Was there something else that was difficult about this hunt?" Coleman asked. Taahso's head snapped back and he looked at Atura. She cringed and slowly shook her head from side to side.

"How do you know that?" Taahso asked.

"I saw the fear in your eyes when you looked at Dubo's wound. I knew that was not the first time you had seen someone gored by a tuntro," Coleman responded.

"You are right, Tondo. I saw the tuntro's wound before. When I was young, I hunted with my friend Tzani. We found a tuntro and it charged us. I was trampled and injured. Tzani was gored. He died, painfully, over many days. It was awful. I wanted to kill that tuntro, but . . ." Taahso paused and lowered his head, "I was afraid."

"Yet you overcame your fear and brought me this gift. How did you prevail?" Coleman asked as he lifted the horn.

"I shared my fear and my shame with Atura. We talked and she gave me the strength to do what I had to do."

"Tell me, Taahso, what have you learned from all this," Coleman asked as Tzeechoe began to understand Coleman's plan.

Taahso thought for a moment. Then he looked at Atura as he answered the question. "I learned that I could not have done any of these things without Atura's help. She was there to support and encourage me. Now, I understand how much I need her to make my life full."

Coleman smiled and said, "That is right, Taahso. Atura will be there to give you counsel and strength when you need it most. You must always be a strong man because you are the taahso of this village. A strong taahso needs a strong woman to help him during the most difficult times."

"Yes, that is true, Tondo. And Atura is a strong woman," Taahso interjected.

"You have overcome old fears and learned new talents. Remember, Taahso, you can never become all you are meant to be without the help of your woman. For you to grow, she must also grow, and you must help her be all that she can be, as well. In that way, you both become better and stronger together."

"Now I see the wisdom in these gifts, Tondo. I thank you for being my teacher." Then he bowed.

"Taahso, thank you for these worthy gifts. You may take Atura from me along with my blessing." Tzeecha began clapping and Tzeechoe quickly joined her. Coleman smiled as he watched Taahso and Atura's eyes locked in an invisible embrace.

"We should not let these habagas go to waste," Coleman finally said as he handed the fruit to Atura. The group chatted and laughed while the fire warmed the fruit. When the delicious treat was ready, they ate and talked some more.

Before he retired for the night, Taahso told the gathering the Matti-mas would begin in five days. This brought more smiles and laughter to the group. They all followed Taahso as he left the lodge and waved goodnight as he walked to his lodge. Coleman turned his head heavenward and watched the blue and red moons in their nightly dance. Munnoga hung alone and low in the sky. He stood transfixed, still marveling at the wondrous sights above. After several minutes, Coleman walked back to the lodge and found Atura examining the ghee wrap.

"Does this really have special powers?" she asked.

Coleman walked to Atura's side and put an arm around her shoulders and said with a smile, "The magic is not in the wrap. It was in its making."

CHAPTER 18

MATTI-MAS DAY ONE

During the next four days, the entire village was abuzz with activity. Extra food was collected and the women began preparing for the Matti-mas feast. New clothes were fashioned as all wanted to look their best.

Coleman continued his daily routine. He hunted or gathered in the morning and spent the afternoons practicing taah. He was becoming more proficient every day. As long as he didn't let his mind wander, he was able to control not only where the fire started, but also the size and intensity of the flame. After each successful attempt, he would set a new goal. Failure brought introspection. He would determine why things went the way they did and work to improve them on his next attempt.

Only Toto accompanied him on these ventures. Tzeechoe was busy preparing for the Matti-mas and found watching Coleman's struggles a bit boring after the first few days. Both felt it was safe enough in daylight to let Coleman continue on his own.

After each practice session, on his way back to the village, he would take a detour to the creek and collect a few gold nuggets. He kept this activity to himself, not wanting the other villagers to learn the true nature of the shiny stones.

It's your fortune. The chief gave it to you, his inner voice harped. *If word ever gets out to the rest of the world that the local creek holds a fortune in gold, the People will suffer from the greed of others, and you will lose this treasure,* he greedily surmised. *This will lead to either exploitation like what had happened on your home world or uncontrollable vanity and jealousy like what had happened with Tzeecha. You may as well keep all this to yourself; including the riches.*

Many times he considered explaining more forcibly to the chief and Taahso about the wealth at their fingertips. But, in each case, by the time he arrived back at the village, he had decided that until he knew more about this new world he was on, he would just keep collecting the little yellow pebbles. He had already seen what mischief a few bright beads could cause; however, he felt his own avarice growing with each nugget he collected.

As the days counted down until the Matti-mas, excitement grew among the villagers. Coleman felt this fervor was akin to New Year's or Mardi Gras celebrations back home.

The day before the Matti-mas was to begin, Coleman noticed most of the women had left the village. Later, they returned with baskets of fruit he had never seen before. Upon questioning Tzeechoe and Atura, he learned the fruit contained mystical properties. After further questioning, Coleman deduced that the fruit contained some type of psychedelic compound that produced hallucinations. He didn't like the idea of an entire village becoming high, but this obviously wasn't the first time they had done this. He resigned himself to being an observer and hoped the three days of activities would pass quickly. *Why be a bystander? You've worked hard and you deserve to have some fun,* was the thought that came to him.

Coleman attempted to gain an understanding of what the lure was and concluded that it was the only fun thing the people allowed themselves during the entire span and there would not be another until a whole span, four hundred days, had passed again.

Also, many important events occurred this past span, including Tondo's arrival, the killing of the gorga, and the visit by Myron, Zoseemo, and their incredible rasters. These events even topped the triumphant hunt for a bataro, which in spans past would have been the most celebrated event.

Late in the afternoon of the day before the start of the Matti-mas, Coleman returned from his daily practice and found Atura waiting for him in the lodge. "These are for you to wear. I won't have any of the women saying I didn't take care of you," she said as she handed him a bundle of clothes.

"What are they?" he asked.

"Tomorrow, everyone will be wearing new clothes and so should you. I hope you like them."

Coleman took the bundle and examined each item. He found a vest of supple leather and a pair of leather trousers. He immediately put on both and noticed they fit perfectly. He then asked, "How do they look?"

"They look splendid. The trousers will protect your legs from sharp brush and the vest will protect your shoulders from the hot p´atezas," Atura advised. Then she continued, "Thank you for all you have done. When the chief gave me to you, I was afraid, but you are an honorable man and a good friend. I wish there were more I could do to show you my appreciation."

"Atura, that is the nicest thing you have ever said to me, and these clothes are just what I need. Thank you very much. I hope you and Taahso have a happy life together." Atura blushed a little. She was about to speak again when Tzeechoe and Tzeecha burst into the lodge.

"Look at you!" Tzeecha exclaimed. "Hoy! You look very handsome." Now, Coleman began to blush and everyone noticed his reddened tone.

"Why do you turn red like that?" Tzeechoe asked.

"That's what happens when my people get embarrassed," he said.

"You look funny, Tondo," Tzeechoe mused and then began laughing.

"Oh, stop it," Coleman growled. "What do you think of the new clothes Atura made for me?"

"Very good. I wish I had new clothes," Tzeechoe said as he glanced at his wife.

"Ha," she said. "I was going to wait until after the evening meal to give you your gift, but I'll do it now." She rummaged through a pile of skins stowed in the shadows of the lodge and came up with a bundle very similar to the one Atura had presented Coleman. "Here. Don't bother me anymore," she said in mock irritation. Tzeechoe took the bundle and quickly slipped into the trousers and vest she had fashioned. "We still have work to do on our own things, so you two leave us alone while we finish," she told the men.

"I think we had better leave before they put us to work, Tzeechoe," Coleman quipped.

"Not before you take off your new clothes. Those are for tomorrow," Atura barked.

"You had better do as she says," Tzeechoe warned.

"You, too!" Tzeecha demanded of her husband.

The men carefully removed their new garments, folded them, and put them in a safe place. The women then shooed them out of the lodge. While the women giggled and laughed as they worked inside, the men bided their time and waited for the evening meal. Tzeechoe started work on a new basket and Coleman passed the time by igniting a dry stick he held in his hand, then extinguishing it repeatedly. Tzeechoe occasionally shook his head but said nothing as he watched Coleman's antics. After an hour or so, the women exited the lodge and headed to the center of the village.

"Good," Tzeechoe exclaimed. "I'm starving."

"Now tell me, Tzeechoe, the entire village will be up to greet the rising p´atezas tomorrow morning, right?"

"Yes, yes. It is the beginning of the new season and the Matti-mas. We must thank the gods for blessing us with another line of life. It is also a time to remember those who have crossed-over since the last Matti-mas. It is a very solemn time, so be prepared. We will pray for Munnari to visit us in our mystical fruit dreams and safely guide us to the next Matti-mas."

It was still dark when the booming of drums awakened the village. Coleman wiped the sleep from his eyes. He quickly stepped through the doorway of the lodge and scanned the early morning sky. It held the promise of a beautiful day. Only a few wisps of clouds slowly moved across the star-studded sky. All three moons had set and the eastern horizon was beginning to turn a warm orange and red. Tzeechoe, Tzeecha, and Atura soon exited the lodge dressed in their new Mattimas garb. Coleman quickly re-entered the lodge and put on the fine trousers and vest Atura had made for him. The four briskly walked to the gathering near the village entrance.

The chief and Taahso stood in front of the seated villagers. Families sat together, unlike the separation of the sexes during meetings in the great lodge. Coleman's group found an open space and sat on the moist, soft grass. Atura was no longer with them for she had found a seat near another group of families.

Coleman noticed that both the chief and Taahso wore elegant headdresses made with colorful feathers and flowers. As he looked around the gathering, he could see that every female, no matter what her age, sported a flower in her hair. The married women wore red flowers and the unmarried women wore pink or white. He then noticed a red flower in Tzeecha's hair and a pink flower in Atura's. As he scanned the gathering, it became apparent that children and young teenagers wore white. Coleman surmised the pink flower symbolized an eligible maiden, while white told the world that the girl was too young or not interested yet. As he continued his scan, he found Namad's family. He could see Nita wearing a white flower. All the other girls her age appeared to be wearing pink. He also could see Ayascho's eyes fixed upon her. Coleman shook his head in dismay.

"Tondo, what is it?" Tzeechoe asked.

"I still see that Nita's scar is covering more than just her hand."

"She feels unworthy," Tzeechoe noted.

"Yes, I can see that, too. I hope she gets over it soon," Coleman said.

"She may never forgive herself. Her transgression was very great and she shamed her entire family line."

The chief raised his arms above his head, and the drumming stopped. "My children, it is the beginning of the Matti-mas. Let us give thanks to the gods for we have been granted another line of life. Let us remember those who are no longer with us this day. Taahso will now tell us our history. Listen carefully and make sure your children pay attention so they may understand the connection to their ancestors."

With those words, the chief sat. Then Taahso began reciting from memory the history of the People. He did not stand but remained seated on his stool. He droned on in a prosaic monotone. As Coleman listened to the words, he became enthralled by what he was learning.

The ancient tribe had grown too large to be accommodated by the land. The decision was made to divide the tribe into two groups, and one of the groups would separate itself from the other by a great distance. Family clan leaders discussed and argued over the details, but in the end, an acceptable agreement was reached. Families who chose to leave were allowed to go, but they amounted to only about a third of the original tribe. The remaining clans drew lots until the agreed upon number was obtained.

Taahso then named each clan and family that departed. As a name was given, Coleman noticed that a grouping of families in the assembly would give a shout of acknowledgment. Coleman realized now why Atura was not sitting with Tzeechoe and Tzeecha.

For the next several hours, Taahso continued relating the adventures of the journey the tribe's ancestors took. Their path was full of danger and a few deaths, but after many days the People had traveled far enough. They searched and finally found the pleasant place where they now lived.

Taahso continued with the history, naming names of those who died and those who were born. He recited significant events, including many groundshakes. He included several events attributed to the blessings of Batru and how the People survived a rainy season that lasted many days longer than usual. They flourished through several generations and then happiness fled. A powerful predator moved into the area—the gorga. The People attempted to kill the beast, but it was too powerful and killed many of the tribe's best hunters. This was so devastating to the village that starvation became a real threat. If a hunter died, there was no recourse but to expel his family from the village to save the tribe. A hunter could barely gather enough food for his own family, let alone another. It was an unpopular choice, but it was accepted by a previous chief, taahso, and group of tusk-men.

Taahso continued naming names and relating events for another hour. Finally, Coleman heard his tribal name, Tondo, uttered. Taahso included the vote for his life and how he had killed the gorga and freed the people from its dread. He also included Myron's visit and Nita's theft. At this, Coleman dropped his head in dismay, knowing now that it had become tribal history and would forever be shared with the tribe's descendants. It would always be a scar of shame upon the lodge of Namad.

Taahso soon completed the history and spoke no more. There was no fanfare. No applause. Nothing. He just stopped and that was it. The assembly sat quietly for a minute or so while they pondered the story.

After a long delay, the chief rose and began to speak. "My children, you have heard the history of the People from the Great Separation until today's rise of the p´atezas. Remember it well and share often what you have heard with your children for they must understand the effort and sacrifice our fathers' fathers have made. It is you and the children who will carry on in the coming days. Batru has given us a great blessing. He has sent us Tondo to destroy the gorga and open our minds to new ideas. It is now time for Tondo-measha. Let us go and feast and give our thanks to Batru."

The assembly began to disperse. As they did, many of the villagers drew close to Coleman and touched him lightly on the shoulder or head. He couldn't tell whether it was in thanks or in reverence, but it made him self-conscious and uncomfortable, though as the families continued to pass by him, he could see the gratitude in their eyes for what he had done for their village. He felt a joy he had never experienced before; the joy of satisfaction in giving the People a new lease on life. His love for them grew even stronger.

After all the families had left the area, Coleman stood and walked back to Tzeechoe's lodge. When he passed by the vacant abode of Atura's father, he stopped. How long had he been living with Tzeechoe and Tzeecha? He had lost track of time; he couldn't recall an exact count of days. Nevertheless, it had been too long. He felt like a guest who had overstayed his welcome. It was time for him to move into his own dwelling place and this lodge would serve him well.

As he contemplated his circumstances, a thought disturbed him. *These are a simple people, but they could be an instrument in your hands to bring your superior knowledge to the rest of the world. It wouldn't take much to train them into a powerful military force and then you could be well on your way to revolutionizing this entire world. You could be a benevolent king and it wouldn't even be that hard,* his inner voice urged. *Many already look upon you as a god or at least a messenger sent by the gods. You can turn that to your advantage, as well.* Suddenly, he heard footsteps behind him and turned to see Atura coming toward him.

"Are you going to skip the meal that is so important that it was named after you?" she asked in a dry, sarcastic tone. "The others are waiting."

He shook his head as if coming out of a stupor. He felt dizzy and stumbled, nearly falling to the ground. He had never had such delusions of grandeur back home and yet now he was thinking about becoming a god-king. That just wasn't in his nature.

In the creation story Taahso had shared some time ago, he mentioned a Tempter who had been loosed upon the world. Could he have just experienced its influence? Was it the voice from his many other worrisome thoughts? Could it possibly be a real entity of evil? So many of the things he had experienced since his arrival were impossible for him to understand fully, not the least of which was the power of taah. If that were possible, why not a Tempter? But that would also mean the Whisperer was likely real, to balance out the whole thing. That was a lot to accept by one not believing in the tribe's religion.

He finally regained his bearings and focus. "Sorry, I was just thinking of moving into your father's lodge when the Matti-mas is over. Would that be all right with you?" he asked Atura.

"I have already told you, the lodge is yours. It needs someone to care for it, and I think you would be the right person to do that."

Coleman smiled and, try as she may, Atura couldn't stifle a smile of her own. "You know, Atura, I'm beginning to like Matti-mas more and more. You keep saying such nice things to me," Coleman teased.

Atura responded with a simple, "Todo!" and walked toward the center of the village with Coleman following like a wayward child.

After the meal, the women gathered, formed small groups,

and began playing a stick game. The game started with six women seated in a circle with about four feet separating each of them. Three such rings were formed. Around each ring, another gathering of standing women collected. All the women were singing a catchy tune and clapping their hands while those inside the circle started twirling the sticks. They would tap the ground with the sticks and, when the singers gave a shout, they would toss the sticks to the person across the circle. This continued for some time and each time the tune was repeated, the tempo increased. When a woman in the circle missed the beat, she was eliminated and had to leave the ring. Those inside the circle would rearrange and the tune would begin anew. If there was an odd number of players, the sticks were tossed either left or right, depending on the sequence of the tune. When another woman dropped her stick or made a move out of sequence, she was eliminated. Occasionally, the sticks would hit in midair, and it was up to those in the outer ring to determine who was at fault. As the games continued, Coleman noticed that sometimes the outer ring voted for the wrong player. This puzzled him until he determined that the vote was more of a popularity contest than it was one of fairness.

As the afternoon progressed, the games continued. After every woman had a chance to participate, two new rings were formed that included only the previous winners. The men did not participate in any way. Only the women played the game and sang the tune while the men stood around the outside of the ring and shouted encouragement to their wives, daughters, sisters, and friends. It was all in good-hearted fun and no one seemed to be upset when they were eliminated.

As the contests progressed, the length of time between each elimination increased substantially. By dusk, there were still some winners of the first round who had not yet played a second time, but the games had to be called due to darkness. Coleman learned that they would conclude tomorrow morning. He also learned that there was no real prize, just the satisfaction of being the best player in the tribe that season.

He had been following Tzeecha's and Atura's progress. Late in the afternoon, Tzeecha was eliminated when she went left when she should have gone right. She laughed and left the circle, giggling and covering her face with her hands. It was evident to Coleman that Atura was taking the competition much more seriously. Her concentration clearly showed on her face. He was surprised that she won every vote even though her popularity in the tribe was not all that great. It soon became apparent to Coleman that her status had changed significantly when Taahso had chosen her as his soon-to-be wife. She would become the taahsa, a most prestigious tribal position. It seemed to him that no one wanted to be on her bad side.

The evening meal was shared under the light of all three moons. Munnoga hung low in the western sky. Munnari and Munnevo danced high in the east. All were at first quarter. The meal was hearty and full of different meats, newly discovered vegetables, and sweet tasting fruits.

It is a feast fit for a king, Coleman thought as he indulged himself until his stomach bulged. He lay on a grassy strip of ground feeding Toto strips of meat. Most of the villagers had grown accustomed to the betzoe by now and they no longer feared him. It had even surprised Coleman that the pup had become such a social creature. He had worried the animal might turn to its wild side as it matured, but much to his relief, it had not, at least not so far. It was probably time to begin training him to hunt. Coleman felt that would require them to hunt together alone until the betzoe learned his duties, but all that was for another day. This evening was for relaxation and the joy of being among people who had accepted him and who he loved.

About an hour or so after the meal ended, the tribal drums sounded, and all the villagers made their way to the great lodge. The villagers assumed their usual places. Coleman thought how curious it was that everyone chose the same location each time they met there.

Not much different from home, he thought.

Soon, the chief stood and welcomed his family to another First Celebration, meaning the first evening of Matti-mas. He said several significant events had occurred since the last celebration, and many of the men had prepared stories marking the events. These stories turned out to be what Coleman saw as campfire skits.

The first involved the death of Atura's father. From what he could gather, Atura's father, Tumtuo, had died of either a stroke or heart attack during a strenuous hunt. The hunting party had been chasing down game when Tumtuo collapsed. It was evident he was a much-beloved member of the tribe for many men and women were shedding tears by the time the presentation concluded.

The next performance took Coleman by surprise. Before it began, Tzeechoe left the lodge, leading Coleman to guess he was preparing for his part in the next skit. Suddenly, Tzeechoe ran into the lodge and leaped, landing in the center of the room near the fire. He was covered in a ghostly white ash or some similar substance. His jaw was covered in brown tree moss, and his eye sockets were painted a bright blue. It was obvious he was playing a caricature of Coleman.

As the drums set the beat, Tzeechoe jumped and stooped, spun and dashed as if he were being chased or hunted. He looked like a clown and his gyrations and contortions added much to his ridiculous appearance. The men laughed and hooted. The women giggled and sounded their long, wavering shriek. Coleman couldn't contain himself and gave a belly roar that could be heard above all the other noises.

Soon, three men from Coleman's hunt team dashed in and captured the crazed Tzeechoe, leading him out of the lodge. All the villagers stood and applauded. Even the chief and Taahso laughed and clapped their hands. Coleman sat amid a sea of legs while the men near him touched his head and shoulders. Finally, he stood, grinning broadly. Tzeechoe returned and came to his side. Coleman let everyone gander at the contrast. Tzeechoe poked and prodded him, much to the delight of the others.

After a short time of this, the gathering calmed down and everyone seated themselves again. The chief stood and invited Tondo to share the story of how he had killed the gorga. Coleman was a bit flustered; he had no idea he was expected to give another performance.

As he sat pulling together his thoughts, the villagers began to chant, "Tondo! Tondo! Tondo!" It was obvious they would not relent. Slowly he rose and, as he did, the men gave guttural shouts and the women ululated. For the next half-hour or so, Coleman related the story of how he killed the gorga, much as he had done the first time several Munnoga moons ago. When he completed his story, the villagers stood and shouted for joy. The men beat their chests and the women trilled even louder.

Then the chant began anew, "Tondo! Tondo! Tondo!" It was evident they wanted him to do it again. After much coaxing, he began retelling the story as the people cheered. After he finished, the villagers clamored for more. Coleman needed to end this ongoing repetition, so he initiated a sly plan.

"My friends, I have shared with you the story of Tondo and the gorga. But now, let me share with you the story of a creature so fearsome, so terrible, it makes the gorga seem like a docile saptur. This beast is known throughout my homeland as Bigfoot," he said using the godspeak term.

For the next half-hour or so, Coleman spun a yarn of terror and suspense that had his listeners hanging on his every word. Not a soul stirred. Even the little children kept silent as they clutched their mothers. Coleman finally finished his story by saying, ". . . and they were never seen nor heard from again."

There were no cheers or shouts, only a quiet pensiveness from what the villagers had just heard and mentally visualized. Children clung tighter to their mothers, who had worried expressions. The men were leaning back in anxiety. Coleman quietly returned to his place and sat, crossing his legs and arms, satisfied that his plan had worked and relieved him from more storytelling.

After a few moments, the chief stood, uttered a few words of dismissal, and the throng exited the great lodge. Men rushed to their wives and children, gathering them in their arms, protecting them from the shadows of the night. The chief and Taahso stood unmoving and impassive until everyone had left.

Coleman remained seated reveling in the moment and stifling a chuckle. His features remained stoic until the chief addressed him, "Could such a beast follow you here? Are we in danger?"

Coleman could contain himself no longer and burst out laughing. The chief and Taahso looked at each other in puzzlement. Then their gaze returned to the elated Tondo. Coleman tried to control himself, but their expressions of worry and concern started another convulsion of laughter.

"Tondo, this is no laughing matter," the chief grumbled. "Are we in danger?" he repeated sternly.

Coleman continued laughing and watched the others' concerned expressions turn angry. As the gravity of the situation became apparent, he told them. "It is only a story. There is no Bigfoot. The village is safe."

"Then you lied to us!" the chief angrily accused.

"No, it is not a lie. It is a made-up story. I did it for fun. My people enjoy such stories. It is called fiction."

"Made-up stories? It seems like a lie to me," Taahso grouched.

Coleman now realized the villagers had no concept of fiction as entertainment. "I noticed you two listening closely. Could you see in your minds what I was telling you and the others?" Both men nodded. "That is why my people share stories with each other. It is fun."

"That story was not fun. It was awful and those poor people died. If your tribe likes such things, they must be of Munnevo," Taahso reasoned.

"No one died. It is just a story. I told it to you because it was a story my father shared with me and my brother when we were boys. We would hike into the woods and at night he would share scary stories while we sat around the fire. I really enjoyed those stories and thought you would too. I am sorry I scared you."

"Stories about big dangerous beasts and people dying is bad. Too many of our loved ones have died because of beasts like the gorga. I never want to hear another story like this Bigfut. Never again, Tondo."

"Sorry, I will not do it again," Coleman promised. He had completely misread the situation and the culture he was now in. He'd have to tread more lightly in the future.

Coleman stood and returned to Tzeechoe's lodge. He let Toto out for a late-night romp and sat on a log staring at the moons while pondering his latest confrontation with the village leaders. As he thought, he wondered if there was a polar star up there somewhere. It should be easy enough to determine. He had always enjoyed stargazing. The only problem here was the plethora of stars; bright stars, dim stars, white, red stars, blue, and gold stars. There were more than he had ever seen on his home world even while camping in the high mountains far from city lights. The only thing that seemed to diminish the stars' sparkle was the brightness of the moons. He wished he had pencil and paper so he could draw a picture of the night sky and mark the brightest stars, following their paths over time. He decided he would start a calendar of his own based on what Myron had told him. Since this was the equivalent of New Year's Day, what could be a better time to start?

CHAPTER 19

MATTI-MAS DAY TWO

On the morning of the second day of Matti-mas, the women's stick game, called schazu, continued. As midday approached, the field had been reduced to the final ring of six contestants. Nearly the entire tribe was in attendance. The women began the song again and the sticks began to twirl and bounce. Atura had managed to make it into the final six. It was obvious she was determined to win this time. It finally came down to Atura and Denta, a young single woman Coleman had never met but had seen from time to time in the village.

The sticks flew and the song's tempo increased over and over until Coleman could no longer follow. It amazed him how dexterous these women were. The sticks moved at a dizzying pace. They were just a blur to him. Suddenly, during a pass, one stick hit the other, knocking one to the ground and the other straight up into the air. Denta knew hers had hit the ground, but Atura was fixed on the stick in the air. The whole tribe held their breaths as the stick seemed to hang for an eternity. Finally, it came down and Atura leaned back, barely managing to catch it.

Denta smiled and bowed to Atura. "Good catch. You are the winner." With that, the game was over and Atura was declared the champion.

Coleman wanted to lift her on his shoulders and march around the village as if she were the winning quarterback in a championship game, but he restrained himself and let the other women fawn over her. Atura wore a smile from ear to ear. He had never seen her this elated. It was evident, she had finally attained the public acceptance she had sought. But this was only the beginning. She would soon be the taahsa with new duties, purposes, and responsibilities. Coleman knew that whatever she set her mind to would be accomplished. Even though she presented a stern and hardened front, beneath her hard exterior was the heart of a loving and compassionate young woman. She was the perfect match for the tribe's taahso.

After the midday meal, the entire village lounged around doing nothing. Coleman soon became bored and challenged a couple of his hunt mates to a foot race. The other men watched and cheered when the racers caught their attention. Small groups of six to ten men formed their own races. Quickly, a new village competition began. When all had run their first race, the victors formed into small groups and ran another heat.

The races went on for a couple of hours until all were eliminated, except for the final five. By this time, the entire village was involved and began cheering on their favorites. Coleman had been defeated in the third heat, along with Tzeechoe. Only Ayascho remained to represent their old hunt team. Taahso had been nominated by consensus as the starter. He raised his hand and let it drop. The men took off in a flash. Coleman had marked off what he estimated was one-hundred meters for the first race and that had remained the official distance for all the subsequent races. By this time, the soft ground had become a quagmire. The men bolted down the foot-worn path, a couple of them slipping and sliding as they went. Ayascho, fleet of foot, reached the finish line first and the chief declared him the winner. Ayascho swelled with pride.

Coleman noticed many of the women's schazu sticks had been discarded and dropped in a pile. He grabbed a few and explained to the runners how to run a relay race. The men nodded as if they understood. Coleman's idea was for the men to run to the previous finish line, turn around and run back to the start line where they would pass the baton to their teammate.

Unfortunately, things didn't work out as he expected. In the first attempt, all the racers rushed to the mid-line, some stopping there and others running back to the start-line. Coleman patiently explained the rules again. When Taahso dropped his hand, only the first runners took off; however, when the first runner returned, all the other runners took off, no one taking a baton. Coleman explained the rules a third time, but this time men started throwing the sticks at each other, so Coleman admitted defeat and suggested another race, a long-distance one. There would be no heats. It would be every man for himself. A short discussion ensued and it was determined that a race to the Sweet Waters and back would be a real test of any runner's mettle. Coleman estimated that it was about four or five miles to the landmark.

"Now, that should separate the boys from the men," Coleman shouted above the ruckus he had caused. By this time, the shadows were growing long and it was evident the event had to be postponed until the next day. The women began preparing the evening meal. After the day's exertions, the men were ravenous. No one was disappointed at the delay and all were looking forward to the Sutro Race, as it was being called.

Soon after last-meal, the drums sounded and the villagers assembled in the great lodge for the evening festivities. They started with tribal singing, like a well-practiced choir. It was a song of thanks to Batru. The singing continued for nearly an hour; verse followed verse with male and female voices blending in consonance and harmony. Coleman leaned back and relaxed, enjoying the peaceful and soothing strains.

When the singing stopped, several solemn-looking men entered the lodge. They were hunt mates of the deceased Dubo. They reenacted the hunt in which he had been gored and killed by a tuntro. Coleman couldn't restrain himself and took a quick glance in Duba's direction. She sat, children in arms, nodding slowly. The presentation was in honor of her husband and that was how she received it.

The next skit was performed by members of Coleman's original hunt team, the same members who had captured him shortly after his arrival here. This time there was no caricature of him, only a studied and practiced hunt for the bataro. When the killing blow was made, the assembly cheered and the villagers jumped to their feet, carrying on as they had when he had pantomimed the killing blow of the gorga. He had since learned that the tribe believed the bataro was a gift from Batru and its flesh strengthened the people.

Soon, the villagers started to chant, "Tondo! Tondo! Tondo!" Coleman resigned himself to yet another telling of the story of Tondo and the gorga. When he finished, the chant resumed. *This is becoming intolerable*, he thought. "My brothers and sisters, I have shared with you, again, the end of the evil gorga. Now, let me share with you another story from my homeland. It is about a yellow-haired girl and three furry creatures from the trees. It is called Goldilocks and the Three Bears."

For another half-hour or so, Coleman spun the yarn of the little girl and her encounter with the family of bears. He held his audience in the palm of his hand for the entire time. They had never heard such a story and, like the previous night, they were enthralled. The chief and Taahso also hung on his every word, but their expressions revealed some annoyance.

When Coleman finished, a low growl came from the seated men. The chief and Taahso glared at him and he realized the child's tale wasn't received as he had hoped. The chief rose to his feet and dismissed the gathering. He looked at Coleman and said, "Tondo, I wish to speak to you after the others have gone." Coleman could tell by the chief's demeanor that the storyteller was in trouble once more. After all the others had departed, the chief asked, "Is this another lie?"

Tondo frowned, "It is not a lie. It is a story; a child's story."

"Do those creatures, the bars from your homeland, talk like animals did in the days of old?" Taahso asked.

"No, it is just a story," Coleman tried to clarify once again.

"Are these the things your people teach their children? The yellow-haired girl entered the bars' lodge without permission. Then she stole food and broke things that didn't belong to her. What she did was even worse than what Nita did. I can't understand a people who allow this," the chief was shaking his head.

Coleman had become more than a little annoyed that his simple fairytale had been so misinterpreted. In frustration, he growled, "Goldilocks did not get away with her vile deeds. The bears complained to the village elders and she was arrested. She was charged with many crimes and found guilty. She was sentenced to ten years of hard labor. It was a fitting punishment for her transgression."

"I'm glad to learn she was punished, although I don't understand what that punishment is. You may go," the chief said.

Coleman was fuming, but he regained his composure by the time he got to Tzeechoe's lodge. After he arrived, he thanked Tzeechoe and Tzeecha for their hospitality and informed them he would be moving to his own lodge the following evening after the conclusion of the Matti-mas. Although they protested and offered him a longer stay, he was ready for his own lodge. Tzeechoe accepted his reasoning and silently turned in for the night. Coleman remained awake, taking a short evening walk with Toto who was romping around him, following many scents.

"Yes, my young friend, we'll soon put you to work," he told the growing betzoe in godspeak.

Coleman and Toto returned to the lodge very late, allowing him only a few hours of sleep.

CHAPTER 20

MATTI-MAS DAY THREE

Tzeechoe shook him awake. "Do you plan to sleep all day and miss the Sutro Race?" he asked.

"What? Oh, yes, the race." He rubbed the sleep from his eyes and quickly rose to his feet. "Atura, please take care of Toto; I have to run," he chuckled at his accidental pun.

Atura took a deep breath and expelled it with a loud, "Oy!"

"Do not worry; this is the last day you will have this duty. Try to make friends with him. He likes you."

"It's a beast! What's wrong with you?" she shouted as he departed, not really expecting an answer.

It wasn't long before all the men and boys had gathered near the village entrance. Only the very young and a few older men would not participate. The chief fell into the latter group, although it was evident he wished he were a younger man. Taahso remained the official starter, and when he dropped his arm, the race was on.

The women clapped and ululated as the men dashed off in the direction of the Sweet Waters. A couple of leaders tripped over each other and several men tumbled over them as the women pointed and laughed. It wasn't long before the runners disappeared into the jungle. A few minutes later, some of the younger boys reappeared, walking back to the village. Shortly after that, another trickle of young men emerged from the trees, slowly heading back, their heads hung low. They could see there was no hope of competing with the adults, so they had given up. For the next quarter-hour or so, many of the racers, including adults, returned to the village, having also quit.

The villagers stood transfixed, staring at the jungle where the runners had disappeared, waiting for the first competitor to reappear. After much time had passed, Coleman rushed through the trees and brush and scampered into the village, coming to a slow trot as the villagers cheered and clapped. Not another runner could be seen. It was five to ten minutes more before a couple of bedraggled runners made their appearance and struggled to the finish line. Over the next half-hour, the racers dribbled back to the village. When all were accounted for, the chief declared, with great fanfare, that Tondo was the winner of the first Sutro Race. Tzeechoe slapped him on the shoulder as Atura stood nearby, beaming like a proud mother or sister.

The men rested and some jumped into the stream to cool down. It had been a grueling race for all but Coleman. He recovered quite quickly, while most of the others took the rest of the morning to regain their strength.

Why is that? he wondered. *I'm fit, but so are these men. Is the gravity in this world less than my home world? Well, it doesn't feel any different. Could there be more oxygen in the air? Maybe that was it. That theory might also explain the larger size of the insects I've run across here. Whatever it is, I feel good about myself this day.*

The midday meal was taken as villagers approached Coleman and offered their personal congratulations. *What a good-hearted people they are,* he thought. No one seemed jealous or upset, except for one. Ayascho, the champion sprinter, appeared to be the only one out of sorts. Coleman chose to ignore the younger man's pigheadedness, again; however, he knew that in time, this boiling pot would overflow, forcing him into a violent confrontation he didn't want, and one which his ego assured him Ayascho couldn't win.

In the afternoon, the families assembled in small groups and began tattooing new age lines on each other. It was done with a flexible stick of about twelve inches in length. Attached to its end was a small, sharp obsidian chip. It was dipped into an ink solution concocted from local plants and then tapped into the skin. It was a painful process and he grimaced as he watched.

Coleman learned the girls received their first line during the Matti-mas after their first menstrual cycle. The boys received their first line during the Matti-mas after their first hunt. So, the lines didn't accurately indicate their exact ages and it was impossible to tell how much older each individual really was. No one here kept precise track of time. It was always referred to as 'many days' or 'many rains.' This was quite sufficient for the People, but it drove Coleman crazy at times. He was used to keeping close track of time during his military years and even before that. It seemed everything then was reduced to a strict schedule, almost to the second. Although he had left the military a couple of years prior to his rip, he still patterned his life on the army regimen to which he had grown accustomed.

Several villagers asked him if he wanted lines, but he politely refused their gracious offers. He didn't think much of tattoos, especially those on a person's face and neck. When asked, he merely said he was thirty lines, though he knew it wasn't exactly accurate. Coleman also noted that Tzeecha and Atura were nowhere to be seen. He guessed they were preparing for the nuptials later in the day. He saw Taahso withdraw to his lodge, for he too needed to prepare.

As the shadows grew longer, most of the villagers simply relaxed. The men and boys were drained after the Sutro Race and needed to recover. Coleman felt good and strolled around the village stopping to chitchat with the villagers. He spent an hour visiting Chashutzo while his children played with Toto. Chashutzo was quite depressed after missing all the action, but Coleman's visit lifted his spirits and was much appreciated by Chashutza, who had to put up with her husband's dour mood.

When Coleman exited Chashutzo's lodge, he noticed that almost all the village women, young and old, had formed a double lined pathway from Tzeechoe's lodge to the great lodge. *The time must be near for the marriage ceremony*, he thought to himself.

He quickly went to the great lodge and found the village men seated on the right side of the room. Taahso, dressed in his best finery, was standing near the seated chief. His head was adorned with colorful feathers: reds, blues, yellows, and greens. A feather necklace hung around his neck. He wore earrings of multicolored balls. The garments he wore were newly made and light tan in color. His shirt had full-length sleeves and his trousers went from his waist to the top of his bare feet. His elbows, knees, and ankles were covered in feathers. He was trying hard to appear unflappable, but his eyes revealed the truth.

He looks like a deer caught in the headlights, Coleman mused to himself.

It wasn't long before the women began to murmur, indicating the bride had made her appearance. The assembled men craned their necks to get a glimpse of her, but no one in the lodge could see her yet. Taahso suddenly gave an audible gasp when he first laid eyes on his bride. A few seconds later she entered the great lodge, paused and looked around, her gaze finally falling on Taahso.

A broad smile filled her face and lifted her countenance. Coleman always considered Atura to be a handsome woman, but today she was gorgeous. She seemed to glide across the ground, with a smile so apparent and infectious that every soul who looked upon her had to return one of their own. A feeling of joy and happiness filled the lodge. She wore a dress of nearly white leather from her neck to just above her ankles. Flowers of all colors of the rainbow adorned her neatly combed, shiny black, braided hair. Around her neck hung a necklace of multi-colored flowers, which matched the flower bracelets on her wrists and ankles.

As she stood at the entrance of the great lodge, the other women passed around her and took their seats on the left side of the lodge. When all were seated, with eyes fixed upon her, Atura glided into the room until she stopped at Taahso's left side. Coleman's eyes shifted to the groom and watched as a trickle of sweat slid from temple to chin and dropped to the dusty floor mat beneath. Nevertheless, Taahso looked the image of the solemn medicine man, with only a slight tremor in his knees.

The chief stood and raised his arms as if to embrace the couple before him. His eyes danced with joy as they jumped from the bride to the groom and back again, more than once. His face beamed with happiness. A small tear formed in his right eye and then escaped, running down his cheek. He paid it no mind. Coleman could see tears of joy on many of the women's faces and a few of the men had to wipe dust from their eyes. Coleman's heart swelled as he took in the joyful scene. He had never felt such love exhibited by a gathering of people before.

The chief began to speak, but at first, his voice cracked and he had to clear his throat. He started again. "My children, we are here this day to share the happiness and joy of our brother and sister. Batru smiles upon the merging of a man and a woman into a couple dedicated to one another for the remainder of their days. Taahso, you have chosen the woman, Atura, to join with. Is this true?"

"Yes, I have," came Taahso's firm reply, with only the slightest hint of a quaver.

"Do you agree to protect her and see that her needs are met all the remaining days of your life?" continued the chief.

"Yes, I do," was Taahso's reply.

"Will you always feed her and see that she is protected from the rain and the p´atezas? Will you always lead her with honor, and will you raise your children to respect her and honor the laws of Batru?

"Yes, I will," Taahso's voice cracked just a little.

The chief's eyes turned and rested on Coleman.

"Tondo, do you find Taahso to be a man of honor and worthy of your trust?"

"Yes, he is an honorable man. I trust him with my life and the lives of my family," came Coleman's loud and practiced reply.

"Atura, my daughter," the chief was now looking upon her, "Will you leave your family and take this man's name for your own? Will you follow him and care for him all the remaining days of your life? Will you teach his children to honor their father, to obey his rules as he follows the laws of Batru?"

"Yes," was Atura's confident and powerful response.

The chief lowered his arms and turned to a small table next to his stool. Coleman hadn't noticed it before. The chief picked up a round, red and gold colored fruit. It reminded Coleman of a mango. The chief then picked up an obsidian knife also resting on the table, as well. He cut the fruit in half and laid the knife and one of the fruit halves on the table.

He lifted the other half fruit above his head with both hands. "As Taahso and Atura eat of this food, they promise to live their lives together, partaking of the good and the bad as life presents it to them." The chief then lowered the fruit and held it between them. Taahso leaned forward and took a bite; Atura followed. The chief held the fruit above his head with one hand, clearly exposing the two bites. He turned and placed the fruit on the table. The chief then took a braided leather cord from around his shoulders and wrapped it around a wrist of the bride and the groom.

"You are now tied together in life. Go forth with one purpose," the chief declared. He removed the cord and then turned the couple until they faced the onlookers. The women ululated and the men began slapping their chests. Everyone stood and began congratulating the newlyweds. Coleman couldn't contain himself and gave Taahso and Atura big hugs. The shocked looks on their faces indicated he had breached some unknown protocol, but he didn't care. He was filled with joy and happiness and he felt it was the right thing to do.

After everyone had offered their congratulations, a double lined pathway was quickly formed from the great lodge to Taahso's dwelling. The happy couple quickly darted down the narrow passage and disappeared behind the door covering.

Drums began to sound and some of the young men and women began to dance around the fire. The p´atezas had set and darkness was closing in. Everyone partook of the meal as they celebrated. Coleman watched as Tzeecha wrapped two dinner servings in green leaves and placed them in a basket. She took the basket to Taahso's lodge and placed it near the entryway.

Everyone was jubilant, even the small children. It was the final night of the Matti-mas, the only Batru holiday Coleman was aware of, and he could see they were not going to let it pass without a wild party. After an hour or so, the children without lines were quietly dismissed to their lodges. The remaining adults and near-adults, all with lines, partook of the mystical fruit. Coleman had no idea what it was and chose not to try it. He had heard from Tzeechoe and others of its magical properties and he was ready to sit this one out.

Even though the villagers had obviously done this before, he wasn't quite ready to abandon himself to whatever happened. *Acting like a fool, or worse, would be a disaster,* he thought.

Go ahead, join in the fun. You deserve it, his inner voice tempted.

He shook his head and uttered an audible, "No!" He only enjoyed the singing and dancing, even joining the dancers a couple of times. The men watched him with interest and then began to mimic some of his unusual dance moves.

As time passed, Coleman was becoming bored with the repetition of the songs and dances. He decided to step away casually and carry out his relocation. He knew Tzeechoe liked having the one favored by the gods living with him, but now that Atura was starting her new life with Taahso, he realized it was time for the visitor to move into his own quarters in Atura's father's old lodge.

He quickly gathered his few meager belongings and moved them to his new home. He then visited Chashutzo and collected Toto, who had been keeping the hunt leader company. Toto ran from place to place, sniffing the ground and chasing his imagination.

After they had entered their new home, Coleman stacked wood, then lit a fire by simply pointing at the pile with his finger. He sat, examining his hand and turning his finger from front to back.

"That's simply amazing," he muttered in godspeak. He watched the flames dance, following sparks as they flew high into the room before burning themselves out. He fed Toto some meat he had carefully wrapped in leaves and saved for him. The betzoe gulped down every scrap and sniffed around the lodge for more. He then nuzzled his nose under Coleman's arm and rested his chin on his master's thigh. It wasn't long before the rhythmic breathing told Coleman that his pet was sound asleep.

Coleman sat lost in thought, feeling his life turned upside down. He had no idea where he was or even how he got here. He had no connection to family and friends. What were they thinking? By now, he must be presumed dead; an unfortunate accident in an experiment that went awry. As he began to sink lower into self-pity, he heard a couple of young female voices call his name.

He stood up and exited the lodge. Three teenage girls stood before him, giggling and holding onto each other for balance. None had any lines, but apparently, they had indulged in some of the mystical fruit.

"What can I do for you, girls? Do your fathers know you are here?" All three girls giggled some more; looking in all directions except toward Coleman. He had seen them around the village but had not yet learned their names.

Finally, one worked up enough courage to speak, "Tondo . . . can we . . . can we . . . I mean . . ." There was a long awkward pause. "Can we enter?"

"I do not think that would be a good idea," he counseled. "I think you three young ones need to go home and go to sleep." There was another smattering of laughter and gibberish that Coleman couldn't understand. Unexpectedly, the girls' eyes widened and they began screaming. Coleman stood bolt upright, looking from side to side, wondering what had just happened. The girls started pointing at something behind him and retreated, two girls tripping over each other, ending up in a heap on the ground. Coleman turned to see Toto's head peeking around the door covering of the lodge. Teeth bared, he began a low, menacing growl. The girls regained their feet and scampered off into the darkness. Coleman stood, a bit shaken himself by the experience.

He looked at Toto and said, "Thank you, boy. You just saved me from a very unpleasant situation. You will get a big reward tomorrow." Coleman returned to his lodge and went to bed, still unnerved by the young girls' bold advances. *This will never do*, he thought.

He determined that advances such as these needed to be stopped before they ever began. He quickly formulated a sly plan. It was evident he would never see home again. This was to be his new life. For the past several detzs he had pushed that realization into the deep recesses of his mind, but now all his pent-up fears overwhelmed him. He fought to keep his mental resolve, but suddenly all his pent up emotional pain burst loose. Tears rolled down both sides of his face. Toto rustled and plopped his head onto Coleman's stomach as if trying to comfort his master. Coleman rubbed the betzoe's ears while he tried to calm down. His new life was totally unexpected and he was certain he would never get back home, but, in the very back of his mind, a small voice reminded him of something he had forgotten. *You have done good*, it seemed to whisper. The thought reminded him of his visions of the young girl who needed his help.

Perhaps this whole experience isn't just about me, he thought. *If nothing else, I can get up tomorrow and help. I can give these people guidance and save more lives. It is not what I expected when I stepped into the rip chamber, but it's not such a bad life, after all.*

The morning after the Matti-mas concluded, Coleman awoke as light from the p´atezas chased away the gloom from the lodge. He quickly rubbed the sleep from his eyes and scurried to the center of the village. Much to his surprise, no hunt party was there. A couple of little children greeted him with a hearty, "Good morning, Tondo," but that was all. It didn't take Coleman long to realize the adults were sleeping in. He wondered if they were suffering from the effects of the mystical fruit. He decided to try to hunt on his own. He grabbed Tumtuo's spear and club, his betzoe, and trotted out of the village.

Coleman knew he wasn't much good with an atlatl. He had never felt comfortable with the lever and he always missed. Toto was a natural hunter and led Coleman to game, but his master always missed. Finally, the betzoe resorted to his own devices and took down a small deer-like animal. Coleman skinned and dressed the beast, feeding its heart and liver to his hunting partner. He deserved the treat for his heroic actions of the previous night.

The two headed back to the village, but at a stream crossing, Coleman paused for a drink. It was a beautiful setting with the verdant greens of the jungle above the fast-flowing clear waters. Flowers of all colors bloomed at the water's edge. A small waterfall plunged about eight feet into a deep green pool. After partaking his fill, Coleman leaned back, enjoying the view and listening to the calming sound of rushing waters. Toto sat on his haunches at his master's side.

After relaxing for a bit, it was time to move on. As Coleman stood, he caught the glint of a shiny object at the base of the falls.

Maybe it's another gold nugget, he thought. *How funny it is to have all this gold lying around, and yet be unable to do anything with it. I'm a poor rich man.*

There was something different about this shiny object; it seemed larger, much larger. He took a closer look and his eyes widened as he tried to pierce the water's ripples. Finally, he dove into the pool and swam to the bottom of the falls. At its base, he found a hole full of gold nuggets. It was a huge gold cache where the heavier gold nuggets collected. He stuck his hand into the mix and found nuggets as large as his thumb.

This is fantastic! he thought. *What a magnificent treasure!*

He soon realized he needed air more than gold and quickly kicked back to the surface. He found an anxious Toto pacing back and forth at the water's edge, barking a sound that was a cross between a bark and a screech. When the betzoe saw his master break the surface, he jumped in and paddled to his master's side.

"Well, puppy, we're rich, but so what!" Coleman pulled himself onto the stream bank and began laughing. "The irony of it all. Rich beyond the dreams of avarice and nothing to spend it on," he gasped. He opened his palm and stared at the nugget he had retrieved. It was indeed as big as his thumb and quite heavy for its size. He rubbed the stubble on his chin and thought. *There may come a time when I go to the Ancient City and I know gold has value there.* He decided to be patient and prepare for the future by prospecting for gold.

Collect it all. You'll become rich and powerful, his inner voice harped.

He then broke the obsidian from his spear and tossed the pole into the pool, watching it slowly drift downstream. "Enough of that. I am hopeless with it, anyway," he grumbled. "No one in the village uses a bow and arrow. It is time I invented them." He looked around for something that would make a suitable bow and chopped it free using his short sword. He fashioned himself a bow using a small air root for the string. When he drew it back, the line broke. "That will never do," he muttered. He then noticed that the reddish p´atezas was nearly at its apex, so he hefted his kill, or more accurately, Toto's kill, and off to the village he and the betzoe scampered.

When he arrived, there was still little activity in the village. As he passed Taahso's lodge, he noticed the untouched basket of food still sitting near the doorway. He grinned and kept moving. A few of the adults were sitting around the village fire, holding their head's and muttering to themselves. Coleman's greeting of, "It sure is a beautiful day!" seemed to hit them like a sledgehammer. He chuckled to himself and started cooking the meat. As it sputtered and sizzled, the aroma rose with the smoke. Several of the stricken villagers staggered from view, holding their stomachs. "Hoy, this is going to taste fantastic. Yum, yum, yum." Several more villagers darted from view. Some of the smaller children gathered around him and, when the meat was done, he served out portions to everyone who asked. He even coaxed a few who were too bashful to ask for a portion.

As the afternoon progressed, more of the adults could be seen. Some were in better condition than others, but all looked like they were suffering by one degree or another. He noticed that many were sucking on a lemon-like fruit. When he tried one, he found it sweet and refreshing. A few of the men gathered their hunting gear and headed out of the village. By the time the p´atezas set, they had returned with enough food to meet the needs of the few villagers who felt up to eating a meal.

The evening was spent in quiet lethargy. Tzeechoe finally made his appearance, but he looked no better than the others. Coleman just grinned and shook his head as Tzeechoe turned his face away, somewhat embarrassed. Before he retired for the night, Coleman told Tzeechoe not to wait for him in the morning. He was going to hunt on his own for a while. Tzeechoe simply accepted his friend's decision, mainly because his head ached too much to mount a protest.

Over the next several Munnoga-moons, Coleman spent a lot of time on his own, accompanied only by his trusty betzoe. He let his beard grow and the villagers began to refer to him as the wild man. He no longer had trouble with girls' flirting advances, though. Toto had gained his total height. His shoulders were well above Coleman's waist and his head-plate was fully formed. He still had a lot of growing to do, but Coleman guessed that it would mostly be in muscle and bulk.

Coleman had also mastered the construction of a bow. It took him many attempts with many dismal failures, but he finally found the right combination of wood and animal sinew. The materials he settled on made a bow of considerable power, yet it was light and compact enough to be useful in the dense underbrush of the jungle.

Tzeechoe taught him how to make obsidian arrowheads. At first, Tzeechoe was puzzled by their small size. He was used to making spearheads, but when he saw Coleman take down a tuntro from three times the range a spearman could, he was impressed but still preferred to stay with his spear. Coleman felt that was due more to his desire of attaining the highest rank for a hunter than it was for the spear's effectiveness. Coleman offered to help others create their own bows but encountered the same resistance Tzeechoe exhibited. Slowly, over time, a few village men came to appreciate the new weapon and, with Coleman's help, they made their own bows and arrows.

About the time he had perfected his bow, a sutro groundshake struck the area. He estimated the shaker lasted ten to fifteen seconds, but he couldn't be sure; time seemed to stretch during such events. The damage to the village was minimal. The worst thing that happened was a child fell into a fire. Coleman examined the child, a boy of about three rains and found he had second-degree burns on his left leg. Coleman concluded the boy would heal in time and wouldn't be scarred by his misfortune. The child was screaming in pain, so Coleman rubbed his hands together and placed them on the wound. The child stopped his screaming and relaxed.

Shortly after that, Taahso appeared, examined the boy, waved his feather fan over the wound, and departed. Coleman could tell, the medicine man was not pleased. Coleman had intruded into his domain and caused him to lose face with many of the villagers. A few days later, Coleman had a meeting with Taahso. He apologized for overstepping his bounds and promised to seek Taahso's counsel before using any of his newly found powers. This seemed to placate the shaman, but Coleman knew it could only be a temporary solution. Also, Chashutzo made a full recovery but would walk with a slight limp for the rest of his life. He was able to resume his role as hunt leader.

The summer was warm and humid. The rain came every day to cool the air and steam rose afterward. Coleman had settled into a routine. He would hunt with his hunt-mates every third day. The rest of the time he hunted alone, accompanied only by his betzoe. On those days, he would practice his taah and retrieve a few nuggets from the cache at the base of the waterfall. He also spent time making arrows and maintaining his bow. He had concocted a glue to secure the bow's layers, but the high humidity was causing it to fail. He resolved the issue by wrapping the bow tightly with sinew straps. That seemed to increase its power, also. No one else in the village could pull the bowstring more than about twelve inches, but Coleman could draw it the full distance of about thirty inches, to the marvel of all the men.

On the days Coleman hunted with his group, he noticed Shadi, the scent-man, seemed to lose his vigor. Coleman finally realized that Toto was much better at following scents than Shadi, causing the man to lose his status in the team. After realizing this, Coleman worked out a plan with the scent-man to capture another betzoe. This they did after tracking a betzoe pack to their den. It took until the next rains for their plan to pay off.

Shortly after, a litter of pups was born, the two men snatched one of the critters while the rest of the pack was hunting and took it back to the village. It was a female that quickly bonded with Shadi the same way Toto had bonded with Coleman. In due time, Shadi regained his status with the team as his betzoe became a valued hunt partner.

It was late in the next span when Shadi's betzoe, whom he named Dada, or friend, showed signs she was pregnant. "What have you been up to, Toto?" Coleman said to his betzoe. The creature cocked his head as if to say, "Who, me?" The pups were born shortly after Coleman's second Mattimas. It had become apparent that the betzoes were looked upon with envy by the other hunt teams. Shadi was able to trade each pup for a valued item.

It was also in Coleman's second summer that the village learned both Tzeecha and Atura (who was now called Taahsa) were expecting. This happy event was the cause for celebration. Many were the days in which the expectant parents found a basket of goodies on the doorstep that included food, a favored hunting tool, or something useful in daily tasks, even a garment for the expected new arrival. No one admitted to the deeds and no one asked. It was a village tradition that was joyfully followed.

The gestation period lasted, as well as Coleman could determine, the same length of time as on his home world, and it was late in the warm season when both delivered. Tzeecha gave birth to a healthy baby girl and five days later, Taahsa gave birth to a bouncing baby boy. When it was announced that Taahso had a son, he puffed up and strutted around the village like the proud father he was. This also meant that the line of the village taahso would continue. The chief called for a day of celebration and the People danced and sang. Stories were shared by the light of the fire in the great lodge. Coleman relented and shared his own story when everyone shouted his name, "Tondo! Tondo! Tondo!"

He told his audience he would only say it once, but when he finished, they wanted more. He thought about telling a werewolf story but decided it wouldn't be appropriate for this celebration, nor would it be favorably accepted by the village's leaders. He settled on the story of Moby Dick. His listeners were amazed by his description of the ocean and the ships that sailed it. They were astonished when Coleman portrayed the immense size and grandeur of whales. These landlocked people never imagined any of these things were possible. They listened to his every word; no one made a sound, not even the infants. Coleman warily watched the chief's and Taahso's expressions, worried he might somehow ignite their ire once again. When the story was finished, the villagers didn't make a move. They sat in their places, contemplating all they had heard.

Finally, the chief asked, "Tondo, are the things you tell us this time true? Are there really such huge beasts and never-ending waters?"

"Oh yes, they are real, at least in my homeland. I cannot tell you if any of these things can be found near the Batru," was Coleman's careful response. The chief grunted his satisfaction, much to Coleman's relief.

It was an excellent ending to a beautiful day, and the

villagers left the great lodge, their imaginations reeling from an overload.

Ayascho remained agitated and sullen when around Coleman. The debt he owed him for not exposing his cowardice gnawed at him like a tick buried deeply in one's skin. He had yet to find a way to repay the great Tondo, nor did he want to, but duty nagged at him. He could only wait and hope that one day the gods would smile upon him and he would be able to discharge the debt proudly.

CHAPTER 21

A NEW PURRANT IN TOWN

It was morning and it was going to take several days to walk to Nevesant's village. On the way, the boy shared his knowledge of the small town while the fourteen marauders and Tangundo listened.

"Purrant Grazius is the hamlet overseer, master. He's the one who ordered you into the mist."

"Then it's time I paid Purrant Grazius a visit and showed him what the gods of the mist gave me."

"But master, he has a gravetum sword; hard and sharp."

"Are there other swords in that place?" Tangundo asked.

"No master, but most men have gravetum knives. They also have quarterstaffs made from hardwoods found in the nearby woods."

Tangundo rubbed his head. "Yes, I remember. I think I'll take the purrant's sword and his dwelling."

"He'll summon the king's men. They have longer swords, charging mounts, and little concern for who they slice or trample," one of the marauders warned.

Tangundo wheeled on him and asked angrily, "Do you enjoy living out here, like an animal?"

"It's not so bad during the warm season, master," the marauder mumbled.

"Come with me and we will live in comfort from now on," Tangundo promised.

Nevesant and the others smiled broadly, but it quickly changed to concern. "Master, what about the king's men?" Nevesant asked.

"By the time they come, we'll have enough men of our own to send them into the mist," Tangundo promised. Nevesant's smile returned.

It took more than a couple of days to reach the village. Tangundo and his followers of Munnevo arrived at the outskirts of the hamlet just as dusk fell. They ate some dried meat and slept. The dawn would bring them a new day and a new life.

They arose before dawn. Only Munnoga cast its silvery rays over the countryside. Nevesant led his master to Grazius's house. It was surrounded by the marauders. Tangundo and Nevesant stood at the door as the first glow of dawn brightened the eastern horizon. Tangundo tightened his grip on the hand ax he was holding. He took a deep breath, lifted the door latch, put his shoulder to the door planks, and shoved it open. The room filled with purple light from his burning aura. A woman screamed and two girls began shrieking in terror.

"What's the meaning of this?" Grazius roared as he threw off his blanket and fumbled for his sword on a nearby table.

"If you touch that sword you will die!" Tangundo growled. He rushed forward, engulfing Grazius and his bondmate in his aura's burning rays. The woman screamed in painful terror and Grazius howled. The couple's two young daughters rushed to them, but as soon as they fell under the aura's excruciating influence, they retreated with howls of pain and panic. Grazius and his woman pressed against the wall while still in their bed. Tangundo snatched the sword from the table and held it in his left hand, the hand ax still in his right. He stood near the suffering couple for several long moments, increasing their misery. Their cries of pain slackened as they began to lose consciousness. Tangundo stepped back and their torment eased. One of the girls dashed toward the door and was intercepted by Nevesant. He pushed her to the floor, and she crawled back to her younger sister. The two girls clutched each other, sobbing in horror.

"Who are you?" Grazius asked weakly. Tangundo pulled his kerchief down, exposing his beard. "You're the beast we sent into the mist," Grazius gasped.

"That was your first mistake. The gods of the mist have made me one of them. Get down on your knees before me," Tangundo ordered. Grazius slowly climbed out of bed and complied with Tangundo's order. "You, too," Tangundo commanded the woman. She also knelt.

"What do you want from us?" Grazius asked, his face only inches above the floorboards.

"I'm the new purrant in town. If you cooperate, I'll let you live," he turned to the two girls quaking nearby. "I'd hate to see any harm come to these young ones." Tangundo waited expectantly.

"I'll cooperate," Grazius finally replied in a labored tone.

"Good! You may refer to me as Purrant Tangundo. Now, you say it."

"Purrant Tangundo," Grazius repeated.

"Very good but that will not do. I am your new master, and that's how you'll address me." Tangundo gave the man a cold stare with his Munnevo-red eyes.

Grazius glanced up and caught the tall man's glare. He lowered his head and said, "Master."

"Woman, I'm hungry. Feed us. All of us! Prepare enough for twenty." The woman stood and as she did, Grazius began to rise, as well. "Not you!" Tangundo growled. Grazius remained on his knees.

Grazius's bondmate scurried around the room, starting the cooking fire and preparing flat-cakes and eggs. When the meal was ready, Tangundo and Nevesant ate the best meal they had partaken in a very long time. He summoned the others in shifts and they all ate, leaving the house with full bellies and huge smiles.

When all had eaten, Tangundo moved to Grazius and stood over him. The deposed purrant looked up and shuddered as Tangundo's wicked Munnevo eyes glared down at him. "What will you do with us?" the villager asked, his voice quaking in fear.

"You will assemble the village men and tell them they are to obey me. Tell them what you've seen this morning. Be sure to tell them I'm imbued with the power of the gods of the mist. If anyone refuses to join me, they will be fed to those gods. Now, summon the men," Tangundo ordered as he pulled his kerchief up.

Grazius rose and exited his house with Tangundo at his heels. He went to a gravetro triangle hanging from the porch rafters. He picked up a nearby gravetro rod and sounded the alarm. Village men came running. When all had arrived, Tangundo counted twenty-five or so.

"Purrant, what's the problem?" one of the men asked. Others sounded their concern.

Tangundo stepped forward and pulled down his kerchief. The gathered villagers gasped. "I am your new purrant. Grazius will tell you what to expect."

The deposed purrant told the men what he had been ordered to say. Several men grumbled their disbelief and prepared to charge Tangundo and his men. The outsider's aura ignited and he swept the air with the sword. A wave of dark energy crashed into the village men, knocking them off their feet and stunning them.

"You have just received your only warning," Tangundo growled. "You now serve me. I am your new god. Now, on your knees and bow to your master!" he ordered. The village men submitted as their women watched from a distance. Tangundo smiled and faced his chosen followers of Munnevo. "Today we have taken a village. Tomorrow, we'll conquer the world!"

CHAPTER 22

HALLS OF THE TEMPLE

Myron's ire was rising as he listened to Zoseemo's complaints. "But master, by the king's order we can't go back. The Pannera will take us and only the gods know what suffering they'll put us through. They do the most horrible things to those who violate the law, especially slaves. I beg you, master, don't do it," Zoseemo pleaded.

Myron, Zoseemo, and their three rasters plodded along, following the temple priest, Tutor Pershon, garbed in his cobalt-blue priest's robe and riding his furry mount.

"What would you have me do, boy, disobey the Sutro Seer? The tutor has promised us the temple's protection. Now, hush before you raise the priest's ire as well as mine!" Myron growled. Zoseemo stopped his vocal complaints, but Myron and the priest could hear his sniveling sobs as the trio advanced toward the Great Teg-ar-mos Wall.

By mid afternoon, they could see the towering bulwark in the distance. The wall was made of massive stone blocks stacked to the height of six men, its towers higher than that. The wall ran in both directions for as far as the eye could see. It was an impressive and imposing edifice, which acted as the kingdom's forward line of defense.

As the small party advanced closer, Myron could hear Zoseemo begin to complain again, this time monologuing his fear to the pack animals. "Zoseemo, stop that racket this instant! You're upsetting the rasters," he grumbled. The young man took a deep breath and became silent.

A short line of travelers had queued up before the Wall's huge gates as kingdom guards examined each group before allowing them to proceed. Slowly, the line crept forward until it was Myron's turn to state his name and business.

"I am Myron and my business is with the Sutro Seer," he declared.

"Myron, is it?" the guard asked. Myron nodded as Zoseemo wiped tears from his eyes with his forearm. "Wait here!" the guard ordered. The guard quickly marched to the gate tower and disappeared inside. In short order, he reappeared accompanied by four other guards, one undoubtedly his commander, discernible by the crest of red plumes on his helm denoting the rank of an officer. The military group stopped in front of the lead raster on which Myron was mounted.

The officer looked up and ordered, "Come down and be quick about it!" Myron kicked the raster a couple of times with his heel and the beast dropped to its six knees and rested on its belly. Myron stepped off the animal and approached the officer. As he did, Tutor Pershon, the priest, joined him.

"My man tells me your name is Myron. Are you the same Myron who was banished by the king?" the officer asked in an angry tone. Myron nodded.

"He is with me," the priest announced.

"Who are you?" the officer spat.

"I am Tutor Pershon of the Great Temple. The Sutro Seer has summoned us," the priest declared.

"This man has been banished by the king. He will not be allowed to pass. As a matter of fact, my orders are to punish him if he dares to return," the officer growled in a threatening manner. Zoseemo began wailing his fears aloud once more.

"This man has business with His Eminence and you will not interfere," the priest asserted.

"Without proper authority, he will not pass. And a tutor of the temple does not carry that authority," the officer proclaimed.

A voice nearby shouted, "I carry that authority and a signed declaration from the Sutro Seer himself." A taller than average man, wearing the blue robes of a temple priest, dismounted and marched up to the officer. The priest's dark eyes bored into the commander, causing a detectable shudder in the officer. The new arrival handed him a leather tube. The officer opened it and slid out a parchment scroll. He read it, rolled it up again, and handed it back.

"Myron and his party may pass," the officer stated. "Please understand, Master Shergus, I was only doing my duty; however, I must report this to my superiors," the officer said deferentially.

"Very well then, we'll be on our way," Master Shergus replied sternly. Myron remounted his raster, and the party continued south, toward the Ancient City.

Myron sat alone in the small room of the temple, the ever-present harmonious chants of the priests wafting through the air like invisible fog. Myron struggled to remember the last time he had been inside the temple. *It has been a very long time. Could it be a hundred spans? Two hundred? And I'm about to meet with the Sutro Seer, the greatest religious leader of the age. Dare I blame the king who banished me? No, that I cannot justify if asked about my dalliance. I've only been banished for the last two spans or so.*

He heard the door latch move. He quickly stood and turned toward it as it opened. In stepped an aged man, wearing the blue robes of a priest, the robe's cowl over his head. He carefully closed the door and turned to face Myron. He removed the hood and let it drape over his shoulders and around his neck. As he looked at Myron, a friendly and warm smile covered his ancient face. Myron didn't know what to do or say. He had never been taught how to act in the presence of His Eminence, the Sutro Seer. Myron dropped to his knees and groveled, "Your Eminence."

"Thank you, my son. Please sit," the Seer offered. Myron sat and waited. The Sutro Seer took a chair and placed it in front of Myron. He sat and stared into Myron's eyes, searching the merchant's very soul. Myron felt uncomfortable under the Seer's relentless gaze, but he dared not look away. Finally, the Seer's smile widened and he said, "My son, I hear you have been to the Wilderness. Please, tell me what you found there."

Myron explained how he had decided to leave civilization for a time to see if he could find business in another part of the world. He admitted to being banished from the Ancient City, although he didn't say why. He had spent time in the great cities of the other two kingdoms but being Anterran limited his prospects in those realms. Maybe the Wilderness held greater promise. Unfortunately, it hadn't. The few savages he'd encountered hadn't possessed much of value, so he returned to his own civilization.

"You met someone in the Wilderness; someone unusual; someone different than the others, didn't you?" the Seer asked.

"Yes, Your Eminence, I did. He's the person I mentioned to Tutor Pershon. He's a big man, a head taller than most king's men. He didn't look like a savage, either. At first, I thought he was Anterran, but he didn't act like one. He appeared to be a man of knowledge and wisdom, too. Even stranger, he had eyes the color of the blue moon. Have you ever heard of such a thing?" Myron asked.

"That is unusual. Did this man rule over the native peoples?" the Seer wondered.

"No, Your Eminence. He deferred to the chief of the village. He was curious about Anterra and all the places I had visited."

"Where did he come from? Why was he there?"

"He would never give me a clear answer to those kinds of questions. I know he was hiding something."

"What is this man's name?" the Seer asked.

"As far as I could tell, he has no name. The savages call him Tondo, the visitor."

"Myron, you have been very helpful. I need to meet this man. Can you fetch him for me?"

"Please, Your Eminence, I have been away from the Blessing of the City for more than two spans. To leave again would compound the damage already done to me, my animals, and my slave."

"I see. Would you be willing to prepare a map for others to follow?"

"Yes, Your Eminence, that I will do gladly."

"Good. I will use my influence and request your banishment be withdrawn," the Seer promised.

Myron dropped to his knees before the Sutro Seer again. "Your Eminence, I will be eternally grateful."

The Sutro Seer stood, helped Myron to his feet, and guided him to the door. "You will be given the materials you'll need to make a map for others to follow. Be sure it's durable. You are to remain here, in the temple, until I meet with the king."

"Thank you, Your Eminence."

Myron was escorted by two young priests and, as they departed, Master Shergus and another priest entered the small room and closed the door. They stood silently waiting for the Sutro Seer to speak. The Seer's eyes were closed and his head bowed. After several moments, he looked up.

"I have seen great evil enter the world. It is a threat unlike any we have faced in this age; however, the unnamed god has brought balance back into the world. He has given us a tool, another man. But this tool can be as dangerous as the threat."

"What should we do, Your Eminence?" the priest accompanying Master Shergus asked.

"All men choose their own path in this life. Please refresh

my memory by reciting the first verse of the Tome of Life for me, Master Varios," the Seer requested.

Master Varios began speaking in a loud and clear voice, reciting temple scripture by rote: "Within the heart of man are planted the seeds of his being: the need to love, the drive to hate; a desire to act with honor, an inclination to act with dishonor; the heights of joy, the depths of sorrow; the reserve of humility, the force of pride; the drive of curiosity, the apathy of indifference; the uplift of hope, the discouragement of fear; the fulfillment of desire, the angst of disgust; the conveying of pleasure, the infliction of pain; the offering of generosity, the hunger of avarice; open-hearted compassion, close-minded cruelty—these seeds and more, are placed there by the gods for man to choose for himself the good seed or the evil seed." Master Varios ended his recitation and waited for the Sutro Seer to comment. The two master priests understood that this exercise was for their benefit and edification, for they well knew that the Sutro Seer didn't need his memory refreshed.

"The first outsider who came to our world has chosen the evil seeds. We must determine which seeds the Tondo chooses to nourish. It will be your duty to determine if the risk is too great.

"Master Varios, Master Shergus, extend an invitation to King Teg-ar-mos. Have him pass through the Hall of the Guardians. I will meet with him in the Outer Sanctum. I will request he summon the Tondo. After this visitor arrives, the two of you will test him, and if he proves worthy, prepare him for the coming struggle," the Sutro Seer commanded.

"And if he proves to be unworthy?" Master Shergus asked. The Sutro Seer didn't answer. He lifted the cowl over his head, indicating the meeting was at an end.

CHAPTER 23

A KING'S SUMMONS

It was late into the second span since Coleman's arrival, when he returned to the village after hunting with Toto. He had a fresh kill slung over his shoulder. As he approached the village fire, he noticed an unusual commotion near the center of the village. Under a light drizzle, he saw a rather large animal standing near the chief's lodge. At first, he thought it was a small elephant-like creature, and then a rhinoceros. As he drew closer, he found it to be neither of these beasts. It looked like a small triceratops. It was as big as a rhino and yoked to a cart with metal shields and other implements of war stashed in it. On the far side of this beast was another one, also hitched to a cart.

Coleman could see, and now hear, what sounded like an argument taking place near the central fire of the village. He handed his kill to a nearby villager and walked past the animals. The one closest to him turned its head and gave a bellow like the sound a cow would make. The villagers turned and saw him approaching. They quickly moved aside, forming a pathway. It was then he noticed a group of remarkable looking men standing in the villagers' midst.

They were dressed in leather armor and carried metal swords and metal-tipped pikes. He counted a total of ten men who looked like ancient Roman warriors to Coleman's eyes. When the soldiers saw the wild-looking man with the hairy face, one turned toward him while the others took defensive stances against the villagers surrounding them. Village men discreetly left the throng in twos and threes, quickly returning with spears and clubs. The women grabbed their children and retreated from the crowd.

Coleman's eyes locked on the man he perceived to be the leader of the expedition and slowed his pace. Toto uttered a low-pitched growl. The commander scanned Coleman from head to foot and back again. Tondo was wearing leather breeches and a loincloth. His obsidian knife hung from the right side of his waist belt. His feet and torso were bare and his skin was a reddish-tan. The gorga fang hung from a strap around his neck. A leather headband kept his long, sand-colored hair from his face. His brown beard was long and scraggly. He held the bow in his left hand, a quiver of arrows protruding above his left shoulder. The pommel of his short sword peeked above his right. The commander's gaze stopped at Coleman's beard. His jaw dropped. He quickly regained his composure and focused on Coleman's blue eyes. A tight smile crossed his face. Then it was gone.

Coleman stopped a few feet from the soldier, slowly scanning him from helmet to sandals. His helm appeared to be made of heavy metal straps crossed over the peak, covering the thick cloth or leather lying beneath. Attached to the top was a six-inch long spike with soiled white streamers dangling from its point. He wore a blue tunic of soft leather, gathered at the waist, making it appear like a skirt that went to his knees. His upper body was protected by a cuirass of hide—leather treated in such a way as to make it stiff and hard. From his waist hung several brass-looking strips that went to his knees, protecting his groin and thighs. He wore leather sandals with straps that wrapped halfway up his lower legs. A sheathed short sword, similar to Coleman's, hung from the man's waist. The other soldiers were similarly geared, except their tunics were white, not blue, and their helms did not have a spike or streamers.

Coleman flexed his back muscles and felt his sword's scabbard laying against his bare skin. The commander's stare looked both threatening and uncompromising. Coleman knew he was walking into a dangerous situation that could erupt in violence at any moment. When he stopped, the two men stood silently, staring at each other.

Finally, the commander spoke with a thick accent like Myron's and said, "Are you the one they call the Tondo?"

"Yes. Who are you and why are you here?" Coleman asked.

"I am Sestardi Titus, emissary of King Teg-ar-mos. He commands your presence."

"Oh, does he? Who is King Teg-ar-mos?"

"He is the ruler of Anterra, the Ancient City."

Coleman paused to ponder these words. He recalled his time spent with Myron, the merchant. He guessed the trader had told the king about their meeting, but why would the king want to see him? Coleman handed his bow to Tzeechoe, who had quietly moved to his side. Coleman raised his arms above his head and, in a voice loud enough for all to hear, he proclaimed, "My brothers, put down your weapons. I will speak with Sestardi Titus. Sestardi, tell your men to put down their weapons." The commander turned and nodded his head without uttering a word. His men lowered their arms and stood at parade rest, eyes scanning the villagers surrounding them.

"Your men are well trained, Sestardi," Coleman complimented.

"Yours are not," came the commander's terse reply.

"They are not fighting men. They are hunters. And I am not their leader." Coleman stepped to the chief's side and said a few quiet words to him. The chief waved his arms in front of his body and the villagers began to disperse slowly and cautiously. Coleman turned to the commander and began speaking, "Sestardi, may I call you Sestardi?"

"Yes, that is my rank," he replied.

"Oh, I thought that was your name. Okay, Sestardi Titus, is that correct?"

"Yes."

"Well then, Sestardi Titus, let your men relax. All of you may join us for our midday meal. You and I can then discuss your mission."

The commander crossed his arms over his chest and contemplated the invitation. He was in the midst of hostile people who were willing to defend the Tondo with their lives. He was grossly outnumbered and knew that although he and his men could inflict grievous casualties on the villagers, his little contingent would eventually be overrun and annihilated. Sestardi Titus was a brave man, but not a foolish one. He had been charged with bringing the Tondo to the king and he would see his duty done. Although diplomacy was not his forte, it would have to do in these prickly circumstances.

"Yes," he finally said, "we will join you." He turned to his troops again and dismissed them. He ordered his soldiers to stow their pikes in the carts, but they were to keep their swords with them. He also ordered them to keep them sheathed unless he personally gave different orders.

A wise move, thought Coleman. He certainly didn't want a misunderstanding to turn into a massacre for either side.

The drizzle turned into a mist as Titus's men moved under the canopy that protected the meal fire from the rain. They seated themselves on a log and quietly talked amongst themselves. Coleman guided Titus toward the two beasts and carts.

"What are these?" he asked.

"They are thrice. They make excellent beasts of burden. These two have pulled these carts for the past six detzamars over some of the most rugged terrain you can imagine."

He rubbed the nearest one's back. The creature stood nearly as tall as a man. Its skin was brown and its three horns were the color of ivory. At the end of its snout was an ivory-colored beak. The frill of its head plate was tipped with ivory-like protrusions, sharp and threatening. Its brown eye—the only one Coleman could see—stared at him, following his every

move. The beast made no aggressive motions and appeared
to be chewing its cud. Coleman walked around the thrice and
touched its hide. It was tough and leathery. The only thing
that looked different from the classic triceratops he had seen
in illustrations, other than its smaller size, was its small tail.
From what Coleman could remember, most large dinosaurs
had long, heavy tails. This creature did not. It reminded him
of an elephant's tail, relatively small for the size of the beast.

Was there no end to the wonders of this place? Coleman
thought.

He then moved to the cart and examined the weapons
stowed there. After asking the sestardi's permission, he
hefted a shield and carefully examined the pike-like
weapons. The shields had a wooden frame, covered with
shiny, brass-colored metal like his sword. They were about
three feet tall and two feet wide with a weight of fewer
than ten pounds. The pike-like weapons, which Titus
called metrens, were around six and a half feet long. They
were topped with a metal tip the color of brass and were
over two feet in length. Coleman also saw a few daggers
and short swords stored in the carts. There were many
wooden boxes that Titus told Coleman were food stores,
a few medicinal supplies, and tents. There were also a few
small barrels in the stash, most of which were filled with
water. There were a few empty barrels, too. These, the
sestardi said, had been filled with his men's daily ration
of gant, which he described as a diluted wine drink. Titus told
Coleman that his men had been miserable since they ran out of
gant over two detzamars ago.

Coleman shrugged his shoulders and said, "We do not have strong drink here, although there is a fruit that can be found that will render a man incoherent in short order."

"I don't need that. These men are hard enough to control as it is," was the sestardi's troubled response.

Some village women began serving the soldiers food in leaf packages. They also brought food to Coleman and Titus. Coleman noticed that the men did not offer a word of thanks, but only snatched the meals from the women, tearing open the neatly folded leaves and gobbling down the contents. They seemed famished or extremely rude, probably both. Coleman thanked Duba when she handed him his portion. Nita gave Titus his share, but he also said not a word of thanks. He unfolded the leaf package and devoured the meat in a couple of minutes. Coleman just stared at him.

It wasn't long before Titus noticed Coleman's gaze. "We haven't eaten in two days. Most of our food stores are infested with creepers that make the food taste horrible." He shoved more into his mouth. "This is excellent."

Coleman just nodded and handed his portion to Titus, who delayed for a second and then grabbed it. Nita trotted off and returned with another meal package for Coleman. He then told her to make sure the other soldiers were fed until they were full. Titus thanked him but ignored Nita. That seemed odd to Coleman, but he didn't say anything. The next few minutes would be crucial to the relationship he was attempting to develop with the sestardi, and he didn't think it was necessary to put him on the defensive, at least not at this time.

Be warned, Coleman's inner voiced nagged, *these warriors could be the ones who enslave the village. Remember your vision. Kill them before they kill a villager!*

He pondered his thoughts and wondered how such a small force could be a threat. *Are they the vanguard of a larger hidden force waiting to pounce?*

After all had eaten their fill, the soldiers relaxed and some napped. It was time to discuss the subject at hand. "Sestardi Titus, tell me about your mission."

"King Teg-ar-mos commands that you return with me and answer his questions," Titus told him.

"How does King Teg-ar-mos know about me?"

"The merchant, Myron, returned to a nearby city and spread the word."

"Oh yes, Myron. What did he say?"

"He told everyone he had found a man with blue eyes, different from anyone he had ever met before. When the word reached the temple, the priests immediately summoned the king to a meeting. Shortly after that, the king commanded me to fetch you. That was over six detzamars ago. We had no idea our journey would take so long and be so treacherous. Two of my men have crossed-over along the way."

"What do the priests want with me?"

"I don't know. I just do what I'm told. I've found asking too many questions gets a sestardi in trouble."

"You said the priests summoned the king to a meeting? Who runs the city anyway, the king or the priests?"

"The priests usually don't have anything to say about the way the city is managed, but they are very powerful, and their Guardians are feared by all, even the king."

"Who are the Guardians?" Coleman asked.

"I'm not sure if they are a *who* or a *what*. I have never seen one, nor do I wish to. The few who have, seldom say much about them. They guard the temple and are so fierce it is said a handful could destroy an army of men. I don't know if these are stories to scare children or not, but our leaders do not challenge the priests in any way. Since they seldom make demands on the city leaders, they are simply left to themselves."

"So, the priests have called for me and why is a mystery. What could I possibly have that would interest them?" Sestardi Titus only shrugged his shoulders. He then rummaged through the cart and handed Coleman a round leather cylinder about eighteen inches long. Coleman shook it and heard something inside. One end was covered with a leather cap, so he pulled it off and looked into the cylinder. There was a scroll inside. It appeared to be parchment. He slid it out. When he unrolled it, he found writing on it. The writing was pictographic, resembling Egyptian hieroglyphics. There was a seal pressed into red wax at the bottom of the document.

"What does this say?" Coleman asked.

"Let me see it," Titus said. "I was told to give it to you when I saw you. My commander told me it is a Document of Summons." He scanned the parchment for a minute or more. When he finished, he said, "I don't read so good, but it says you are to come back with us to Anterra and report to the king. I am to protect you. It says you are a guest of His Highness. My commander told me, if you don't submit, I'm to take you by force."

"On one hand the velvet glove, and on the other a steel fist," Coleman muttered in his native tongue.

"What did you say?" asked Titus.

"Tondo sometimes says things that no one understands. He is using godspeak," came Tzeechoe's words. Coleman hadn't noticed his friend had joined them.

"Godspeak, is it? I have never heard such talk. What did he say?"

"When Tondo uses godspeak, no one knows what he says. Only Tondo and the gods understand and sometimes he doesn't share the gods' message."

"The Tondo," Titus said, "what is that on your face?" as he reached to touch Coleman's beard, but he quickly withdrew his hand.

"Just Tondo will do. It is called a beard. It is only hair. Go ahead. You can touch it." Titus grabbed his beard and gave it a tug. "Oy!" Coleman shouted. "It is just like the hair on your head. Would you like me to give your hair a yank like that?"

"I have never seen such a thing. At first, I thought you were some kind of wild animal. Maybe you are," Titus continued.

"I am no beast unless I get angry," Coleman said with a coy smile. Titus looked surprised, but then he could see Coleman's humor and smiled.

"What is that thing your slave is holding for you? I noticed a few others carried one as well. What are they?" he asked, pointing to the bow Tzeechoe still held.

"This is Tzeechoe, my good friend. He is not my slave. Tzeechoe, give Titus the bow."

Titus examined it carefully, pulled the bowstring, but he had no idea how to hold it properly. Finally, he asked, "What does it do?"

"Here, let me show you," Coleman said as he took the bow from Titus. He thought this would be an excellent opportunity not only to show off his bow, but also to prove to Titus and his men that he was no one to trifle with. He took one of the shields from a cart and leaned it against a tree trunk. He then stepped back fifty feet or so and nocked an arrow. He looked around to make sure the other soldiers were watching and, when he was certain he had their attention, he let the arrow fly. It easily penetrated the shield and sank deeply into the tree trunk. Titus went to the shield and examined Coleman's work. He attempted to pull the arrow out of the shield, but it was so deeply embedded in the tree trunk, he couldn't remove it. He then slid the shield over the arrow's shaft and feathers and took a close look at how far the arrow had penetrated the tree. Coleman watched the commander's reaction closely. He wanted Titus to realize the power he possessed, and if he chose not to go with him to the Ancient City, he and his men would not be able to force him to comply. "So, what do you think, sestardi?"

"I have never seen such a weapon. It would be devastating in battle. Where did it come from?" he asked.

"From the gods," Tzeechoe chimed in. Titus ignored Tzeechoe's remark.

Coleman walked to the tree, grasped the arrow shaft with his right hand, and gave it a quick, strong tug. It popped out and he examined the arrowhead. "This looks okay. I can use it again," he said as he slid it into his quiver. He glanced at the other soldiers and saw their worried expressions. They were whispering among themselves. *Good,* Coleman thought, *let them digest that for a while.* "Sestardi, would you like to give it a try?"

"Yes," came his simple reply. After some instruction, Titus nocked an arrow and pulled the bowstring back as far as he could. He couldn't draw the bow all the way back, but then neither could any of the villagers. He let the arrow loose and it flew wild, disappearing into the trees. Coleman and Tzeechoe smiled. Titus returned the bow to Coleman who nocked another arrow and again pierced the shield, sinking deeply into the tree trunk. He retrieved his arrow, then took a moment to find the one Titus had lost. Toto was sniffing the air and ground until the wayward arrow was found.

"I see it takes a very strong man to use this weapon," Titus admitted.

"His bow is the most powerful in the village. I have seen Tondo take down a tuntro from here to those rocks over there," Tzeechoe advised as he pointed to a small group of boulders nearly one-hundred-and-fifty-feet away. "He is the Sutro P´oez, the greatest hunter of the Batru!"

"With a weapon like that, I can see why," Titus said.

"He killed the gorga with only a club and a knife. That is its fang hanging from his neck," Tzeechoe went on, as Titus studied the large incisor.

"Gorga? What's a gorga?" he asked.

"The most dangerous beast the Batru have ever faced. It

killed many hunters over many rains, but Tondo killed it all by himself. We ate its heart," Tzeechoe stated proudly.

Unexpectedly, a woman screamed, and everyone's attention shifted to the sound. Nita was in the clutches of one of the soldiers. She was trying to escape his grasp, but he was too strong for her. She bit his arm as hard as she could, so he slapped her and pushed her to the ground. With cat-like reflexes, Coleman dashed to the scuffle and punched the soldier in the side of his head. The man crumpled to the ground. Toto faced off against the other soldiers, keeping them at bay with an intimidating deep-throated growl.

Titus scampered up, surveyed the situation, and smiled warily. "It doesn't look like any harm was done here. Apparently, the wench was causing trouble," he stated in a matter of fact tone.

"You had better control your men or I will," Coleman threatened, as the fallen soldier staggered to his feet. He shook the dizziness from his head and then glared at Tondo.

"Sestardi, I demand satisfaction. He struck me when I wasn't prepared, like a coward would," the soldier grumbled as he glared at the hairy villager.

Titus smiled. Now, it was his turn to see what this Tondo was really made of. Was he as tough as his man Tzeechoe boasted? "By our rules, you and he must resolve this dispute until one gives up or can no longer fight. Are you willing to do that, Tondo?" Coleman looked at the quaking Nita and anger filled his heart. The sestardi could literally feel Coleman's ire emanating from the wild-man like waves of heat. He subconsciously took a step back and asked, "Yes or no?"

Through clenched teeth, Coleman growled in his native tongue, "Let's get it on!"

Titus looked around at the villagers nervously before finally saying, "I'll assume that means yes." He brought the men to a cleared area near the village entrance. The soldier, Bardas, stripped down to his warrior's loincloth and wrapped his hands with leather straps. He then began pounding his fists together as his comrades shouted encouragement to him. He was a burly man, around five feet eight inches tall, and approximately two hundred pounds. Coleman exceeded him in height, weight, and reach but would it matter? By this time, most of the village men had surrounded the two combatants, forming a large ring. Coleman removed his weapons and declined the sestardi's offer of leather straps.

Coleman asked, "What are the rules?"

Titus replied, "The only rule is you cannot kill one another. Broken bones, dislocated joints, gouged eyes, all of that is acceptable."

"Very well then. Let us do this," Coleman grumbled.

The two men circled the ring, each taking the measure of the other. Toto barked his screechy bark, but Tzeechoe held him back. Coleman soon stopped moving and assumed a defensive stance with his feet planted one behind the other, his arms and fists prepared to take an assault. He wanted to see if the soldier was a skilled fighter or just an unskilled brute.

It didn't take long for him to find out. When Bardas saw that Coleman had stopped moving, he charged. Coleman popped him in the nose with a quick left jab, then quickly stepped aside, avoiding the charging man. Bardas could now feel Coleman's aura of rage, causing him to lose some of his resolve. But encouragement from his fellow soldiers bolstered him and he charged again. Stepping into the charge, Coleman caught the man's leg on his hip and rolled him to the ground. As Bardas hit the dirt, Coleman smashed the heel of his right palm into Bardas's face, hitting him in the forehead with a loud smack. It looked like Bardas lost consciousness for an instant, but he quickly scrambled away, jumping to his feet; it was a quick and dexterous move that surprised Coleman. Before he could set himself, Bardas charged again, grabbing him around the waist from the front in a vicious bear hug. The soldier's comrades shouted their glee as Bardas squeezed Coleman with all his might.

"He's finished now!" called one.

"No one ever escapes the death-grip!" shouted another. A wry smile crossed Titus's face at the hairy savage's predicament. Coleman felt as if he were in a vise and he couldn't take a breath. If he didn't extricate himself quickly, he would pass out for lack of air. Bardas's mistake was he hadn't pinned Coleman's arms, so he rubbed his coarse beard against Bardas's face, surprising the Anterran. He then crashed his fists down hard on both sides of the grappler's neck, stunning the man and causing him to weaken his grip. Coleman then gave him a head-butt that bashed into Bardas's left temple, knocking him senseless. He crumpled to the ground again.

He's down! Finish him! Coleman's inner voice growled. *A quick knuckle punch to the throat or the bridge of the nose is all it will take!*

Coleman quickly reasoned that this was a fight and not a battle, so he wouldn't be so vicious. He stepped back and waited for Bardas to regain his feet. The soldier staggered up, glared at his opponent, and charged again. Coleman was ready for him this time and he grabbed Bardas by the arms as he fell backward, placing his right foot on his opponent's abdomen as they collapsed. When Coleman felt his back hit the cold, damp ground, he straightened his leg with a jerk, and Bardas flew through the air, landing on his back with a crack, several feet away. This time, the man didn't get up. His head had hit a stone and he was out cold.

Coleman stood up and looked around the circle. Titus and the other soldiers were clearly disappointed that their man had lost so decisively. The villagers didn't know what to think. They had never seen such a violent contest, but it was evident to all, Coleman was no one to be challenged.

He walked over to Titus and asked, "Is it over?"

"Yes, Tondo, and you have won. I have never seen such moves before. Are you a warrior?"

"You could say that, but it was some time ago. It seems I have lost some of my speed," Coleman said as he examined a scratch on his left side. "I wonder how I got this," he said to no one in particular. He was splattered with mud, and his skin was beet red. A slight trickle of blood oozed from the scratch.

Bardas moaned and then sat up. He rubbed his head and watched as blood dripped from his nose and ran down his bare chest, mingling with the mud that covered most of his torso. Coleman walked over to his vanquished foe and extended his arm. After a short delay, Bardas took it, and Coleman pulled him to his feet. He then stared into the man's eyes and threatened, "If you or any of your friends so much as touch one of the village women again, you will have me to answer to."

"That will not be necessary. I will see to it that the women are left alone," Titus said with the voice of command. His eyes darted from soldier to soldier, pausing as each man nodded in recognition of his order. The villagers then began to disperse, Ayascho being the last to leave.

"I need to clean up," Coleman told Titus and Tzeechoe. He then departed the village and jumped into the stream, washing off the mud and blood. He returned to the village much cleaner and a little sorer. He had been in some real knock down hand-to-hand battles when he was in the Rangers, both in training and combat. Bardas was hardly a challenge, but Coleman knew he could have done better, having forgotten some of his moves and losing a little of his speed over the years and spans since his military days.

Titus realized getting Coleman back to the Ancient City would not be an easy task. The hairy savage was a bigger and more powerful man than he expected to find, and he carried a weapon that flung deadly missiles great distances. Nevertheless, Titus had his orders and he would do all within his power to see his duty done. He refused to return empty-handed.

Titus and his men set up their camp about a half-mile from the village. The villagers wanted nothing to do with them after the events of the first day. The soldiers were not allowed to go near the stream. That was considered sacred ground,

Coleman told them, and he threatened to punish anyone who disobeyed his dictate.

Coleman and Tzeechoe refilled the soldier's water barrels as needed. They would pass the men's camp each morning but would not stop unless the soldiers had left an empty water barrel to be refilled. This routine went on for several days, all while Titus and his men stewed and complained amongst themselves at the delay.

"Sestardi," Teness began, "what are we going to do? Are we just going to sit here and wait for that hairy savage to meet with you again? I'm tired of waiting, and all of us are aging to death ever since we left the Blessing of the City. We're all tired of waiting and I'd guess you are, too. You're the king's representative. If this Tondo doesn't respect that, it is our duty to force him to."

"No need to remind me of my duty, Teness. This is a sticky situation. We're outnumbered significantly. If he won't go with us voluntarily, it will take some planning to take him by force. I'll give him another day or two to come around. If he doesn't, this is what I want you and the others to do in preparation . . ."

Coleman ignored Titus and his men; however, he continued to fear that a larger force of king's men was lurking nearby, preparing to attack the villagers. His nagging inner voice continued its warnings, urging him to force Titus and his men to leave or ruthlessly eliminate their peril altogether.

This threat won't go away. They're here to conquer the village and turn everyone, even you, into slaves. Kill them, kill them all! Display their severed heads at the village entrance as a warning to any others of their ilk hiding nearby.

Coleman's soul froze at the thought. He began to ponder his options. The idea of killing these invaders without due cause was abhorrent. Yet, it became harder to ignore the warnings.

It's just a matter of time before they strike. Titus will surely summon his other warriors, the ones hiding in the trees. Then what can you do? Strike now while his force is divided. Gather all the hunters and lead them in a quick, overwhelming strike. End the threat now!

Coleman's worry and consternation grew. He recalled his vision, remembering the men and beasts of war. In his mind's eye, he saw the villagers shackled and chained. He could not—he would not—allow that to happen to his adopted family. He decided he must act and a preemptive strike would be the best solution.

Good, very good, his inner voice goaded. *Now, gather the hunters and plan the attack. Take no prisoners! This victory will be the first of many. You will be hailed as a great leader, a savior, a god!*

"What am I thinking?" Coleman exclaimed aloud in godspeak. "This can't be right."

Unexpectedly, Coleman's inner agitation was pushed aside and a calming influence embraced him.

Listen to the promptings of your heart. All you need to do is to choose what is right and then act upon it. Why anguish over the unknown. When you choose to nurture the good seeds, you will be supported.

Coleman relaxed and drew a deep breath. The idea of slaughtering Titus and his men suddenly became repugnant.

How could I have thought such an evil thing? Am I being influenced by some wicked force? Could the Tempter be real? Could the Whisperer also be real? He continued to ponder his feelings and thoughts for quite some time. Finally, he said, "I must be true to myself. I cannot go against that which I know to be right."

Although mollified somewhat, Coleman still worried that a larger force of king's men was hiding nearby. He searched far and wide for the dreaded larger contingent, but none had been found. The jungle was huge, and he knew it would take little effort to hide a large force within its trees and bushes.

He chose to let Titus stew for several days, making it clear to the king's messenger who was in charge. He was certain that this irritated the sestardi significantly, and he reveled in the thought. He knew the commander was in a hurry to get back on track and resume his mission, but that wasn't going to happen anytime soon. Coleman knew it was late in the season and, even if he wanted to go with these men, the rainy season would soon make travel nearly impossible.

Several days had passed since Titus and his men had arrived. Coleman had let the Anterrans chafe long enough. It was time to meet with them again and discuss the future. Late in the afternoon, just as he was getting ready to head to Titus's camp, Teness and Bardas entered the village and marched up to him. Toto started his low growl of warning.

"Tondo, we need water," Teness declared.

"Why didn't you leave an empty barrel out this morning?" Coleman wondered.

"We had plenty this morning, but that stupid male thrice kicked over the barrel, and by the time we noticed, all of the water had drained out. Do you mind fetching some for us before it gets dark?" Teness asked.

"Okay, not a problem. Toto, stay. I will be right back," Coleman commanded. Then he and the two Anterrans marched out of the village.

When the three men arrived at Titus's camp, Coleman asked, "Okay, where is the barrel?"

"Just over there, between the tents," Bardas told him with a smile.

Coleman moved between the tents and picked up the small barrel. He noticed two of Titus's men move to block his path to the front. He turned around and saw Teness and Bardas blocking his path to the rear. He stopped and examined the men's demeanor. He quickly realized he'd been ambushed.

"Where's Titus?" he asked angrily.

"Here," Titus said as he stepped around the back of one of the tents. "You're coming with us, whether you like it or not." Coleman threw the empty barrel at him and reached for his sword. Four men jumped on him before he could draw it forth. Coleman got in a few good strikes with his fists before his arms were pinned. Then Bardas punched him hard in the face, stunning him. While he was shaking off the grogginess, the others quickly wrapped him in a rope, pinning his arms and legs. He was soon gagged, and they picked him up, carried him to a thrice cart, and dumped him in it. Coleman began growling his angst, a mixture of his new language and godspeak; however, no one could understand a word he was saying with the gag so firmly placed.

Titus and his men dropped the tents, collected their things, and hitched the thrice to the carts. After arming themselves with metrens, the party was off, driving through the thick jungle as a misty drizzle began to fall.

Titus pushed his men through the night, moving as quickly as the thrice would allow. By morning, everyone, including the thrice, were reaching exhaustion, but Titus would not stop. He had to put distance between his party and the Batru village.

Coleman grumbled all night long, his garbled speech being ignored by the other men. Finally, at midday, Titus called a halt to give man and beast a rest. He had Teness remove Coleman's gag and, after he did, the prisoner blasted Titus and his men with a barrage of godspeak curses and epithets. He finally calmed down enough to make coherent sense.

"What are you doing? This is todo!" he exclaimed. "You are going to get us all killed."

"Shut your hairy mouth or I'll bust your face again," Bardas threatened.

"Titus!" Coleman yelled.

The Anterran commander moved to the side of the cart. "What?"

"You are going to get us all killed," Coleman repeated.

"I doubt your savage friends are going to attack us with you as our prisoner."

"I do not know what the villagers will do, but I can tell you this, the rainy season is upon us and it will end your mission in death. All of us will die in the muck," Coleman warned as he struggled to keep his temper in check.

"We've been through rainstorms already. We can handle it. Now, you want some water?"

"Yeah," Coleman growled through a dry throat. Titus held the waterskin while his prisoner drank. When he finished, Coleman continued, "You have not experienced anything like what is coming. Rain will fall day and night, day after day. And it will not be like the drizzle you've seen so far. It will come down in torrents. The ground will become a bog. Your thrice will become exhausted and die. Then your men will start dying of disease. None of us will survive to see the Ancient City." Titus's expression turned to concern as he pondered Coleman's dire warning. His men noticed the change in their commander's demeanor.

"Sestardi, don't trust that hairy savage. It's all a lie. He'll say anything to get us to stop and let his savage friends catch up," Bardas warned.

"Bardas, you're an idiot," Coleman spat in godspeak. "You have no idea what you are in for. If we leave now, we will be dead in thirty days."

Teness and Pontus dashed out of the trees and went to their commander, frantic expressions covering their faces. Teness was the first to speak, "Sestardi, fifty or more savages are coming. The prisoner's beast is leading them to us. What should we do?"

"Untie me!" Coleman shouted. "Let me talk to them before someone gets hurt," he offered.

"Shut up!" Titus ordered. "Men, prepare for battle!" Titus and his men fetched their shields and prepared to engage the hostiles.

"This is stupid!" Coleman grumbled in godspeak. "Titus, you cannot be serious. You are going to get all your men killed this way. Stop and think."

"If that's the way it's to be, we will take a bunch of them with us," Titus threatened. Just then, the first of the Batru villagers came into view, quickly followed by many more. Tzeechoe was restraining the angry betzoe on a leash. Coleman watched nervously as Taahso stepped forward.

"Come no closer or I'll order my men to attack!" Titus shouted.

Taahso raised his staff and without warning, a small fireball shot forth. It hit Pontus's shield, sticking to it like burning tar. The Anterran cast his shield aside and shouted in fear, "He's got the power of the priests!" The Anterrans and the Batru villagers stood facing each other, neither wanting to step into the eye of the storm and initiate combat.

Coleman knew he had to do something and do it fast before someone got killed. He focused his taah on the rope binding him, and it soon began to smolder and burn. Unfortunately, the flaming rope was also burning his skin, but he knew he had to endure the pain in order to escape his bindings. It only took seconds for the rope to burn through. He managed to wiggle free as the coils loosened. Then he stood.

"Tondo's free!" Bardas yelled in warning and rushed toward the freed prisoner. Suddenly, his shield burst into flame. He quickly tossed it aside as he turned and faced Taahso, assuming the savage sorcerer was the one who had ignited his shield.

Coleman stepped down from the cart and quickly strode

into the space separating the two groups. Toto moved to his side and the huge beast began growling at Titus and his men, unnerving them as much as the savage sorcerer had.

"My Batru brothers, stop this before someone gets hurt," Coleman pleaded.

"Tondo, are you all right?" Tzeechoe asked as he lowered his club.

"Yes. Taahso, let me talk to the Anterrans."

"These invaders have no honor. I will see them punished for their attempt to steal you from your home," Taahso declared.

"They made a todo mistake. I stayed so I could counsel them. They wish to travel through the great rains." Several of the villagers scoffed at such an idea, a few voicing derisive comments.

Coleman turned and marched up to Titus, the massive betzoe at his side. They stopped a few feet from the Anterran commander. Coleman's expression grew stern and Toto bared his teeth, exposing his huge canines, grumbling his irritation and warning. Coleman could easily sense Titus's rising distress.

"All right, sestardi, now what are you going to do? You are overmatched, so think before you answer."

"I've got my orders," Titus simply replied.

"So you do, but what you just did could have gotten us all killed. I am serious about the hazards of the coming rains. I am inclined to return to the city with you, but I have no desire to die because you are too stupid to listen," Coleman sternly stated. All the time he was speaking, Toto continued his grumble and threatening stance.

"How long will these killing rains last?" Titus wondered.

"Probably a hundred days, maybe more."

"A hundred days! I can't wait that long. I won't wait that long."

"You can leave whenever you want, but as I said, you will all die," Coleman warned again.

"I won't leave without you."

"Then, you will have to wait for the rains to subside. After the rains, I will go with you."

"You will come with me, willingly?"

Coleman nodded.

"All right, we'll wait. We will wait here and see for ourselves how bad these rains really are." Coleman gave the Anterran a wry smile, turned on his heels, and walked away. Toto gave a snort and followed his master. Everyone made their way back to the village, grateful that no blood was spilled.

Word quickly spread throughout the village that Tondo would be leaving with the Anterrans. There was sadness in the villagers' hearts, but somehow, they knew his work here was done and he needed to follow the path Batru had prepared for him. It was their duty to let him go and they prayed to the gods to carry him in safety.

Coleman desired to learn more about the Ancient City where he had decided to travel. He invited Titus to his lodge and the two men discussed things over last-meal while Pontus and Teness stood guard outside, suffering under a light drizzle.

"Sestardi, why are you in such a hurry to return? You made a foolish decision to rush back. Why?"

Titus stared into the fire and Coleman could see he was reluctant to answer the question. Finally, he replied, "The longer we are separated from the city, the faster our lives pass."

Coleman was confused. He asked, "What does that mean?"

"How old are you?" Titus asked.

"I am around thirty-two spans. Why do you ask?"

"I'm eighty-four and I look younger than you. All my men are older than me. One is almost two-hundred spans. As long as we stay near the Ancient City, our lives are prolonged. When we leave it, we age like other men. Didn't Myron tell you this?"

"No, he did not. Why, then, would he leave the Ancient City? I cannot imagine it was simply to ply his wares at the cost of shortening his life."

"Myron angered a baron, one of the king's relatives. It had something to do with a transaction that went wrong. The baron petitioned the king, and Myron was banished. No one ever expected him to return because to do so would certainly mean severe punishment; however, he did return with stories about you and was forgiven. The king allowed Myron back into the good graces of the kingdom at the urgings of the Sutro Seer," Titus explained.

"The Sutro Seer?" Coleman wondered.

"He's the senior priest."

"Did you and your men volunteer for this mission?" Coleman asked as he studied the sestardi's face.

Titus looked embarrassed as he admitted, "This duty is a punishment for me and my men. We were assigned as guards for the king's cousin, a baroness. She was traveling to an estate on the outskirts of the city. We had to cross a small stream, so I and my men had to steady the royal's carriage. The water was swift and we lost control. It drifted downstream and rolled onto its side. Although we were able to save the baroness and her friends, I was reduced in rank from officer to non-officer. Also, our punishment was to go and find you; a hopeless and deadly mission everyone said. To make matters worse, for each day we are away from the city, we will age ten. That is why we must hurry back. I'm sure the Blessing of the City will fall upon you, too, when we arrive."

Coleman sat in silence, pondering the sestardi's revelation. The promise of near immortality was tempting, but travel during the rainy season would certainly kill them all. After weighing the options, he spoke. "You and your men can leave anytime you wish. I will follow when the rains end, but be forewarned, if you leave now, you may not survive to see the Ancient City again."

"I will not leave this place without you. Above all, it is my duty to bring you to the king," he stated in a firm and uncompromising voice.

"Spoken like a true soldier. Well then, we will all leave when the rains end. Are there any other soldiers nearby waiting for you?" Coleman asked, reading the man's face and feeling his inner-power reaching out, searching for deceptions or secret plots; he perceived none.

"We are all the king sent. He wouldn't waste any more on a hopeless mission. Two have already crossed-over." Titus leaned back, "I will accept your counsel and wait. I must now return to my men."

"Before you leave, tell me about the Ancient City," Coleman asked.

"Where would you like me to start?" Titus wondered.

"How many live in the city?"

"I'd guess between twenty and twenty-five thousand in the entire kingdom. There's also several thousand slaves."

"Tell me about slavery in the city. I would think a city as renowned as Anterra would not allow such an awful thing," Coleman stated.

"Slavery is probably the same there as it is everywhere. Undoubtedly, the same as it is in your home city."

"There are no slaves in my homeland. Slavery was ended hundreds of years ago."

"Eerz?" Titus wondered.

"I mean spans," Coleman corrected.

"Your kingdom has no slaves?" Coleman nodded. "That's incredible! I can't imagine how a kingdom can survive without them. Slaves keep all the kingdoms prosperous. They perform much of the labor."

"Myron's slave was a white man. Are all the slaves white?" Coleman wondered.

"White man?"

"The same skin color as you and me."

"I've never seen a slave of a different color. I've heard of dark-skinned men working in caravans, but I've never seen one. These savages are the darkest people I've ever seen," Titus explained.

"Go on, tell me about the city," Coleman coaxed. For the remainder of the afternoon, Titus explained many of the aspects of life in the Ancient City as Coleman asked questions.

CHAPTER 24

HONOR BOUND

Titus concluded his exposition of Anterra, leaving Coleman with a thousand more questions, but he could tell the sestardi wanted to get back to his men, so he politely thanked him. Titus quickly dismissed himself and left the lodge.

Coleman sat, contemplating what the next few detzamars would hold. *Idleness is the Devil's workshop,* he thought. If he and the soldiers were to survive the rainy season without coming to blows, he needed to suggest a project that would occupy their time. The men were living in the leather tents they had brought with them. The two thrice were tethered and had no shelter at all. Coleman settled on a construction project that would see several log cabins built. He thought he could even convince the soldiers to create a wooden stockade to protect themselves from the wild and dangerous animals that prowled the area from time to time, or so he would tell them. It was certainly a stretch of the truth, especially now that the gorga was dead, but he wanted these men to remain busy until they departed.

When he proposed the idea to Titus, the sestardi quickly accepted it. He, too, was concerned about his idle men. Although he didn't share this with Coleman, he had been very concerned about his party's vulnerability to attack by beast or man. On the following day, work began. The soldiers had two gravetum, iron-like axes, in their stash of equipment, which quickened their work. The first structure completed was a ten-foot square log cabin. The soldiers were the only ones allowed to work on the project, not that the villagers wanted to go anywhere near these awful men, but it had been made clear to the villagers by Coleman. By now, Tondo's status in the community was such that his words were good enough, no questions asked, though Coleman guessed, the chief understood the underlying reasoning. The cabin was erected and roofed in ten days, which the soldiers called a wernt. It would meet the needs of the men, but just barely. It was crowded and smelly.

After a day of rest, construction began on the second cabin. By then, the rains had arrived in all their vigor, surprising the Anterrans and causing them to accept Coleman's dire warning as unfortunately accurate. The deluge of unrelenting water fell both day and night; however, construction did not stop, though it became much harder to handle the muddy, wet, and slippery logs. The second cabin took two wernts to complete.

The next structure was built for the thrice. It was larger than a cabin but had only three sides and a slanted roof. When that was completed, the men built a third cabin for their commander. After that, they started working on the stockade.

During all this time, Coleman saw to it that the soldiers received a portion of each day's hunt. He didn't want them tramping through the wilderness unescorted. After a while, Titus became suspicious of Coleman's rules, but he never said a word about it. It wasn't worth getting on the hairy savage's bad side or causing him to change his mind about peacefully going with him to the Ancient City.

One day, while returning from his morning hunt, Coleman found Bardas hitting the female thrice with a stout club. The creature was bellowing in pain, but Bardas kept hitting her.

Coleman quickly approached the man and grabbed his arm. "Why are you beating this creature?" he demanded.

"It stepped on my foot and nearly broke it. It'll never do that again when I'm finished with it," he yelled in a pained and angry voice.

"If you do not want to get stepped on, keep out of her way. You are supposedly smarter than she is," Coleman scolded. He watched as Bardas contemplated his next move. Coleman perceived his thoughts and warned, "I still owe you one for punching me in the face. I am ready if you are."

Bardas was in no mood to listen to a lecture from this wild-looking, hairy man-beast. He considered using his club on Coleman, but recalling the beating he'd already received at Coleman's hands and not being backed up by any of his comrades, he thought better of it. He threw the club as far as he could and let out an ear-splitting yell of anger and frustration. He then limped away to his cabin and brooded. Coleman examined the beast's wounds, made a poultice of medicinal herbs he had learned from the villagers, and treated the creature's injuries. He then found some food pods and fed them to it.

"That a girl," he said as she munched away. The other thrice, a rather dimwitted male, gave a loud bellow of his own once he realized he was missing out on the treats. Coleman gave him a pod and he crunched in sublime bliss.

"You are such a doofus," he said to the now placated male thrice. "That is what I will call you, Doofus." Coleman had a penchant for naming creatures of the wild, so why not a couple of domesticated beasts of burden. He'd noticed that the soldiers did not personalize the creatures in any way. They only referred to them as 'it' or 'the beast'.

"Now, what shall I name you?" he said to the female thrice. "Ah yes, Lulubelle. How do you like your new name, Lulubelle?" The thrice gave a grunt and a snort, and pushed her beak into Coleman's arm, nearly knocking him over. "Now, you are the smart one, are you not? So, you want another treat?" he said as he fed her another pod. He then chuckled to himself. Lulubelle would be unpronounceable by anyone but himself. He laughed at the thought. *That will probably drive Titus and his men nuts, and it wouldn't bother me in the least.* Coleman wasn't particularly fond of either Titus or his men. Titus wasn't as bad as the others, but all the Anterrans seemed crude, rude, and disrespectful toward the Batru villagers. He detected an air of superiority in them or was it bigotry? He wasn't sure which, but he didn't like it.

Time passed and so did the torrential rains. As the rains ebbed, the sestardi's impatience waxed. Some days, little rain fell, but on others, it fell in a deluge. When it was evident to Coleman that the rainy season was nearing its end, he told Titus to prepare his men for departure in three days. He had picked that day because it preceded the Matti-mas celebration by two days. He wanted the soldiers miles away by the time the village merriment began.

Coleman's last three days in the village were bittersweet. All but Ayascho wished him well and thanked him for all he had done for them. The chief called for a special gathering the night before his departure. The People sang songs of thanks and happiness in the great lodge. Many skits were performed, culminating with another rousing round of "Tondo! Tondo! Tondo!" And again, he told the story of Tondo and the gorga, over and over, until his voice grew raspy. Finally, the chief intervened and he was spared from yet another telling.

Early the following morning, Coleman gathered up his few belongings, his betzoe, and departed the village for what he was sure was to be the last time. All the People assembled to wish him farewell. He even caught a glimpse of Ayascho watching his parting from behind Taahso.

Tzeechoe struggled with a heavy leather sack the size of a man's head. "What's in here?" he asked, but Coleman gave no reply.

When the two men arrived at the soldier's stockade, Coleman placed his gear in the cart Lulubelle was pulling. He embraced Tzeechoe but said nothing. He feared his voice would crack and he didn't want that to happen in front of Titus and his men. He gave a hearty wave to the People, then turned to Titus and nodded. The sestardi gave an order, and the party slowly made their way into the jungle. The villagers saw Coleman turn and face them, taking one final look, giving one last wave. Then he disappeared into the green wall and was gone.

Travel was difficult. The ground was soaked and the carts' wheels got stuck in the mud several times a day. By the end of each day's journey, the men were exhausted. Coleman scouted ahead with Toto and brought back fresh game for the men's meals. After five days, Coleman found firmer ground. It was not nearly as soaked because it was on a slight slope.

About midday, Titus took two of his men aside for a short conference and sent them armed with metrens into the jungle. Coleman thought it odd that they hadn't returned by the time the rest of the party started moving again. It wasn't until late in the afternoon that the men approached. Coleman thought he could see through the dense foliage and shadows another man with them. The soldiers poked and prodded him with their long, pointed metrens. When the men caught sight of the rest of the party, one of them gave their captive a vicious blow to the back of his head with the butt of his metren. The man collapsed face down in the muck. Coleman and Titus ran to them to find out what was going on.

"Sestardi, you were right. This fool was following us. We laid a trap and captured him quickly." The man moaned and rubbed the back of his head.

"Who is this, and why has he been following us?" Titus demanded of Coleman.

Coleman kneeled, turned the man onto his side, and gasped in disbelief. It was his village nemesis. "Ayascho, what are you doing here?" Coleman asked in amazement. The young villager sat up and continued rubbing the back of his head. Coleman examined his wound and found a small cut that was starting to bleed. "Oy?" Coleman asked again. Ayascho continued to rub his wound, his eyes wide as he looked at the host surrounding him.

"Why are you following us?" Titus demanded.

"Let me beat an answer out of him," interjected Teness, one of the soldiers who captured him. He made a move toward Ayascho, but Coleman blocked him with his arm. Toto growled a warning.

"We need an answer, Ayascho. We do not have all day," demanded Coleman.

"Is this one of your slaves?" Pontus, the other soldier, asked.

"The Batru have no slaves, and neither do I," stated Coleman sternly. He grabbed the groggy Ayascho by both shoulders and gave him a strong shake. "What are you doing here?" he demanded again. He felt a surge of energy pass through his torso, then through his arms, and into Ayascho's shoulders. Both men jumped in surprise. "What just happened?" Coleman asked. Ayascho looked no less bewildered and said nothing as he weaved groggily. Coleman asked again, "What are you doing here?"

Ayascho shook the dizziness from his head and just replied, "Honor."

"Honor? Honor! What are you talking about?"

"I remain in your debt. I cannot find peace until the debt is paid."

"What is this moron talking about?" Titus growled.

"I can only guess, but he has a strange sense of honor and holds strongly to the traditions of his people. I never thought it would lead to this," Coleman told the sestardi. "Ayascho, you cannot follow me. I may never return to the village. I thought my departure would put you at ease."

"I will follow you until Batru grants me a way to remove my shame," Ayascho said. Coleman stood up, crossed his arms over his chest, and pondered this unexpected situation.

"You must go back!" Titus shouted at him.

"No!" Ayascho shouted back, defiantly.

Coleman tried a more reasonable approach. "It may take many rains before Batru grants your wish. Let me save you some time. I release you from your debt. Now, go home."

"No!" the young man replied again.

"After a good beating, he will change his mind," Pontus shouted. Then he began to laugh. "Let me have him, Sestardi," he begged.

"Stop, you have done enough already," growled Coleman. "Return to the others and let the sestardi and me work this out," he ordered. Pontus and Teness were not about to be ordered around by this hairy beast of a man. They waited for their sestardi to endorse or countermand the order.

"Do as he says," Titus said after a short pause. The two men marched off in the direction of the carts, grumbling. "All right, Tondo, what are we to do with this fool?"

"Ayascho, how have you survived for all these days? Where are your spear and knife?" Coleman asked.

"I've been hunting at night after you stopped. I haven't

eaten in two days. Those men took my knife and spear, then threw them into the trees.

Coleman turned to Titus and said, "We have to take him back to the village."

"We're not going back!" Titus shouted. The soldiers turned and stared at the three men.

"If you go back, it will be for your own sake. I follow Tondo," Ayascho told them.

Coleman was losing patience with the young villager. He knew he wasn't going to be able to convince Titus to return to the village and, if he insisted, there would be a major confrontation. Titus and his men felt they were aging ten days for each day that passed while they were away from the Ancient City and they were in a hurry to get back. Now that they were on their way, they were not about to turn around.

Coleman reached down and pulled the young man to his feet. He searched his eyes and could see his irrational obstinacy. "Okay, you can come with us. You may never see your home again, though. I want you to remember, it was your choice," Coleman lectured. Then he turned to Titus and said, "He will be coming with us. I will be responsible for him."

"As you wish. We've lost enough time because of this idiot. We need to get moving," Titus growled, very much annoyed by the wasted time.

Since Coleman had a bow and a short sword, he gave Ayascho his obsidian knife. The young man now had a weapon to protect himself, if necessary. Coleman also saw to it he was given some food as they all started their march again.

CHAPTER 25

CHITTERING DEATH

Titus carried a leather scroll with a map burned into it; the one Myron had made, which Titus showed to Tondo. The two men examined it often, but nothing was to scale, making it difficult to gauge distances. Coleman, Ayascho, and Toto scouted ahead of the main party, searching for the easiest route. Nevertheless, their progress was maddeningly slow because the carts the thrice were pulling sunk into the water-soaked ground and became mired several times a day. Coleman estimated their progress at only three or four miles a day, sometimes less.

After several days of such poor progress, Ayascho climbed to the top of a tall tree, searching for an easier way. After scrambling down, he briefed Tondo on what he had seen. "There is no easy way. It's thick growth as far as the eye can see; however, I saw mountains in the distance, toward where the p´atezas rises," he explained.

"We should move in that direction. It will lead to a higher elevation and, hopefully, firmer ground. Let us go and tell Titus," Coleman advised. The two men and the betzoe took off at a trot. A few minutes later, Coleman reported to Titus and he redirected the party in a northeasterly direction.

A couple of days later, the party noticed the ground

becoming firmer and they could tell they were climbing in elevation. The going became easier and their pace increased each day. As they climbed higher, they noticed the vegetation changing, as well. The swampy growth gave way to plants and trees requiring less water. As the party advanced, they began passing through meadows. It was a much welcomed relief from the dense growth they had been struggling through up until then.

As they advanced, they began seeing huge mounds as tall or taller than a man scattered across the landscape. After examining a few, it was determined that they were creeper mounds, most likely termites. The creepers were huge; most were between one and two inches long. Soldier termites, identified by their enormous heads and large mandibles, approached three inches or more in length. These creepers could give a man a painful bite, as Teness discovered while teasing one. The men also passed animal skeletons stripped of all flesh, hinting that the creepers could do more damage than just what Teness suffered.

Occasionally, the men also caught sight of other gigantic creepers. Huge spiny spiders like the one that had greeted Coleman upon his arrival to this world and even giant black scorpions over two feet in length.

Creepers preferred leaving the safety of their dens and mounds at night. Sleeping men felt the insects crawling over their bodies more than once, startling them awake. Coleman also suffered because he used Lulubelle's cart for his nightly bed. He allowed Toto to join him in the cart. At least a couple of times each night, Coleman would awaken to the snap of

Toto's jaws as he crushed a creeper that had invaded their space. Titus and his men resorted to reducing the length of their tent poles and pinning down the sides of their tent walls with logs and heavy rocks. Still, a few creepers managed to get in, causing a soldier to jump to his feet in the middle of the night, stamping and jumping up and down in a wild, panicked dance, which included a round of curses. Everyone was looking forward to putting this part of their journey behind them, but no one knew how long it would take, and that made their suffering all the more intolerable.

Travel was slow during the day as they dodged the creeper mounds, and the nights continued to be filled with annoying interruptions. The men were becoming exhausted physically, mentally, and emotionally. Their tempers began to flare at the slightest provocation, making Coleman grateful he and Ayascho spent most of their time far ahead of the main body, trailblazing a path. The nights, however, were just as restless for them as for the others.

After eight days of struggle through the creepers, things had not improved. Then one day, the two thrice awoke in bad tempers themselves. Something other than creepers had their nerves on edge. They bellowed their angst and resisted their harnesses, but eventually calmed enough to continue the trek.

About midmorning, a low rumble was heard in the distance, stopping everyone in their tracks as they craned their necks and listened. Tondo and Ayascho bounded back to the main party.

"You heard it, too?" Titus wondered. Both trailblazers nodded, their eyes wide. Unexpectedly, the ground began to roll, and the rumbling roar returned, only much louder this time.

"Groundshake!" one of the soldiers yelled.

Everyone stood in their places, swaying back and forth, attempting to remain on their feet. The two thrice bellowed in fear as they hunched down and dropped their heads in a defensive stance. Groundshakes were not uncommon and Coleman had felt several since his arrival; however, this one was particularly strong, knocking several men to the ground and causing a few nearby trees to topple. Small fissures opened in the ground, as well.

The ground rolled like ocean swells for nearly half a minute, maybe more. Birds took to the air and wild creatures ran in panic, bolting past the men. One four-legged, deer-like creature slammed into the side of one of the carts and lay unconscious for a few moments before standing and staggering into the brush. The fissures grew, swallowing trees, bushes, and boulders. Every man began to fear being swallowed by one.

The shaking and rolling finally subsided and the men looked at each other wide-eyed, sporting huge smiles of relief. The two thrice raised their heads and bellowed their relief, as well. Just as everyone was getting their bearings and preparing to resume the trek, buzzing and chittering could be heard coming from all around the party. Coleman strained his eyes and ears, searching high and low for its source.

"There!" Ayascho shouted, pointing to a fissure that had opened not far from where they were standing. Swarms of creepers began pouring forth. The jungle floor turned into a pulsating carpet of white legs and pincers, and it began rolling toward the men.

"Move it!" Titus ordered as he began shoving his men into action. Everyone took off, including the two thrice. They crashed past bush and tree, attempting to put as much distance between themselves and the swarm as they possibly could. As they moved, they noticed other fissures vomiting forth more of the chittering and snapping creepers. Huge black scorpions were disgorged from the colossal crevices, and it wasn't long before the party began encountering giant multipedes, six to eight feet in length, with large mandibles powerful enough to crush a man's arm or leg.

"Tondo, Ayascho, clear the way!" Titus shouted over the cacophony surrounding the party. "Teness, Pontus, support them! Move out!"

The four quickly looked around, searching for the safest route. Coleman was the first to dash forward, Toto at his side. They were quickly followed by the other three. As Ayascho rushed past a cart, he snatched up a metren and continued after the others. Coleman reached over his left shoulder and extracted an arrow from his quiver. He nocked it on the run and was soon facing off against a large multipede. The beast arose like a threatening cobra, daring anyone or anything to come closer. Toto barked, bounding forward and quickly jumping back, avoiding the multipede's dangerous snapping mandibles. While the monstrous creeper was distracted by Toto, Coleman launched his arrow and it struck the creature's underside just below its head. Surprisingly, the huge creeper shrieked, emitting a high-pitched scream that sounded like a woman's wail. Coleman was taken aback and he hesitated, but just an instant. He quickly recovered, reached over his right shoulder, pulling his short sword from its scabbard as he charged forward. With a mighty swing, he cleaved the keening monster in two and watched as it collapsed at his feet, the two parts writhing in its death throes. While he watched it wither, an unnoticed black scorpion scuttled toward his bare right foot. Toto dropped a massive paw on the creature's tail, pinning its stinger to the ground. The betzoe smashed the scorpion's body with his headplate and its legs twitched as it died.

Ayascho had thrust his metren through another giant multipede and was struggling to keep his feet as it twisted from side to side, trying to free itself from the impale. Pontus and Teness were standing side by side, slashing a horde of monstrous black scorpions blocking their way. As soon as one was dispatched by the sword, another appeared. Coleman re-sheathed his sword, nocked an arrow, launching it into the head of the multipede Ayascho was struggling with, dropping it to the ground. He then rushed to aid Pontus and Teness in their battle with the scorpions.

Titus had deployed his remaining men around the thrice pulling the carts. They were drawing closer to the trailblazers as they battled more creepers scurrying out of the brush, every man glancing over his shoulder, gauging the distance between themselves and the white carpet of doom advancing from the rear.

Coleman grabbed his sword once more, but before he could reach Teness and Pontus, a giant multipede rushed out of the undergrowth, fleeing in fear from some perceived threat, crashing into Pontus's side, knocking the man off his feet. Instinctively, the monstrous brute clamped its enormous mandibles around the man's right thigh, cutting into his flesh and causing Pontus to scream in pain and terror. Coleman jumped to his rescue, slicing the gigantic arthropod in two, its head and three feet of its body still hanging by its mandibles from Pontus's leg, the creeper's many legs wiggling and squirming as the body twisted in spasms of death on the ground. Pontus continued yowling in pain and fear, his blood covering the creature's mandibles, still clamping his thigh in a vise-like grip.

The other men and thrice reached Coleman, Toto, and the two lead soldiers as two other soldiers picked up Pontus and dumped him into Doofus's cart. The party delayed only long enough to help the injured man. Then they quickly trudged onward, attempting to escape the onrushing chittering and snapping wave of biting termite-like creepers drawing closer every second. As the cart rumbled over the rough ground, Pontus pried the monster's mandibles loose and tossed its remains over the cart's side. He grabbed his thigh with both hands, rocking back and forth in pain, uttering a low growl of suffering as the cart bounced onward.

Coleman took the lead again and drove forward, hacking and slashing at the impeding brush and threatening creepers as they scuttled toward him. Toto continued to protect his master using tooth and paw. Ayascho and Teness moved to his side and the three men cut a swath through the brush wide enough for the thrice with their carts and the others to follow. They'd advanced less than a quarter-mile before they were confronted by another horde of black scorpions. The men were tiring and so were the thrice. Things were beginning to look bleak and everyone was starting to lose hope. Even Coleman was beginning to despair as he hacked and slashed at the black horde of stinging, poisonous peril blocking their route. The white wave was relentless. Even the shortest delay would result in the creeper tide washing over them.

As they were dealing with the horde of scorpions, a colossal multipede skittered out of the undergrowth. It rose half of its body off the ground, towering over the men, its mandibles snapping and its many claw-tipped legs wiggling. Coleman faced off against this new and deadly foe, slashing with his short sword. His blade struck the huge beast just below its head and glanced off; the gigantic creature's exoskeleton was as hard as metal armor.

The area was suddenly engulfed in blazing white light and nearly instantaneously, the men's ears were assaulted by a shattering boom and a continuing rumble that rattled the men's bones. Lightning had struck nearby, adding confusion to the men's fear. Within seconds of the flash, the heavens opened and a torrent of rain drenched the men and the ground. So heavy was the downpour, the men could hardly see each other. The thrice bellowed while the trees and bushes roared as the deluge poured over them. The creepers threatening the party quickly withdrew, seeking hiding places—places of refuge and safety from the drenching bombardment. The black horde of scorpions dispersed. The gigantic multipede lowered itself and skittered away as a couple of other multipedes scurried past the party, ignoring the men and thrice in their search for shelter. Most importantly, the white-colored carpet of threatening creepers advancing on them thinned and eventually disappeared.

The men spent several minutes scanning for more threats, but it became apparent, the rain had driven the creepers underground once again. As they came to this realization, broad smiles began covering the men's faces as they stood in the drenching rain. Ayascho dropped to his knees, raising his outstretched arms above his head.

"What's he doing?" Titus wondered.

"He's thanking his god for sparing our lives," Coleman shouted above the roar. Most of the men simply watched as Ayascho offered his silent thanks. A few men nodded their heads in acknowledgment that divine intervention had saved them. Two of the soldiers also dropped to their knees, bowing their heads in gratitude for their god's help.

The downpour began to slacken, so Titus let the men rest for a while and collect their thoughts. It had been a near thing, but they had survived. As the heavy rainfall abated and turned into a drizzle, they examined Pontus's wound and Coleman treated it. The cuts didn't need to be sutured, but Pontus was still in great pain because of the crushing power of the multipede's bite.

Coleman rubbed his hands together until they warmed and glowed red. He placed them over the bandage covering the injured man's leg, drawing away the man's pain as one would an invisible poison, leaving Pontus and the other Anterrans in awe of the hairy man-beast's magic. They wondered between themselves what other powers might this unusual savage possess.

At midday, Titus ordered the party onward once again. Coleman, Ayascho, and Toto took the lead. They continued moving through areas of creeper mounds, deepening everyone's worry about a repeat of the morning's experience. Fortunately, there was no recurrence, although they endured several aftershocks, but none as powerful as the original groundshake. Nevertheless, the tremblers unnerved everyone, including the two thrice.

The party plodded on for the remainder of the day under a rainy mist. Coleman thought they were continuing to gain elevation, but it was hard to tell for sure. Toward late afternoon, Ayascho pointed out a four-legged creature grazing in the distance. It had the appearance of a very large moose without antlers.

Coleman took careful aim with his bow and launched his arrow, striking the creature in the forequarter. It galloped off, and Toto bounded after it, barking. The two men took off at a trot, following the betzoe's calls. A few minutes later, they came upon their prey's carcass, Toto sitting on his haunches awaiting their arrival.

When the rest of the party reached him, Titus called it a day and they made camp. The men gathered what little dry wood they could find and a smoky fire was started. They managed to tear open some rotting logs and use the dry wood within. The creature Coleman had slain was prepared and roasted, a tarp of skins protecting the fire from the constant drizzle. The men gorged themselves on the fresh, tasty, roasted meat. Then everyone retired.

The rain had stopped, and the sky cleared somewhat. Coleman lay in Lulubelle's cart gazing at stars appearing through scattered clouds. He could hear the soldiers conversing in the tent nearest him. He thought they acted like ordinary soldiers of all times and places. Their crude and disparaging remarks were no different than those Coleman had listened to long before on a distant world. It wasn't long before the soldiers' crude conversation shifted to the hairy savage, Tondo. One scorching remark followed another, while the men's voices and laughter grew louder and louder. It really didn't matter to Coleman what these men thought of him, but their bluster was keeping him awake.

Bardas, Teness, Rao, Gheedan, and even the injured Pontus, whom Coleman had treated and freed from his pain, continued their insulting banter until they heard a loud thud coming from the front of their tent. Bardas got up, curious to find out what it was. He lifted a log holding down the tent flap and pushed it open, grabbing the front tent pole as he did. He uttered a profane yelp, examined his hand, and found it was bleeding. He looked at the tent pole to see the tip of an obsidian arrowhead poking through the wood.

He quickly pulled the flap shut and retreated into the tent. Coleman could hear Bardas's gruff voice as he quietly explained what he had found. There ensued an exchange of whispered words, and finally, the tent fell silent. Coleman rested the bow by his side, pleased with himself. He heard

Ayascho rustle in Doofus's cart and then the young man said, "Thank you." Tondo surmised the rest of the night would pass in relative quiet and peace.

Coleman returned to his stargazing, and as he did, his thoughts ran wild. What an amazing place he was in: amazing creatures, amazing people of tremendous age, amazing powers. He thought about his inner-power and how it had developed. He was certain he had only scratched the surface. What other great abilities lie in wait for him to discover? When he reached the Ancient City, would he too live for hundreds of spans? What would that be like? Why had he been summoned by the king and the Sutro Seer? What manner of men are they? All this was so exciting; it almost made him whimsical, just like when he was a child waiting for Christmas to arrive.

And yet there were terrors of untold horror here as well. Would he and his party even survive their journey? The Anterrans seemed to be surprised they had made it this far. What other dangers were they yet to encounter? Whatever they might be, he would willingly face them. Something at his center was urging him onward. Was it simply curiosity? No, it felt to be much more than that. Was his inner-power driving him on? To what end? For what purpose? He had to know the answers even at the risk of his life.

CHAPTER 26

EPILOGUE

More than thirty days had passed since Coleman's party had departed the Batru village. He had guided Titus and his men in a northeasterly direction, slowly climbing in elevation and finding firmer ground. Majestic mountains could often be seen through the trees. The mountain range snaked along their right flank for as far as anyone could see, both to the north and to the south. Coleman thought the mountains were no higher than five-thousand feet, but they were very rugged. He could see clouds bumping up against them and now he knew why it rained so much on this side. Rain continued to plague the party, but the going was getting easier day by day.

The days were becoming longer and the p´atezas was nearly directly overhead at midday. Coleman had no idea how far they had traveled and neither did anyone else.

On the fifty-fifth day of their travels, sometime before dawn, while it was still dark, Coleman awakened with a start. Toto was sitting up and sounding a low rumbling growl. Coleman grabbed his bow and poked his head above the sideboard of the cart, his eyes straining to see through the gloom. The moons had set, but the brightness of the stars gave a slight glow to the immediate area. Toto continued to growl, but it was obvious it wasn't about something he saw; more likely it was something he heard or smelled. Coleman placed his hand on the betzoe's back to comfort him, but he continued his grumble. Suddenly, the betzoe sounded his screechy bark, a signal Coleman knew meant danger. Through the brush, he could hear movement. He stood up and fumbled for his quiver. Before he could nock an arrow, he saw a spear tip floating in the darkness, hovering just above his heart.

PRONUNCIATION

GUIDE

b´ This low-pitched popping sound is made by pursing the lips together, rolling them inward, and releasing them, creating a low-toned pop.

p´ This high-pitched popping sound is made by pursing the lips together, extending them forward, and releasing them, creating a high-toned pop.

t´ This clicking sound is made by placing the tongue against the palate, and pulling it down, making a sharp, clicking sound.

ă	ask, bat, hat
ā	ate, bake, late
ä	are, bar, call
ch	chain, inch
ĕ	end, fed, led
ē	eat, beat, meat
g	golf, pig
ĭ	it, hit, tip
ī	ice, dice, pie
ŏ	opt, pot, top
ō	oak, boat, own
oo	took, moot
ŭ	unlit, lump
ū	use, rule, mute

Anterra	ăn tĕr´ rä
Atura	ä tū´ rä
Ayascho	ī ä´ shō
Bardas	bär´ dăs
bataro	bä tăr´ ō
Batru	bă´ troo
Ben-do-teg	bĕn´ dō tĕg
betzoe	bĕt´ zō
Chashutza	chă shoo´ tzä
Chashutzo	chă shoo´ tzō
Dada	dä´ dä
detzamar	dĕtz´ ä mär
Dondi	dŏn´ dē
Du	dū
Duba	dū´ bä
Dubo	dū´ bō
Dumas	dū´ măz
gant	gănt
ha	hä
habaga	hä bä´ gä
hoy	hoi
Icee	īs ē'
Munnevo	mŭn nē´ vō
Munnoga	mŭn nō´ gä
Myron	mī´ rŏn
Namad	nä´ mäd
Namada	nä´ mäd ä

Nevesant	nĕv ĕ sănt´
Nita	nē tä´
Nu	nū
oy	oi
p´atezas	p´ āt zăs
p´oez	p´ ōĕz
Pannera	păn nĕr´ rä
Pershon	pĕr shŏn´
Pontus	pŏn´ tŭs
purrant	pŭr rănt´
Rao	rā´ ō
raster	răs´ tĕr
regum	rĕg´ ŭm
schazu	schä´ zoo
sestardi	sĕs tăr´ dē
Shadi	shă dī´
Shergus	shĕr´ gŭs
sutro	sū´ trō
taah	tä
taahso	tä´ sō
Tangundo	tăn gŭn´ dō
Tanzi	tăn´zē
Teg-ar-mos	tĕg´ är mŭs
Teness	tĕn´ ĕs
Titus	tī´ tŭs
Tondo	tŏn´ dō
todo	tō´ dō

Tu	tū
Tumtuo	tŭm too´ ō
tuntro	tŭn´ trō
Tuz	tūz
Tzani	tză´ nē
Tzeecha	tzē´ chä
Tzeechoe	tzē´ chō
Uragah	ooh rä´ gä
Varios	vär´ ē ŏs
We	wē
wernt	wĕrnt
zanth	zănth
Zet	zĕt
Zoseemo	zŏ sē mō´
Zue	zū´ ĕ

GLOSSARY OF TERMS

creeper	An insect; a pest
cross-over	To pass away; to die
detzamar	Also referred to as detz, it is a period of forty days. There are four wernts in a detzamar and ten detzamars in a span
gant	A wine drink diluted with water
gravetro	A metal similar to iron
gravetum	A metal similar to steel, having the color of brass
ha	World-speak for yes; also an exclamation similar to okay, oh, or well
hoy	A world-speak exclamation of surprise or despair
measha	Food; meal
munna	A moon
Munnari	The blue moon; known as the good moon
Munnoga	The silver moon; known as the neutral moon
Munnevo	The red moon; known as the evil moon
Munnoga-touched	An insane or deluded person

oy	A world-speak exclamation of surprise similar to *oh* or *ah*
p´atezas	The planet's source of light and life; equivalent to the Earth's sun
p´oez	Honored slayer of prey
purrant	An authority appointed by King Ben-do-teg to oversee local affairs; the hamlet constable
regum	A large gold coin of the Teg-ar-mos Kingdom
span	The duration of the planet's orbit around its star. One orbit takes 400.33 days. One day is added to every third span at the end of the first detzamar of the span
sutro	Greater, senior, superior
taah	The inner-power that grants an individual special abilities
thrice	A three-horned domesticated beast of burden
tuntro	A bovine-like creature similar to a large water buffalo
wernt	A period of ten days
zanth	Gold

THE MUNNARI CHRONICLES

MUNNARI

ASCENDING

NOVEL TWO

Coleman continues his dangerous and deadly trek to the Ancient City, facing an old threat and many new ones. As shocked witnesses watch, shaking in fear, Coleman contends with the gods in a life and death struggle, demanding them to restore life.

Can he succeed? How will he deal with a new reality when an unexpected event requires him to become a reluctant slave master? Temple mentors arrive to test him and determine if he is worthy to lead the forces of Good in the coming era of threat. Deadly encounters, vicious creatures, new magical powers, and an unexpected romance await him. *The Munnari Chronicles* continue with *Novel Two, Munnari Ascending.*

MunnariChronicles.com
MLBellanteBooks.com